BUGBEAR BLUES

BY ANI FOX

Delphi having departed the City and returned alive barely makes news. Delphi having stopped a small invasion and returned alive makes his fellow janjacks nervous and curious by turns. Especially when word of a hatless drunk Delphi haunting the streets at the witching hour reach them. The sisters are their spokeswomen. In all things related to Austen's janjacks, the sisters are the ascendant powers—determining the social and cultural agenda of their micro-society, which is always less than two dozen souls. They arrive to find a dressed, sober, reflective monster, decked in grey and wintergreen, wearing a different top hat perhaps a trifle dusty and sporting an obviously new set of ribbons. Today Delphi has worn the house colors of Kizervexius, gold and green with the requisite second ribbon of midnight doublestripe. It's as much a Vanguard as he needs ever deliver, and for a moment even the brash Vorskla stands agape.

Then she greets him in her peculiar style: "The count is fifteen." By this, Delphi knows none are dead, missing, or born anew. There were fifteen janjacks of Austen yesterday and there are fifteen today.

Who are these women, who have say over the inimitable Footman? Vorskla and Dnieper, twins from The Free Duchy of Kyivan Rus, veterans of the Fourth Slavic War and subsequent escapees from a Soviet prison camp, apparently ageless and perhaps cursed by Romani magic, experts in Tejano lore, warcraft, diplomacy and music, the reigning queen regents of Austen's dueling circles and the most militant knitters in the Western hemisphere. It is said that you need to kill a man to be invited to their Thursday Evening Stitch and Bitch. Austen has a nineteen-page waiting list, and potential international guests regularly send photogravures of their dueling wins.

DEDICATION

For the women in my household: Katya, Marina and Suliko, each of whom appears in this book…

CHAPTER 1: A BROKEN AXLE

Gerhard watched the dying sun with growing certainty—no help would come. His children had already fallen into familiar patterns of bickering and blame. Zoe, his rambunctious teenage daughter, had already set upon the younger Max with glee. He hauled more wood for the growing fire.

"I just knew we were stranded." Zoe gave him a fussy look. A few years ago he'd interpret it as fear; now he could not be so certain.

"If we had left on time," Max huffed about kicking stones into the fire. "If you hadn't got caught ..."

Gerhard sighed and they both stopped moving. "Enough. We need to gather as much wood as we can. Right now."

They knew the tone and obeyed. Years on the farm had taught them all what a broken axle between the village and city could mean. Night fell hard and the dark consumed unwary travelers. There were wolves and worse out there. The road would be deserted until dawn—not even the worst of humanity dared venture out once the sun disappeared.

The little family gathered in silence, though Max let it be known that his seven year old's sense of injustice would soon overpower his good nature. Then it was too late—they had as much wood and gear as they would gather when the sun, a thin wick of scarlet, dropped and black flooded like fingers between the trees.

Gerhard had hauled out enough of their goods to build a makeshift lean-to of bales and baskets, with some blankets to keep them warm. Food they had, in abundance since they had been bringing dried and fresh goods to market. He stoked the fire higher, counting the wood. It seemed more than enough to keep the fire at full force until well past dawn. With a small child and a near ton of fragrant food, he dared not let the wild things of the night smell weakness.

He occupied them for a time with dinner and washing up, with using the latrine by makeshift torchlight which was an adventure all in itself. But then with stomachs full and the whole of the darkness to keep them company the night sounds began encroaching. Flying things flittered past on bent wing almost silent but making themselves known. Howls and scratching erupted too close while something urgent that growled in the distance. The kids huddled and for a moment forgot their animosity. He could see their fear.

"Would you like to hear a story?"

"Is it a sad story?" Of course, Zoe would ask that.

"Sad and happy and full of danger, adventure…"

"Will there be swordfights Daddy?" Max's voice barely rose over a hush.

"Tons of swordfights. And there will be elves."

This time Zoe smiled. "I love elves."

"Well these elves might disappoint you Zoe." Here Gerhard frowned thinking of the story he had in mind. It was long enough perhaps to get them to midnight.

Max gave him a shake of the head. "If they have swordfights and battles and demons it can never be disappointing."

"Yeah Pops, if there are demons and wars and evil magic, they won't disappoint us."

This time Gerhard leaned forward, letting the flames cast warm shadows across his dancing eyes. He smiled a rare smile, feral almost and began:

"This is not exactly a true story. Or maybe it is. But it happened long ago far from here in another place where the elves had banished darkness with their spells. In this place there was a lonely city with dusty streets and on such street, in the blazing sun of high noon there sat something, not quite a man and yet with piercing eyes…"

CHAPTER 2: DELPHI'S TALE

It is a truth universally acknowledged that a proper gentleman must be in possession of a good hat. In the year 1983, on the dusty streets of Austen, Tejas, that hat happens to be an Elven silk tapestry top hat in the classic Brummel lines with feather for a dandy and a ribbon for a swordsman. Under just such a hat Delphi sits in the Café Ragueneau on Sixth Street looking for all the world like a posh boulevardier, hat beribboned appropriately in simple red and touched by the janjack midnight double stripe. He's taken a table on the actual avenue, back to the cool brick wall. His Caffé Cyrano steams before him. His brim tilts over predatory eyes hiding where he casts those grey monsters, clearly waiting.

The Cyrano proves a popular drink here; arguably perfected by the Ragueneau's staff. The sharp Kentucky bourbon and smooth Elven coffee dance with just the right touch of cream, sugar and absinthe. Delphi knows by the hush and sway of the crowd that Things are Happening. Knows by the way that men who can wear hats are wearing them, tilting them just a little more than needed. They say *throw down, challenge me*. It's a swordsman's café, so it's to be expected. Duelists need duels. But they move as if expecting someone to give offense. It's the way of Austen.

Austen sets itself apart by tradition and choice. Free state, city state, micro-nation, call it what you will. Built on dreams and access to a Door. Delphi serves this place as a janjack, a word defying exact translation and perhaps stemming from some bastardized Russified Elvish. Fixer, tour guide, assassin, city official, negotiator, private badge, babysitter, confidante, advisor, gentleman's gentleman, to borrow some words: consigliore, mamzer, gunsel, vor. Generally to a city or a guild. By express purpose and by definition, janjacks never serve men; they serve ideas and places, generations and houses. Except for one: the errant Footman, a mysterious servant of the notably ruthless and arrogant warlord Elven Lord Protector Kizervexius.

"Wait Daddy, what's a gunsel?"
"A criminal of sorts Max. It means he's kind of a mobster but also tough, a little cool maybe, dangerous."
"Does he have a sword?"
"Shh. Wait and see…"

Lowly Delphi, mercenary, problem solver, janjack has been a resident of Austen since 1863 just twenty years after the Texians achieved independence from the Greater Elven Cohort of Extenso Mexico. He stood at the Battle of San Antonio, where the Footman cut down the Black Grimalkin and ended its radioactive plunder of the Tejas capital. Delphi even resembles said myrmidon, being of the same species and of roughly the same legendary size, resembling something part bear, part cat, lissome rather than hulking. Alas, he cannot be the Footman because everyone knows this hero has been dead for well over a century. He disappeared shortly after San Antonio, gone to legend and dust and whispers across the Doors, much like his great vicious magnificent and deadly lord, the late Kizervexius.

"Pops, what the hell is myrmidon? And who are the Extenso exactly?"
"Right, it's a fancy word for a soldier."
"Then why not just call him a soldier?"
"It sounds better to change your words, to add depth to the story."
"Yeah seems needlessly confusing to me. "
"Ok Zoe, no more myrmidons."
"And this Extenso thingee?"
"It's an elven creole word for the empire that stretches from the tip of southern continent to the edge of Tejas, where Austen sits. And creole means a mixed up language."

"Like what we speak?"

"Exactly so my smart child. The next part you're going to like a lot."

Another truth less universally acknowledged and thus more powerful—The Street has its own uses for magic: drugs, sex, profit, beauty, prestige, gossip, scandal, revenge, even murder. Delphi smells unauthorized Shine before he sees the Glamer; his nose has a taste for this itchy kind of excess. By scent, Delphi even knows the man's name: Coralaviere. An adjutant to the King's Seneschal, he's an Elf of Sacred Rank, a named man, a bearer of the Sancurion and the Star, two of the most valued badges of the known worlds and generally a serious swordsman. Coralaviere requires people to know it, hence the Shine.

Delphi understands. It cuts down on fights. The elf lord isn't bad *per se* and he doesn't want to make widows just to notch his belt. He's older now, some say two thousand years, and as much as he's got a thirst for power and rank, he's not the killer half his peers are. To them, cutting down a few mayflies constitutes a hobby. So the Elf struts his stuff and arrives everywhere armed for bear and looking Fabulous, as only a Glamered and Hammered court noble can.

Coralaviere doesn't really understand what's about to happen. Certainly he's connected and a King's Man, but he's been dawdling around on other planes, doing the work of Chafrium for a couple centuries. Terra, for all its charms sits on a cul-de-sac of low Potential and thus is a backwater. Delphi tosses back his drink, the bitter finish lingering on his tongue. He will need both hands soon.

His fanfare announces he elf lord three blocks away with lackeys ushering stray automobiles and carriages aside. A horse spooked by some annoyed goblin's car-horn bucks and Sixth Street tenses. Behind the cortege comes the muscle, thin cloaked outriders with ominous guns. Elves aren't fond of guns, so those that use them tend to arm themselves with very lithe, very deadly little things.

"You said they'd have swords. So far it's just guns and automobiles and shiny stuff."

"No Max, Pops means Shine is a kinda spell. It makes everyhting extra shiny."

"Oh, so they are all glowing?"

"Just the one guy, the big elf lord general who everyone reports to. He has spells and a bunch of medals he earned with a sword. That's the whole dueling part."

"That sounds cool. I hope there's more of that."

The throng grows. Hangers-on, genuine squires, goblins trying to do business or on an errand or there to pick pockets or catch some intelligence. There are faces from a thousand worlds mingling. Around Delphi the immune system of Austen, its vagrants, mercenaries, duelists, musicians, thieves, and lovers, swarm the cortege. Inside the Ragueneau, The Word has just been passed. Swords rattle as scabbards are checked and men itching for a fight begin a slow, delicate scratching.

"Finally! Are they cool swords?"

"Very cool Max, thin dueling blades meant to kill an opponent with a slash or stab."

"Okay but what's a scabbard?"

"The hard shell that guards a sword. Just like mine."

"Yeah, okay. But theirs have to be cooler than yours. With colors and gems and stuff."

Coralaviere arrives and takes in the sight. To the untrained eye an enthusiastic crowd has appeared from nowhere, good naturedly edging in the nobleman's contingent. Everywhere Goblins swarm, sliding in waves and shudders among the dangerous milling elves. Lord C has spent over two thousand years in training and his eye takes in the reality: his little army has walked itself very cordially into an ambush. He nods and flashes the crowd a gorgeous smile. *Very well,* one can intuit him saying, *I've underestimated Austen and certainly the famed chevaliers of Sixth Street*. Delphi, at his table, slowly tips his hat back and meets the elf lord's eye. Neither man smiles. In this situation one might construe that as an act of war.

Coralaviere takes the initiative, perhaps because Delphi has neither moved nor acknowledged him. By every standard except one, Delphi has just spit on the man's shoes and called his mother something terrible. The elf must decide if the ensuing bloodbath merits a response or if he must in turn allow Delphi that one exception. So he makes a short bow, almost to equals. Delphi does not move.

"Pops you're doing it again. Using the fancy words and not explaining stuff."

"Which things?"

"Like I get chevaliers is supposed to be soldiers again but Max might not. And what the hell is this little eyeballing thing? Is this a man thing?"

"Yeah Daddy, why are they going to have a war?"

"Right, so I'll start adding some stuff about their rules and etiquette and all that. Might take half the night."

"As if we didn't have it..."

"Yeah. So the rules of this game are very complex but basically elves are very polite in their own weird way. Normally one would bow or salute or act scared of a general, especially a scary guy like Coralviere. But Delphi does nothing and it's an insult. A big time snub. Unless he outranks the guy. In which case it's totally good, even expected."

"Got it Pops. But knock off all the wordy word stuff huh?"

A small army arrives, headed by one of the deadliest, most peevish Elf Lords ready for Trouble, yet Delphi does absolutely nothing. He watches and waits. Coralaviere rates high enough to have an army but low enough to need one. It's the Elven paradox that the very greatest of Lords command by reputation and style. Coralaviere, for all his majesty, still requires a blade.

It's a strange moment by most standards, out of place even among the tough posturing duelists of Sixth Street. Lives, perhaps hundreds if not thousands of lives and certainly the immediate future of several square blocks of Austen, rest upon the shoulders of these two men, the adjutant and the janjack. The Elf lord has made the gesture, the allowance, the soft acquiescence to necessity. In his silence, his opponent has forced the entire Elven contingent in Chafrium to blink and make a short bow, almost to equals.

The sinews of the warriors around the street creak as guns, blades, various molotovs and potions are gripped, waiting. The elf lord squints in surprise. It is as if only now, standing here ready for all-out war, does he discover something is amiss. It's a small thing, a thing which is only conspicuous in its absence. Elves take great pride in their Vanguard—that little floating constellation of awards and badges over the left breast that serves as shorthand for rank, power, class, and caste. In an instant one can determine the relative position and merit of the person facing them. It saves eons of tedious conversation and politesse. For elves, coached in etiquette and layers of polite nuance, the Vanguard saves everyone's face.

But men and their ragged humanoid counterparts—the goblins, orcs, half bloods, and such—often lack a Vanguard. Men who deal with elves tend to sport one, often a Shined one like Coralaviere's, dandified and made just a little illegally better so that Everyone knows just how ferocious and interesting the man in question really is. When you're a mayfly that little edge matters. If you have a weak Vanguard you might try to jigger it, adding random and obscure awards through illusions. It will fool the common folk. But once across a Door, it fades. That is what makes Vanguards useful. They display only real achievements and honors.

Delphi has no Vanguard. In his time and travels Coralaviere has met very few tough men without them. The adjutant has been sent to take this man back to Chafrium, to escort him back to the Lord King, master of Chafrium's elves. When he arrives, the elf finds himself trapped, insulted and perplexed. Delphi appears to command these mayflies' ... respect, if not loyalty. Where is the Vanguard then? Curious. His sword too merits respect—serviceable, spotless and like Coralaviere's own, of very high quality.

"Daddy, does this Chafrium place make vanguards?"

"No Max, a vanguard is magical image that glows—that's why Shine works—it shows all the cool things you've ever done and tells people who you are."

"And they both have cool swords."

"That's because Pops is trying to make them equals. So in the story they wear the same imprtant thing—a sword—which has the same purpose. They are both super deadly duelists, right?"

"Very good Zoe. That's why he's so confused about the Vanguard. Because it's the key to etiquette. Without it there's the risk of making social mistakes. Which are worse than getting stabbed."

"Oooh. So these elves are feminine. It's like a pack of nasty girls."

"It's more compli... no maybe it isn't. Yes, a pack of ultra competitive women who live for thosuands of years competing and fighting and cooperating while doing their hair and having fashion shows. But as Max said, with swords to also stab people."

The heat of the morning has begun to play with the asphalt of the street. It offends the elf lord that a city as nominally grand as Austen uses such a cheap substance for a thoroughfare. Like its peoples, the street pavement comes and goes and is replaced by the next generation.

Coralaviere says something sharp and powerful. A nauseating wave of blue magic ripples through the air, over the bar and street. Everywhere hidden things begin to pop into view. Little things glamered away, trashbins and pimples, reappear. But the thing the elf wanted, the Vanguard roaring like supernova, does not appear. Nothing whatsoever appears and suddenly the elf of sacred rank shivers. The shadow of suspicion rakes its venomous claws down his noble back.

Here, in the sere arena of Sixth Street, Delphi surprises his opponent with glorious anonymity. All that marks him are a superb gentleman's top hat and a nondescript sword of long and loving use. He exudes a deep unnerving sense of things greatly amiss.

Perhaps a small detour into etiquette can explain. A proper Vanguard glows like a daystar. Among them are awards, titles, and even Keys. With Keys one can open and close Doors—both an honor and a mark of power. Aside from Keys, there are five awards that mark a person of distinction and are known across all the worlds of the City of Doors. Five specific interplanar sigils of glory:

The Sancurion—roughly equivalent to every army's big medal for courageous stupidity. Coralaviere owns one himself among other greater honors. It is why to this day Elves of Hidden and Superior Rank nod to him as he passes.

Above that the Holy Leaf, emblematic of some kind of direct act of glorious mercy, preferably involving widows, orphans, or horrifying audacious disasters. It says something about Elves (who set the social agenda of the Known Worlds) that mercy trumps courage. There are of course many more Sancurions than Holy Leafs and for the same reason.

Next the Star, a combination of the lesser two, involving outrageously stupid courage in the face of something requiring more than violence, preferably with widows, orphans, or defenseless maidens. It helps if you slay a demon or have the demon award it to you. Coralaviere earned his for stopping a sentient plague ravaging nine worlds.

Above that comes The Sun—a direct marker of appreciation from somebody bigger than a local king and meaning "you saved my life, kingdom, girlfriend, pet dragon and/or treasury" and with it comes the assurance that if someone messes with you, Big Muckety Mucks will be Displeased.

Last and greatest comes The Arrow. The Arrow more rightfully goes by the wordy title The Most Holy Elven Arrow of Supreme Sacrifice. If your courage, stupidity, exposure to bodily harm, and knack for saving important orphans and widows has gone beyond all measure, if the Gods themselves have taken notice and the tide of Fate has been turned by your little stunt, then one of a select few Elven nobles at the direction of the Oracle of Chafrium awards this to you. It is the most exclusive club in the known universe.

"So he's going to have one right?"

"That's what Pops is trying to imply, that he's this famous guy who did stuff, bigger and cooler than just war. Dmon stuff and saving drgons and maidens right?"

"Well, yes and no. It's a complicated story. Telling you would ruin it but..."

It gets better. The list being short and the invitation being given by one specific oracle of one specific species in one specific city, the club members are pretty much known to every self-respecting elf and elven hanger-on as well as every soldier across every Doorway. It's not hard. There are among the three hundred and eighty major civilizations with Doors no more than a thousand living recipients of the Arrow. Count in the few thousand backwaters and Doors to deathlands, and you have less than two thousand total of the things awarded among hundreds of billions of sentients.

There are only fifteen people who have ever earned more than one. The Elven King has three, a feat equaled only by the Lady Apocalypse of the City of Arachnids and the Footman. His master Kizervexius alone managed before his unexplained and untimely death to accrue four of the damned things. It is said that the thieving god Lomar before ascending to godhood garnered five.

None of this matters except that in not yielding Delphi has called to mind the strange terrifying rumor that Kizervexius and his Footman still persist. That they hide in plainest sight, taking the elven view of life and playing out some millennial game of cat and mouse with the King and his sister, Lady Ashlelani Greyleaf, Highest Elf in Chafrium save the King.

Coralaviere of House Etris Chess has just found a janjack who vastly resembles the Footman and insulted him. His Lordship the King generally takes a dim view on antagonizing

Great Heroes. Until today the elf had a promising career and the King's ear. He must call the bluff, spill the blood, murder the man he seeks to bring home or face disgrace. All for a man who will not bow. Both men know the limits and conditions of his duty. With a sigh, Coralaviere bows again and drops all pretenses. "I am sent by his Lordship the King to escort you to Chafrium."

Delphi bows to an equal and motions to the table. "Might I offer you the welcome of Café Ragueneau, Lord Coralaviere? It's quite an honor for a bearer of the Sancurion and Star to be here." It's his emphasis on the awards and not the elf's rank or species that twigs the man to where he is. The adjutant has come within a stone's throw of the dueling grounds of Austen and as such has not just insulted Delphi but brought an aggressive force into the most heavily armed and defended section of a city famous for daily duels between killers. Coralaviere sits and it is the signal for his men to stand down. The crowd thins a bit. A waiter arrives with menus as if signaled. In reality, Duchamp Half-Elven has been watching. It says everything about Duchamp that he has been prepping the staff to fight the fire and repel ambushers rather than, say, run like the cowards two streets away. This is why his café is the one that serves both the best coffee in Austen and the men with blades who must drink it.

In the end, both Delphi and the elf lord opt for the daily special, a hastily concocted drink of Elven rum, bitter espresso, goblin spice, and steamed milk called the *Caffè Coralaviere*. Lord Coralaviere falls in love. Smell and taste—for elves the tongue is the organ of memory. Somehow the day when he drove back the Lord Defiler and earned his Sancurion chasing down the Undead Necromancer has been captured. He tastes the moment he faced the demon with no more than a spear of alder and jade, *here*, in this café, the dust blowing around him and the rough men who for a moment are his social equals.

The rum he's drinking is from the same case Duchamp dragged across the desert so many human lifetimes ago never quite knowing why he saved it for so long. Austen and Chafrium: some say the cities themselves are rivers of time and magic.

Certainly coincidences of the highest and most organized order happen in a regular and (one might infer) regulated manner.

An intuitive person might ask—why did the King Sæceæn XIX Lord of of all Elves summon Delphi? Delphi is asking himself this thing right now. Think about what is known of the King who, fighting a war of silent assassins, has already outlived his predecessors by centuries, who threatens to die in bed satisfied and successful.

Among the Elven Matriarchs he stands alone, the descendant of descendants of the mythic Lomar. Supposedly of his blood, named after the god's closest friend, the godfather of his own twins Sedilia and Sylmaxis Grey Elven of the Houses Lomar, Lyska and Zoëæ. One King among the Worlds, one Man and his City against an entire civilization of women and women's rule. In the history of Lomar's regal line there have only been nineteen Kings, all of them named Sæceæn and every one of them dead before his time. History agrees that the Worlds change when a Queen is not on Chafrium's throne. For all their prescience and wisdom, elves hate change. A thousand queens but nineteen kings, every one thankfully dead before their time. Until now.

"Daddy, they had my name in their name! Sylmaxis has Max you know."

"I do know, Max. What an amazing coincidence."

"Sure Pops and the house also includes a Zoe? If there are two tuxedo cats and a woman with flowing blonde hair, we'll know you're just adding stuff from home."

"I said it was a mostly true story or a false one. But I'll keep that in mind."

"Still, it was a nice touch adding our names…"

"Thanks Zoe, glad you like it. Wait until you hear about these elves before you decide for certain."

Lady Ashlelani Greyleaf's lover, the famed Kizervexius, disappeared less than two centuries ago. Of him there has been no trace save one: his servant the Footman, to whom he willed his sword and his suite at the palace. The King has asked

Coralaviere to find him Delphi—one of the better known and respected of Austen's dozen or so janjacks, but just a janjack without rank or power. Does he, like the elf lord, suspect him of being the Footman in disguise?

If either man now considers how outraged Sæceæn will be knowing the Footman has been for all intents and purposes hiding under the King's nose and, for those keeping social score, snubbing the hell out of him in a very spectacular way, they must then also consider whether Lady Ash has claims on Kizervexius's man. Would she be angry or pleased?

After another few sips and a rather detailed conversation in High Elvish about the best way to behead a gorgon, Delphi rises. Acting the host, he bows low and impishly to Coralaviere. The City of Jane knows and prides itself on being polite. Delphi, as the city's janjack, has just made a wonderful gesture to a man who on any day would be the most famous hero within several thousand miles. "Lord Coralaviere," his voice cuts through the afternoon din and if it's possible the quiet grows. "On behalf of my city, my guild and the esteemed Café Ragueneau, may I humbly thank you for your official visit and bestowal of your seal."

Oh the raw audacity! Delphi has in one sweep honored, dismissed, trapped and swindled his opponent and dare one conjecture, friend. The High Lord Adjutant Coralaviere of House Etris Chess has just been told he needs to endorse the Café, bestowing a vital seal—itself a kind of award and prize—or be called out for being a boorish hamhanded thug. The social death involved would be colossal.

The High Elf waves for his batman. Slowly he rises and then bestows the ultimate courtesy. He requests Duchamp to attend him. An hour later Duchamp Half Elven walks away not with some nearly anonymous Elven Seal which would be displayed on his front door and attract The Right Crowd. The elf lord has instead given him a personal letter of praise, sealed in a ForverCharm. For decades men and elves will come to Austen to read this, to sip the famed drink made in the Elf Lord's name, and to hear stories of how this came to be. More than that, Coralaviere halfway through has remembered the limping café owner, a man who among other things helped sew the Lord back to life. Duchamp, who has never spoken of that day nor intimated he ever did more in the Elven army than cook, has come face to face with his Lord General once more. He even knows the man's intimate nickname—Ral.

Does it matter how Delphi and the Great Lord happen to be on Congress Street, making way to the Door? Cafféinated and liquored up, perhaps friends, perhaps something a little closer to the Elven notion of *Desideralla*—variously translated as "trusted rival", "predictable opponent" and "warm foe".

"Pops, are there going to be lots of these Elvish lessons?"
"Yeah Daddy, because they are cool."
"They are?"
"Yeah. It makes it all super real. Like it happened and you were there and knew them all."
"That would make Pops super old."
"But he speaks Elvish, Zoe, so he has to be old right?"
"Maybe we just keep going..."

Fate has placed them on opposite sides of what promises to be a significant conflict. Even at a supposed 200 years old, Delphi can be expected to understand the complexity of the situation. Ral, his newfound friend, is also Coralaviere, the man who has pretty much ruined his day. For two Desiderallae like them, this comes as a source of mirth and good natured word play. The talk stays light in the elven low tongue. Across the door lies Chafrium and several painful conversations in very formal High Elven. The King waits and by now everyone in the retinue knows messengers have relayed the salient facts.

Chafrium: the Great Whore, the Shining Jewel, the Eternal Bastion, the City of Gates and Doors, the one and only anchor among all the known worlds. In every land, in every single place where sentience reigns, there exists a Door to Chafrium. Or as the Chafriumites like to say—*from* Chafrium. Ruled by a group of warring clans blessed with near eternal life and mind-boggling innate magical talent—in a word, Elves—the City has thrived for as long as anyone has kept records. There are 436 types of Elven sapient subtypes known among the planes. All ruled by one species only: the Great and Known Grey Elven Clans of the Chafrium Sylvan Vale and Mount, Houses Lomar, Lyska and Zoëæ. These tall thin grey eyed malicious backstabbing charismatic fiends built Chafrium from stagnant mud and standing stones a million years ago. At some point there came a reprobate king, the greatest among a tribe better known for its assassins than its manners and culture. Demon slayer, petty thief, honey tongued liar, seducer, filthy assassin, lover, planar runner, chaos lord, ringleader, and then king: Lomar. He was a legendary monster who became a more legendary king and then stole the very stars to become some kind of strange heartless god. They say Lomar and Chafrium share a soul.

For a janjack on duty, as Delphi is, Chafrium will do nearly anything to keep him alive. No one knows exactly why and every attempt to determine more about this oddity has been met by the City itself with a swift indelicate eviscerating series of *accidents.* Inquiry has been sporadic and halfhearted at the most curious of times.

What? You discern that somewhere the next Queen in line perhaps encouraged those brash young rulers to exert their power. Cynical already? We've barely begun and you're not even across the gates of the City and already making accusations, albeit correct ones. Whose story is this exactly? Is it Delphi's or Coralaviere's or some other as yet undiscovered protagonist, perhaps a dark heroine or the kind of anti-hero Chafrium delightfully keeps by the dozens, lurking cravenly in various shadowy alleys? Right now it's Chafrium's story and Austen's, because their servants ride proxy: pieces on the board of the Great Game.

The Door itself looks almost like any other archway or gate. Almost. By elfsight or if you have those pesky red eyes the Supreme Soviet so adores, then the Door gleams like a newly won pearl in the Caribbean sun. For those with Keys, the Doors sing. Each Key and each Door have their own mutual song that with the keeper becomes a kind of symphony, a mingled euphony or cacophony that for the sensory-prone elves bonds to memory.

It is not an exaggeration to suggest the Chafrium Guard knows the song of every keeper at every door. The defensive value of that knowledge has been sufficient to keep the the 435 types of elves not directly ruling the City in positions of trust and power for over seven hundred millennia. Before that they just posted a bunch of orcs with spears and let the situation sort itself out.

As the Desiderallae ride through children ring bells and beg for sweets, coins, and bread. Some are starving, some crippled, some cunning thieves and killers, some all this at once. The outriders shower the urban vermin with distractions of copper and sugar. The gifts prove to be cheaper than fighting. No one doubts the cortege's willingness to do so should the bribes fail, which convinces the much larger than usual throng of scum and villainy to move aside and let the host pass. Ahead, an even larger mob fills the street.

This much becomes clear—messages have passed not just to King Sæceæn but to the Guilds and their adversaries. The Guilds are a whole world unto themselves and style themselves the true rulers of Chafrium. The Elves, The Guilds, and the Academy—with its worlds of wizards, scientists, bokors, mechanics, inventors, conjure-men, engineers, and shamans—are the three legged emperor of Chafrium: a trio of blind old women clutching for one eye to see.

The Guilds' have adversaries who style themselves literally and politically as the humane opposition to that three legged power base. They eschew the Elven braid, the matching house colors and trappings of rank. Recklessly tattooed, shorn-haired, and rambunctiously eclectic in their fashion, these clash-colored anti-fops capture in their ensembles a sneering sardonicism. The Elves call them the Drowning Ones. They hoard guns, bake their own bread, own their own printing presses and worldwide web; they are the undisputed rulers of the City's proletariat.

Imagine for a moment the vortex of men and beasts, shadows and bells, politics and deadly earnest struggle. Drugs, sex, profit, beauty, prestige, gossip, scandal, revenge, even murder convene in the Street. Whatever small affair the King had in mind, every faction in the known worlds from demigods and demon lords down to the crackpots in the sewers seems to have

sent an emsisary into the street turning Coralaviere's errand
into an Incident.

The Desiderallae by this time must of necessity slow their
gait and take note of what could be the most dangerous ride
through Chafrium's streets in the last century. Delphi knows by
the growl and churn of the crowd that Things Are Happening.
He stops his horse, stands in his saddle, and doffs his hat. The
sun breaks the clouds and for a queer moment he alone rises
from the shadows and din, bathed in the long clean flame of
afternoon.

Delphi stands just under eight feet tall, long-armed and
hefty of torso, his every inch of skin covered by a fine thick
fur of forest colors—green, brown, grey, and shadow blue.
His hands bear long aristocratic fingers gloved in rich brown
leather which cover claws sharper than eagle talons. He wears
a comely emerald frock coat of the classic Austen style, cut for a
swordsman and worn by loving use. At his left side the expected
scabbard with plain saber, crossdraw-holstered dueling pistol,
and wakazashi. He has opted for simple laird's riding trousers
of dark grey with below-the-knee black boots stiff, decked with
combat knives, and knob-spurred. Like many duelists, he wears
a silk shirt fetchingly stitched in red and white stripes sans
collar and open at the neck. To this he has added a handsome
brocaded vest of lighter green that sets off his frock and seems to
pronounce his regal top hat. But all eyes are on his magnificent
head festooned with great ears that shame the lynx. His massive
jaw packs a smile of jagged teeth whiter than dinner china. His
brows recede like any bear's or cat's and under them rest two
grey eyes, old, wise, and perhaps dangerous. He turns the horse
in a tight circle, lets it prance and raise him higher, showing the
full of his braidless head. The crowd cheers loudly and several
who had perhaps edged too close to the cortege back away from
dangerous hooves.

Delphi has had a good look at the multitude assembled to
greet his party. In one turn of horse, the janjack has scouted
several teams of snipers, a small contingent of goblin anarchists
(complete with molotovs and pamphlets), three slithering
abominations, some kind of ominous splinter in reality, at least

a dozen cultists, a lone demon red with slaughter, and several figures Elven, human and otherwise whose posture, dress and piercing gaze denote magicians and agents of divinity.

He bows crisply in his saddle, replaces his top hat at a jaunty angle, and hies his steed forward to a trot. The crowd spreads before his bow wake. Once he's broken free, he loosens the reins and opens up to a near canter upon the roadway. By his side ride the the Elven outriders who understood his movements and intent. They are making an escape. Chafrium gives itself over to wide but cramped avenues, generally of indestructible cobblestones not quite worn smooth by eons of use, clear through the middle and swathed on the sides by makeshift homes, squatters, and merchants with tents, stalls, automobiles, and firepits.

Coralaviere matches his gait and gives him a wide smile. "A good day for a ride, one suspects." He has opened the conversation in English.

Delphi gives an acknowledging nod. "Your Lordship has provided me with a fine horse and an inviting avenue with which to admire such a creature. Who am I to disappoint the machinations of destiny?"

"Who are you indeed? That, Sir Janjack, promises to be the central question of the day."

Delphi winks and lengthens the stride of his horse. They are moving past canter into charging speed, scattering passersby and carriages as they proceed breakneck towards the crenulated inner fortress of Sæceæn the Nineteenth. "Ah my Lord, you have answered your own question. I am by my promise unquestionably a janjack."

Both Desiderallae share a small smile and then, rushing past a wave of gunfire, they cross the King's threshold and enter the first of many layered sanctums. Here they may rest and render themselves presentable as gentlemen and servants of their respective masters. The Elf Lord soaks up his demesne, almost shining as he acclimates to his reacquired equilibrium. Within these walls Coralaviere requires neither army nor sword; his Vanguard precedes him.

For those unfamiliar with Elven etiquette, the next few

moments so saturated with meaning and nuance will seem perhaps quiet, unusually relaxed, even auspiciously friendly. They would be deadly mistaken. Like the Vanguard, etiquette armors the elves. When lives are more likely to be lost to accidents and violence than age, disease, or injury, one by necessity develops a certain calculating vigilance. For the elves it is a prison of rigid expectations. Elves above all require predictability. They have a saying—The Moment Makes the Man, the Legend Makes the Lady. Coralaviere has arrived at his moment; perhaps Delphi as well.

The Elf Lord has, perhaps through no fault in his manners, intent, or direct actions, bungled a delicate and relatively minor task. Twice Delphi, the lowly and unranked janjack of the lowly and unremarkable Terran dimension, has rescued them both from an ambush. Twice the Adjutant has almost gotten Delphi killed and neither time with good reason. Elves keep score, and to his credit, Delphi has not yet compromised his friend Ral.

Coralaviere drops from his horse and gives his charge an unabashed smile. "Well then, by our own estimations, we could turn for home and admire our stallions a second time."

A groom of Orcish stock helps Delphi dismount. Another dandies the tall swordsman down with a livery brush, knocking dirt from his boots and taking the grosser layer of road dust from his coat and trousers. "As you say my Lord. And yet..." Here Delphi returns the smile. "I am powerfully inclined to speak with your King. We've come this far together. Might we not trust to luck and walk the last of it?"

The Elf sighs, his killer's eyes sad and soft. "If only you had a Vanguard, my Lord Janjack, I might find some small favor to add to it."

Delphi, made presentable again, does an elegant quarter bow and taps his spurs like a proper hussar. "If only... and yet, by the hand of Fortune, it appears that I do not." There stands a quiet moment between them as the arcane nuances of their conduct filter through the complexities of language, posture, and thought. Delphi matches his smile to the soft sad deadly eyes of his again adversary. "When I do again sport one, perhaps you'd do me the courtesy of resuming this discussion. I'd be honored at any such time to host your Lordship for a good hour over a *Caffé Coralaviere*."

Then the men do something out of bounds in an Elven fortress. They firmly shake hands, swordsman to swordsman, equals before the great Lady Death. Their speech shifts to High Elven. It is the Elf of Sacred Rank, the High Lord Adjutant Coralaviere of House Etris Chess, who speaks. "I regret muchly what may come next."

Delphi shakes his head, adjusts his hat to a perfect angle, and touches his saber, perhaps by sheer instinct, perhaps to emphasize his next point. "I do not." The Moment Has Made the Men. The janjack has stoutly refused to take the advantage provided by the King's enemies and down this man. He greets his Desideralla with friendship, esteem, and audacious courage. Ral will forever be Delphi's man, even if Coralaviere cannot. It has been a day of unexpected twists.

CHAPTER 3

JANE AUSTEN MAKES AN ENTRANCE AND EXIT

Poets and travel writers have long attempted to impart to the multiverse the splendour, cacophony and opulent intensity of The Court Royale of Chafrium. On the day of her death, Jane Austen, the beloved writer laureate of Tejas Libre, famously put it thus: " 'Tis an estate unschooled by time, rather touched by a savage inclination humbling those whom education, taste and society have little assisted. I had naught but once even imagined where Nature had done more, or where her eternal beauty had been so little counteracted by an awkward taste. Its remembrance surely will provide enduring pleasure."

Having heard this pronouncement…

"Pops you made that up."

"Jane Austen's quote? Certainly not. You can check any number of texts and see exactly what she said."

"So you're tellin us this is a true story? C'mon Pops… there's too many coincidences for this to be random."

"Well Zoe, you'll just have to take it on faith. Or not. Because there will be lots more. There's even those pernicious cats coming."

"Yay, kitties! Please Daddy tell us more."

"Zoe? Okay then. Having heard this pronouncement…"

… the King had it translated into Grey Elven and inlaid on the Outer Foyer's welcome stone. A few hours before her demise, Jane witnessed its topping out. It is upon this very stone that Delphi stands, waiting with the Lord Adjutant and a small guard of nine silent armsmen. No one has asked him for his firearm and if asked he would politely refuse. Beneath his boots, Jane's words trace gold whispers across the red flecked marble slab. Great thick doors of bronze, jade, and a wood whorled in iridescent pinks stand between them and the inner foyer. If he is pondering the court, he most likely recalls not his city's patroness but the ancient words of Senior Assassin Rexor the Revenant, who, happening upon Lomar's court in its full glory, remarked succinctly to his former friend: "I left you a rogue in filth, seeking the splendour of kings, and find you a king whose splendour is all rogues and filth."

A servant in royal livery of black and red claps them forward and the doors part inward to reveal a wide stairway of interlocking platforms, each dais of different motif. The colors are muted but intense, a paradox that speaks to elven sight's higher reds and lower violets. Delphi sees all, his eyes keen. The room has been built to glow, providing progressively brighter steps leading to the near gleaming doorway that, blocked by two flat jet doors etched with arcane symbols and death wards, stands between the inner foyer and the outer court. The Elf lord confers with the servant then motions Delphi to follow. The small group navigates the opulent steps and with a ring of a hidden bell, the black maws of King Sæceæn XIX's court open to them.

From within come the strains of an a capella quintet, the specialty of the Moon Elves of Ka-Aten-Nur. Their mournful cantillation washes over the assembly. After a respectful time, the servant ushers them forward into a dimly lit avenue where stand sculptures matching the outer dais themes, enacting various historic accomplishments of the Court. Pillage and rapine, while excellent subjects for French romantics, have been excised from the family gallery. After many long steps, the party arrives at a set of doors whose battle scars and utility cannot be belied. By tradition, the detritus of every unsuccessful coup and assassination has been conspicuously displayed here. These doors hold flame scorches, battle axes broken at the haft, arrows by the dozens, and ominous scratches, dents, perhaps something like bite marks. Beyond lies the court proper.

Delphi detaches from his guards and lays his gloved hand upon a particular welt, a crater of dull brass and bloodstains. The doors' magic includes a powerful sigil of stasis—the blood almost runs where it has been splattered. This bullet gave birth to the Free State of Austen. He takes his top hat and taps it upon the wound. A small patch of blood smears the front edge of his topper's crown. Someone stifles a gasp; the Terran janjack Delphi possesses a memory hat, a rare and valuable artifact of exclusively Tower Elven manufacture. By the time he turns and rejoins the cadre, the offender has been either silenced. Later, when duties have been discharged and the guard disassembled, whoever shamed the King will be upbraided. For now, etiquette demands no one take notice that Delphi has just smudged Jane Austen's blood across his warrior's hat. As gestures go, his has been unmistakably direct and bellicose. The Lord Adjutant gives an almost imperceptible bow and gestures his charge forward. Ten thousand silent eyes take note. The King will be informed.

The doors heave on their old rusted hinges, squealing like gelded pigs as they arch outward threatening to knock the men down. Both Desiderallae stand stock still. It's a game of swordsmen to test themselves against such contrivances. Recently three hyena godlings from the Chafrium provinces lost this duel: their brown incompetence demarcates nicely where not to stand. The doors grind outward, gaining speed, and by the time they pass the warriors they have enough heft to splatter a Soviet battlewalker. Delphi's hat tips back, kissed by the inside edge of the left-hand door. And then, the court.

The court of the Grey Elven of the Houses Lomar, Lyska and Zoëæ stinks of power and wealth. The King has toned down the almost defiling penchant of his relatives for garishness; his sister Lady Ash has lent the court a strong and abundantly tasteful hand. It was to her that Jane paid the compliment. Given all the wealth of 380 interplanetary empires and uncountable thousands of abundant worlds, the Court has wrapped itself in a restrained decadence that, despite its self-possession, strains credulity. The floors are jade, the walls swathed in complex tapestries of spider silk and gemstones, the ceiling lit by the captured breath of dying suns. Magic courses through every molecule of the place; technology smoothly disguises galactic power sources, communication devices, and a panoply of necessary conveniences as objets d'art. Great gilded foo lions with pulsar eyes mark the Court Royale's exclusive dais.

The room could hold tens of thousands but has been pared down to an intimate few hundred nobles attended by a simple thousand or so servants, guards, and golems of stone, steel, rare wood, and nanotech. In the center rises a simple pure white stair of widening steps. Delphi, who has studied the history of Chafrium, knows that they are in fact bones. The dragons of Kentium sought to murder the upstart Lomar, having heard through an oracle that he would be their extinction. They called down an army of demons and in their gamble lost. Lomar had their bones converted to his throne, dais, and stairwell as a threat, promise, and reminder to his subjects. Their ghostly screams can be heard if one levels an ear to the floor. In the dead center of the high platform sits an elf garbed in black silk coat and trousers. He wears no shoes, instead sliding his pale elegant feet along the tortured remains of his forefather's enemies. His long, spiderlike hands are unadorned save the simple platinum ring of office. Elven kings do not wear crowns. From the distance his face seems kind and open.

Lord Adjutant Coralaviere gestures to Delphi and guides him towards the stairs. The crowd does not part so much as conveniently thins as they pass. By tradition no Elf of the Blood stands below the Queen's Dais (or King's as it is presently and temporarily styled) and no elf of any other house stands upon it. In practice they come and go with enough frequency that some fifth cousin prince minor might be holding forth on the floor and a page, field marshal, or other such power might be on the Dais speaking with the Sovereign. Today the line between elves has been fiercely drawn and the full glory of Lomar's house has arrayed itself. A good four hundred haughty, long-nosed elves of infinitely elegant attire and tasteful wealth position themselves in abstrusely complex relationships of power and meaning, the most conniving, dangerous, and important of them near Sæceæn himself. Among them weaves the unranked baroness Dvorhah bedecked in stark black, handing out drug laced macarons with her silver encrusted fingers. Even the servants are elite royalty.

Next to him, standing by his right and touching his arm, his sister Lady Ashlelani Greyleaf, Matron of the Stars, Keeper of the Broken Ankh, Oracle and Priestess, Elf of Supreme Rank watches the retinue as it advances. Like a binary star, his black clothing has been eclipsed by her grande luxe couture. Lady Ash has draped herself in yards of spun gold and blood. Her dress courses with the beating of a diamond heart, glowing in tendrils of blazing crimson. Her Shine decimates the room with unfolding light, a sharp painful thorn of inhuman beauty that stabs the sensitive eye and forces it by dint of its majesty, ferocious luminance, and magical intensity to look away. She has layered herself with charms and glamers so thick they cling to her like a cloying musk.

Delphi keeps an even pace and advances without expression. Any strategist might infer that the Lady and her brother have in their dazzling way made assassination all but impossible except face to face. She obscures and bends the target of the throne—no killing missile can hit what cannot be seen, and the guardians of technology and ageless soldiering will have removed the kinds of weapons that might damage an area. More than that, her beauty shines forth so gloriously that the elves near her weep. Small delicate handkerchiefs have been made available by some handmaiden; they match exactly her ensemble, calling attention to her influence. Silence accentuates their hauteur.

As the escort walks Delphi towards the bone stairs, they are touched lightly by Elven fingers, a greeting, a warning, an affectation that unnerves the uninitiated. In days before the nineteenth king, in the court of the first queens, it became clear that outlanders from beyond the Assassin's Guild's sinecure meant the Throne harm. Every manner of illusion, deception, shape shifting, suicide vest, and the like had been employed to bring Death and the Sovereign face to face. It became habit to verify outsiders, habit became pro forma, and in time, as the millennia passed, it became a thing unto itself, a conversation of sorts between these amoral people and the outlanders who invade their demesne. Fingers clawed with stylish jeweled razors, elaborate nails, and gloves of various alien pelts compete with the softer and equally dangerous skin of the elves. By turns delicate, savage, or probing, the assembled viscerally coerce and influence outsiders who run their gauntlet.

"Whoa, Pops, did you just really…?"

"Yeah Daddy, did you really? But Zoe, what did he do?"

"Ummm, so Max, the elves are into some adult stuff. Like they are aren't just bad, they're naughty. Kind of seriously naughty."

"Like go to bed early naughty?"

"Exactly like that Max. From the mouth of babes, eh Zoe?"

"Yeah. This story just got kinda cool Pops. Keep going."

"Less interruptions?"

"More elven kink?"

"Zoe, it's nothing but kink for the elves and there's whole long tale to be told…"

"So yeah, Max and me want to hear that. We'll be quiet and just listen. Right Max?"

"Yeah, bad elves are cool."

Those who touch Delphi flinch. Austen's dying agony preserved these long years by the defenses of the court reverberates from the stain on his stylish hat like an echoing wail. By the end of his approach, the elves have actually parted from the cortege's path. Fear, anger, outrage, disdain ripple through the ocean of ancients followed by something more primeval and thrilling. Is it Him? Does it Matter? The King shall prevail? The City dares? Do we fight? Can he be finessed? Can he be stopped?

A new face arrives, one not yet noted in our little tale. Now steps forth onto the stairs descending the King's Own reigning duelist of Chafrium, the avowed rival of the warlord Kizervexius, his *Vrashnaralla*—variously translated as "future betrayer", "lovingly despised", "bloodbound enemy" and "ardent opponent"—the Great and Good Supreme General,

Revered Intimate of Inner Rank, King's Own Swordbearer, Blade of the Throne, Viscount and Minister Absolute, Lord Duke Dahnstalyon of House Rexor. The Lord Duke embodies every arrogant excess of Grey Elves: swaggering down the stairs fully confident in his legendary prowess with both blade and love, loathsome in his layers of regalia, medals, and baroque ornamentation, glamered, Shined, perfumed and powdered with some kind of Enhancing Dust. He has personally murdered over 1,000 Austenites between the dueling plaza and the battlefield, each death lovingly commemorated on his scabbard by a small carved diamond with the foe's name, the method of dispatch and a date. If he were not the most beloved, dangerous, and powerful man in Sæceæn's palace, the nobility would despise him. He has the ear of the king and the bed of the king's sister demanding pride of place as Chafrium's foremost general. He prances down the alabaster stairs delicate, ferretlike, and full of menace.

Coralaviere does not bow to this man. Dahnstalyon has everything a man of his birth and opportunity could possibly seize and dominate, but he does not have much in the way of a Vanguard. Oh, his citations and regalia stagger. His placements, his official awards, his ranks and honors astound. But in battle this soft murderer has accrued not even one Sancurion; nor in court life has he secured anything greater. So he must bow to the Lord Adjutant, which he does with irony and a giggling wink to the courtiers. He then ostentatiously ignores the escort, concentrating on Delphi himself. "You came as called, janjack." The words cascade over the audience hall, bright with Vox in syrupy insulting English.

Delphi gives a bow to the throne and Lady above and to his left, then answers, throwing his High Elvish up the stairs. "I have come as requested to hear the entreaty of Chafrium's King."

The Viscount hisses and descends to the floor, standing within inches of Delphi. His fury overcomes him, and for a moment all illusion of weakness dims. His feet purchase the floor with deadly certainty, his hands loose and threatening. "I am speaking to you." Gone is the English.

Delphi looks down at the smaller, angrier noble. "But, Lord Duke, I am not speaking to you." Before the eye can blink, The King's Own has grabbed the janjack's coat and attempted to throw him. Instead Dahnstalyon lets out a howl of pure despair, flying back onto the stair and then, dignity stolen, he vomits helplessly upon his own finery and the stairs around him. For those who notice such small changes, one diamond on his adored scabbard turns a dim cloudy red. Delphi takes his hat and, to punctuate his feelings on the exchange, slaps the bloodstain against the swordsman's face, crumpling the crown. In reply the Minister Absolute screams in anguish, the stink of his burning flesh filling the room. Sound and smell amplified hundredsfold by his layers of enhancing dust and Vox. Polite choking and gasps of displeasure fill the vicinity and the elves skitter away like insects.

Delphi takes a moment, toys with the crown and brim until the hat proves again serviceable. Placing it upon his impassive brow, he bows gravely with full courtly splendor to the King and his retinue above watching. Having served Jane's memory, her whimpering murderer insensate and humiliated, he turns to Ral, tossing him a quip in French. "The man clearly needs better spies."

Ral, for his part, looks with utter disdain upon the ersatz warrior who let pain cripple him, involuntarily flexing his left arm. His Sancurion flares. Memories. "And better perfume."

The bon mot filters through the throng of jackals and some amused predator starts to snigger. Soon the assembly teems with laughter and loose gaiety. Small ardent applause escapes a band of cuirassiers on the far right, assumedly old loyal swords of Kizervexius's party. A pair of pages hoist the fouled Duke and carefully convey him to a side hall. Life resumes and the coterie again nears The Elf Lord and his charge.

A solemn Elven lady descends, her eyes tearful, her hands gripping the expected kerchief in her left and a vellum envelope in her right. The kidskin matches the King's bone dais. Where Dahnstalyon entered fey and full of malicious glee, she saunters with hips swaying and carries with her the effortless sensuality of her Lady. She wears layers of gossamer and stars, glowing, revealing and laying into shadows her hourglass body. For the lean Grey Elves she seems almost Rubenesque, being heavy of hip and breast, her arms full fleshed and bare. Coiled along them are snakes of silver and gold, worked in gems and, to no one's astonishment, still alive. Little bells and the smell of Spring morning accompany her. Small faeries flit about her, tousling her raven hair and forest gown. Her eyes are Death Herself, still, empty and calling. First Lady in Waiting, the Contessa Principale and Personal Confidante of Lady Ash, Princess Meleyasza drifts down to the floor accompanied by a cool breeze and the quiet symphony of scent, light, and warmth that comes with her sylphs.

Coralaviere gives her a smiling bow full of appreciation and, one detects, interest. Many suspect she keeps the King's bed. None know save her Lady and Sæceæn. It is of provident interest and worth several pounds of alchemical gold in Austen to have proof. The Princess bows back, displaying her glistening cleavage. Delphi waits until she addresses him, and upon receiving her eye, he sweeps off his hat and drops to one knee. Before she can react he places his head upon her feet and bestows a small kiss. At once submissive and audacious, Delphi has also done a very clever thing: the Court's Assassins, seeing Meleyasza neither flinch nor falter, recede into the full shadows of the hall, no longer training their deadly sights upon the janjack.

Her court Elven sounds old-fashioned and terrifically elegant. Unaugmented by ridiculous Shine or Dust, it lingers at the foot of the stairs barely within earshot of the closest courtiers. "You grace me with a boon, janjack, in making my necessary precautions needless."

Delphi rises again but holds his hat in his right hand. Again the signal clear: *My sword hand is occupied.* That he still holds a weapon escapes few. "The Lady compliments me overmuch. Your fame and beauty are known across all the Doors of the Worlds. Who blessed with such temptations would not dare steal a kiss?"

Here the Contessa smiles, but her eyes are still shadowed whorls of infinity. No smile touches those or perhaps ever has.

"But why then, Mister Janjack, did you not try stealing one from my lips?"

Delphi does a curt bow with accompanying boot click, his spurs musical in the near silence of the eavesdropping gallery. "I was not thus invited."

"Nor were you invited to touch my hem or kiss my leathers. Still you advanced upon me, sir."

Here the janjack finally smiles, revealing his many sharp teeth. "You hold me to account, then?"

She seems to examine him, letting the silence speak for her. Her eyes rove across his immaculate presence, his well-worn Elven style saber, his stained top hat, his unsmiling eyes, grey and sad. "Perhaps I invite you to dare my lips?"

"That," he announces with a loud and crisp voice, "would put me into deadly opposition with all your many and varied paramours. No man could survive the audacity of your favor."

"But you'd attempt it if it were offered? I imagine this of you, Delphi Janjack of Austen."

Again the bow, again the small click of boots and then a narrow genuine smile for the Lady only. "On duty, no, my Princess, I cannot. In my official capacity as Delphi Janjack, never. As a man who admires a woman, a swordsman and a gentleman, I'd hazard almost any obstacle to win the charms of someone as lovely as thee."

Here the Lady Elf surprises the hall and gives him a curtsy. She extends the envelope to the janjack and the perfume of the letter proliferates everywhere instantly. Roses, lavender, myrhh, and witchcraft with its whiff of hunger, spite, and sensual frolic linger. Summer, love, certainty, loyalty, delight, and evanescence. The Lady Herself. "And so you have, Sir."

He cracks the seal and reveals the warm red paper within. Delphi, Janjack of Austen, may in the company of the Personal Confidante of Lady Ashlelani Greyleaf approach the King of all the Known Worlds to confer and be heard. Did they expect the Lord Duke to fail? It's a question that matters to the astute watcher of the Court. When word passed to the King, did he follow the intent and logical consequences of the memory hat? Did he send his man to such brutal humiliation?

All worth knowing and none known. On such mysteries the elves will dine for many moons, and if the affair should blossom into something sticky and repulsive like a war or scandal, then it shall be discussed incessantly into the years and decades beyond.

Her eye sharp and imperative, she turns to the Lord Adjutant and then begins to rise. Coralaviere motions politely to Delphi, and together the friends climb towards the judgment of Sæceæn XIX. While they mount the stairs, the hush of the room returns. Was there ever any question of the King and Delphi meeting? None. But where—that matters. Usually, and this confuses outlanders, the King comes down from his aerie, which signals your lower status. Your ruinous presence cannot be allowed upon the sacred Dais, and while it inconveniences the King, his discomfort and irritation are necessary because you've shown up without having the good grace to be Elven, well dressed, and acceptable to court. Occasionally you are allowed to rise to meet the King and witness the regalia, the throne, and the secret doings of the Great Master Race. Your inconvenience is a great honor, you will be told, and your being made to traipse up and away from all hope of rescue or protection should not in the least discomfit or alarm you. No, meeting the King on his Dais honors and enhances you. The rumors of supplicants being thrown from the high step should be ignored. In Lomar's day, they were said to leave the bodies to rot for a full lunar cycle. Petitions to Chafrium's Lord diminished greatly thereafter.

Delphi climbs the stairs, hat still tucked under his right arm, followed by Coralaviere, who will execute him unthinking should his King give a nod. Both smile peculiarly, a look common to a certain class of gentleman and therefore to duelists. The time has come to pay for their intransigence on Sixth Street or be rewarded, as the case may be. Below them, the elves begin to mill and gossip. The resplendent electronics coupled with some simple Magewalls make the upper platform utterly inaccessible to easvesdroppers. Clever little spines of various drugged liqueurs are passed around and the retinue recommences its frivolities as if this were any gala soiree—and perhaps it is. In contrast, the grim silent faces of the King's House come into view. Here all eyes are grey and no one dares smile. The kind face of the King gives way to his real visage, one of a patient, dangerous monster able to tame the whole room with lifted finger.

Lomar, ever the joker, etched his throne with various comical ribald motifs, portraits of monsters and admired women, adding a small table to hold food, drink, and dice and on the left a small chessboard filled with platinum and gold figures, frozen mid-game. His strategist Smith used to pull up a common wooden chair and play. A man matching Smith's description, human, plain and unassuming, occasionally plays with the present King. Sæceæn has added two swords in scabbards hanging off the right throneback and a small astrolabe-like device set upon his snacking table. He holds a platinum goblet of something steaming, sipping now and then indifferently. His sister, upon closer direct inspection, burns with magnificence. Around her weep her relations, stern and stonefaced.

Meleyasza turns and elegantly sweeps behind her Lady, whispering as she goes. The Matron of the Stars nods and her eyes sharpen, sending the corona of her solar storm flaring out. Below, murmurs begin. Delphi simply stops upon the Dais exactly one stride from the edge of the perilous stairs. Next to him, Lord Adjutant Coralaviere makes his heartfelt bow to his King. "As you requested my King, the janjack Delphi of Austen."

As an elf of sacred rank Coralaviere may dispense with the usual hour of pleasantries and honorifics. He may require an army, but here, elf to elf, he comes as close to equal with his King as he ever should or will. Sæceæn motions adroitly for him to rise. "I heard the anarchists came out in force."

The Adjutant nods and makes a small sweeping bow. "Spies, my Lord. The Guilds in all force and every House came out. Whatever thing you intended, this will not be a small or quiet affair."

Lady Ash intrudes, her voice so strong with Emphasis and hanging with so much Vox that it cuts the skin in little prickles. "Do you doubt, Messenger, that my brother the Sovereign would not apprehend this?"

Coralaviere turns and does not bow nor flinch despite

blood running from his eyes. "My Lady Priestess, I serve the Seneschal who serves your brother our Beloved King. I neither doubt nor assume anything of my liege. I am honor bound to fulfill my duties including giving counsel to my lord when he so requests."

The King lays a hand on his sister's. "Enough, Ash. It's not his fault Stalyo got ambushed with a hat. It's certainly not his fault the man fouled himself in public. Or is it, Coralaviere? Could this have been avoided?" A chill runs through the air and all seems thicker.

The Adjutant considers for a moment, looking over Delphi impassive and stock still next to him, the offending hat under his arm. "I did not surmise that this janjack had acquired Hoode's hat." The faces of the impudent nobles begin to goggle and squint with varieties of curiosity, shock and disbelief. Hoode's hat. The God of Chaos. Lomar's *Desideralla*. The betrayer of Chafrium and its patron saint. The sacrament of the Proletariat. His wizard's hat should have been lost when Lomar exiled him to outer dimensions. The first memory hat, the father of all such devices, the masterpiece of alchemy, eldritch rites, sorcery, and alien technologies. Hoode's damned hat. Coralaviere asserts some two-bit no-name janjack from the pleasure provinces of Elvendom has acquired this priceless artifact.

"Perhaps if I had sent ahead this news it would have changed how the Viscount greeted our entourage."

The King considers, sipping from his drink. On his hand, the ring of office glints dully, and he thumbs it, turning the band around his thin bony flesh. "When did you ascertain it was Hoode's?"

"When his flesh burned, my Lord Sovereign. Only the original has this property. Hoode's Incantation of Thirteenfold Return. He incorporated it into his hat and it killed many men who dueled him until Toki Ojawa gave the secret to our Master Strategist Smith."

A wry smile and a motion of the steaming cup. "After, we note, the General had been struck by the hat. But Lord Adjutant, you certainly knew what touching it would mean to him."

Here the statue of the janjack moves and with a cough and

a crisp bow from the waist interjects. "Your Majesty. He could hardly have anticipated that I'd provoke him."

The Lady turns her face upon the bugbear who stares back uncrying and unmoved. "And why is this, rude janjack from the plane of Terra?" Her brother's hand appears upon her wrist, a clenched tether of steel.

Delphi gives her a delicate nod. "Because, Madame, *no one* provokes your lover."

"My lover you say. Not General, not Hand of the King, not Greatest Swordsman, not Viscount. No one provokes him because…"

"He is your lover and no one dares provoke your Ladyship."

She advances, her arm pinned to the throne, but her sharp menacing eyes ferociously magnified within the constellations of her magic. "Yet you clearly have."

Delphi laughs softly and gives them a smile, all fangs. "I am, after all, no one, and thus the only person who can."

Sæceæn releases her and begins to clap as he bursts out in buoyant laughter. His merriment carries across his discomforted relations and down into the greater throng milling below them. He curls into a catlike ball on his throne, feet dangling off the left arm and weeps with delight. "You are not at all what I expected."

Delphi then gives the King of the Universe a deep proper bow. "And you, my Great King, to the contrary, are exactly what I expected."

The Lady breaks into a thin, terrifying smile. "And what did you expect of the King?"

"Unpredictability, my Lady."

She nods and, looking over her brother, smiles slightly more intensely. "This will be precisely what he says of you as well."

The King rights himself, wipes away a laughing tear and with it all evidence of emotion. He could be stone. "Delphi Janjack, I have a problem that both lies within and beyond my jurisdiction."

"It involves Austen?"

The King nods and waves for refreshments. A tall majestic elf of some woodland extraction traipses toward them bearing a diamond tray with ruby goblets bearing something dark and murky. Delphi accepts the cup and sips without question. Everyone knows the rules. When he does not drop dead it appears no one dares anger the City.

"It involves Austen." The elf gestures to his anguished sister. "And The Lady. Her daughter has gone missing."

And here the room goes silent. For however long Qelniasherah Greyleaf has been missing the secret has been strictly kept. The Lady Who Waits, the Silent Princess, the Green Queen; Qelniasherah in Elvish means "bittersweet memory." The angry root, the fiery headstrong vicious petty defiant and at time terrifying *infant terrible*, Qelniasherah. Lady Nia to her intimates. Gnash to her detractors. Absent, mislaid, or abducted. The whispers rise and fall like the heaving chest of a dying giant.

Delphi gives a short nod and clicks his spurs. "I crave your pardon, your Majesty, and perhaps your indulgence, but am I to understand that the heir to the Skeleton Throne has gone missing in Austen?"

The Lady's eyes darken into storms. "She left us a note. Our trackerbeasts followed her scent to your shores and have lost all traces."

Sæceæn swirls his drink and sips. "Within your city my heir resides. She has not left it and somehow she has found a way to mask her Vanguard and avert all scrying." Four hundred pairs of solemn hateful eyes look upon Delphi, silent, weeping and intent. Behind him his Desideralla waits, sword arm free and poised. War has been declared in all but name.

A moment, an aside, for those less versed in the intricacies of Lomar and his clans' eccentricities. The Grey Emperor, the Ravager of Worlds, never lost anything he ever wanted found. Indeed, to this day questers and huntsmen revere the God of the Distant Stars as the Patron of Retrieval. Through his bodyman Sæceæn, Lomar tracked down his every friend and enemy, even the unfindable Hoode who once ruled Chafrium's undertowns. In the history of the Skeleton Throne there have been a handful of incidents where a Royal went missing, either by skullduggery or whim. Chafrium's armies, its assassins or its shriveled overlords of the Academy have found them and brought them home, often from the charred ruins of whatever fortress or sanctuary in which they found a place to slum. Chafrium has never lost an heir, and until the nineteenth King gets some elf with child, Gnash the Rash inherits the Lands. Her mother the Lady cannot; the inheritance rules are so abstruse it makes even elves cringe whenever the relevant documents are untombed. And this young woman has just gone missing in a small city-state adjacent to Chafrium, conveniently connected by multiple Doors and utterly incapable of resisting a full onslaught from the most ruthless centralized power in the Known Universe.

Delphi takes a thoughtful sip of his drink (perhaps wine, perhaps something more exotic) and does nothing. The collective elves wait silently, the King impassive, the Lady a hawk with golden talons outstretched. His voice sounds like a wave crashing upon some alien shore: "This speaks of an accomplice, one would suggest."

The King nods and his smile breaks into a thin cruel line. His feet brush the floor made of his dead enemies. "One would. One takes note that you, Janjack, also do not sport a Vanguard."

Here they turn facing one another, the janjack outmassing the slight ruler by a goodly foot and a half of sheer ferocious muscle. The King has already flexed his considerable might with aplomb. Delphi sets one obvious implied challenge aside immediately: "There are, as you rightly suggest, a limited number of ways to mask a Vanguard. Death and rebirth as a janjack could satisfy the conditions, but my City would know her and thus, so too I." He makes a significant and utterly correct bow. "I give you my sincerest word of honor that I alas do not and most fervently wish I did."

Here the Lady moves in for a closer kill. "So that you might avoid unpleasantness, Janjack?"

"No my Lady, so that you might." He gives another slight click of his spurs and bows to her gravely. "The remaining possibilities are few and all devastating. She may have taken one of the cloaking orbs of Norlexenj'ar; she may have mastered the incantation of Nod or had an accomplice with sufficient skill to do so for her; or, she may have acquired within the Palace

Royale one of the Nine Songs of Hoode. All of these require a powerful patron—each a direct relative of yours."

Ral moves closer. "What nine songs are these? How is that we have not heard of them?"

Here the Lady smiles and surprises the entire ensemble: Ashlelani Greyleaf actually knows the Nine Songs themselves and has touched them, sung them, spoken in secret to Hoode. Next to the bonfire of war with Austen, this small confidence trick of hers looks like a supernova. Kizervexius, her lover, gone, and possibly she helped him? Or slew him and covered him in a Song. Her own child has disappeared and now, the ominous truth dawning upon the silent and sepulchral Dais high above the world, The Lady herself has become the prime suspect in a mystery at turns murderous, fascinating and utterly scandalous.

Almost the entire ensemble. Several faces register recognition or acquiescence or mere curiosity, betraying foreknowledge or perhaps suspicion. Coralaviere for his part has always known despite his protests otherwise. He serves the Seneschal whose business is to know and to never say. The Contessa Principale keeps a stone face and the King sighs, but it's clear he has pushed his sister to this painful revelation. Clear to all four hundred relations as well, and thus the wheels behind their slate eyes churn. War has been declared in all but name and Sæceæn XIX stands to lose his neck. Delphi simply listens; he has a face built for poker and he plays Austen's hand all-in.

The story so simple, so despicable and Elven. A few decades before the disappearance of Kizervexius, Lady Ash decided to take another lover—in itself not a burden on the Elves nor a danger to the Throne, though as the King's prime man and trusted Voice, the Lord Protector had enough social cachet to make the ensuing public kerfuffle...difficult. What's a manipulative, brilliant, decadent woman of several thousand years with nigh unlimited power to do? In this case she sent one of her handmaidens to find the God of Chaos, her family's mortal enemy and sometimes occasional salvation, and consort with him. For in her Palace hung nine shadows of star, song and entropy—The Songs of Hoode. Like Lomar, Hoode once walked among the living and amassed in his adventures a coterie of artefacts, nanotech, and magical enigmas. He experimented upon his enemies and sometimes unfortunately upon men who called him friend. He manipulated peoples and nations, time and memory. He built illusion upon deceit upon betrayal and bones. And he found many things in secret pockets of the universe which elevated him beyond mortal ken and transformed him into a huge, dangerous, profound blasphemy—a god. As a god, a small bloodthirsty human minded deity, he wove the Songs, little snippets of empty cold hate folded upon themselves. Each hideous vortex sings its own mournful dirge to the Universe from which it has been ripped, a raw wound calling to its birthplace.

These Songs only gods can hear. Lomar, the elf, stole a god's talents and then he removed the treasures from Hoode's fortress. None knows how but all know why. The enmity between the two beings had grown and festered. Hoode loved the Songs and so his beloved must be taken from him as Hoode had so often taken from Lomar. They hang in a small hallway within the Donjon, forgotten to all but the inner family, casting their eerie emptiness into an already dark and morally void place. They also whisper and if one can learn their language they teach of many terrible things, among them death after life and life without death. One of their small talents that so possesses the privacy-obsessed Grey Elves came to Ash's attention. Brushed just so with skin and song and blood sacrifice, the recipient might for a period go unseen by the Universe—erased from consciousness itself.

So it came to be that Lady Ashlelani Greyleaf, Matron of the Stars, Keeper of the Broken Ankh, Oracle and Priestess, Elf of Supreme Rank gave her flesh to Hoode for a time in exchange for a few crucial secrets, and thereafter she stole in her lover, Lord Duke Dahnstalyon of House Rexor, a man now acquainted with mysteries and secrets sufficient to displace Kizervexius on all fronts. This simple revelation casts into doubt every agreement, secret alliance, backstabbing side venture, and double cross the whole House Royale has been planning within itself for centuries. The missing Lord Protector reemerges as a point of political contention. Now the heir, the possibly compromised

Lady Nia, has vanished, through magic so similar to her mother's dark pact it casts a stain of indelible rumor. How delicious all this war and intrigue and blasphemous treachery, how perfect for the season if one has the right clothes and matching drugs, which of course any elf (even the lower orders milling about in Chafrium's streets) will certainly possess.

Delphi (who might also be the Footman), confronted with what the observer might infer is damning evidence about Kizervexius's complete undoing, gives away nothing. He manfully scratches his chin and reflects, looking down among the glittering snake of bodies that wait for news and opportunity. "And am I to also surmise that your Majesty called upon me specifically because I am rumored to know the location of Norlexenj'ar?"

Lady Ashlelani shakes her head. "No. In frankness, I asked for you." Can he be finessed? Is it Him? Can he be stopped? Does it Matter?

Delphi bows to her. "I am at a loss as to imagine why you would ask for me, Your Grace."

She smiles grandly, sending blades of beauty through the crowd. Several of the weaker relations on the edge faint. War has begun—or perhaps, as many watchers of the court remark, it has never ended. "Fourteen years ago you found a small girl, Melissa Betancuriana, who had been kidnapped from her home by a group of cultists." She flicks her hands and a small cameo appears with the likeness of Gnash engraved upon it. She places it softly upon Delphi's hat. "My men told me you tracked her across three Doors and unraveled several conspiracies to find her." As Delphi begins to speak she holds up her delicate hand, so pure in the glamered light. "And then spent the better part of the next decade hunting down the cultists and dueling those who would not submit to arrest. In all," she theatrically consults memory and her closed eyes bring a momentary relief to the besieged elves, "you killed seventy-three men, nine of them wizards of some renown, and among them four very famous sabreurs. Another dozen or so rot in your jails."

The King stands and the crowd begins to rustle, rippling backward and out of his path. "As you can imagine, I am beyond concern with my heir's welfare. My time, by nature of her manner of evasion, proves limited. I must make Austen my jurisdiction far too soon."

"Unless Austen cedes your heir to you." They lock eyes, each a grey whorl of indefinite emotion.

"Indeed." The King gestures with his thin fingers. "Unless she returns."

Delphi coughs, places the cameo in his right jacket pocket, and doffs his hat. He makes a sharp, almost mocking bow. "Your Majesty, to serve my nation I must slight yours. You have a saboteur within your House. How do you suggest I divine this?"

The Lady holds out a bone-colored scroll with a blazing seal upon it. "No, Delphi Janjack. We instead ask what you suggest and require." She has placed within his reach a Writ of All, the skeleton key of social power. With it he may come and go as he wishes, speak with anyone, and most impressively, speak with the Sovereign. With it he may presumably solve the mystery and save his City: he becomes, briefly, a member of the Court Royale granted power over Chafrium and its demesnes. With it comes Death.

To whom does the Court Royale think they have handed this precious object, and more intriguingly, why? Why give it to him, whichever *him* you believe Delphi to be? The elves aflutter with looks, hand signals, imperceptible sighs and a thousand other utterly crass gestures of conviction, have begun their unfolding argument. In time—perhaps minutes, perhaps hours—the revelers below will perceive the truth and all hell, as the Austenites so fondly put it, will certainly break loose. Have not the Guilds and their antagonists assembled in force? All of Chafrium rises for War.

The Lady surprises the assembled a second time, something so alien to the Court (in its long fastidious love affair with predictability) that several aristocrats, having misread their cues, actually break step and shamefully collide with their fellows. A glass falls and shatters, raining embarrassment and omen upon the gala below. She closes in to Delphi and places the Writ in his hand with both of her hers; then, leaning she might kiss him, she begins to whisper. "You've met him? That's where you got the Hat?"

Delphi ponders, his eyes darkening in thought. "Say rather, Lady, that I stole it from him in a fair fight."

"Then you know…" Her eyes meet his. "You know the prices I have paid. She's a child still."

Delphi leans down and kisses her hands, still clasped upon his sword arm. "Chafrium has my word as Austen's janjack that I will not rest until she returns to a place of protection."

Still she does not release him. "Find her, Delphi. For me."

The Contessa Meleyasza approaches and begins to guide her Lady down the bone steps to some other part of the Palace. As she departs, she turns her head and gives Delphi a radiant smile. "As a man who admires a woman, a swordsman and a gentleman, will you do it for me?"

Delphi places the Writ with the cameo and bows to the departing Ladies, so perfectly he might be an Elven courtier. He turns and gives the King of All Lands a curt martial bow. "I will do it, of course, because it is my pleasure to do my duty and my duty is clear. And forgive me, Ladies, but I will do it for Qelniasherah Greyleaf—who, though Silent, deserves a voice."

CHAPTER 4: THE INN OF THE HORNY GORGON

The flight from the Palace proves a simple thing. With the Writ and Coralaviere serving as his keys to entry, Delphi quickly navigates a series of servant corridors and hidden passages meant to aid assignations and murders. He arrives upon a nameless backstreet within the high sloped slums of Chafrium. His Desideralla has loaned him a cheap, weatherstained cloak and some local coin. Ral, good to his word, has not sent men to spy, though Delphi knows the assassins and wizards will soon be on his tail. For a brief moment he stands disguised, anonymous and alone, in the parts of the City elves generally do not tread. He has a chance to take stock.

In times like this he has taken to talking to himself. "Delphi, you are most certainly screwed."

A low and deadly little voice sings out from atop the nearest wall. "You are more than *screwed,* my lovely. You are in danger." Delphi swivels to see two small shapes astride the wall, roughly his height from the ground. The larger shape lurks slightly in the shadows, its outline a study in black and white fur. Two small, very green eyes gleam from within the smaller shape's catlike face.

He knows without knowing that the smaller, sleeker, black-and-white cat has done the talking. To call her a cat is, in a way, to mangle language. This creature, a thin magnificent prowling thing, is to the average cat as a charging bull is to, say, a sausage—infinitely more alive, dangerous, and powerful. She weighs all of fifteen pounds, yet even Delphi feels little pits of fear in his stomach. Her pale green-gold eyes sparkle with intelligence.

He tries not to smile. "And who invited you to this party?"

The lady cat swishes her tail in a distinctive manner that *feels* like annoyance. "I am of course Senior Cat. I invite myself, Delphi." She lifts a lazy paw to the behemoth of cat behind her, now lumbering out of the shadows and more than double her size—perhaps forty or so pounds—but intriguingly similar in black and white coloration and pattern. "Junior Cat... does what pleases him. Which almost always means following me."

Senior Cat flicks her tail in a way that seems to say *decisive* and jumps down in a motion so fluid she appears to fly. She lands upon Delphi's shoulder and curls around his neck. "Shall we dispense with the formalities?"

Again a detour of sorts seems in order. These are not *cats* as one would know them. Say instead they are the mother and father of all cats, the ur-felines of eternity. Among the many whispers that are the history of Chafrium it has been said that these two are immortal and nearly eternal, having been there when light and dark separated. Nonsense, of course, but indicative of how powerful, ancient, and ultimately pure in essence these two really are—senior and junior, mother and father, void and absence of void. They are gods of sorts, watching angels, demons to many, and last, perhaps most importantly, they are aligned to a cause so old and broken they are out of step with modernity as it was defined before the rise of Lomar. The Cats serve the memory of Arüne, the sleeping god.

Delphi laughs and for a moment his feline essence seems ascendant. "Where do you want to begin?"

Junior Cat lumbers closer on the wall. "Why didn't they ask if you were the Footman?"

His partner flicks her ears with exasperation. "Tch. They *know* he's the Footman, or suspect it. Hence the Writ. Asking shows their weakness."

Delphi rubs a small corner of her ear with his gloved hand. "And puts The Lady in danger. The Footman would be honor-bound to avenge Kizervexius. Even all these years later." He hears the bitterness in his voice, and it surprises him.

Senior Cat bites his fingers softly. "Self-indulgent, your species. Pay attention. We know who you are. We have known you your whole brief life, *Delphi.*" Her emphasis on the last word sends prickles of fear down the spine. Delphi remembers suddenly with whom he has the pleasure to pass the time.

Then he smiles and rubs her chin with tenderness, eliciting the kind of nine-alarm, rumbling earthquake that might level a city. She has begun to purr. "Indeed you have," he says. "So they gave me some tools, asked no questions, and clearly must be desperate."

Junior Cat has inexplicably arrived in front of Delphi, standing on a broken gate, his weight slowly bending it. "Will you stand by Sæceæn? Without Gnash, he falls. It's not your fight, but he was your friend once."

Delphi shrugs. "Austen falls unless I bring her back. For all her spoiled excess, she's still a child. Gods of below, she isn't even two hundred. And with a father like Stalyo, it's a miracle she hasn't taken to carving the ears off servants for entertainment."

The purring stops. Senior Cat rises onto his shoulder, nipping at his neck. "You will not let Austen fall, child. Instead, you shall keep your petty disputes out of this."

In a flash Junior Cat rests upon his other shoulder, a bulk delicately balanced and immovable. "It is a thing that must be fixed. You might be the only one who can help the lost empress."

"She has Sæceæn."

"Who is constrained, you fanciful idiot, by his own Court and by Chafrium itself. Don't play stupid."

Delphi holds up his hands in mock surrender. He must soon move into the slums, putting narrow corridors of desolation between him and the professionals who want to find him. "You said you were dropping the formalities. How long are we going to pretend you haven't come to beg a boon?"

This earns a swat from Junior Cat's paw which, even slight and playful, draws a mild welt upon the skin. "You started this with your ridiculous costume changes and running around heartbroken and making Senior Cat fret. She actually fretted about you."

"And here I am to assuage all concern. I come here often, don't I?"

Senior Cat flicks her tail with admiration. "So well done,

changing the subject. Almost a cat, and so young." She disappears to some shadow on a wall. "Mark our words: we like Austen too much to let it fall because of the wrongs done you. We shall expect success from thee."

Junior Cat drops to the ground and bites his ankle. To a normal man it would feel something like being crushed by a vice; Delphi knows he's just been shown the closest thing to love Junior knows how to deliver. "We cannot be expected to worry about you twice in a millennium. Listen to Senior Cat." His tail slaps Delphi's boots. Then both cats are shadow and only the soft danger of their musk lingers.

Delphi begins a careful dance through the slums. Throngs of the Guilds' men have begun to move in force, the streets growing silent and empty as their little armies pass through. The Writ has made him twice the target he was when he entered Chafrium. While his name stains the page, a competent forger armed with a few essentials like unicorn blood and some nano weave can replace it with another name. The value of such a thing might be nearly unlimited for someone needing to undo a single command, bend one rule, or pass one barred gateway. By tradition, such writs are never passed to persons incapable of stopping anyone with such absurd and larcenous intentions.

Time, he realizes, to do something magnificently drastic. The Cats have seen him and called in debts old and unspoken. This was his City once, until he joined Austen, and he knows it as few living men can. Why have these ancients put themselves into play? He needs more understanding, more insight. He might as well face the next puzzle piece head-on. Whatever old hatreds he has discovered within his hulking heart, he must now push them aside to find Gnash and bring her home. Chafriumites know The Inn of the Horny Gorgon for three things: bad beer, worse criminals, and a back room where Hoode and Smith play chess. He must get there alive.

The geography of Chafrium baffles experts. The sewers alone merit five different degree programs at the Eternal University, and the Head of Sanitation, Public Safety and Vermin Relations must possess all of them. The City morphs over time, adding news places, altering locations as suits it. Sentience in Cities has been of academic interest for millennia. But the actualities of finding, say, Dock Twelve or the Cotton Warehouse on Dead Crow Avenue matter equally, and those facts are subject to change. Chafrium has three Dock Twelves in three different locales, each of which believes itself to be the ONLY Westward High Docks. Luckily there's only one Dead Crow Avenue, but its length varies on every count. It has, depending on which map one consults, six thousand and five buildings, seven thousand thirty eight, or on the Transplanar Guild's quantum flux map, nineteen master structures of hypercubic penteract origin.

The location of the Horny Gorgon should be questionable. But it is not. There are clear, inviolate fixed points within Chafrium which never move, never change, cannot be destroyed, and between which the distances have not varied in a million years. The Palace and the Hanging Gardens (where criminals are fed to the carnivorous plants of Ninebo Plane for public amusement), the Inn of the Horny Gorgon and the Northern Sewer Grate leading to Arüne's upper temple, the Doors and Central Market, all of these stand exactly as they always are and were. City layouts differ month to month, but they are there, exactly as expected and required. The spine of the City, perhaps. Which makes reconnoitering Chafrium an act of aplomb and memory, where one spelunks from one fixed point in time and space to another.

For a fee, the devious and unhelpful tour guides Azmael and The Corsair will provide unsatisfactory services to the very lost or very desperate at exorbitant prices. Still, no one dies when using their services. Chafrium has an unacceptably high fatality rate for residents and visitors alike. Were it not the only place that connects all others, and were it not the richest, most magically advanced, technically sophisticated, and socially important location in all of known existence, it would be despised and avoided at all costs.

People die there for good reasons and bad. Muggings turned to murders. Plagues, demons, revolutionary skirmishes, terrorism, counter-terrorism. Corruption of the City Guard, paid assassinations, missteps, road hazards, magical experiments, runaway magical experiments, necromancers, undead of every stripe, vampires in specific, undead hunters who use explosives, undead who use necro-balls on those hunters, and so on. It's an endless parade of carnage.

In Chafrium this means armored carriages and mercenaries who dissuade would-be brigands and such, but also a peculiar form of legal code, the Lex Vendetta—the reciprocal principle of sanctioned retribution that has been the backbone of the Guild system and the various royal families over eons. Kill the least of us and face our best killer or wizard or abomination.

Allegiances inside Chafrium are like the maps, shifting and subject to change at some universal whim. Few souls belong to only one guild or family, one single source of the loyalty. There are exceptions. The janjacks, for example, are such monofocused creatures. Some of the Higher Court and such are as well, by definition men like the Seneschal and his lieutenants. But for the most part the fickle Elves and their imitators like to layer loyalty and veins of power such that someone somewhere will be quite put out by your little stunt involving a bodkin and a dram of blade poison.

People who travel to Chafrium but fail to understand this nuanced field of crisscrossing, often contradictory loyalties make a hash of their business. They lose money and fingers, sometimes their lifeblood. Nor does any amount of warning or explanation help. Simply put, most living beings are too short-lived to really grasp why Elves do what they do or how abstruse their relationships and interconnections might be. They underestimate the probable damage done by hurting someone seemingly vulnerable. It explains Coralaviere's Shine that much more, a compassionate warning to the overzealous.

Does this stop the flow of people inward? Certainly not. Like any lottery, Chafrium represents a tax on those who cannot understand mathematics. But they pay with their bodies and souls rather than a few coins. It's an all or none game out there in the hideous streets. Tourists return to hostels to find the room or building simply no longer exists or has moved, or that they have been replaced by demonic shapeshifters or face brigands who, with a bribe, have been kindly ushered into their rooms. Does it stop tourism? Absolutely—for a few weeks in a few places. Until the story mutates and gossips have a field day tacking on resentments and speculation as to who did what to whom and why the dearly departed really got scratched from the worlds. Then, curiosity and impudence getting the better of the many fearless stupid roiling billions who live outside this little pocket of chaos and crime, they send more sacrifices to the altar and wait for the gods to answer.

Because in Chafrium, gods do walk. One street might host slums that make dungeons look appetizing, and then across the wide cobbled street a walled palace thick with guards and hostile magics towers over the whole of the block. Under which a teeming society of rat lords and verminous scorpioids trawl for treasures among the sewer trash. There are sewers and tombs and libraries and hidden vaults of gold and magic swords all the way down endlessly—just as impossible towers and floating castles and chateaus of mist and platinum float many hundreds of paces into the sky, occlusive and at times painfully oppressive to the sprawling urban poor. A place of a many, unthinkably many persons folded up and down, around miles of twisting roads that turn this way and that, some back on themselves in an endless figure eight. There are nine roads, three avenues, two boulevards, one route, and six alleys that are longer than many rivers all named Infinity.

This is what Delphi rushes towards, this snakepit of complex and inconsistent laws and morals. He knows the place well enough to make it from his fixed point to the next, to find the Inn within a few streets of where it stood last time. There are griffon riders already in flight, searching for him. Likely there are snipers on the rooftops and a bevy of scrying mages seeking him at all costs. He puts his mind into overdrive and rushes headlong into the baleful night, saber in hand and with a terrifying assurance that serves to pass him safely and without incident among the more feral residents lurking in the poorer neighborhoods.

It speaks much about the reach of the Guilds that Delphi does not reach the doorstep without a brace of pistol shots, several bolts from silenced crossbows, one ray with some kind of sizzling necromancy, and at least three types of homebuilt grenades being tossed his way. He leaves a cheerful wake of corpses and smoldering buildings behind him. By Chafrium standards he's been discreet.

The smell of a burning corpse always makes one's entrance to the Horny Gorgon. Add in gunshots and the screams of gutted men as you blithely step across the threshold and you have said something powerful, something that the rotgut scum of the foulest dive bar in the multiverse (a title to which no less than forty bars lay claim) respect to the point where they generally refrain from trying to mug, murder, rape, hug, proposition, eyeball, or otherwise interact with you. But being Chafrium, all bets are officially off. Delphi's boots track gore, fire, anguish, and some lingering mustard gas across the dark floor. He flicks blood on the nearest table, sheaths his dueling blade, and with a deft motion fires a single lethal shot behind him with his repeater. Some foolish wizard strangles on his missing throat and crumples half in, half out of the doorway, blocking the huge cobalt wedge that serves as emblem, threshold and occasional door. Then Delphi orders a milk.

The bartender, a mutilated orc by the charming name of Bloody Alice, smiles ear to missing ear and hands him a bottle of something brown with a skull for a label. "Obliged, Alice." He tosses the King's gold on her counter, far too much and glistening like falling stars.

Alice stares at it, her smile fading. "Delphi." She makes an obscene gesture to something knotted and hideous with limbs like tree trunks. The troll mutters, heaving itself towards the door and pushing back the small army of outraged and now terrified agents of various competing Guilds. A few gunshots, someone torn limb from limb, some shouting, and the judicious application of brute force resolve the battle for the door. Tock the Troll closes it behind him and begins to snack on his victims. Until he's done, no one goes in or out of the Inn.

Delphi considers the appalling mess Tock has started making across the floors and tables, then tosses a few more gleaming coins onto the counter. "Buy yourself something pretty." Behind him the troll burps up teeth.

Bloody Alice smiles again, rubs a burn scar with her dirty

finger, and motions Delphi to a door off the main room. "They're in." She hands him a glass.

Delphi turns, leans against the bar, and uses a handkerchief to clean the glass before pouring himself the smoking brew and taking a hefty swig. He can feel the alcohol punching the back of his head even as the magic kicks in and lifts every hair on his body for a moment. Icefire started as a poison, employed by the Assassins as a way to deliver a special message: we won't just kill you, we'll humiliate you in the most agonizing and long-lasting fashion possible. Human consumption of the beverage results in loose bowels, seizures, uncontrollable screaming, enlarged organs, eyes and tongue literally catching fire. But it happens in a kind of frieze of slowed time, where the victim spends hours trapped dying. It works to a greater or lesser degree on other species, and it has a special acidic quality when it touches Elven skin.

To prove the point, Delphi pours himself another and, with great precision, splashes the contents on a figure to his left. The elf stumbles into the light howling, his every contortion slow and spectacular. Weapons clatter to the floor as the man grips his melting chest. His screams hang in the night, echoing through the dull room.

Delphi carries the bottle and glass in his left hand and advances unmolested towards the door Alice has indicated. Since he has entered, with the exception of the tyro assassin he has just struck down, not a single person in the Horny Gorgon has approached the bar. They wait until he has knocked and entered, finally returning to business and pleasure when his bulk slips under the low frame into the bright room beyond.

Does it surprise you to find Hoode, the God of Chaos and arch-nemesis of the House Lomar, playing chess with a simple ageless man—Smith—the same man who plays the King, the same man who played Lomar? It should not. Our *dramatis personae* now sports two mysterious Cats, an immortal mad wizard, the chessmaster, a god who was asleep when Lomar acquired Chafrium, and perhaps the shade of absent Lomar himself. Add to that the self aware cities of Chafrium and Austen, things more and less than these gods. So many sticky poisonous fingers in the pot. It should astonish no one that old friends might meet and pass on the news. Survival requires it. There are things larger than even the local deities, things so vast in comparison that to them, the gods are like the mayflies of Austen.

Hoode looks up first. He sighs and hands the plain man a small sum of gold coins, Smith having predicted that Delphi would arrive at more or less this time and place. Delphi and Hoode are not exactly enemies, but they do not much enjoy one another's company, for reasons different to each man. The Footman has been unable to forgive the Old God his wiles and deceptions which shamed Kizervexius so thoroughly and to such devastating effect. Hoode simply wants his hat back, and by the abstruse rules of the game he and the Footman have played, he may not ask for it nor steal it nor, worst of all, have it stolen back. It must be given—and by the cruel smile of seething triumph Delphi flashes the Old Bastard, today will not be his day.

Smith takes his time with the chess board, moves a bishop, and then allows his plain brown eyes to fall upon the Footman. The entirety of what is known about Smith can be told by any child of any major world. He has always looked the same, a plain, dark haired man with brown eyes and medium build. He moves with neither grace nor speaks with exception; a thoroughly average specimen of humanity: tall, healthy, flat-faced, ethnically mixed and of entirely forgettable aspect. By *always*, some skalds of Chafrium claim he arrived with Lomar while others claim he knew the original Sæceæn thousands of years prior to Lomar making his way upon the scene. Regardless, he and Hoode are contemporaries and both men eons old. Last, he plays chess and plays it well. Not perfectly— and often people suspect he plays to lose, or to watch and learn—but well. He plays at or slightly above the ability of his opponent. He plays urchins and thieves, merchants, whores, Guild elders, Queens, and gods. He plays chess with everyone and he plays everywhere. If there is one City—Chafrium—in every world, then every place with a chessboard of any kind and game resembling it has Smith. That is all that is known.

He may or may not give advice; he often makes comments, little insightful suggestions about a given situation. But since one never knows with whom Smith plays this greater game, the advice is worth as much as Delphi's namesake. Some few also know that he had in his time very few friends: Lomar, Sæceæn, and Hoode counted as his closest among all the millennia of relations. The Footman has played Smith, having won and lost, and suspects he plays him still. Which pleases him and draws a grand smile from his sharp jaw. Despite himself, despite the presence of Kizervexius's destroyer, he smiles and extends a warm hand to the Chessmaster.

Smith rises and takes Delphi's paw and shakes it. He speaks first. "Smoojak sends his warm regards."

Delphi smiles harder, shakes harder, and gently pats Smith on the back with his encumbered left hand. "Well met—and tell my friend Smoojak that I shall lay out some fine salmon for him at Winterfall."

"I shall." The man gives him a bow and sits back down, his face again a study in studying. It is said that when Kasparov met him for the first time, he laughed and left without playing. Later he admitted to his friends that, compared to Smith, any Russian's face was an open book and he knew he had already lost the game.

Hoode changes his appearance the way most divas change between opera sets. Even as he stands there, looking over his glorious hat and the wretched villain who had the audacity to swindle it from him, his cheeks sharpen, his eyes lighten and he starts becoming a new species. Some feel he has played in the primordial chaos too long and it now clings to him like some lichenous symbiote from places beyond reason. There's no mistaking his general dislike of Delphi nor Delphi's own disdain.

"Hat thief." He offers Delphi his hand.

"Whiner." Delphi takes it and finds himself slammed against the opposite wall before he can let go. Hoode has grown claws which now impale the Footman's wrist. With his clenched left hand Delphi brushes off the dust and splinters from the shattered wall that leans upon him and carefully adjusts his top hat. "I correct myself. Pathetic whiner." Then he slams the bottle of Icefire against Hoode's head and watches as the god's skull burns. For safety he pours what remains upon the interlocked battle that is his wrist and Hoode's hand. Letting a dark god take your hair and blood would be suicidal. The acid staunches the wounds shut, fills the room with a distinct stench of burnt fur, and most importantly, forces Hoode to let go.

It takes him nearly a minute to remake his face and head. In that time Delphi sits down and accepts a mug of what turns out to be Darjeeling from Smith. After a sip he lets out a yawn and waits. The hellos are over.

Hoode, when he can speak, mutters something to Smith and takes a mug of tea like any civilized guest. Then he again sits down and, ignoring the damage, burnt stink, and obvious wounds inflicted on both himself and Delphi, studies the chessboard. He decisively takes the bishop and groans as Smith then takes his exposed queen. Check and mate. He grumbles and then hands the man another sum of old looking gold. Only then, his business with Smith resolved, does he deign to address Delphi.

"So Herr Katzenjammer, you come for answers." He sips the tea and makes a face. "You know I despise Darjeeling."

Smith smiles a rare smile and nods. "I have arranged dinner for us." A knock and then Bloody Alice opens the door with a tray of sausages, bread, and beer. A wheel of fine cheese and some dressed watercress lay upon a platter in her left arm. She hands them in and wordlessly leaves. For a moment it appears that she has winked to Delphi.

"I brought her here, you know." Hoode has spoken, and for a moment it takes Delphi's mind through a series of women until he realizes that the god means Jane herself. He gives his adversary a curt bow from his chair.

Smith hands him a mixed plate with sausages prominent and nods. "It's true. She came twice and played a very fine game of chess… the second time. The first, I believe, she spent a goodly portion of her time with Alice, asking questions and making notes."

Delphi smiles. "The bar scene in Duty and Danger. Where

younger Darcy meets the masked Granville and slaps him. It's the Horny Gorgon?"

Hoode's eyes sparkle. "Watered down and the stabbings in the corner perhaps mislaid to another book, but yes. Jane found the place astonishing. Far more than the Imperial Gardens."

Delphi tackles a sausage. He's eaten here before, but never with Hoode and Smith. The expected mix of sawdust, spoiled meat, and perhaps arsenic are missing. Apparently Alice knows a supplier that can make a decent meal. He downs the brat in three bites. "Other than showing off, why tell me about Jane Austen?"

"It seems to be her night." This confirms a suspicion of Delphi's, that Hoode and his hat are more than creator and created. He knows. Knows where it's been and what it's done, who it has touched. Which rather puts a new spin on the janjack sporting around town clandestinely investigating the disappearance of the future Empress of the Known Worlds. It's part of why he's here, why he pushed Hoode instead of showing the god some respect as anyone with a healthy self-regard would. Which begs another tier of questions and internal debates. Does Hoode know, does Smith, and is it some ploy within a ploy? The truth doesn't change his course of action. Duty, awareness, self-restraint limit a man until his path knows only one direction.

It does, however, change how one might consider Hoode and his relationship with Jane. With Jane's town and with her death. And for that matter, with Kizervexius. Delphi has another sausage and some cheese, drinks the good cold beer. Smith watches, an amused statue, and Hoode, ever warping, has become some kind of lizard creature with forked tongue and discordant blue eyes.

Smith breaks the spell. "What exactly are you hoping to conjure here?"

The Footman shrugs. He doesn't really know where to start. For the first time in a long time, he has come to a place where new, unpredictable things have occurred. In his long life, that has not happened often, and not since he remade himself as a simple janjack from a simple city. He takes off the hat and scratches one of his ears. He finds that, unexpectedly, he has changed—that while he went about his bitter business, mourning the lost Kizervexius, he gained a new spirit, a new self of sorts. He enjoys being Delphi, enjoys his trade, enjoys being baffled and lied to and lost. He knows Smith might wait a year for an answer, and he feels set up. Hoode looks on, reptilian and distant. A thought, a sudden cascade of What If kind of daydreams, a certitude born ten thousand tiny steps down a winding path. Hoode.

He hears himself speak and stares down at his beer. "I aim to reckon whether Hoode here dons this mask of faces merely to deceive, or if they represent some greater set of experiments on the psyche of his pawns." It is a statement of bold fact. It jumps whole lifetimes of guesswork and lands clearly down some rabbit hole. It calls upon all his selves at once, and for a brief moment Delphi remembers what it feels like to not be angry.

Hoode starts to laugh, and the face he wears sloughs off in what can only be described as bundles of stardust. They tinkle like faerie bells as they touch the floor and evaporate with a puff of light. His clothes, his voice, his very being slowly melt away, leaving a smaller, older, tempered man as human and forgettable as Smith. Then he picks up his tea mug and sips slowly.

"Before I knew more than a man's limited mind could contain, I learned a simple fact: people only tell the truth in how they lie."

Smith scratches his chin. "Think of it as a gambit, Delphi. A series of opening moves to probe your opponent. Except that the way Hoode's magic works, you create the faces, not him."

Delphi listens and tries to hear the lesson. He's clearly out of his depth, starting at last to see that Kizervexius's ruin was itself a gambit, a piece on a board of a longer game. Perhaps larger still, and beyond the ken of a mortal mind, as Hoode has inferred.

"All his magic?"

This time Smith sighs and hands a sum of old pressed gold to Hoode. The old wizard merely smiles, and the moment seems to hang in time. Delphi doesn't know what's weirder—that Smith has lost a bet or that these old men have bet on something so random. It occurs to him that he really doesn't know how far out of his depth he really has foundered. When, for example, did these two make this bet?

Hoode pours more of the abhorred tea for himself and nods. "Yep. All of it. Imagine if you will that the conservation of matter and energy includes magic. That you pay for everything you get and that it must be a purely even exchange."

Delphi ponders this grade school lesson in magistry. A god with access to levels of power and reality unseen by the dying, a deathless entity of absurd reach—might see this limit as something different. It might view the exchange as a lever, a means to build speed and vector, a way to alter the fabric of the world while playing at the very edge of the universal constant. He nibbles on a chunk of cheese. "How many questions do I get, exactly?"

Smith smiles, and it looks sad on the man. "As many as time allows."

"So this is really about who killed Jane and why, and not about Gnash?"

Hoode nods with a strange expression of satisfaction. He mutters, "less than three centuries" and then stands. Outside, there are voices and a small explosion. He gives Delphi a slight, crisp, ever-so-sharp bow. "Say instead they are all one question. Ask yourself why the Minister Absolute trifled with murdering an innocent woman and had the ill luck to do it at the Main Door."

Delphi cocks an ear and hears the voice of Kizervexius's *Vrashnaralla* calling for a battering ram. The hat. Stalyo has tracked his own stink to this place. With a sinister laugh, Delphi bows low to the old trickster and hands the hat back to its master. "I knew I'd only get the one use." He sighs as he runs a claw along the sensuous brim. "You should have seen his face."

Hoode gives him a blank stare that reveals all that Delphi could hope. Even gods tell the truth in how they lie. This amuses Smith, and he hands Delphi some of the gold. Nonplussed, he stares at the gelt, suddenly afraid he's holding temple coins from the ninth millennium, when Arüne had a working priesthood. They weigh upon his huge paw, cold and alien. "I didn't realize we had a bet." Then a moment later. "Nor really know how I just won said wager."

Smith stares him in the eye, and a cold deep fear seeps into Delphi. "But we did make a bet, Katzenjammer. Long ago, but I still remember."

And then he knows.

If not for the insistent cries of men rising as the Horny Gorgon's door shatters and a cohort of elite troops spearing their way inwards, he might dare ask dozens more questions. As it is, he experiences a feeling akin to all the bones in his body freezing for a quarter second, shivers, then looks for an exit. Later he will vomit all the fine food he just ate into a gutter and shake with raw terror at what he has just learned. Later he will stare at the stars and wonder how he could be so blind, so angry, so lost. Later he will laugh and cry and spill absinthe on his vest as he swaggers down the avenues looking for a fight. But just now his body aches to survive. He gives both gods a sincere, low bow and holds it three full agonizing seconds. Then he whispers a word of power, blowing out the far wall, and leaps into an empty street. In their zeal, Stalyo's men have abandoned the rear guard. Delphi races into the night, burdened with secrets and a certain joyful whimsy. Somehow soon he must make his way back to the bar and have Alice regale him with the full story of the moment armed and snake-angry Dahnstalyon corners and attempts to take revenge on the current owner of a certain top hat.

When he trails out of sight, a third man appears from the shadows within the room, watching the mayhem below as the elves regroup. To outward appearances he seems human, dark of skin with worked dreadlocks of hair, ribbons, totems, and small bells. If he shakes his head, the hair becomes a delightful musical instrument all its own. His eyes, though, are grey and uncanny, old beyond measure and unlike anything resembling human. Neither Smith nor Hoode give him the slightest regard. They cannot see him, after all.

How has this been accomplished, here in the heart of these immortals' own aerie? With just a hint of misdirection and no small measure of stealth. It's clear from his movements—the way he casts his head, the way his eyes take in the world around him—that Chafrium and this stranger known one another well. He waits without sound, his breath unperceivable until the Viscount and his men mount a spirited attack on the outer door.

Hoode sits down and composes himself, the look on his face a mixture of amusement and cruel desire. Smith stands aside, watching as the door explodes and the stranger, taking his cue as all eyes turn to Dahnstalyon storming across the threshold, drops out of the building through the hole Delphi made.

He lands like a cat, supple and silent upon a nearby roof, and dances away towards the docks. He's a ghost tonight, a spirit of the City who has witnessed the undoing of Delphi. Whatever struck such fear into the janjack, the shadows seems to understand.

Behind, screaming and explosions have begun at the Inn. Men are thrown through walls and the ever expanding holes made therein. Gunshots fire; lances of fire and frost cascade off neighboring buildings. The dousing brigade and policing guild are hailed; the City Guard begins to arrive. They will wait until the numbers promise a short unfair fight with the entirety of the bar and the Minister Absolute's remaining soldiers.

The shadow would like to be there, to watch a scion of House Rexor face the music with the inimitable Hoode. But he has business of sorts across town, in the sunken temples of Arüne. An old friend to meet and a debt to be paid. He pads across the spine of a church roof, laughing as he goes. Below him lies sacred place dedicated to the House of Lomar and its descendants, a cultic temple where the elves may see and be seen, take blessings, and share communions via drugged wine and hors d'oeuvres consecrated by some overpaid fifth cousin for whom no better occupation could be found. The kind of place a thief such as him would delight in robbing of its gemstones and platinum had he the time. He marks the location and steals off, onwards towards the sewer entrance known only to him.

By now Delphi has made it across town and through a Door to his homeland. We shall find him tomorrow, once his guts have been vomited out and his heart reconciled. This shadow takes us, dear reader, somewhere else—somewhere far more sinister than back through to Austen. This man, faceless in the night, slinks towards an ordinary storm drain which opens to main sewer line of Chafrium.

The thief glides through the opening, never touching the slimy sides. He's that sinister and dextrous, a lithe dagger of shadow and intention. His feet slosh in the standing water but make little noise. Only ripples show his passage as he pushes a certain discolored brick on a false wall, opening a long, well-lit passage adorned with glowing double ankhs. An old temple entrance for the priests of Arüne.

Experts know that Chafrium has been built layer after layer on top of itself. The marshes sink and adds another layer. The original sewers are now ten stories below the present surface. Somewhere below all this lies the original temple of Arüne, sunk when the god went to sleep. This thief, however, remembers the way, knowing every turn, every stair and doorway to take. Even here in the abundance of light, his dark face and pale eyes are lost within the smoke of his passage.

He makes another turn and heads through an ancient antechamber to tackle the last long staircase when he finds he is not alone. A tan-skinned human woman stands in the center of the room, her eyes a resplendent green and her hair the deepest shades of red. She's tall, well-shaped but slender. On her right hip rest the requisite sword and pistol of the duelist. She carries what appears to be a letter on fine parchment bound with a proper wax and ribbon seal. She bows and he bows. She seems harmless enough, but he is not fooled. He knows her kind well enough, if not her. They wait, neither speaking.

He chooses English to begin the conversation. "Is that for me?"

The woman nods. "She can't make it. Detained, I am told, by the events unfolding."

She offers him the letter and it disappears. It's not so much that he takes it as the shadows grow and it now sits in his hands a few paces away, being read by his pale merciless eyes. He sighs and then perhaps smiles. If so, it's the thinnest of indications. "How are Kyi, Shchek and Khoryv, by the way?"

She shrugs. "Am I to know?"

He nods. "Yes, you would. Doesn't matter. Just making small talk, really. I haven't seen them in so long it's, herm…" he seeks a forgotten word, "irrelevant."

"Anything you'd like me to tell her?" If she has any feelings about this creature of darkness, her face shows nothing.

The gloom about him grows. For a long moment he does not speak, does not even breathe. The light sifts into his world and bends away from him. "She already knows it's started."

The woman nods. "She does. The whole of the worlds know."

"Not yet they don't, but they will." In this his voice seems resolute, as if etching stone. A prophet's voice, perhaps. Or a demon's. In Chafrium they are often the same thing. "Tell her soon there will be new stories worth her time. New players and songs never imagined. Things she will want to see and people she will wish to meet, to interview like she did before…"

"I will tell her."

A smirk breaks out from his gloom. "Of course you will. But she knows already, I'm sure."

The lady gives him a formal nod. "Then why send me?"

"Isn't it obvious?" A slim hand covered in dark blue leather makes a gesture, almost as if he were saying 'come hither'. "She wants you to be seen, for me to understand. Why else send you instead of another one of your kind? Another sister, perhaps, or one of the elfbloods?"

Again a formal nod, her face blank of any discernible emotion. Less and less she looks human to his eye. It makes her if anything more severe and thus, to him, more elegantly striking. Not quite beautiful in a human sense; this woman before him proves too refined, too stark and absolute to be coventionally attractive.

"And what have you learned, having seen me?"

He smiles, a genuine cruel smile of immense charisma, and for a moment the light seems to pierce his dark skin. "Why, everything important. Tell her I accept her proposition and consider myself at her disposal."

Then he's gone. In the blink of an eye, as the red-haired lady moves to give him the slight bow of acknowledgment, he fades from living sight. Neither sound nor smell of him persist. He is truly gone.

Why has this been seen at all? Who among the many players in the worlds wanted you to see this? Is it Chafrium or Austen? Something out there wishes to be understood and takes us away from Delphi's story long enough to witness the enigmatic meeting between two persons who give no name, have yet to be recognized, and who've said nothing that explains where to find the absent Qelniasherah. What could matter more than that?

CHAPTER 5: THE FATES

The Footman sits in Pemberly Park, sipping spiked lemonade with janjacks Vorskla and Dnieper. Around the Great Oak, enthusiastic refuseniks dance and drum, celebrating Eeyore's Autumn birthday with cake, hard drink, beer chilled in the nearby Cascade Creek, and a healthy dose of *take-that* to the fools who insist on the Spring version of the fete. A goodly two thirds of these ersatz pagans celebrate both holidays, and the haze of dreamsmoke speaks to a spiritedness that heralds the faster, more indulgent 21st century speeding towards their City. Delphi hands Dnieper, fairer and without a facial scar, a slice of Janecake, a peculiar Austen recipe that's a mash-up of red velvet and ratafia cakes: a massive dose of extenso-style chocolate, apricot kernel flour, beetroot, and Kyivan saffron doused in liqueur and slathered with soured milk frosting. She, in turn, hands it to Vorskla—dark of hair and eye, blessed with a long dueling scar along her left eye and cheek—and then accepts a second plate for herself. The two are twin sisters famed for their Slavic tempers and encyclopedic knowledge of all things Tejano.

Vorskla informs him that the saffron grows on duelists' graves, a peculiarity of Austen that feeds the mystics and cranks. Years ago, immigrants from the Kyivan Rus brought the crocus morutu and planted them at the edge of the Boggy Swamp, and as they drained the floodplains to build the city, the flowers, despite all logic, thrived. Some suspect the local Traveler women plant the crocuses on fresh graves; others claim the turned soil revives old dormant bulbs. By tradition, the University of Austen dentro Tejas dyes all its sporting and dueling uniforms the peculiar burnt orange hue of the Kyiv saffron plant. Austenites thrill in using the spice and the color in every imaginable place, and once a year, on Jane's day—conveniently also Darcy the Younger's Birthday—they dye the river orange.

It's a kindness to divert him. The sisters arrived at his door a few hours earlier, concerned by the change in the Song. Some janjacks simply go about their jobs, distantly connected to the City, but ultimately mere men and women who do a singular kind of job and do it well. Some, the queer death-touched few, hear or speak with the City. Vorskla and Dnieper sing to it and in turn hear its song. The Europeans call Austen the Living Music Capital, and in a way it's true. So many elves vacation here that a whole series of magically enhanced artforms have sprung up. Holographic paintings, interactive motion picture films, the famous bleeding violins of Ossetia, speedjazz, and pyrotechnic funkpop, along with some dozens of barely emerging hybrids, offer the aficionado of loud, soft, thrilling, or sublime experiences a whole range of endless diversions. The sisters hear a simple melody, sung in a child's voice, that reveals untold amounts about every inch of the place. And the song has faltered, the child stammering her lines.

Delphi having departed the City and returned alive barely makes news. Delphi having stopped a small invasion and returned alive makes his fellow janjacks nervous and curious by turns. Especially when word of a hatless drunk Delphi haunting the streets at the witching hour reach them. The sisters are their spokeswomen. In all things related to Austen's janjacks, the sisters are the ascendant powers—determining the social and cultural agenda of their micro-society, which is always less than two dozen souls. They arrive to find a dressed, sober, reflective monster, decked in grey and wintergreen, wearing a different top hat perhaps a trifle dusty and sporting an obviously new set of ribbons. Today Delphi has worn the house colors of Kizervexius, gold and green with the requisite second ribbon of midnight doublestripe. It's as much a Vanguard as he needs ever deliver, and for a moment even the brash Vorskla stands agape.

Then she greets him in her peculiar style: "The count is

fifteen." By this, Delphi knows none are dead, missing, or born anew. There were fifteen janjacks of Austen yesterday and there are fifteen today.

Who are these women, who have say over the inimitable Footman? Vorskla and Dnieper, twins from The Free Duchy of Kyivan Rus, veterans of the Fourth Slavic War and subsequent escapees from a Soviet prison camp, apperently ageless and perhaps cursed by Romani magic, experts in Tejano lore, warcraft, diplomacy and music, the reigning queen regents of Austen's dueling circles and the most militant knitters in the Western hemisphere. It is said that you need to kill a man to be invited to their Thursday Evening Stitch and Bitch. Austen has a nineteen-page waiting list, and potential international guests regularly send photogravures of their dueling wins.

The three janjacks are watching the people of Austen dance, drink, and innocently make good-natured fools of themselves. An effigy of the famed Eeyore stands near a newly kindled bonfire, and some drunken drummers have tried to start a Maypole conga line around a sacred ash tree. It's a typical party for the season: cooler heads prevail and the most intoxicated are dumped in the creek when drugs, drink, flaming clothing, or clumsy sexuality overcome them. No one will drown and Janecake will be served. Children with balloons and an honest-to-god newly built six-wheeled Rolls Royce automobile complete the party scene.

Dnieper asks Delphi again about the Writ. He shows them both, certain Vorskla, who rarely speaks, has as much interest as her more luminous sister. Dnieper produces a jeweler's loupe and reviews the entire document line by line. She nods to her sister, who grimaces. Vorskla slugs back her drink and sighs. "They don't yet realize you still have one."

Delphi nods. So much of the unfolding plot has lain before him, there to be discovered but—and this requires some explanation—until now essentially secret owing to the unwritten laws that govern janjacks. For example, the sisters arrived in Austen after him, but how long they lived in the Free City and what they know of the older world he has never bothered to ask. Caught upon the horns of Hoode's little dilemma, he finds a whole cast of potential ancients lurking about in what until yesterday the Footman would have categorized as a quaint city in a minor province distinguished by its peculiar brand of tourists.

Another detour, then: The right of sanctuary exists in this world with abundance. Right and guarantee are different things. The Powers have colonized so many corners of the Earth with their little cancers of magic, wealth, and influence that genuine asylum requires almost slavelike devotion to the Supreme Soviet, the Great Raj, the Extenso, or (for the right kind of politico) the American Union or the Middle Kingdom. This subtle and terrifying imposition of will from beyond warped the laws and ethics of a world which had far too little compassion when Spanish Conquistadors re-opened the door to Chafrium in 1609. For the average refugee, criminal, asylum seeker, or plain old runaway, the options proved dangerous, limited and uncertain. It was, and remains still, a buyers' market; even the Soviets, once the beckoning arms to many generations of revolutionaries and anarchists, have put up an iron wall and closed off their borders to all things new and foreign.

Early on in the reintroduction of magic, cities started to develop sensibilities—*mentalities*, to calque from the French. These places required servants of an unusual sort, smart people to do the will of intelligences alien and perverse. Asylum seekers reeking of desperation found a blood bargain they could stomach and janjacks were birthed. Assuming a *nom de guerre* and the identity that went with it, these naked souls clothed themselves in duty. The city became their armor; to the extent that they served well and honestly, their own former lives faded.

Imagine the social dilemmas involved as the first of these new creatures emerged into the world. What questions can one ask this defaced man? As of yet, none were women—the elves would eventually bring equality among the genders and then more genders to confuse the hapless humans. From asking the local janjack to tea and sitting him at the banquet table to addressing legal last wills and assessing liability for property damage, the common law and mores of the seventeenth century grappled with a wholly new kind of phenomenon. Never before had human will been thwarted by otherworldy forces, verdicts overturned, and most relevantly, soldiers of every kind subject to summary judgment by sentient geographies. The trees, rocks, and rills fought back. Industrial regions found their own cities no longer under control. Mills and machines independently tendered alliances with elves, wizards, spiritual forces beyond the planes of existence, and, most dreaded, lawyers.

Humans being a practical species, much given to what the uncharitable might call a penchant for taking the easy way out, adopted the cultural practice of forgiving a janjack all their old crimes and transgressions—asking no questions. Police stopped their pursuits and even *omertà*-driven vengeance was abrogated for the janjack. How? The man lost his name, and by consensus, his soul was forfeit. The new man, the janjack, owned the body, but the mind and essence were deemed to be new, unique and legally different from the entity prior. Codswallop, certainly, bolstered by a raft of half-truths, rationalizations, and self-serving intellectualizations but effective and pervasive. Ultimately, this clean slate attracted the suicidal, the romantic, the unhinged and distraught as well as the starving and defeated. In two generations, *janjack* became a word in most languages; in two more, most major cities sported one or two. By the mid-eighteenth century, janjacks had become a fixture of the modern world.

Humanity, like the many peoples conquered before them, created the same solution to the same problem. They followed the same rules and adopted shockingly similar legal fictions about janjacks. No one in the 380 worlds or the provinces beyond has had the gall to push the point. The limits of this psychic taboo astonish even the most cynical.

Nothing is what it seems. Clearly to his detriment, Delphi tacitly accepted the limits of his society. This cold, aching fact calls to his pondering mind Hoode's strange injunction: reexamine the laws of magic. You pay for everything you get and it must a purely even exchange. Magic requires power given and power taken, cost and return. Delphi and all his generation have understood this limit in a very physical, four dimensional way.

Until Dnieper and Vorskla hint at their own past, it never occurred to him to consider if silence and taboos are not the cost but the product of magic. Magic has become a commodity, produced and sold in bottles and charms and tied to the limitations of species. The Raj deploys apartheid and empire; the Soviet Supreme uses proletarian eugenics and aggressive breeding with goblins and ogres as well as the dog soldiers; the Americans have their potion factories and opium clippers; the Austro-Hungarians their wind demon dirigibles and universities for ritual occultists. It amounts to a pittance. On this plane, magic barely works.

Only those of the Old Blood—species from offworld—have any real ability to manipulate spells and the like, and all of them serve the elves directly or through proxies. A few human descendants inherit enough rogue mitochondria from eons old castaways and planar explorers to be minor Powers. The great unwashed bulk of the world simply buys its magic and moves on.

What has the magic industry done to the people of Austen? It's no longer an idle question. Somehow Lady Nia lurks within their borders, unseen and beyond immortal ken. Who bought and who paid for that? If the effect of a potion is the price paid and not the result, if the magic dehumanizes to pay for the actual sorcery, it makes the whole process significantly more sinister.

Normally he'd ask the Lady Sawyer—occult expert, speaker to Elders of all species, and not coincidentally, a stalwart critic of humanity's headlong rush into industrial magics. Every few months she passes through as she tours the various regions of the American Union and its borders. Delphi is cognizant that this may be unwise, that she may not know the answers he seeks—or worse, may be in danger for answering them. Where creatures like Hoode are involved, woe and misfortune follow. In keeping with his present run of both rotten and extraordinary luck, he need not worry—the Lady has been detained in a temporal prison by the Misi-Zaaging peoples. It seems while in Mississauga to consult on the rampage of an abusive Djinn (a loathsome creature who'd been preying on lonely women, marrying them and then taking their souls), she miscalculated, and instead of unmasking him she'd been bound by some kind of blood-oath from his home world, ugly stuff that attacked her soul. Some kindly local medicine woman had thrown her out of time to prevent the curse from taking full effect—an unthinkable honor for a human, but then, Lady Sawyer has few peers on Terra and many admirers. Locals managed to secure the help of the region's foremost scientist-sorcerer, the Lord Roberts, as well as a priest named Slater renowned for his preternatural calm and miraculous ability to absorb curses, a genuine sin eater and exorcist. Eventually Lord Roberts will free her with the help of Slater—but the threat to her immortal essence being paramount, that looks to be months if not years in the making.

He might ask Steinmetz the Clever. If the Shaman really does talk to cats, he might have an answer worth hearing. Or for that matter, Delphi can query his rival: the absurdly successful cat therapist, toastmaster, and dreamspeaker for the Jaguar Clan of the Greater Extenso, Lady Deandra the Great. More commonly known among the Extenso and her feline clientele as *Y'ulen*, The Dewclaw. For a human among the Southern Elves, she's almost famous.

Still, he hesitates. It all comes to the same problem. He needs both information in a timely fashion and secrecy despite the speed. What he knows, his enemies will know. Anyone important and knowledgeable enough to ask will be spied upon and mindthieved minutes after they speak. He needs secure access to wise counsel he can trust without question. Smith and Hoode gave him more information last night than he knows how to manage—much of it conflicting, hard to swallow, and perhaps just a little on the side of the impossible.

He downs his lemonade and gives Dnieper a smile as she tops off his glass. To himself he says, perhaps a trifle too loud, "And one more to cut the cloth once spun."

Vorskla smiles a wide and toothy grin and winks at her sister. "So, Footman, you want to know if we have a sister?"

The Footman gives her a sitting bow. "Something like that. Say instead that I suspect the count is sixteen."

Dnieper takes a bite of her Janecake and suddenly her smile

resembles nothing modern or human. "The count is seventeen..."

Then she cocks her head and Vorskla gives her a sudden stare. Delphi knows that the song has begun anew. He waits. They sit like statues, eyes locked, their faces blank and mildly horrible. He has never been able to watch them so closely as they listen, and he finds himself reminded of Smith or (and this comes unbidden) Sæceæn. From the periphery of the party, a figure slowly approaches.

In Austen there are several professional ghosts. Take Drowned Leslie, the on-again, off-again patron saint of masquerade and drama, who appears during music festivals and post-duel celebrations asking for scarves to make a dress. She's either a real person, a local myth, or a real ghost. Like the Kyiv Saffron, no one agrees which, and yet the sightings of her are fairly common. There's Lady Jane, the supposed remnant of Jane Austen, a woman in pure white with Regency perfect English saber and dueling pistols, always looking prim, crisp, and aware. Some swear a monster horse named Three Legged Pete haunts the river and tries to trample boats. And everyone agrees that at all times somewhere in town the Red Lady can be found wandering.

Janjacks don't take the rumors too seriously. In his centuries here, Delphi has seen Leslie once—he reckoned her a living man dressed as a woman—and once had to ride Pete, whom he knows to be a ghost. He has never seen Jane, and he always doubted the existence of the Red Lady… until she shows up, sits down next to Dnieper, and takes a slice of cake. She greets them with a flat Slavic smile.

Delphi rises and bows. "Lybid, I presume?"

She gives him a cordial nod. "And what name are you going by today, Delphi Janjack?"

So and so. So much tumbles into place and he knows at last he's gone too far out of his depth. "What name would you like to call me, Lybid Janjack?"

This brings a very slight smile to her face. It gives him a moment to study her. She's the duplicate of Dnieper and Vorskla, save her green-grey eyes and hair every color of red. We have seen her just the night before conferring with Mister Shadow.

Vorskla sits by her side and he sees the trio: the spinner, the allotter, and the inevitable.

"You said there were seventeen. Even with Lybid, that's only sixteen of us."

Vorskla shakes her head. "You know this already, Footman. Jane makes seventeen."

He does what feels most natural: he stands and gives them his most formal sweeping bow. "Forgive me, ladies. I am beyond my depth. Am I to understand the ghost of Jane is our Jane and a janjack all these years?"

Lybid makes a sound like laughter or derision. Perhaps both. "As if these years mean anything to you. All these few centuries, you meant to say."

Delphi ponders and realizes that, contrary to Lybid's assertions, he in fact does mean what he says. And this surprises him anew—that he has changed and that he cherishes his brief time among the humans and their City. That he feels such delicious jealousy and embarrassment to have grieved so long and publically as to miss obvious clues strewn about him by the Powers. He bows a second time and holds it as one does for elders and queens. "No, Madam, I meant as I said. Color me discomfited if you will. I paid homage to Saint Jane only yesterday, so the idea that she's been walking the city for a few centuries…" He shrugs. It makes him feel small and helpless. If one of the sisters hands another a bag of coins, he imagines he'll scream.

Dnieper smiles as warmly as anyone can expect of a Slavic reaver and waves her delicate hand, full of dueling scars. "Be still, Footman. *Mir*, I say. *Mir*." She takes a moment to stand, then carefully replenishes the Janecake and lemonade for the four of them. Once civilization has had a moment to reassert itself, she sits as prim as Lady Jane and gives him her endless eyes. "The Song calls you the Lord Forsaken. Do you think it means you have been Forsaken by your Lord or that you forsook him?"

It's an honest question, and one with extraordinary depth. In his grief over Kizervexius, Delphi has long hidden from the hardest truths. In love with Sæceæn's sister, the Elven Lord pursued an ill-fated romance whose collapse rocked the political universe. In a heartbeat the King lost his champion and his brother in law, his chief general and his closest friend. More than eight decades of Elven dinner parties were given to gossip about the juiciest details: did Sæceæn engineer this betrayal to prevent a coup? Did his sister bring Dahnstalyon upwards and into key circles to effect her own vicious attack? What crimes could cruel arrogant Kizervexius have committed that were so foul even the gods conspired against him? And so on, over drinks, tapas, naked bodies, and tripdust.

The man most likely to rule as the next king, a four-thousand-year-old warrior prince with unlimited resources and the most ridiculous collection of medals ever seen on a mortal's Vanguard: Kizervexius just disappeared. He vanished one night, leaving the Footman in his wake. No message, no reply to satisfy the elves or the worlds for that matter. He managed one of the more dramatically singular exits in historic memory. Forsaken by his master and in turn forsaking his sacred duty, the Footman followed, and then he too vanished. Into the bowels of Austen with a new name.

Delphi sips his drink and thinks about who these women are. Terrans have many names for them—the Norns, the furies, the Valkyrie, Shakespeare's three witches. How long have the wandered Terra? The Paleo-Indians sealed off the Door some fifty thousand years ago. Have they been here all this time? Are they recent manifestations and the legends mere coincidence? So many questions and he still has to find the missing girl. Now, here, he learns that besides playing the fool for centuries, he might really have always been a fool, from his first years in Chafrium.

Lybid places a warm and supple hand upon his great paw. He finds it shockingly erotic and, more shockingly, fulfilling. He feels *seen*. Because, of course, he has been.

Why did Jane die? It's a different question than why Dahnstalyon might have killed her. A better question, he realizes. He needs to understand and perhaps properly avenge Jane's murder.

He releases her kind fingers and stands, facing what suddenly look like a tribunal. Well, he's dressed for it. He flashes them a sharp grin and unconsciously bows like a proper magistrate. They all know that time wanes for the missing heir. "She's in our city and I must find her. Quickly. Preferably before someone else, perhaps the accomplice, finds her." He discovers himself unaccountably angry.

Dnieper nods sadly—or does Delphi simply imagine it so? "Everything has a price. Janjack to janjack, we can certainly help. But we suspect you ask in another capacity."

Does she mean his former life or hers? Does it ultimately matter? He has given his word, and now angry, obsessed, and sober after a wretched night of fear and paranoia, he has come entirely resolute and prepared to swiftly battle his way to Lady Nia. "What do thee ask of me?"

Vorskla cocks her head and all three listen to the song. "Your name, janjack. Tell us your name."

Magic for magic, every exchange even. His name—his true name. Around him the mayflies whirl and laugh, cavorting with their kin, drunk with brief life. He sees a path and knows upon whom he must soon call.

He bows low and cocks his hat just so. It says everything about him, the way his ribbons flutter, and he assumes a quiet swagger. Already he begins to think ahead, to consider where he might find the man in question. He does not need the Norns after all, not for this. Still, he has been asked, and he finds great pleasure in the answer. "Today, ladies, my name is Delphi." He clicks his heels and winks at the sisters, and with a swordsman's turn, he strides away before they can reply.

He does not see Lady Jane approach. He has gone seeking smaller prey. Nor does he see the four women, janjacks all and yet something more, convene. Janecake is once again handed out along with some old and valuable wine Lybid has brung with her. The Norns and Jane. What do they discuss? It would be so easy to assume it's the man who has left them, or any man for that matter. In Chafrium, women rule. But in the earthlands, in this farflung little corner of nowhere? Oh, it's all about men. Not necessarily in Austen, which presents another strange and glorious aberration. Here, among these four women, it might be about any of the nine gendered folk and not situated on the maleness of power. It's resolutely certain that the Four discuss the Cities and Fate, and strangely, not one scintilla of their concern is for the Footman. Or any other combatant for that matter.

How and why has this meeting come to pass? Dnieper and Vorskla gave us all a clue—the Song has changed. If the Norns own the Song, then Jane, poet laureate of Tejas and mother of this strange little city, knows all the words. And what of Jane Austen who has be returned to us at the hands of some strange, perhaps profane magic?

While we forget Delphi for a moment and leave him to the quiet avenues of Austen, walking now to a destination with some obvious purpose, let us draw back and see the whole of the multiverse. After all, we've made it our business to watch this little backwater, but it's only that—a place of minor Potential, made exceptional by its queer connection to the real center of all worlds, Chafrium. To some degree, its very value has been the anti-magical nature of the place. Magic dies quickly here, as do nanotech, invert physics, and a dozen other quantum anomalies. Other places deliver palaces of dark matter and bridges of living despair; here magic provides a few potions, some uptempo music, and perhaps slightly improved surgical techniques. Earth still struggles with barbaric inconveniences like influenza and dirigible travel. Disease, distance, dust, and despair: it's how the Demodian Ambassador explained her trip to Moskva Prime, the capital of the Supreme Soviet, arguably the most magically and technologically advanced of the so-called Earth Powers. Apparently she liked alliteration and hard consonants.

There are rules, immutable certainties that bind all of creation to a standard in which magic does exist, in which transplanar quantum submechanics does in fact harmonize with the multi-string vibration of sentient entropy. Gods can and do go anywhere, perhaps even anywhen as well. The universe cheats: while magic and superphysics and nanoparticle matrices vary by planar Potential, they do so only as an expression of geographic contour. Which is to say, there's no real speed limit for a god. Or a wizard. Or, for the point of this discussion, a resurrected set of eternals.

Junior and Senior Cat, should they deign to enter the locality of Austen or Free Kyiv or Moskva or London or even West Poughkeepsie, would have the full panoply of the Universe's might at their disposal, to the limit of their own capabilities and expressly not to the limit of the local Potential. That's the real dividing line between mortals and immortals. Some can break the rules; but most can't. It's a truth well understood by those who can break the rules that few ever do; it's just the nature of sapience. We obey limits entirely of our own manufacture.

Take janjacks. What an odd thing to exist. How are they made? No one knows. Truly. Every attempt to dig into the mystery has been met with a series of fascinating accidents, made more intriguing by the scale of their obliteration. Gods accidentally imbibe a dark star that unbinds them like a spool of baling wire. Immortal wizards trip and drown in a sea of superlava. Over time the smart money has been on leaving the issue for future generations. Still, the mystery does create some questions. Does a janjack really gain or lose a soul? Unknown. How did the Footman become a janjack for a man when it's forbidden? Unknown. Why do janjacks even exist? Unknown.

But the speculation fills libraries. It hints at a universal creator, a supreme god with a bold sense of humor. We know janjacks transform from one essence to another; there's an exchange where something is lost and something gained. Often but not always, that's identity. It's not uncommon for janjacks to forget their old lives, old names, to become subsumed within the oeuvre of their new duties. But, exception, some do retain the whole for their identity. Often but again not always, the janjack starts out dead. It's not spoken of in polite circles, but cities often collect their servants from the river banks, sewers, and morgues.

Resurrection usually goes hand in hand with memory loss; a dead body and the sentience of the land handshake with the Universe to create a janjack. Or so the theory goes, because it could just as easily be random chance, a demon god's prank, the Tuesday study break hobby of some alien species, or any of a few hundred thousand other proposed possibilities. The elves have been debating this for a million years. The orcs who predate them in the multiverse by a factor of hundreds have been debating it since before they conquered fire. No one knows.

Take Shakespeare's *London and Juliet*? And how did the immortal bard really make it to 1764 without turning into decrepit bones and mummy dust? Romeo dies and stays dead, but Juliet becomes London's newest janjack. How could he even have known? The Extenso doors opened in 1609 and somehow old Billy, struck by the mercurial arrow of Fate, begins to live beyond his years, to write stranger and stranger plays, to prepare the English and the World for future truths.

A pattern emerges. Everywhere there is life, there is Chafrium connected to it. There are janjacks and Smith playing chess. There are gods and demons and magic and exceptions to all the rules above, regardless of which rules are in play. Let us not forget what the Grand Wizard of Kyiv, the amazing Singer and Maker Bulgakov theorized: that all the worlds are but stories, that God exists to Listen and The Devil, he's the librarian. Manuscripts do not burn.

Now here, at old Waterloo Rocks, we find some odd exceptions. Three women fitting the exact description of Hecate's forms, of the Norns, of Shakespeare's much-mentioned witches. Are the sisters that old, or like Juliet, possessed of a spirit given them by the Universe recently? Jane likely knows that answer.

Jane who was slain upon the Great Door of Chafrium and whose body was supposedly interred within the crypt of the slumbering god Arüne. The elves consider the god that ninth gender—*Llywiss*: formless, shapeless, eternally shifting yet immutable; a gender that changes with the company, that adapts to circumstance and need. Some think ihm once was the One True God or perhaps more likely a splinter of that unfathomable super-reality.

In this day and age, the local earthlings who cannot speak Elvish use *Ihm* as the universal pronoun for the multitude of genders that they cannot easily bucket into him or her. Dative, possessive, direct and indirect, in any location, in every language, *ihm* has taken hold as a loan word.

The King decreed Jane have a state funeral, and to his credit, Dahnstalyon gave her one. But he had to be clever, to one-up the

Lord of All Doors. He gave her an ancient funeral rite along the simplest of Chafrium sacraments, inviting the absent priests of Arüne to provide the ceremony. When no one came, he dumped her lifeless corpse in the sewer that feeds the tomb, conveniently transformed a few hundred millennia ago into a storm drain by the PAWs. At the Queen's behest of course.

The upshot? Dahnstalyon gained a loyal following among the purists, who think of humanity as some kind of mud-blooded cousins to trained monkeys. Maybe kissing cousins at that. To his credit, the King took it in stride. He had through the Minister Absolute's machinations suddenly gained ground among those most staunchly opposed to his rule: the Matriarchs of the Grey Elves. He never commented on the event, and that silence gave the young upstart room to begin a campaign of terrific ambition. He now beds the man's sister, after all.

All this means that as these four women form up ranks and share a meal, they are in a world outside the rules and expectations of our story. Or are writing it. Or both. We cannot fathom all they say, but we can listen and perhaps, if you've been paying attention, watching the players come and go, thinking some about the Game and the stakes, you will draw your own conclusions. About Austen and Chafrium, about Lady Nia and the Footman, about a great many complicated things.

Vorskla begins. She pours the wine and speaks: "To absent gods and present company."

Glasses clink and Janecake gets eaten. "Have Thursdays been going well?' Lybid wants to know. Jane nods, also interested.

Dnieper shrugs. "It's knitting, so we like it. But it's not the same without you."

Jane laughs. "I haven't knit much since I took up writing. Still, a lady needs something to do with her hands."

Lybid winks at her. "There's always sex, Jane." This brings a round of laughter among them. Vorskla and Dnieper both have wives, something known only among the janjacks and their families. Lybid beds whomever she pleases, and frankly no one has ever seen Jane exhibit the slightest interest.

"I'll stick to writing, perhaps." They laugh again. What kind of writing does this janjack do, and for whom? It's a central question—one that has occupied scholars for the better part of a century. Had she lived, what would Jane Austen write next?

The Elven School led by High Emeritus Zief van Kizerllyl believes she is still writing. That her immortal spirit creates works for the gods. Hokum. But delightful hokum that continues to sell her existing manuscripts and not coincidentally allows the elven world to control Jane's legacy and canon, to co-opt her works as essentially High Elven culture rather than human-made art.

The Seditionists genuinely believe Jane was done, as in DONE, never to write again, and as a result she was struck down by the Viscount in act of divine justice. Her High and Complete Grace the Supreme Priestess of Beloved Understanding, Lady Row'yndyrc leads the Graveyard League, which ascribes to the notion that Jane never existed and she, like Shakespeare and Homer, is a fiction invented by humanity to lend the feeble species some credibility in the wide and far more cultured world of Elvenkind. They're named the Graveyard League precisely because they put so many critics there, and when it comes to the Austenite rebuttal, they lose a fair number of hired hands and scholars to those in Jane's Town who take exception to the genocidal smear. Her High and Complete Grace pays one guild an astonishing three million gold talers annually to keep their famed assassin from making a visit.

In rather refreshing contraposition, The Black Elven Cadre insists Jane was in fact an elfblood of black elven origin and spends inordinate resources and time linking various pieces of circumstantial and imaginary evidence together to prove she's one of them. They've spread her across the worlds like few others.

For Terra, there exists only one legitimate school of Post-Jane Austen scholarship, and they have a peculiar theory about what Jane would write if she had lived. They point to frequent legends of a Saint Jane or Lady Jane walking in her namesake city. Based on their most solid scholarship, they argue we should go and ask her, since she's not dead in a total sense and should speak for herself.

Located at the far northern Extenso University of Kumeyaay

at Santo Miguel across the border from the American Institute of Oceanic Magic and Technoscience, their nominal leader is a polarizing figure, Professor Anna Joy X. Every year she takes a new last name related to theme of her scholarship. Presently she's Anna Joy Nonlinear and her work digs into the nature of metanarrative, subtext, manipulation in writing, and self-deception, as well as ways to remedy the situation through alienation, asymmetry, involution of plot and narrative, and such. Her student suicide rates are much lower than most Extenso professors, but she's still considered "as bad as any Elf," which among humanity puts her in an intellectual class open to heretics, geniuses, the insane, and the openly sycophantic. No one would mistake her for an elven sycophant. She's won nine duels on that front, killing two rivals who would not accept first blood.

Anna Joy X has made five trips to Austen over the years—interviewing various janjacks and Jane scholars, taking time to visit her home and archives and seek out Lady Jane herself. How she would wish to be here, to see that she among all the various schools might be more correct about the murdered author. Mind you, none of that answers the crucial question. What does Jane Austen write now that she's Lady Jane and a janjack? These four assembled know, and if we count the shadow without footfalls, then at least one soul in Chafrium has strong suspicions.

And what do they wish to discuss, when alone and unencumbered of Delphi? What do they say that Anna Joy and her various rivals would pay eyeteeth to hear? Dnieper starts the process by coughing as if she were to give a formal speech. "The Song."

Jane makes a statement but also asks a question: "Yes, the song. It has changed, you say? All three of you agree?"

Dnieper nods while Vorskla tops up the wine. These women drink hard, even when it's expensive plonk. "The Weave speaks of a new fire and many broken souls."

Lybid rubs her eyes and thinks. "I hear something else, a kind of joy peeking through. Something will be born soon, something not yet seen."

Vorskla: "Something wicked, something wild…"

Dnieper: "Changes stride and having died…"
Lybid: "Kneels when it may once more stand…
Vorskla: "A willow of fire, steel, and land…"
Dnieper: "Once a slave and yet now freed…"
Lybid: "Unified, reborn in deed."

They talk of other things. Births and deaths, duels and chores, paying bills and raising children, of back pains during their periods and the way silk drapes when knit just so. Into the hours of the night and early morning they watch the children of the 20th century frolic, making chitchat, exchanging ideas and recipes and combat tips, comparing notes on criminals and potential legal problems. They consider how to align the other twelve janjacks; no one speaks of Delphi. His time in Austen has come to an end. When he finds the The Lady Who Waits, she will kill him one way or another.

They've known for decades, waited for the day to come. Soon the count will be Sixteen.

CHAPTER 6: LIES, SUBTERFUGE, AND DECEPTION

Delphi returns to Café Ragueneau and waits. Duchamp hands him a simple double espresso and departs. The avenue bustles and someone screams in anguish or perhaps triumph from the dueling grounds. Delphi has eyes for one man—Lours the Watchman. It's a triple entendre, because Lours does in fact repair timepieces as well as serve on the city night guard. But among a select few, he is perhaps best known for his obsession with elven genealogy. He knows the names of every queen's relation down to ninth cousin stretching back millennia. The dark angel of Grey Elven heraldry, Lours has long watched Chafrium—ever wary, ever drawn, a moth to irresistible flame.

Delphi, a watcher of sorts himself, knows Lours takes lunches at the café now and again and has sent the man an invitation. In this case, he has handed several bravos a wad of banknotes and asked them to kindly escort the Watchman to his appointment. As courtesies go, this lacks finesse; but Delphi has a timeline, and Lours now stands between the Footman and a lost child. Besides, no one much likes Lours; having him dragged through the street will improve everyone's mood.

Presently the man and his none too gentle bodyguard arrive. Lours has a split lip and no hat. Delphi shrugs, offers him a seat facing the wall and signals the waiter. Lours, the bastard, orders the full filet with truffled potatoes. Delphi considers, then orders the same with garlic toast and a hammer of quesadillas as well. In Austen, for no etymological reason anyone has ever been able to discern, the practice of serving seven of any item is affectionately called a hammer.

For a few moments there reigns tense silence. To you, the

reader, it might seem unremarkable; to any Austenite, the problem sticks out like a stray nail. In his or her own City, a janjack never pays for anything. The only tax a City imposes upon its people are these small courtesies. Misuse can break a merchant merely by depleting inventory. In just such a manner many moneylenders and swindlers have discovered that janjacks administer a subtle justice. Consequently, janjacks often take pains to not impose too greatly upon anyone. Lours, as Delphi's guest, has broken an unspoken rule and been greedy. It's clear that Lours knows something.

Delphi slaps the pissant hard enough to knock the little clockmaker into the street. Then he's around the table, a blinding locomotive of raw strength. He lifts Lours from the path of an onrushing carriage and tosses him back, shaken, into a waiting chair.

"Let me be clear, Watchman." Delphi's voice carries the stink of death. "I have exactly as much time as lunch takes me and no more. Answer all my questions by then or I will break every bone in both your hands." From a table nearby, one of the tougher duelists chuckles. Then, his face a trifle too ashen, he makes a quick bow and swiftly departs.

Lours spits a bloody tooth and nods. A welt has begun to rise along the left side of his face. On cue, the waiter brings a whisky double and a cloth with some chopped ice. Duchamp has a sense of the urgency at hand, and as a good host, he plans for every contingency. That his guests have ordered the most expensive of his menu items worries him not at all. Delphi has earlier made Duchamp a very rich man for life. The Footman's ribbons fluttering from the janjack's top hat ensure that Duchamp will become an outrageously rich man and for the same reason. He finds deep pleasure in being able to provide his benefactor Delphi with a fraction of what the lord deserves. Lours does not know this and sees only the face of desolation, dressed neatly and sipping a coffee.

"Ask me then, Delphi." He avoids the monster's grey piercing eyes and the ribbons that have terrified him since he arrived. He stares at the chest of his abductor and shakes with uncontrolled terror.

Why terror, when Delphi has so far been likened to some kind of oversize, highly adored stuffed cat or bear (albeit one who recently leveled a section of Chafrium)? We must revisit the the fair city of Austen's early history. In all of Terra, and indeed to some serious degree in all of civilization, there has never been a city like Austen. That's not to say Austen has some extraordinary claim to exceptionalism; rather, it's been a disappointing confluence of the opposite. In the 1600s, as the elves began their merciless expansion into the Mexican territories, slaughtering hapless Conquistadores, they expanded first to the southern limits of the continent. Only after they'd set up fortresses from the Country of the Lords of the State to the City of Palaces did the elves look northward. It took them the better part of a century to dislodge the suicidally ambitious Spaniards, who in their hubris built Armada after Armada in an attempt to invade Chafrium itself. What would become Austen consisted of a puddle cossetted by hills west and south with barren flatlands for endless kilometers north. Friars and traders set up a series of temporary encampments, a few missions, some scout towers for swapping horses and watering men, and as an afterhthought a crude hospital. Armies came and went: the French, the Germans, the heretic Czechs and their Hun allies, the rogue navy of Li Zicheng. All of them felt the wrath of the Elven outriders, and each contributed another layer of dead, dying and maimed to the hospital districts of Waterloo Rocks along the Colorado.

The elves found it convenient to also drop their wounded there and were delighted to discover the feeble human's would succor injured and dying enemies. They were doubly delighted when in 1704, Archangel the Fell, Assassin Apprentice of the Fourth Rank, stumbled upon an unused Door from Chafrium into the heart of Waterloo, killing his mark and advancing to Assassin of the Outer Queue. Gatemen were established at the newfound Door, outposts and outriders were encamped, and Waterloo Central became a convenient place for elves and men to informally meet. It took another three decades before they accorded it neutral ground. Consider, then, that Waterloo had several unique qualities good and ill: it existed in a plane of limited magic, it bordered an active war zone, it accessed Chafrium directly, and it provided a place where soldiers could gather without fear. How, then, to manage so many egos, so many armed and aggressive souls? Residents set aside a few places for duels, codified the Assassin's Guild for Waterloo, and established a tradition of amnesty for the combatant that lived.

What better for the elves? Neutral ground close by the City with hospital facilities for the survivor. It became a favored place to settle offworld scores, to pit champions against one another and end wars along the planes. Where elves went, swordsmen, flunkies, merchant princes, and con men followed. Waterloo grew—but not evenly and not well. Too many killers, not enough farmers. In time, the maimed and war-weary set down roots and Waterloo became a haven for swordsmen made obsolete by the encroaching Powers with their twin gifts of technology and magic. The Cossacks, the Samurai, the Mongol Horde, the Saracens of Moroc, the Musketeers from Guyenne and Gascony, Clan Gregor, the rogue Shaolin, and then hundreds of dozens of smaller clans and mercenary companies sent their masters, their sole survivors and their embittered few to the dueling place. They became its unofficial army and its quieting influence. Waterloo became the City of Swords.

The elves kept the city small and contained; the human empires sent assassins to keep it leaderless and neutral; the duelists kept it orderly and polite; and Jane Austen, arriving in late 1816 to battle death at the Waterloo Hospital for Bilious Maladies, survived to give the city her name. In 1821, the first chronicle of Darcy the Younger, grandson of Fitzwilliam Darcy and Elizabeth Bennett, seized the popular imagination. *Travel and Turmoil*, the saga of the Darcys moving to New World, established Jane Austen as the preeminent writer of her planet and sold through one hundred and eight printings in the first year. It was translated into Elvish four months after publication and became required reading for most of the universe's intelligentsia soon after. She followed it with *Honor and Honesty*, which situated Darcy the Younger in Tejas and became an overnight sensation, exceeding the first book threefold. Jane Austen toured the planes and was received in Chafrium. Then *Duty and Danger*, the famed dueling scene, and immortality. It was the book that launched a million swords—duelists from every walk of Civilization arrived doubling Jane's Town size within months.

Austen's janjacks met the challenge with aplomb. Slowly but surely, they developed a consistency of character beyond being the finest duelists living or dead. They earned acclaim as peacemakers, as educated and ennobled ambassadors of taste and politesse, the unofficial arbiters of interplanar janjack style. Why does such a thing matter? Because the phrase "cool, calm, and collected" originated at Waterloo. *Sangfroid* was coined on the banks of the Colorado after a grueling duel. *Snubbery* and *snobbery* are words long attached to the Esplevian (the Spanish Elvish creole of the Extenso) concept of a snob who snubs: *El Deslache*—shortened to Eldes. The janjacks of Austen are all masters Eldesiors by trade.

Think now of those queens of janjackery, the sisters Dnieper and Vorskla who take Eldessery to its limit. With a look they might freeze a man's soul and thus save a fight. It is said that in her day, the janjack Lady Suliko had a side-eye so piercing, assassins wept when she showed them disfavor. Vorskla wears her saber for a reason.

These women set a stern agenda among their own, and for Delphi they have made it clear that he, the towering hulk among them, must be twice the gentleman and three times the imperturbable mediator. Over time he has tamed the fearless duelists and cultivated among Austen's citizens a deep trust in his essential goodwill to the City. To the dangerous and hot-tempered grandchildren of murderers and rogues, he is something of an overgrown plush toy.

Poor Lours only now comes to the heartrending place of truth. Austen produces nothing soft; its janjacks are all razor blades and poison under their velvet scabbards. The Footman perhaps least of all. Lours wets himself disgracefully and prays his voice will not fail him.

Delphi begins. "Who has been asking about the line of succession?" He need not expand upon the question. Lours and he both know that only one line counts—the Imperial line, Lady Nia's next of kin.

Lours lifts the ice from his jaw. "Archangel came by last week and paid me for a full chart." Just as humans adore a good horoscope and pay exorbitant rates for their full start chart to be done, genealogists like the Watchman run a steady business of family charts for elves and their hangers-on.

The Footman scratches his chin and finishes the espresso. "The Merchant?" It's as fitting a snub as any. Archangel, the previous celebrated cutthroat of minor fame has in the last centuries become something of a gold-counter; his fees exceed those of better practitioners and his rise among Assassin ranks never materialized. He remains an Assassin of the Lesser Gate. In other words, an also-ran. Locals call him the Merchant; he only works hits where he can loot his victims for a second payment.

"Yes, Delphi." Lours has begun weeping softly. "He paid me double my fee. I found it... I thought it odd. My lord."

"You had him tailed?" Among the janjacks few secrets are kept, and most know Lours, a shady and despicable specimen of avarice, employs a cheap network of goblin youths who ferret out liaisons and spy on suspected bastards of royalty. It makes the best kind of sense. Sooner or later the elves send monetary support to their half-breed offspring despite never claiming, often never even contacting the child. But good manners dictate that the bastard of an important man not live in poverty. Lours cares nothing for their vices, yet, obsessed and meticulous, he has the whole of the Elven species tailed from brothels and mistresses, ever seeking that one more line on his master chart. He had Archangel followed to discover which elf was looking for a byblow, and thus whom he had missed.

The Watchman nods and then grows silent as the waiter returns with the food. The uniformed man, a lad named Pol with nine duels under his belt and a reputation as a card sharp, hands over the food efficiently, pours Lours a glass of healer's wine, then spends a moment rearranging the table before setting a Caffé Coralaviere before the Footman. Delphi sips it, takes immediate note, and lets a slow, vicious smile run across his face. He whispers something to Pol and hands him a coin.

"So?"

Lours sips the wine and lets the mild magic do its work. His teeth stop aching and his terror has given way to a numb acquiescence. "Blind Napoleon paid him, but... but the trail ends there."

Delphi considers as he devours a quesadilla. "Assuming Qelniasherah fails to ascend the throne, who would?"

Here Lours smiles, forgetful of his missing tooth. His love of the subject eclipses all other things. "Well, that's an interesting question, and if Kizervexius were alive it would be particularly thorny."

The Footman feels a thrill of fear run his spine. "The Lord Protector has no children."

"Correct. But he legally invalidated several of Lady Nia's cousins through his bloodline and his relationship with her mother. As it is, with the Minister Absolute installed but not declared, the succession falls to Duchess Bezeltine."

Delphi scoffs. "Guinevere? Surely you jest? How would she possibly be next in line?"

Lours gives the janjack a look of abject despair. "It will take me hours to explain. But the shortest way to say it would be that The Lady herself implemented some small legislations in hopes of child with Kizervexius, and when he disappeared, she never rescinded them."

Oh the great game, the sly dagger of Hoode slips deeper. It has been an elaborate con of eons. Guinevere the Base, the reigning gossip of Chafrium and avowedly the tawdriest of the highest of high elves, has been afforded a rare shot at absolute power.

"And if Dahnstalyon were declared? Certainly Lady Nia's his child."

Lours shakes his head. "It gets better. If he is not, if neither he nor Kizervexius fathered her, then two things may happen which are... dangerous. Both frankly unprecedented. Were her father to be outside the Grey Elves, as some conjecture, then Lady Ashlelani again becomes the heir should her daughter fail to ascend. If she ascends, then were Dahnstalyon, the man not her father, to marry her, he would rule as King, not as consort."

Delphi pushes back his hat. He considers and then takes a

massive bite of the filet while he considers his next few meetings. "Perhaps you'd better walk me through the whole story, Lours. We'll order dessert and linger. I have invited a guest." Here he smiles so chillingly the Watchman fouls himself anew and unconsciously rubs his hands as if washing them.

The Great Lord, the Footman's Desideralla, has arrived. Coralaviere seats himself, allows dessert (in the form of pears and cheese, his own eponymous drink, and some bittersweet chocolate) to be presented him, and listens. The two friends tap glasses and exchange courtesies while Lours looks on, a rabbit frozen between wolves.

"You got my message?"

"Certainly, Lord Footman, and came forthwith." Then he almost rudely looks over Delphi's choice in haberdashery and smiles. "A goodly choice of hats, methinks."

"You have my thanks. On all fronts." Both men share a small nod. "I hope the discussion will be to the King's profit. Certainly it helps me locate the child."

Ral smiles severely. "That is to all our benefit I regret to say." And so he does. Time runs short for Austen and both men know it.

Lours, prompted and half-drunk on a second glass of the wine which Pol has made materialize, launches into a complex tale of political compromise, legislative maneuvering, and lust. Between bastard children, succession conspiracies, and the bizarre legal narrative that crowns the reigning sovereign, the friends uncover all manner of suspects—the foremost being the Duchess Bezeltine of the House Zoëæ, Last Priestess of the Great Void and Imperial Auditor, nicknamed Guinevere for her love of human romance tales and he proclivity to cheat on her various husbands. One of the few Grey Elves taken to fatness, she is a loathsome and predatory virago who plays the political game so well even the Viscount treats her with respect—in public. Behind closed doors, no one but the lady's reluctant allies speak anything but ill of the woman. It is said that Roald Dahl, the Poet Laureate of Earth and veteran of the Great Pan-Slavic War, the queer wonderful bard of the improbable, modeled his Whipple-Scrumpets after Guinevere. She certainly thought so and had him assassinated for the effrontery. Her opponents take every opportunity to display the rotund little characters on any propaganda involving her and hand out chocolate at protests. To no one's surprise, her liberal opposition style themselves Vermicious Knids. Lady Oompa Loompa, scourge of freedom, has become prime suspect in the disappearance of Sæceæn's heir.

Worse, Kizervexius' sworn enemy Dahnstalyon stands to gain whether Gnash the Rash ascends or not. How so? Guinevere has mothered two bastard daughters with the randy champion. His daughters are the heirs of the heir, so he has a history with both pretender queens. In essence, the removal of Kizervexius has put Sæceæn in the care of man who needs him dead more than alive. For this reason, Coralaviere has been invited to lunch. Three coffees and a second plate of cheese and chocolate later, Lours has walked both men through the frightening paths that a succession battle might take. One thing becomes resplendently clear: every minute the heir remains at large, the life of the King of the Known Worlds hangs by the thinnest of threads. No one believes Dahnstalyon won't act to secure his self interest.

As the young turks escort a soiled and emotionally broken Watchman home, Ral turns to his friend the Footman. "It proves the guilds sensible after all."

Delphi nods. "So Lours was not the only one who had him followed. Nor followed the implications. It would seem the Imperial Auditor moves quickly but not subtly."

Ral considers. "I have seen communiqués, which as writ-bearer I may share with you." He smiles and it seems even the street sighs. Only yesterday these two men almost started a war. It's Austen, however, and duels often give way to lasting friendship. Duchamp brings his new elven patron a slip of a message. The adjutant scans it and grunts. "I will have them couriered to you rightforth. I am, however," and he rises in a liquid motion, "called before the King."

The Footman stands as well. Equals of their rank do not skimp courtesies. Both swordsmen give the proper bow and shake hands, and Delphi holds the elf's hand a moment longer.

"Ral, things will move quickly now. We're at midgame, I suspect, and it would be well, my good friend, to call out your own personal guard. I am muchly regretful, but I ask it in the King's name."

It's a subterfuge of a sort. Both warriors know that their faceless opponent will begin to apply violent pressure now that Sæceæn has openly thrown down his gauntlet and driven the conspirators, whoever they are—the list from Lours dazzles in its breadth of possibilities—into open and immediate conflict. By asking in the King's name that Coralaviere call out his own picked men, Delphi has preserved his friend's face and thrown out his own challenge. He has, by the strange rules of elven etiquette, committed himself to the fight. Until this moment, he's been an employee of the Court Royale, a foreigner shanghaied into service through threats and guilt; the Footman just crossed that line, issuing legal orders to an elf of rank. He has also just used a rare and extremely valuable feature of the writs which, as Kizervexius's picked man, he can take advantage of in the extreme. No sooner has the request fallen from his lips than it has been conveyed through the Doors and across the worlds to Coralaviere's own Chief of Staff.

More than that, Kizervexius's palace comes to life. In the heart of Chafrium, a dead place shrugs off the centuries and begins to call home its servants. Spies for every side, the guilds, the House Royale, the anarchists, the conspirators, even the clowder that is Senior and Junior all now know several things: Delphi is the Footman, he has issued legal orders in the name of the King, and thus he's made definitive and dangerous progress on the case. Even now, Kizervexius's trusted lieutenants stream towards the staging pavilion within his outer courtyards; his red ravens flock to their sacred roosts; the absent lord's house priests are recalled from their monastic retreats; and thousands of the most cutthroat mercenaries and adventurers who owe him allegiance are being alerted by an ingenious spell—the Vanguard Whisper—to return home. Delphi has in a microsecond told the entire known universe that Kizervexius's entire political and social majesty has been thrown into play. Vanguards long asleep now wake, and Kizervexius's standard turns from grey to brilliant gold and green. In every office and palace, his dead colors breathe again. Wherever the conspirators are they know the Footman comes for them and that he has invoked the full wrath and fury of his master's heritage. In the words of Saint Jane: "Surprises are foolish things. The pleasure is not enhanced, and the inconvenience is often considerable." Delphi has just laid the most considerable inconvenience at the feet of his enemies; if they are wise they will kill him at once—anything less spells disaster.

For a splinter of a second the Footman's absent Vanguard flickers, and one would not be remiss if they thought Ral especially observant. The Lord Coralaviere owes much to the King and to his own master the Seneschal; whatever he can glean from the momentary exposure of a thing hidden and forgotten by the universe, he shall. For instance, the mere fact that it exists and that it flickered into being says much about the magic involved in masking the Footman. The Desiderallae consider one another for a moment, and Ral gives his opposite a sharp bow. Delphi has just handed his friend a tremendously valuable gift. The Footman could have issued the same order in a number of ways so as to hide the Vanguard flash. He must have known precisely what his friend and rival would see. He sends the Seneschal a message—one so labyrinthine in purpose that we shall set it aside. For did you see the flash? You did not, nor did anyone else on the street. Only Ral, sole witness, exactly as the suddenly terrifying Footman has clearly planned it. Note too that years ago, Smith and this monster played chess often. Delphi held his own to the degree anyone can with Smith.

What does it mean that Kizervexius's whole world has been resurrected? Delphi is only a janjack, but the Footman is a warlord. Not just a warlord; an extremely dangerous, legendarily incorruptible warrior who will shortly command the fifth-largest army in the known universe. His own personal army no less, beholden by supreme vows, bindings, oaths, and subtle sinister corruptions to no one but him. The Footman, in turn, answers to no one save Kizervexius, who is of course gone, dead, dust, or worse. In this universe there are fates significantly worse than oblivion and death. It means Austen just got an army if it needs it, and that Chafrium must now go to arms while the mass of its potential enemy moves freely about within it. Oh the chilling realization that must come to those who seek to thwart the King. With a few words, the Footman has just not just changed the game—he's upturned the table, kicked his opponent in the delicates, and blinded them with the edge of the board.

Still, Delphi, who owns the body and perhaps the soul of the Footman, does answer to Austen. Bookmakers and gossips are even now licking drugs from their naked playthings and weighing the odds. The Guilds must be in upheaval. Every secret council will be sending flurries of messages and spies swarming like flies on a battlefield. Kizervexius's people will come home, will mass, will arm, will send their own outriders and spies, and will soon clothe Delphi in an invincible curtain of bodies and information. Delphi has painted a target upon his naked back the size of Tejas itself. Around him the cavaliers of Sixth Street nod as they pass, grinning and cocking their hats just so. Hundreds of times today, men will check their pistols and sabers, adding a luck charm, a bandolier, or perhaps the token of their beloved. War has come, and in Austen, where war has never really left, the duelists defy the entire outlying world with their swagger and good humor.

Delphi takes leave of Ral and the café, hastening down the street and through a dark alley. And there we lose him. His trail simply goes cold. The huge bear cat fades from view. One moment he turns into the shadows, the next nothing. For minutes, Delphi appears to have left the known world, to somehow have absented himself entirely. It's magic on a scale that reminds watchers The Footman is a Power rather than a native Terran.

He arrives across town, near the hills of the Liqueur District: a mélange of wine houses, vineyard fronts, and distilleries banked near the edge of the Colorado as it wends towards the sea. It's the far edge of the City, the graveyard-hemmed access point to the outer world of the Extenso and its oceanfronts and ports. Here enter men and elves by foot, travelers not from within Chafrium but the world at large. Here are inns converted to fortresses or nightclubs at a whim. It's not a dueling place per se, but duels happen here. One might say it's the working man's equivalent. Gentlemen (of every gender) prefer the open, civilized, and very public avenues of Sixth Street. Here a boot knife has a better chance of bringing down the target than any ersatz duel. Honor takes a back seat to success. Death by sniper or back-alley muggings happen here more than a fight between fair-minded equals.

Blind Napoleon owns a nightclub-cum-fortress-cum-smugglers' warehouse at the edge of the district—a huge, sprawling affair consuming three houses and four large buildings in a single bricked nightmare of red silence. He has his own moat built from the slow shallows of the river. With the clever use of grates and fencing, he has managed to encamp a large clan of crocodiles along its banks. To enter you must use an honest-to-god drawbridge transported in pieces from Merry London at exorbitant expense, guarded day and night by minions in a uniform of punked-out spikes, black leather, and extravagant hair. Delphi heads toward the complex.

The hit goes down as he reaches the property. Or more accurately, all three hits happen within seconds of one another, a cascade of deadly efforts. First the Merchant plows a massive twelve wheeled truck through a fence, having hidden the revving beast within a shack some forty yards uphill and upwind. The vehicle rams through the shack's wall, carries a six meter section of iron railings across the scrub, and slams into the spot where Delphi stood just moments earlier. The Footman leaps out of the way and finds himself subjected to a peppering of large-sized automatic weapons fire, the bullets sweeping ahead of him and into his path. Divots of brick, dirt, and minion splatter everywhere in a hail of screams. Delphi staggers backward, having taken several rounds at the chest and abdomen. He falls to one knee, his saber dropping, and that's when the Black Cat sets off her bomb, shattering the entire frontispiece of Blind Napoleon's imperial headquarters and wiping the image of the Footman from the planet.

Who is this new player, this Black Cat? Simply the finest assassin in all the known universe. Driven by relentless perfectionism and a complete lack of ego, she has to be one of the most dangerous creatures living or dead anywhere and likely at any time in history. She works for the Plumbing, Aqueduct, and Watersmithing Guild. Don't laugh. There's not a culture anywhere that doesn't value indoor plumbing, not to mention fresh potable water. Water, sewers, and the comfort of plumbing saturate the core of every civilization and are the most universal necessity of all societies. Consequently, the PAWs are the most powerful guild around. It helps that what their wealth cannot acquire, the Black Cat, a fanatic unionizer, can obliterate.

Should it surprise you that the Black Cat calls herself a woman? Among the nine Elven genders, they would consider her a *Sleytahsh*, a non-reproductive woman who lacks a mothering instinct. As genders go, it suits assassins well. Divorced from the core instinct to protect children, they can imagine horrific scenarios and with some emotional distance carry them out. Likewise, they can be all woman, appearing as soft, sexual, weak, and receptive as the culture and species dictate. A razor blade embedded in a slice of cake.

There she stands, dressed in midnight blue, covered in combat leathers doused with resins and charms from the Elvenlands, her eyes a freakish green from a recently imbibed potion. Hyped on some exotic and dangerous chemistry that gives her uncanny speed and accuracy, the Black Cat floats down in a series of impossible contortions across sliding wreckage to her own personal ground zero. She smiles, and her blue teeth lack a gleam. She has taken no chances with the Footman's superior vision, having chosen the color that mutes her heat and night signatures, that calls her into the shadows. The alchemists call it Precious Blue, a pun on Prussian Blue, which makes up the base of the liqueur akin to healer's wine.

The Black Cat has done several poor souls a favor. Archangel the Merchant has been splattered across a few square yards of charred pavement. Journeymen behind him can move up in the guild; the killer's three terrified wives can now breathe easier; and perhaps most satisfying to her, she has nicely saved someone a fee for killing Delphi. The second assassin arrives a moment later and surveys the wreckage, his eyes a flame of red flickers. The Black Cat knows him. Murat Hunthausen, a rogue sebakni soldat, exiled from the Supreme Soviet after it was discovered he was so addicted to the hunt he started killing children. Known for his scandalous lack of decency and inherent cowardice, he honors no guild and has no license to stalk within the demesne of Austen. He does not see her as she runs a clean blade through his spine. The Black Cat might be wholly for the PAWs and loyal to them beyond all reason, but she respects The Code.

It bothers her that three hits were convened here; she did not know about the gunman and ponders how Hunthausen has come to be in this place, smuggled quickly perhaps, into her kill zone. Someone outside the Guilds has contaminated her operation. Someone desperate enough to hire unpredictable scum. Worse, the potential collusion that such a capability reveals makes her question whether killing Delphi serves her guild. This is why she is the best. She never lies to herself, never backs down from a painful truth. Nor fails to learn from it. She sifts through the wreckage, using vital minutes to find Kizervexius's saber. She will need it as proof of her kill.

First the Precious Blue wears off, then the speed charms and finally the shot of Greenstride ebbs out of her, leaving a woman of indeterminate species, mostly human in affect and curiously plain for someone so profoundly electric. Her face and eyes show none of her inelastic will. She continues searching, bearing an everlamp on loan from her guild. After another ten minutes, as the hordes of defenders begin to creep from within their shuttered walls and rattle their weaponry in a useless show of bravado, the Black Cat smiles again. She has calculated down the fraction of an inch where Delphi's body should be; neither hat or blade nor smirch of blood indicate the slightest trace of the man. She has missed.

A single shot pierces the night as her left leg drops beneath her. The lithe Cat finds herself tottering and on the uneven rubble, she nearly falls, turning her descent into a kind of athletic stumble punctuated by the blood pumping from her wound. Without thinking her hands have started triage, slapping special bandages and a crème with a variety of stimulants, pain deadeners, and uncomfortable unguents that will contain the damage.

The Footman stands just beyond sword's reach, his dueling pistol in hand but not pointed at her; instead the deadly instrument threatens the ground at her feet. He gives her a small bow, his eyes full of respect and something else, something murderous like a boiling cloud. Flecks of ash litter his top hat and boots, dusting his coat. The Cat might be on her back foot, but she can reason. It takes her but an instant to realize he avoided her blast entirely, his clothes showing that he walked here as the firestorm abated. The Black Cat has been had. Hoodwinked or—if one will (etymologically it stems from Hoode's Wink)—she has been Hoodewinked in the most Zen-simple fashion. Delphi was never there; she and her peers have decimated several blocks to assassinate an illusion.

The Footman whispers something and despite her extraordinary senses, The Cat cannot hear him. She considers. The Footman cannot be matched in a fair fight, let alone one where she has only one good leg. He can kill her without effort and they both know it. Yet here he stands, immaculate given the firestorm raging around them. Waiting and more importantly, speaking.

She gives him a small bow and fighting the pain keeps her rather ugly high pitched voice steady. "I did not hear you."

He gives her a full courtly bow that brushes his maddeningly pitched top hat on the debris at his feet, then approaches. When he is within range of her most lethal defenses, he smiles fully, his fangs a river of white terror. He winks at her mischievously and begins to speak. His voice has a leathery quality which she has always liked. She has not seen him for over a century, not as the Footman. He stands entirely before her, somehow taller, more magnificent, and utterly regal, every inch the servant of the most arrogant, most cultured warrior in living memory. A quiet wind blows back his clothing as if on cue. She knows it's just the side effects of her bomb, of the fires and the interplay of vortexes, but in this moment, as the shadows and wicks of light play up his epic stature, he looks like a god granting her an audience.

"I said 'Sandoval Prestige, I honor thee.'"

That son of a bitch. Oh, he has murdered her in the most backhanded and unexpected fashion. Worse, he has stolen her only joy. Even as he says it a second time, Sandoval Prestige, the Black Cat, feels what he has already set into motion. Her repressed Vanguard, paid for with many millions of gold coins and dead bodies, flares back into iridescent life. It has something worse than Shine; it has a Grace.

One of the properties of a Writ, coveted so deeply by the masses, lies in its ability to confer permanent honors on behalf of the issuer. As the Footman bears the Writ of All, granted by the very lords of Chafrium and affirmed by the King, he can and by law must bestow honors at the highest level. In thanks for her service, the sigil glowing before them explains all in a heartbeat—eliminating the vicious thug Hunthausen and the rogue assassin Archangel—the Court of the True King in consultation with the Seers of Chafrium and the Confrattery of Elven Legions bestows now and forever upon the person of one Sandoval Prestige the permanent rank, honor, and privilege of The Butterfly Order, Knight Commander of the Blazing Sun.

Archangel was not working on orders nor being paid for his services. For once, the Merchant went rogue, and she has done a major service to the crown twice over. Damned and damned again, for an agent of said Crown stands before her, having caught her in the act of doing a Right Thing. He has rightly and justly given her the proper due—and destroyed her in the process. It's a thoroughly elven thing, and on the scoreboard traveling by gossip and whisper along the Doors, Delphi and Austen have just counted coup majorly, diminishing all their enemies, punching the Plumbing, Aqueduct, and Watersmithing Guild so hard it will take it decades to recover, and pretty much terrifying anyone sane. It's so subtle, so egregious, so beautiful and elegant, especially as Delphi's first major move. It signals a kind of absolute warfare that will force many to simply retire from the game. Perhaps even Guinevere.

How you might ask, has the Footman done all this in a moment? For her entire life, waking and sleeping, everywhere she goes, the Black Cat's Vanguard will display a burning sun sigil more intense than the brightest day and more compelling. It cannot be suppressed, nor hidden, nor ignored. It marks her location, her name, her presence, and her value; it screams from the top of every shadowed rooftop the whole of her deep worth. Almost the entire universe would give their legs and several of their children for this singular honor. It's not a war honor like the Sancurion. It's worse than that. The Writ has transformed Prestige into elven nobility and given her a Key to Court. And by Key, understand that she now must arrive when summoned, must serve the King. The Sigil compels her, hijacks her very soul if needed. No one in the entire history of the award has ever wanted it less; it has been the most sought after kind of award, a patent of nobility, where something as obscure as occasional fealty to the King seems a fair exchange for endless life and unthinkable power.

The Black Cat loves her trade, and the Footman has put her forever out of business. No assassin can be effective with a giant sun following her around, with bugles and angels announcing her progress. More than that, she will be suspected by her Guild—cast out for the sin of future disloyalty. Were King Sæceæn XIX to command her, the Black Cat would obey. Without question.

He has given her a signal honor she will despise and blessed her with an almost endless life in which to ponder how deeply loathed she will be by her most beloved friends. If he has done this to someone he might consider a friend, someone he respects and shows mercy, what will he do to the people who have taken Gnash? What revenge can he wreak upon the King's enemies that trumps death by a few millennia of hellish suffering? Whatever it is, it will make the Courts shake in their boots; the Guilds seeing what he has done in less than a minute to their eldest Union will be paralyzed with the keen understanding that he can and will destroy them without pause.

Watch now the complex interplay of emotions as she realizes this, as her genius intellect takes in the awe-inspiring deviousness of what has been done. The rage, the fear, the total despair. She can kill him, this she knows. A last defiant act. But she has been a tool of reason, a total vessel of her Guild for so long, that even this hideous future does not control her, nor break her emotional resolve. Killing the Footman is not necessarily the right thing to do for the PAWs, and Prestige cares for nothing else. She must parley. They speak of course in Cant—the argot of killers, brigands, organized criminals, and similar entrepreneurs.

The words are almost unintelligible, encrypted in millennia of warped rhyming slang and triple entendre, of shared meanings across a dozen pitiful corruptions of language. They convey whole books' worth of knowledge and inflection with a word or tone. Hence their use of the tongue—it keeps conversations focused and meaningful.

Cat: Skragged moi yuk minnow slaggin' Vornik shelving.

Footman: Two twice done jackeroo shankin' hey? Tick tick swap.

They have had a conversation, an argument, an agreement and set rules, given and taken hope, insulted and praised, all in a heartbeat of phrases.

The Black Cat has just spit on her attacker—how dare you push the rules of war so far, break the essence of our code working as some lackey? Screwed me over entirely you have, and with no purpose but to serve the worst of elven conspiracies, to make us all dance like puppets.

In return Delphi simply stares at her: Says the woman who broke all the rules to assassinate a janjack on duty within his own city? The enormity of the trouble you've brought upon yourself and your guild are without measure or foreseeable end. Still, I am a reasonable man, willing to trade an hour or two of truce for some concessions you neither deserve nor have any chance to properly earn.

To which the erring Cat, her position weak and full of justifiable shame simply nods with a sorrow inexpressible.

"Come now Lucky, you got duped fair and square. You've been fighting linearly for so long, you forgot what I can and will do." He taps the Writ and her eyes explode with understanding. Sandoval Prestige surges with hidden hope. The Footman has made her an unprecedented offer, a mercy of radical value.

Writs have many powers, many uses—a Writ of All foremost. But all of them die when the writ has been stamped or the owner dies. What Delphi has done to her, he can in his lifetime undo. He can rescind the honor or add more, modify her Vanguard, and so on. As well as hundreds of other powers he might invoke. She's known both Delphi and before him the Footman for so very long that he knows her nickname, is as close a friend as she might ever have outside the PAWs. She knew deep down that the job was wrong, but her obedience to her guild overruled her own desire to talk first and kill second. He stands there, his eyes grey flickers of wisdom, compassionate to her incredible struggle. She has earned her Scarlet Letter, but he has all but promised to consider leniency for a simple price: her absolute unswerving help.

For if the Footman dies now, Sandoval Prestige stays put, a humanoid nightlight on a supernova scale. The Black Cat, the most dangerous assassin in the whole of history, has just been recruited to serve, and she cannot rationally decline. The potential long-term value of her survival outweighs any immediate loss of honor or face; even betrayal of her guild for a day or week or year would be a small price to pay for her eventual freedom. The Cat could go back to her fold, serve the PAWs once more. If she did, if he overturned his vicious little sentence, the mere legend of it, the strange circumvention, would increase her own suggestive prowess so much as to give even her most stalwart enemies serious pause. How could she threaten the Footman and the Grey Elves enough to overturn a righteous act of supreme outflanking? What can the PAWs do that would drive an elf in possession of total victory to back down? Delphi winks.

"Speaks the Ottoman." She smiles and he smiles back. Very few people alive would dare call him a hassock. Sandoval gave him the nickname eons ago and they have been allies and friends, true bonded warriors, for many centuries. She speaks to the Footman, of course, and it's implied she's hurt he didn't tell her; that his hiding has brought stress upon the relationship unfairly.

He shrugs. It was needed, you understand. His eyes all but scream: Think, Think, Think! "Parley then, fair and true, for an hour?"

She spits on her sword hand and extends it: "By the many

gods and holy truth I extend a full and absolute truce to thee, let two hours come and go, to thee and thine I shall offer no harm." He takes it with the most solemn nod and they shake three times hard and fast.

The Black Cat has offered more than a truce, she's committed herself to total non-aggression for two hours; if Delphi attacks she must flee, must not even scratch the least of his followers, must surrender or escape. She has extended him trust and as befits her intelligence done the exact right thing given her situation. She senses his need for speed and has bought them two hours where no one has to look over their shoulder. After all, she's just volunteered to watch that back and save his life; her future depends upon it. She has openly and ritually bound her lifeforce to that truth.

In return he slashes the air causally and the Vanguard disappears. No one is fooled. It will blaze back once they cross a door or he wills it or he dies or any other of a dozen contingencies both fair and foul. But for now, her mark of shame dims and disappears, leaving them in the creeping darkness where they feel more relaxed. Then he whispers a word of power and the wound in her leg stops throbbing. Later she will examine the injury; there will be no sign it ever existed. The Footman has given her a clue, a quiet and very personal message. Lucky squints as she ponders. She's already oathsworn for the next two hours, already fanatically committed to getting the Silent Queen back on her throne. Why then reveal more to her than necessary?

They stand quietly. Delphi incongruously pulls a lit pipe from his vest and takes a puff. "You have a question?" But in Cant he's also asking and demanding: come at me, challenge me if you will; make what you say worth it; hurry, hurry, hurry; and not least, be careful, everything from here on will be important. She knows they are watched. The word of power reminds her how far the reach of Chafrium extends. The Writ's presence makes spying inevitable; it all but guarantees that the agents of their enemies, embedded so incestuously close to the King, will be watching, listening, looking for an opening.

She knows too that the pipe means something, likely many

things. She has never seen Delphi smoke one; nor for that matter the Footman. In the four centuries they've been close, she has memorized his habits, if for no other reason than to spare him the embarrassment of having to chase her should she kill someone on his watch. On any given day or night, the Black Cat can predict with perhaps seventy percent accuracy where Delphi will be in Austen. Until today, until she realizes, when it has really mattered.

You magnificent bastard. She smiles then, really smiles. On Sandoval Prestige it looks like a death threat. Perhaps it is. Few things please her as much as killing. She has recognized the pipe at last. That he has brought it along, already lit, speaks to how much he's thought this through, how deep within the sinister twists of the elven mobius he has already gone. She thinks of what her spies have told her of his travels, his previous meetings. Of course. He has told her everything in these few minutes—in fact, more than he may know himself, given her specialty and her reach within the criminal underworlds.

Relieved of her pain, the Black Cat has extraordinary senses. While the worlds look on, certain that she has been bullied, beaten, hurt, and cowed, she and Delphi alone know he has taken her entirely into his confidence and asked her, janjack to assassin, servant to servant, to assist Austen. He is after all smoking Darcy the Younger's pipe. It's so random, so trifling that only a local would think of it.

She sees it now. The hat, the moment with Dahnstalyon, the mysterious meeting with the extra janjacks, her own reversal of fortunes. Delphi has decided to play for it all... to permanently change Austen's position with Chafrium. He's been waiting for such a fulcrum, a rare moment where his unique prowess could be hauled into play. How? Regardless of how this all ends, the Footman will be killing The Minister Absolute. Jane Austen will be avenged.

She already knows about the lineage issues. As if the Watchman could hide from her. She's known for weeks. The Black Cat has operational understanding of every major conflict and scheme in the known universe. For a multiverse this large and convoluted, it's a feat which defines most geniuses. For her, it's not even her most extreme capability. On a moment's notice she can exploit a weakness in security, a trifle of vanity or fear, a single indiscretion. Luck is the residue of design, and no one is more lucky than she. The ultimate designer, the watcher among watchers, the highest hawk. Her whole assault on the Footman had to be planned in an hour. She thinks on this.

He would know she would be coming, had planned on her coming. He had brought this prop, had moderated his lethal response, had neatly trapped her. It meant that Guinevere and her disgusting paramour had their sticky fingers in her guild, had prompted this. When the Footman rushed them with his flexing of Kizervexius' muscles, the conspirators had swiftly set their hawk upon him—revealing their weaknesses, opening the whole of their influences. At this moment, sitting here in the rubble of her failed attack, in the foreshadowing of a dynasty's downfall, he showed her a simple pipe made to honor a literary character. A beloved lie.

What if? It's a powerful moment between them. He has told her to trust he will be for Austen. That he is not yet the Footman, that he will be Delphi, and as mindboggling as it seems, he's really in this to find a lost child. Just that—and while there is more, he's smoking the pipe, telling her where his truest loyalties lie. Forgteting Cant she spits a curse in common English: "Blood and Martyrs!" Then in Cant she tells him what he must know. "Do we kill Napoleon or simply capture him?" Which conveys to Delphi many things: I will follow your orders; message received; I know we're being watched; I'll play along; I can keep the secret. But also, and this remains important—do not let their casual aplomb fool you—she has more to say: I'm not done with this; I won't be put off; I am on to you, you tricky bastard; you need me; you have no clue how deep this goes; and most importantly, I suspect you of lying to me.

He smiles, snuffs the pipe with a casual finger, and puts it back in his vest. "Let's see how it all plays out." Which means just that—to every question. They nod as duelists nod. For her part she limps, putting on a brave face to hide her perfectly functional leg. Actually, she stumbles behind him, light and silent, trying to hide her entirely transformed body. The Word he has spoken has dispelled centuries of combat damage and strain; in a heartbeat he has erased the detritus of a hundred dozen sorties and misadventures. Missing now are the shrapnel in her left shoulder, the scars along her spine, the orichalcum nail driven through her right metatarsal, the marks left by poison wine along her esophagus. She blinks twice, hides a thrill of jagged astonishment, and keeps walking like a hurt girl who must pretend she is not. She has to sell her tough act for the millions of eyes that even now prey upon the battlefield, watching their every word, hanging on nuances within nuances.

CHAPTER 7: ORLENZEN SCUM

It's a good thing the Black Cat has gotten herself under control behind a world-class acting face, because Kizervexius' retinue appears without fanfare or warning. One moment there is only smoke and ash; the next, five tall men, thin and perilous, stand near the wreckage. In the lairs, living rooms, and observatory towers of the Guilds, a collective gasp has just escaped the lips of what we shall term "interested parties."

Delphi gives the men an arrogant bow, then thrusts his pistol back in its holster. As signals go, it's unequivocal: *Try me then—I fear you not in the least.* For their part the terrifying shadows advance without sound into the flickering light, to be seen and officially met. They are Grey Elves all, each one a very important man, a small god of his own world and royalty even among the royals of the Court. Their faces are brick sepulchers of spite and purpose. The shortest man, an old-looking specimen of pure arrogance and malice, returns the bow, his inflection a mere scintilla lower than the Footman's.

Delphi waits until each delivers their bows. The younger they are, the lower they go, each a fractional bit more than the father of them all. When they have delivered obeisance and shown the worlds their grudging sympathies, he gives a smile full of teeth and threats. The occasion calls for Elven Battle Talk, a kind of creole of Cant, High Elvish, and Symbolic Logic. As programming languages go, the high performance stack within Chafrium's main data citadel prefers it. Computers have not yet come to Earth; they have Babbage devices and a Lovelace Engine, of course, but these are still mechanical things, unsentient and lacking in the kind of extraplanar complexity one expects of a proper computer. Battle Talk won't mean much for a Lovelace engine; not yet.

"The last shall be the first."

The old man grimaces as if slapped, then gives the Footman a better bow, respectful of his destructive capability if less heartfelt and loyal. "And the last shall be all you need." He smiles as Delphi bows back.

The Black Cat has kept her face entirely blank. On any day but this, in any place but the edge of Austen, these five newcomers would mean death to her. They are no one's friends, least of all hers. They have a blinding hatred of all things female, for that matter for any gender but those two which are wholly masculine. Their incalculable cruelty wraps about them like a second cloak, bathing them in the crimes of their millennia-long lives. A mere minute ago, Delphi Janjack saved her life. The truce she offered will alone preserve her existence and prevent what could have been the destruction of the PAWs. Whoever within her guild decided to slay the Footman failed to consider the political ramifications of the act.

In this case, those consequences include the House of Orlenzen, of which five of the six heads stand before her, ready to transfer heads to pikes. They are Kizervexius' paternal grandfather, father, older and younger uncle, and one living cousin, the son of the eldest uncle. All are oathsworn to the Lord Protector, who among many honors won the Chair of House Olrenzen. These five are among the deadliest wizards living, dead, or in between. There are a pair of cheerful Vampires in a deadland who might rival them for sheer punch; inside the guilds of the City there might be a few dozen scholars with their knowledge and finesse. But no one anywhere equals them for crazy.

House Orlenzen has to be the most despised and feared entity of the Royal Court. Founded fifteen minutes after the mud bricks cooled in Chafrium, these men (and it's only men who survive) have gang-raped, murdered, kidnapped, blackmailed, and enslaved their way through a million years of elven history. They didn't start out Grey Elves, being of some hideous extraction that mingled with demons and fiends. The Stained

Ones, they are called. As ruling powers waxed and waned, they abducted and mentally crushed an appropriate mate, and then, after stealing the offspring, extracted the victim's legal titles, goods, and social power before exterminating her entire family tree. They are the locusts of Royalty; serial killers each and every one; sadists and psychopaths. Even Lomar disliked them.

The men standing in the ruins of Blind Napoleon's façade are the latest generation of nastiness. Grandfather Orlenzen, the nominal head of the House though he owes his sword hand and heart to Kizervexius, goes by the charming name of Deathtooth. In Grey Elvish it sounds lyrical: Llyndrindl. Old Deathtooth has seen eleven thousand years of desolation. He's famous for absorbing the power of his enemies through necromancy and cannibalism, stewing them in a huge steel cauldron made from an army of offending orcs: iron extracted from their blood; the carbon their fire choked corpses. That feat alone required hundreds of thousands of combatants.

His three sons stand behind him like scythe blades poised to fall. Razorheart, the eldest son, specializes in the art of serial murder and does genocide for hire; business has been brisk for millennia. His child, a boy of six thousand years has been clinically insane since puberty, and has lately taken to calling himself Void. No one quite knows what Void will do, save that he has thus far not crossed his own family. Mostly Void works in antimatter physics and erasure. He expunges things—people, names, places, ideas. Removes them forever from the universe.

Next to Razorheart stands a scarred elf with pale eyes and a sneer made permanent by the disfiguring welt on his left lip. The Black Cat watches him intently. If the balloon goes up, this grizzled elf will be the first to betray them. Everyone just calls him the Gorgon, often with the kind of wink one makes when discussing, say, Vermicious Knids or Hoode's memory hat. Goragovexius is of course father of Kizervexius, the former Chair of Orlenzen and a very bitter man. Half the scars on his body have been lovingly delivered by his own son, presently absent. He has no specialty; he simply takes what he wants and kills anything that gets in his way. There are epic songs that detail his almost romance with the haughty Lady of Ultimate Rank, the splendid beauty Tisifahn, mother of the Lord Protector. For a brief century the Grey Elves of Chafrium held their breath as that savage monster The Gorgon stalked her, winning her favor and perhaps her heart. So patient, so restrained, he killed less than half her suitors and ate none of them.

Next to him stands the reason he failed: his younger brother The Silent Wrath. The Gorgon ate his treacherous brother's tongue after he abducted Tisifahn. Once he removed her from The Silent Warth's possession no one ever saw The Lady alive again. The Gorgon walled her away in a demiplane and used her piteously for a few decades, got child upon her, and once she had given his seed shape, extinguished her for the sin of not dying at his brother's hands. The Silent Wrath has no free will; he's a very dangerous mindslave to the Gorgon, his lapdog.

These five killers, the very worst scum of Elvenkind, are here to guard Delphi and Sandoval. Had they come for some other kind of social call, the Black Cat reasons, they'd already be dead or fighting. Orlenzens don't do subtlety unless they must. Ponder now the scene: the world's deadliest killer and the man who handily defeated her, attended by five of the most depraved murderers the universe admits to owning. It is they who bow to the Footman. Suddenly Lours' lack of sphincter control makes some sense.

Then Delphi speaks: "Deathtooth, I extend to you greetings from the Houses of Orlenzen and Zoëæ. If it pleases you, I'd like a report on the mustering." If it pleases you, hah. So delicately worded and so polite. Having met insolence and threats with courtesy, the Warlord establishes control. Wherever Guinevere hides, she must be shaking with inexpressible fear. For over a century the Elves have played out every What If scenario regarding the Mustering of House Vexius. Smart bets have long been on a sudden and violent change in leadership. Yet here they are, the harbingers of most apocalypses, all but genuflecting to the Footman. Lady Oompa Loompa has gambled and lost.

The ancient elf smiles, revealing sharpened teeth. "Even now the armies congeal, a thick pudding of violence, my Lord. I can have them anywhere, Door or not, within an hour. My sons can arm them and provide the spice they need. Nothing stands in our way. We shall eat the heart of Chafrium itself should that be your pleasure."

Delphi looks at the Black Cat, his face empty, his eyes a dance of amusement. She smiles faintly back, wondering, calculating. "Bring a full cohort here, outriders with swift horse and several scouts. Then stand to. You may send Razorheart to the Fortress to organize and take up my banner." Which means of course taking the Void as well.

The eldest Orlenzen flicks a hand and the two wizards fade almost instantly. No fireworks, no big hum of power, just magic. He gives his Lord a shallow bow. "And when your cohort appears? Orders?"

Delphi nods to the Black Cat to go ahead. Once she passes him, his body shielding her from the remaining three, he commands his men. "Stand to and wait. If I need help with the old man inside, you will know. Guard the perimeter. Allow no one within our territory, start no fights. Kill anyone who defies us." He has set policy; a coolheaded one at that. Assassins within the Court Royal will report to the King: House Vexius arms but does not advance. One of our own stands next to the Warlord's throat and in one hundred minutes' time can slay him at will. Their weakest general commands them by proxy and the Footman stays in Austen. We have them contained.

Then he follows the lithe killer as she wends through the rubble to the barred door that leads to Delphi's original target. Incongruously, the big man knocks and waits as various bars, locks and deadbolts are thrown back, then the beast of a door pulled inward, only to have it stick in place no more than three feet open. He and the Cat slide inside, taking up residence within a cool interior lit by a soft radiant glow Delphi knows to be ambermoss from Altunia.

We have left his story for a while, lingering with the women and listening to their conversations, their thoughts. The Norns and the Black Cat, Saint Jane makes five. Five Orlenzens, five women of valor, and Delphi, the Footman, the Lord Forsaken in the middle. What does Delphi think? What has he done here, tipping his hat to Sandoval and Coralaviere?

It's an important question, for after all, he appears to be

the star of this little show. Assuredly, we know as much about Chafrium and Austen, about the character and feelings of those two cities, as we know of Delphi and his emotions. That's about to change. Following the etymological logic of the universe, Blind Napoleon turns out to be neither blind nor a man. They've been playacting out there, in the battlefield. Putting on a show for the residents of every world but this, for the outsiders who do not treasure Austen as the janjack and Cat so deeply do.

Napoleon, as irony would have it, is a really a pair of rather clever goblins: Merciful and Quickwit Valuta, a married couple who've run a careful business of spycraft, smuggling, anti-terrorism, and policing. They are in fact nationales if one wishes to be precise. Blind Napoleon's warehouses are everything a criminal enterprise should be, with the added benefit of also being the headquarters of Austen's national secret police and counter-espionage unit. Merciful runs the police while Quickwit runs the crime, and ne'er the twain meet, save on the Dais.

They have a frontman, a gibbering old goblinoid from offworld who will say anything for his daily dose of narcorum. He's huge, fat, blind as could be hoped, and really really colorful. For the residents of Austen and the world beyond, he's as much of the truth as anyone sees. But the janjacks know better; Sandoval and a handful of likeminded elites also know. Trained by The Owl, she and all his other apprentices know the names of every secret service, spymaster, and intelligence unit in the civilized world. As well as every mobster, warlord, sequestered wizard and Power, every ranking god, every vampire or mummified archmage, every last significant player in the game which makes up Chafrium's daily affairs.

Austen, having long been under the brutal foot of Elvenkind, has taken its subordinate status in stride; using goblins as its lever, it has found a way to embed spies of every stripe into the worlds beyond—without, it should be added, ever getting caught. Janjack Everstrong will be standing within the hall, ihms presence a certainty. Either Everstong or Bootknife stands fast within the citadel at all times; when they die, another janjack with their skills will replace them. Austen had been providing just such a pair of janjacks since the institution arrived at the shores of Waterloo. They absorb memories, bend scrying, mutate ESP and nanomnemonics and the newest toy of the Chafrium Assassin's Guild, the brainwrench. In their presence these devices do more than fail: they lie to their owners.

Couple that with the Dais taken from Chafrium's old throne room, the one used by priests of Arüne, and you have the makings of a great spy service. The Dais, of course, should compel absolute truth. But Austen sits too far from the dead god's bleeding carcass; instead only truth can be spoken upon the platform. It's a minor distinction in the hands of, say, an orc or a human or those pesky lovers of espionage the Garuda. Elves fair better, having long danced with the Fay and learned something of deception. But the Fay themselves have only one equal in fraud, trickery and the masterful ruse: goblins. Eighty percent of the Austen Underground are goblins or their near kin; the rest are Fay, human, some elf-bloods, and the occasional bored elf, though none grey. They alone understand the less than perfect magic of the device.

Merciful Valuta, that cardsharp of mortal affairs, has honed her craft to a masterwork. One recent interrogation on the Dais:

MV: So we agree to all the binding terms of the contract?

Rube: I intend to honor them as long as I feel you are living up to your end.

MV: But you will break your word if you suspect us?

Rube: Promise me you will be abide by the terms.

MV: I am offering to do so.

Rube: Excellent, then yes, I agree and will be bound by them.

MV: Good. Moving on to the next item…

In such a fashion Austen has survived any number of plots by the elves and their enemies to wipe the small city state from Terra. More than that, it has parlayed its geographic predicament into a massive strength, taking bribes, taxes, and trade excises hand over grasping fist from the ruling empires of the planet. Neither the Extenso nor its human opponents have taken her yet, and thanks to Blind Napoleon, few think they ever will.

Into this place stride Janjack Delphi and the Black Cat, long friend of Austen. The huge door, warped by the recent blast, scrapes on its hinges as several strong men push it closed.

Nearby a troll sleeps, its rumpled tabard over armor evidence that many of Quickwit's killers have been called home for the fighting. Ambermoss glows and around them footfalls come and go. No one pays them much notice except the janjack standing in the main hall, ihms eyes a cauldron of fury. Everstrong has long black hair, braided with flowers, a cuirass of blue leather, two sabers, each belted with a dueling pistol and across ihms back a pair of hunter's axes with long tapered handles of giant elk horn, done out with brass and lapis lazuli. Some say ihm came from orcish stock but that would be erroneous. Humans are so provincial. There are a few thousand major species across the known worlds, and all they ever think is elf or orc. The Karg produce some of the toughest desert warriors ever met. They also occasionally produce a child like Everstrong, begotten from a fiery union of a lost aristocrat and her bodyguard one dangerous Spring many moons ago. The Kargish penchant for flat noses and almond eyes remains, but ihm looks mostly human, standing nearly six feet and being proportioned fairly. Ihm can break someone's arm with a flick of the wrist.

The janjack advances, ihms face a study in wrath. "You bombed this place?" Everstrong's finger jabs out at the Black Cat as the janjack advances, murder on ihms mind. Before ihm can get closer the Footman leaps forward nearly forty feet and hammers the fool into the cobblestone floor. As strong as the janjack might be, the Footman can crush ihm easily. Still, no harm done. The cuirass, designed by the Wizard's Guild, protects the stunned janjack.

"Hello, Everstrong." He speaks in proper English with the slightest Tejas drawl. Here the polite Delphi takes over, stepping away and bowing janjack to janjack.

The disoriented janjack locks eyes with ihms counterpart, and whatever those grey monsters convey, they calm the furious warrior into conversation. "Delphi. What is the meaning of this?"

Another player arrives, quiet and small, her English accented with the tones of many decades offworld. "He's saving our lives, aren't you, Footman?"

Delphi bows to Merciful, far more respectfully than he did

to those murderous scum outside. "Maybe. Or maybe I'm going to blast this place to rubble myself." The Black Cat smiles anew.

Mericful, for her part, raises an eyebrow and gives him her poker face. She's stared down gods and elf lords with that face. "This I must hear." She motions to Delphi and they collectively walk, Everstong taking the rear like a bailiff ready to toss them in the nonexistent brig. The light in the place reveals much hidden to the outside world. Merciful herself proves to be a revelation. She wears a green cotton dress, hem to the floor, wrapped around her spare goblin frame and covered with a grey wool shawl. Her hands bear simple rings of platinum, barely ornaments by Goblin standards, and she wears neither tattoos nor cosmetics. Her grey hair has been tied back with a leather thong, a single long tail down her back.

Around her the place reflects this Spartan sense of style, being barewalled and empty except for the moss and the agents who pass to and fro. The floors are cobblestones, the walls brick covered with plaster and old paint. No one has bothered to repair them in a long while. Anything not immediately useful seems have been forgotten, neglected and dusty, or in the case of furnishings and the typical goblins pleasures, absent entirely. They proceed to a greyish room, faded and dim, where a round stone floor rises a foot from the cobblestones, forming an absolutely perfect circle thirty-three feet in diameter. The sacred numbers make no sense to modern eyes; once long ago a radius of 198 inches meant something to worshippers of Arüne.

The leader of the secret service steps onto the platform, takes up one of the half dozen chairs arrayed on its surface. They are low-backed affairs made of wood and faded tapestry, built Roman style with ornate backings and claw feet. Each is a mismatched antique, dented, chipped, faded, and glued back together haphazardly. In every way that seems to matter, Blind Napoleon's appears to be exactly the opposite of a Goblin place.

Delphi and the Black Cat join Merciful, and their janjack guard stands fast at the edge, ihms eyes alert to movement. Everstrong doesn't quite put a hand on a weapon, but the threat has been leveled. Delphi gives ihm a level stare and then smiles with all the sinister pleasure he can muster. The janjack flinches and moves that offending hand a few inches further from the pistol.

Merciful sighs something fierce. "So you've blown up my front walls and called in the cavalry. To what does Austen's national police owe the pleasure?" It's an acerbic salvo, meant to throw the janjack on his most well behaved backfoot.

Delphi blinks twice and gives her a carefully blank face. If Merciful thinks she can fool him, she has been disabused by his eyes. They boil in a way Everstrong's cannot. The Footman could personally level the warehouse and the brutes outside could level the neighborhood with a whisper. "How long have you known the location of the heir?"

Merciful jerks in her chair, her face a portrait of shock. The Black Cat has taken a chair where she can see all of them, even their miserable bailiff. She has already intuited the answer, or suspects she has, almost from the moment she arrived. There has been a decided lack of agent traffic in and out of one region in Austen and one group of shops particularly.

The goblin smiles. "I can honestly say I have no direct knowledge of the heir being here at all."

The Footman spits at the woman's feet. "And yet we both know that you've done everything in your power to avoid knowing. So where have you intentionally not sent agents to make sure you don't find out she's been here?" Everstrong gasps outright, and this from a stalwart warrior who practices fighting with Vorskla. Ihm has been made accomplice to treason, betraying Austen itself.

Merciful laughs robustly and claps twice, bringing Quickwit with a tea trolley. Behind him loom several sinister types armed with a motley assortment of guns and crossbows. The Black Cat gives him a look and the crime boss shrugs, as if to say: they really wanted to help and I didn't have the heart to stop them. The boss, with the help of his wife, lifts the service onto the Dais and starts to serve. Everstrong joins them, sitting next to Delphi in solidarity, ihms face a storm of disgust and wounded dignity.

Quickwit serves them all in uncomfortable silence, then kowtows to the janjacks in a style that would impress a Mandarin. He starts to speak, finds the Dais choking him, and starts again. "You have to understand, we've known for a long time—for decades—that the Extenso was gaining the upper hand." Sandoval nods. She knows this and suspects that the janjacks, for all they know their city, do not really understand its limited place in the worlds.

Merciful continues: "We needed to do something drastic, something that would change the balance of Power for millennia. We took a risk."

The Footman sips his tea and nibbles on a cookie. "So you lured Sæceæn into a war?"

The Black Cat coughs, and when they look at her, she smiles. "They allowed Dahnstalyon to smuggle her out of the City without reporting it. They lured him and Lady Oompa Loompa into a fatal indiscretion."

They all consider this, and as promised, here Delphi's story will take a turn. Here we will reconnect with our absent hero, if he can be called one. "You knew I'd have to take action, that I'd come out of hiding?"

Quickwit shakes his head. "We were ordered to do it. Both Mercy and I felt it was an insane gamble. But she has final say, and she promised it would work."

Merciful sighs again and puts down her antique cup. "Of all the ops we've run, this has to be the worst. Not improved, I might add, by our recent bombing. We're pretty cash-strapped to fix this over the next decade."

The Footman rises. "So where is Gnash?" When no one answers, he frowns and smashes the tea trolley with a light kick. The pieces go flying onto the floor beyond, little shards of cookie and ceramics wobbling into the shadows. "I am no longer in the mood to be patient." He places his left paw upon his saber, and behind him Everstrong has ihms arms up, hands to axe handles, ready to back the senior janjack.

Merciful nods. "She's staying in the cheese shop above the Elephant Room."

"Was that so hard, to be both forthright and civil?" He looks back at Sandoval and flashes a smile. They both know he's been playing.

The goblins exchange a look. Merciful starts to speak and

finds her voice absent. It puzzles her, and then she smiles—a real smile, something alien to human eyes. When goblins smile it resembles something like a hungry wolf who happens upon a nest of undefended ducklings. They are not bad people, goblins, but they are neither good nor moral. What drives them differs from human motivations. Even the elves, those haughty masters of everything, forget this too often. Goblins are artists—often of dark things like murder and extortion, or amoral pursuits like stealing corpses and raiding tombs, but as likely benign or fanciful as cruel and destructive. They seek perfection, nuance, The Moment. They are defined by their lusts. Lust for symmetry; lust for sequence; lust for an exact right combination of luck, planning, skill, and élan.

"Apparently it is. We cannot help but try to deceive you; it's in our nature." Here Quickwit nods and flashes his own hideous smile. They look as if they might drag an orphan to a riverbank and drown her. Delphi knows they are experiencing pleasure and showing great trust. Goblins do not bother him, and in his present state, even if they did, he cannot afford such petty emotions.

Delphi waits as the gunsels and secret agents clean up the detritus of his faux tantrum and another cart wheels forward, this one with steaming buns. Goblins love buns; they stuff everything into them, including money and weapons. With access to all the grains of the known worlds, these little tinkerers have formulated just three dough recipes that are communally acceptable across all the Doors and which have dominated the culinary ghettos of Chafrium for millennia.

Butterflax mix has Enadian sorghum and Garudan golden butterflax with some strains of buckwheat and a gluten rich kind of seagrass that has no homeland—some wizards killed the place eons ago. Half a dozen seascapes maintain the crop to feed Goblin tastes. Most Earthlings think it tastes like a kind of chewy taro, but with a hint of rye. It's a favorite among elves.

Red rice has just two ingredients: red rice and Califawks starch. Both can be grown anywhere there are shallow paddies and the right breed of white carp. Presently two-thirds of the Middle Kingdom and Proper Siam grow these crops, supplanting

Terran rice for the heartier, richer, and far more valuable red rice. The starch comes from crushing the shells of beetles that live in the rice paddies and boiling them with husks, ash, and some spice for taste. The resultant slurry delivers three things useful to goblins: coagulant for rice buns, a small layer of contact poison, and a beautiful ochre paint base. The Mandarins of the Middle Kingdom have adapted right along with the times, and they've taken many cues from the Goblins, who eat like them, write using a symbolic script, and have the Long View.

Last and preferred in Austen, Emmer flour dough combines any number of old wheat strains with some earth maize and a hint of Norg root from the outer provinces of jungle worlds. The resultant mix has been the basis of tortillas in the Extenso for four hundred years, and as a bun, it stands up to the thickest, juiciest, often spiciest cuts of meat, chilies, and stewed vegetables available. Local Austen goblins make a goat, red chili and nightroot bun that outsells every other kind of bun combined. They call it the Tongs. As in hammer and tongs, which when one orders in Austen gets you seven delicious buns and a nod local to local.

The cart holds several stacks of buns, some the familiar Tongs, others with odd colors and shapes, marked in the goblin way with delicate folds and designs that alert the bun fanatic to contents. A good goblinologist can read a room by the buns served and the way the diners respond to them. Delphi reads them, as does the Black Cat. Everstrong has a knack for reading rooms, as befits ihms role in the Clandestine Service. The janjack frowns as the cart wheels onto the Dais. It's a funereal assortment. Between these buns, this service, and the way the Valutas are staring at them, they expect to be murdered by the Footman, for the whole of the secret police apparatus to be demolished by the Orlenzen thugs looming outside waiting to kill something. Without conscious thought, ihm reaches out to restrain Delphi—so softly, a touch of pure love and concern.

Bootknife Janjack arrives, her face flush with exertion. She has used the tunnels that run parallel to the sewers and the underground version of the Colorado—the place where Austen has several secret-ish Doors to Chafrium. She takes in the scene:

the bun service and Everstrong's pale face, the frozen moment as they all watch Delphi in raw fear, the subtle tension in the Black Cat. If she turns now, she can live yet, report back, save some of the people. The Legend Makes the Lady. She bows, apologizes for her lateness (although all know she is not), and rises onto the Dais, proudly proper, taking a seat next to her partner, the third janjack in the line, loyal even unto obvious death.

As one, the council gives her varying nods of appreciation. Delphi rises, clicks his spurs, and formally greets his colleague with a tip of his hat and a wink. A gorgeous, very obvious wink.

It's been close to ten minutes with no conversation, a thing unthinkable to humans with their need for loud and constant language, their incessant drive to faster faster now now speak and persuade and drive and push. No one here feels that, and in their civilized fashion they have been communicating properly, slowly, carefully on this dais of almost pure truth. No one has even moved to eat the buns.

"Answer me this, if you please." The Valutas stiffen as the Footman's voice rings out. No one feels Delphi in the question. "Saint Jane told you to do this?" Sandoval and both janjacks swivel like toys on springs, their eyes supernovae of disbelief. The Norns have apparently told him something so secret, even the Black Cat has been snookered.

Quickwit nods and snatches a bun. "Just so." His movement cues the group; in a moment of prescient mercy, Sandoval Prestige rises and offers service to her fellows. No one can fault her exact movements, nor her perspicacious assumption of duties that leave the Valutas and junior janjacks free to draw a weapon when the fighting starts.

"And she assured you I'd get angry. Call down my legions?" Merciful clouds, her face a storm of strange expressions. Delphi reads conflict and some confusion. "Well, not exactly. She said your response would be terrifying and lethal. Then she laughed." By her tone, all know that Saint Jane laughing scares the living crap out of the Valutas and they've interpreted this, perhaps rightly, as their imminent death.

The huge warrior snorts and, using a claw, flips a bun from the tray into his mouth. He chews twice and swallows it nearly whole. Something hot burns his palate pleasantly. He turns to the nervous Bootknife, a strange babydoll of human with uncanny blue eyes and blond hair cut short in a bob to accent her rosy cheeks. She's deadly with anything bladed and got her name taking down a cadre of Tonikan assassins with a bootknife and some Kargish *honejitsu*. She often wears slightly girlish clothing and plays up her harmless-schoolgirl looks. She has never lost a duel and the swordsmen of Austen universally tip their hats to her with a depth of respect.

She gives him a defiant rise of the chin, a deep and unnerving stare that fails to do much. "Yes, Delphi? You ask something of me?" He can read her fear, knows she must feel a kind of nameless hate. She has guarded over this place and these people for decades. Now it appears he has come to destroy it and she has to help him, is honor bound, perhaps compelled to serve. But she doesn't have to like it.

"Ask me my name. Please." Again the wink, this time quick and subtle.

"All right, what is your name?"

He smiles and gives her a proper seated bow. "Delphi Janjack." This time the Valutas swivel. No one can lie on the Dais; they must tell the whole, absolute, entire and fully real truth. They can omit, they can evade, but they cannot, even within a shade of meaning, lie. They look at his hat, see the midnight double stripe, see the restraint, the kindness, the time spent here when he has pressing concerns elsewhere and the heir's location. Yet Delphi tarries. Delphi Janjack, servant of Austen, stands fast with his fellows.

Merciful rises, tears in her cruel unfeeling eyes. "How may we serve you, janjack?" Her husband drops to one knee, a feudal gesture of the deepest sincerity. They don't know what will happen next, but he's just told them he's not here to kill them. This whole sick, twisted plot, this labyrinth of subterfuges and ploys, has unraveled for them in a moment; they had reached endgame, and now Delphi offers them a road unseen.

The Black Cat looks at her watch. She has another hour, no more. Outside, the Orlenzens will have their troops organized and the fire will have died. They are surrounded and here she is, within an hour's striking distance, on the verge of a pivotal moment in Chafrium's history. "Perhaps you could explain this whole Saint Jane thing." By which of course she means make sense of why the two scariest goblins in town are acting like sentimental fools.

Delphi nods and begins a complex, multilinguistic journey that draws them all in until there's twenty minutes left on Sandoval's pledge, no more buns, no more doubts, and no more time to dally. To capture the actual words would cheat you. It's not what he said, it's how and why and what he left out. He's not doing this to be kind. He has a plan, a terrifying and lethal plan, just as Jane promised. So chilling that it makes the collection of murderers and cutthroats shiver. Not all of the Orlenzens will survive the week; nor will Dahnstalyon ever see the throne. The Footman in the service of Austen will be making a radical change in the balance of Powers. Permanently.

But that's not why it matters. It's what the Elves call Fitted Fate: *glildwimmir*. All the pieces have unnaturally fallen into a pattern, set out long before by unseen hand. This goes back to Arüne.

Once before time was time and Chafrium existed, before there were worlds per se, entities of vast capability and intelligence differentiated. They ground and slapped, beat worlds into being and then destroyed them. All the while the dust and debris of their encounters swirled and fell to the metaphoric bottom of the Dreaming Sea. These jagged edges of super-reality became their own lesser gods. Still greater than anything that we might see as a deity, certainly vaster than could be accounted for with words or pictures, these proto-universes nonetheless shared one thing with our present predicament: they were more or less linear. They experienced time. As time in turn ran its ragged fingers across their shadows, some small tired bits of these beings dropped into place, anchored in stasis. They became gods with names, bodies, and places; they existed as real life, moving forward with memory, words, and the need to create.

The passage from there to here, the long tunnel of multidimensional reality came to be known as the Fulcrum. On it Chafrium was born—the single splinter that ties the Dreaming to Time. Someone entity allows that toexist; or more essentially the cosmo-empiricists would term it "the unwilled will which cedes agency." Chafrium somehow creates or allows or enables this. It kills anyone who looks too closely into the metaphysics of the process.

Arüne exists in all places at once. She or he or it lives both in the Dreaming and the Lands; her blood flows through the fulcrum and the sewers of Chafrium, and most importantly, from the Dreaming into the Truth of beyond. Arüne might have made janjacks or be a janjack. It might be The One True God, creator of all realities and the ultimate Truth. Or just some strange immortal being who did the equivalent of getting a hand caught in a storm drain. Regardless, random or intended, true to Humanity or simply an unlucky bystander, Arüne has architected the existence of humanoid sentience and civilization. Sometimes, quite without anyone knowing why or how, the sleeping god intrudes upon the affairs of elves and therefore Terran humanity. Lomar revived the god for a moment and from that rapture drew near endless power; so too Hoode and the dark thief's other companions carry the blood of the One within them.

Arüne more than any other force of divine malice employs *glildwimmir*. It seems to be a prankish delight to foist little reversals of fortune upon ones we must label "evil". Arüne has one agreed-upon trait: whatever the god might or might not be, by every moral and ethical standard devised, the god seems to act in the name of Good. Alone among all the Powers, the sleeping god, the only conduit to the Dreaming, alone administers genuine moments of justice, mercy and abject decency from the inner sanctum of the most foul and corrupt cesspool that is Chafrium. Arüne might be Chafrium, one notes. No one, not you, not me, not the learned scholars of the Endless College or the Spiresward Institute or the deathless wizards of Katan know.

The dreaming hand of Arüne reaches out and strikes down ihms enemies now and then. Often thousands of years in the making and with the most delicious of ironic agents, ihm strikes once and well. Lomar was one such victory. What's all this bowing and scraping and formal boot clacking got to do with ancient gods, a lost girl, and the war for power? It is 1983, the eve of a new world, a new millennium, and there are conventions, perhaps a bit stilted and dramatic, to be upheld. It is the age of the top hat and formal bow, rakehells dominate an era where fastidious, style-loving elves have given themselves over to an indulgent epoch of high society, the social season, and the endless gossip that comes from the friction between haves and have-nots.

Delphi has revealed himself to the Black Cat and shown his Vanguard to Coralaviere, to achieve some finite linear result. Be clear—he might be ancient and subtle, but he wants things we can imagine. If not revenge and desolation, as the Austenites have feared, what? This he has explained to his fellow janjacks and the nationales on the Dais. This binds Sandoval to him for life; she cannot betray him now, no matter what happens to the PAWs. She suspects a great truth. Sandoval believes Delphi owns two Writs and now has possession of three total Writs of All, as well as an army and the location of the heir. She also suspects he will do something so unexpected by elven standards it will buy Austen another few centuries of peace.

The Norns know he will die, but does he? Yes, yes he does, and he has found peace in what comes next. He plans to kill many, including himself, to bring Gnash home. More precisely, he will bring the Lady home and do some very awful things, many avoidable but for the rapacious pride of his enemies. He will be Nemesis personified striking down the most Hubristic of the Grey overlords. Arüne has brought this into being, for the commonweal. Adrasteia upon them, they kneel and show their obeisance to the formal nature of the process. We are rare witnesses to mystical bliss, to omens and prophecies coming true.

His plan requires a change of location. It takes him and Sandoval a good fifteen minutes to negotiate with their own generals that movement. The Orlenzens don't like what he has proposed but must eventually cede to his will. With a snap of fingers and use of a little witchcraft, Delphi, the Black Cat and a small contingent of goblins appear down the street from the Elephant Room, a cellar ringed by two carved columns of rare blue jade (from the Temple of the Bright Sword in the Himalayas) emblazoned with sacred elephant motifs. They are downtown, amidst the hubbub of the streets, the night hanging lightly upon their skin.

Deathtooth must follow, burning power in this powerless land to approach his rightful master and report. It's a small reproach, but sufficient to draw a better bow from the old monster; he shows his lord the Footman a true moment of honor, then motions to the hills beyond. The Gorgon and The Silent Wrath have taken strategic points on the north and south banks. With armies of outriders numbering in the thousands, they can repel any number of Terran invasions. On their side of the border, the responding Americans have mobilized a few contingents of pikemen and a small ironbound unit with steam tanks and a bomber dirigible. The Yanks have established a mobile alchemical factory thirty miles behind the lines; at Deathtooth's behest, the goblin irregulars from Kizervexius Fourth Scout Retinue have been gleefully pillaging the factory and smuggling the whole of the contents back to Austen through a shadowgate. The dueling grounds now hold unholy plunder sufficient to drive back an elven force from the Austen gates. Within Chafrium, millions of armed killers have arrived and now control every major passpoint and street corner within the Great City. They won't hold it for long once the Guilds and the Grey Elves respond in force, but the Footman may rely upon his armies to continue returning. Also, word has come from Chafrium: both of Guinevere's daughters by Dahnstalyon have committed suicide. Apparently, Razorheart had the good sense to send them flowers. The Duke of Rexor marshals before the wide gate to the South of the City and waits.

Delphi nods and agrees to a few more pickets, counsels restraint, and then delegates several tasks to a saner General, a gleeful warrior named Van Landingham, who once roamed the streets of Chafrium as a skateboard-toting Drowned One, which include the recruitment and deputization of any sword within Austen behind the Footman's banner. Even now members of his cult, priests of gold and green, walk the streets with ribbons, sashes, and bags of lucre. Café Ragueneau becomes the unofficial headquarters of Austen's irregulars, all of whom have suspiciously acquired gold and green garb as well as gold coins and greenbacks. In a moment of focus, Delphi makes certain Ral may send and receive messages to him via Duchamp, adding couriers, horsemen, and radiominds to the entourage. He also sends four wagonloads of gold from the vaults of Orlenzen. It's a subtle insult, but well received by Deathtooth, who administers the command by robbing his sons and grandson of their treasure.

Then he descends with just the assassin into the jazz house below the pillars, The Elephant Room. It's a small place with low ceilings, smoke, and wood stained by time; everywhere the hot sweaty rhythm of jazz sticks to the skin. Magic, such as it is in this world, erupts here, a prickle on the flesh. It's a full house tonight, with someone billed as the Barefoot Ramblers playing frook, a combination of Elven sonata waltzes and free jazz. Three men, two with Elven blood and another with some hint of angelic lordling to his dark face, hook into the licks with gorgeous ferocity. The tempo races the blood and colors bounce across the room, creating little rainbows betwixt the smoke and refracting glass. The tables are smooth affairs, high and narrow. They exist to hold alcohol of every known variety. Around them stools, chairs, and spidersilk hammocks stand mute, almost all covered by bodies. These grey quiet things have almost no color but forgottenness and are simply there, magically null. The furniture has absorbed decades of bravado, madness, joy, and tripdust. It now sits stolid, an entropic dampener that keeps the room from erupting into boiling madness. The crowd here tends to be bohemian by local standards; there are local houngans from New Orleans and the Acadian alchemists guild owns their own corner. Elfbloods sprinkle the crowd, many here with dates of high name; this is a place to find escorts and buy them for a night or week. But most of the folks here are jazzists pure and simple. Russians, North Africans, local Austen musicians, the croppers from the Mississippi, the Brazilian drummer lords from the Extenso, the rum dancers of Morocco—all here and all in love with the beat. At the bar, a long low piece of nameless wood, there stand two fast moving locals. They augment themselves with memory drams and coins of speed, creating a cheerful blur of hands and pouring bottles. The Elephant Room serves only two beers on tap—Lvivske, a favorite of locals, brewed using the original 1715 recipe and Vault, the highbrow ale preferred by guilds and Drowning Ones alike. "Let's drink a Vault before we kill one another" has become the colloquial expression of cheerful agreement in the region. The bartenders pour tulips of beer at an almost constant rate.

In the near center there dances a girl, her feet muddy and bare, her body covered in flowers, rags, and the detritus of a dozen trades with fellow jazzists. Other than her preternatural acclimation to the tempo, she looks like any of the multitude of young modern women here: bubbling with raw joy, free within the safety of this small world, and utterly given over to the aesthetic. But her human skin has cracks, beneath which shine Gnash. He has found her, as we knew he would. What comes next should be simple enough. Bugbear grabs girl, bugbear returns girl to her own lands and saves queen, kingdom and city.

Perhaps, if this were a cinemascope plot at the theatre or some novelistic storyline, Delphi would build fight after fight, challenge after challenge to the crisis, and then denouement— exit Ral and Delphi at some relaxed café with spiked coffee, swapping some wise or trite phrases of false depth. But this is life; life turns as it wishes, and in the hands of the sleeping god, with destiny threading itself like a parasite through the quantum signature of time, nothing will go as hoped or planned or as literature might demand it. It will be messy and embarrassing. Someone will pee themselves or tear their breeches, there will be mistakes and idiotic conversation and all the tawdry miserable trivialities that intrude upon grand moments.

It's the unspoken wish of the sisters that the janjacks of Austen project an elegance and calm to match every situation. Delphi has this majesty within him. Behind him, silent and swift, comes the Black Cat. How exactly does one greet a queen? Carefully.

If the history of janjacks has been littered with little amusing incidents of death and humiliation, the history of the Elven queens of Chafrium marches forward waist deep in the sorrows of their enemies. The queens collectively represent a league of murderers that shame the Orlenzens in their audacity. If the Orlenzen men are like locusts, rapacious, and keen to chew through all things in their path, then the line of Grey Matrons are tigers, supreme prowling machines of beauty and death. The least of them, unarmed and unaware, walks with thousands of charms laden upon her skin; a dangerous fruit however appealing the aroma. If that were all, if the Queens merely slew as they passed, they'd be awful creatures, assuredly, but not things of legend to be feared. But where go the queens, all their hideous admirers follow. Lomarista is a term much abused in Austen and it covers a whole slew of Eldessery. Mostly it makes clear that the sycophant in question has had the malgrace to support the Elven queens like a pitiful groupie. Sometimes tossed at beautiful men, women, and concubines of middling genders who flow from the beds of Men into the embrace of some foul elf. Occasionally more focused when, for political or economic reasons, some Power or organization or coterie of social influence advocates for The Queens in contraposition to their own human allies. A snide jibe that burns away the irrelevant issues of species, gender, politics, life, or death and hones down to the that critical inflection point where decisions are made: Lomarista means you hold a knife to all our backs.

How much of the room would die for Gnash? Most of it. Some instantly, some with hesitation or by foolish alliance made in prior weeks or a lifetime ago. Being the third lover of a lesser runner of an involved house is enough to spread both scandal and death squads. The Lomaristas adorn themselves in paraphernalia of adoration. They tattoo their skin and wear badges, they shine their pitiful Vanguard and seek out tokens of approval. For them, someone like Ral is a god and Gnash beyond holy. The room, packed as it is, makes space for the girl and, around her, adoring eyes stand guard. Any fight in this little place would spell massacre or riot.

Delphi takes a table that has miraculously opened in the

front and signals for two beers. A hassled-looking cocktail waitress emerges from the rear long enough to drop their tulips and disappear. Gnash dances without noticing him or the Black Cat.

When the song ends and static permeates the room with a low buzz, the muddy-footed girl turns and sees them. All of Austen knows Delphi has been hunting for someone. Many know it's about a lost girl. She understands and her face reflects a complex cascade of thoughts. Ponder now this new actress who has stumbled into our play. She is playing at being human on this backwards little plane where power still favors the physically strong and the grossly over-weaponed—in a word, men. Of course, in Austen, women matter. So for us she must be introduced, her voice realized and her inward life acknowledged.

That little difference hasn't rubbed against the story yet. Austen, like Chafrium, adores every gender and accords what we call women the same honor and respect which men all across the tinpot empires of Earth think their natural right. So here Gnash has been fully woman and fully human. Important and respected while free and unseen. Suddenly Austen's choice as an Elven playground makes more sense. Here, elves may be themselves without the burden of being elven.

That exposes another truth about magic: it has delivered radical equality among peoples—except for those whose natural sorcery far exceeds the biological average. The nasty, glorious Grey Elves fit that exception. So do some rare geniuses of magic and that limited handful of adventurers, soldiers and heirs who acquired some object of power or nanotechnology. They are anomalies in a system which has two tiers—the rulers and the ruled. Wealth difference, birth origin, and religious merit, long the determinants of mudball civilizations everywhere, have been warped. True, the rulers still rule and the ruled still kneel before their vicious might. But among them there no longer exists any real difference in raw punch among genders.

This explains why elves and their groupies so desire a Vanguard. When the distinctions of power are entirely individual and often petty, then social force becomes real force and social death the only one that matters. It's not a mistake that even as the King rules, his sister sets the universe's agenda on Style. Do not make the mistake of thinking it works in reverse. Like the Orlenzens, male elves must over-exaggeratedly seize power via style, panache, deeds, marriage, or force. They rarely exert the kind of subtle social poison that defines the daughters of Lomar—with very recent exception. If we forgive Dahnstalyon, who has imitated greatness and achieved no small measure of social leprosy for his efforts, then his former enemy, Kizervexius had at his disposal a woman's worth of social influence. His Footman, that faithful creature to so treacherous a social lord, bears his cutting suasion as much as he bears his crest and saber.

It frames The Lady Qelniasherah's story. Here arrives no mere janjack. He's her social equal. Gnash in the body of a girl, mud-footed and plain, facing a king of sorts whose every word matters. She cannot snub him nor allow him to snub her. Suicide by Eldessery it would be. The impeccably dressed Footman, so famous when he was mere Delphi, bearing a history of loyal service and suave finesse, has outmaneuvered Gnash in every tangible sense. He need say nothing; his restrained presence has already set tongues wagging.

She smiles sadly, her posture a trifle rigid, and her eyes become beacons of defiant rage. *I will not come,* she screams in her silence, *I am not done here.* She has invited him to knock her down and carry her back to Chafrium over his enormous shoulders like one of the Persian rugs so favored by the Dirigible Men. She chooses to be petty and childish, rash even.

Instead of grabbing her, he bows low to a queen and affords her the coverage of his enormous social grace. Wrapping her in social approval and honor, he motions her with infinite politeness, janjack to highest lord, to join his table and be served by him.

When she stalls, he takes an extraordinary shuffle step forward, makes a kind of curtsy while doffing his hat—the janjack stripe prominent to her jaundiced eyes—and takes her stunned hand. "My Lady." His voice carries across the whole of the hushed room. "Your king, the wise and patient Sæceæn, has tasked me directly with your safe and immediate return."

She cannot refuse. To deny him now would be high treason. This is the truth of Elvenkind: that while their customs cut down the mayflies in riddles of abstruse nuance, they are really meant to prolong the endless lives of the Grey. A janjack has just formally extended a legal order from her sovereign. The Writ in his breast pocket makes those words law—absolute, unbreakable and inviolate. The Lomaristas in the room immediately side with the highest ranking elf alive, Sæceæn, the living embodiment of their rapt adoration and starstruck hysteria. Delphi owns the room.

A clear message has been sent to the spying universe. She Has Been Found. Duty served, his formal responsibilities are essentially complete. Were he struck down by the gods, or the Green Queen—Qelniasherah Greyleaf—to escape, were an army to invade or Dahnstalyon to kidnap her, still Austen has been saved. All know she has been found and the legal incontrovertible order made on behalf of the one true and right king of all civilization. Chafrium cannot now safely wage a war. The loss of social face would be too fierce.

She takes it all in silently; it's a sheer measure of her childish audacity that she considers her options. She may choose death or imprisonment. Be disqualified from the succession. She might flee, might fight and lose, might shame herself more by continuing her rude charade. She has options that, with the exception of acting her age and rank, represent irrevocable losses both to her Vanguard and her person.

The young can be so full of tedious certainty.

Think now how much physical control it takes to hold that position and deny his mind the subconscious pleasure of recruiting muscle groups, of taking her even a fraction of the way to the table. Everyone he cares about needs her out of Austen; every moment increases the danger. Dahnstalyon knows her location and cannot be expected to respond well. So too the Orlenzens have within their guarded perimeter the ultimate physical prize of Elvenkind. She stands isolated within the sudden grasp of a million enemy agents who need only dash through a few Doors and seize this rare moment to assassinate the heir. She endangers peace in her defiant stance; she calls down every malicious agent of Nemesis. Three such women live within walking distance of her position. She has defied the nature and fabric of gods, elves, and sanity.

Qelniasherah's been rude, childish, defiant, churlish even by the standards of elves. But she's also a child in their world, not even really a young woman. Delphi is making allowances and in so doing providing her some brief moments that are all her own. Beneath the dancing girl, there stands a solemn soul, the skin slowly sloughing off and a radiant creature emerging from the cocoon. She seems at a loss to speak, to make a decision. What causes Nia such pain, that she would risk death?

Delphi wants to know. His shoulders shift, letting the Black Cat knows what he wants. Wordlessly, she breaks a small clay tablet, and silence descends upon the Elephant Room. Cold, absolute quiet.

Then Delphi does lead the Lady to his table, where Sandoval has arranged three glasses and a silver bucket with recently chilled Domaines Vinsmoselle Crémant Poll-Fabaire, the mythic '63 black label variety, where a rogue dweomerstorm turned the grapes a rare shade of amethyst and the sugar content gave them a slighter faster rate of fermentation. The stuff retails at something close to the price of a good house per bottle. Two lie in the bucket, one breathing and ready to be decanted. She pours for the stunned heir and then sits, waiting for Gnash to take stock. Delphi stands in attendance, his huge clawed hands upon the chair he offers The Lady.

Nia sits and accepts the crémant, sips, and nods with a demure assurance. Then Delphi and Sandoval also sip, and the three share a nod as they drink one of the finest wines known to humanity—sufficient to be imported in some small quantities to Chafrium. They wait, as we wait, for the future Empress to explain. "So my king has bid you take me home?" She opens in plain English, her timbre and diction that of an ancient line of linguists. She is at once perfect and casual, calm and devastating in her inflection. She implies a thousand shades of meaning and can be called to task for none of them.

Delphi dips his head another time and places his top hat back upon his brow at a rakish cant. He's played this game before and usually won. He played just this afternoon to reasonable success. He does not step into her manifold traps. "Precisely, my Lady, he has requested I expeditiously return your presence to the Skeleton Throne. Do you reckon that your home?" His smile shows sharp teeth.

She considers and switches to Great High Elvish. "Does anyone conspire to call the Throne home? I mightn't not." She gives him a wicked grin. It's a language spoken solely at court, full of slippery idioms and contradictory grammars. Mightn't not has seven meanings and she's implied all of them. What rapscallion thug with a saber can even parse what she's said?

He lets her sit in glorious triumph for a good three seconds, glances at the Black Cat (who, like him, speaks fluent Great High) and then pours the girl more crémant as he responds, "One might, if so inclined, instead suggest that family makes a place home. Or a living hell for that matter."

Qelniasherah Greyleaf frowns and then considers. She looks at the room, then at the duo before her, the black swathed woman of indeterminate age and a hulking gentleman whose manners exceed hers. In simple Elvish this time, pretense over: "Whom do you serve?"

"Delphi Janjack at your service, madam." He gives her a curt bow. "You might also know me as the Footman, servant to the enemy of your father, The Minister Absolute, Lord Duke Dahnstalyon of House Rexor." He expects her to take the news poorly—his loyalties, whether known or not, place him squarely opposite her. Given his renown for ruthless swordsmanship, she'd never dare pull this sequence of childish taunts if she felt him an enemy of her kin.

"He's not my father." Neither Delphi nor Sandoval react, but the words hit them as hard as any physical blow. If possible, the silence deepens.

"I am sorry, Your Grace, did you just tell me Dahnstalyon is not your father?"

She nods and begins to cry. Future ruler of all known reality, she sits and openly weeps, slowly and without grace. "He is not." Then she wipes her face in a most juvenile gesture of artless sorrow. Both the Black Cat and the janjack involuntarily offer handkerchiefs. She accepts one with a small curled cat in the corner and blows her nose, then dabs her eyes. "I was waiting for him here."

"Until we interrupted."

She nods and we see the girl in a new light. She has not run away for pleasure or indulgence. She has fled the horrors of the court to find her real parent, to meet a man she had never known, who by contrast must be better than the Minister Absolute. Finer, one hopes. Kinder, almost certainly. "You came before he could find me and now he has not."

Now speaks the Black Cat. "Does he normally come?"

Lady Nia nods and tries to dry her eyes. "Most every night. He's a musician." The pride in her voice tells a story—one that would be hard to understand were we not already acquainted with both the High Throne and Highest Elves of the Grey. Art and mercy trump mere war; talent and genius together hold more value than a set of Sancurions. Perhaps it's the rule of women; perhaps a lingering presence of the sleeping god's blood. Beauty and magic together pervade Elvish art. None perhaps more than music.

She's in Austen, the Elephant Room no less. A place exclusively for jazz. Jazz being a human phenomenon, this means that in her blood flow human genes. Whatever species Qelniasherah's father ultimately proves to be, he cannot by definition be Grey Elven. There are no Grey Elves playing jazz. Such a musician would be tracked, would be haunted and extolled and worshipped, emulated and battled and challenged: the font of a thousand controversies and stylistic identity crises. He would, without doubt, be famous. Extravagantly so.

Ignore issues of species. Legally, the Lady Nia is as a Grey Elf. The magic within their veins will slowly occlude every aspect of her foreign ancestry, until only her line remains. But her succession can no longer be assured. The rules of lineage are abstruse but absolute—they define every potential circumstance. Delphi has seen the prolific lists of candidates and knows suddenly why Gnash has a roguish fearlessness. She's not the royal heir; once she knew the nature of her father, she slipped inexorably to seventh place for the throne. It's a secret shared by so very few. Understood likely by even less, at most a handful of conspirators and experts.

"His name?"

"Barefoot Jackson." She pushes her lip forward defiantly. She knows Delphi understands the string of implications. She is every inch her mother's daughter. Selfish, magnificent, cruel, sentimental, and desperate for love. Above all, desperate to find some anchor in the storm which defines the inner sanctum of Chafrium. A victim her whole brief life who, in escape, found the illusion of respite. With Barefoot Jackson, the most despicable talented womanizing alcoholic court jester of a jazz genius that any thirty generations have e'er produced. His vocal pressings sell even in the Deadlands. He's legend. Once word spreads he's fathered a bastard under the nose of the Court, and by implication enjoyed the flesh of Lady Ashlelani Greyleaf, Highest Elf in Chafrium, he will become the most vaunted musician in the known universe.

Delphi laughs and laughs. He pounds the table in mirth. It's so perfect and terrible. Kizervexius, who spent all those years circling his rivals yet was replaced and belittled by the presence of the Lord Duke, the mincing cuckolder...only to be hoodwinked *twice*. It changes the way he must approach his endgame; it changes many things. He raises his left arm and circles it thrice cancelling the silence, then issues curt orders in Battle Talk. *Clear the room. Cat secure Princess. Exit fastest rear door. Be not seen.*

The bartenders stop pouring and begin ushering bodies out two basement exits as well as the cramped stairwell that leads to the front door. In seconds, the Orlzenzens will be met with fleeing patrons. He should be there to explain, lest they take unilateral action and overturn the will of Van Landingham.

Lady Nia grabs his arm and holds on with the will of eons. "I won't go back without him. I won't stay once returned." She has the intensity of her mother. As he looks at her earnest face, he sees too the passion of her father. Delphi knows Jackson, after all. He's drunk with him, fought by him and against him, carried the limp and muttering fool home over his shoulders. He sees now, in her certainty and exasperating overreach, what makes Barefoot Jackson the plague of the streets as much as he's brilliant in the sheets. Sandoval Prestige has her other arm and looks ready to knock Gnash senseless. She has been given clear orders to preserve her life.

He considers and then nods. "I will what I can if it's both your desire." He has given his word. What the Footman can do with three writs proves extensive. Nia nods and allows the assassin to rush her towards the exit. Delphi turns and begins to make his way through the small crowd of stragglers waiting to climb the stairs.

That's how they kill him. Delphi Janjack, loyal servant of the City State of Austen since 1863, perishes. As the setting sun paints the sky in dark blood, the count drops to sixteen.

It's bleak, excessive and absolute. The roof shears with a tearing sound reserved for shattering bones and tornadoes. Great black tendrils darker than absence stream down, eliminating matter and energy alike. They wash through the throng with the smallest imaginable resistance. Time slows and Death Herself, a faceless shadow of entropy and rot, reaches up from the cracks of the Worlds Below.

By the time the implosion settles, three of the Orlenzens stand near the rubble with Dahnstalyon. The Great and Good Supreme General, Revered Intimate of Inner Rank, King's Own Swordbearer wants to see the body. Demands it from them. Deathtooth, Razorheart, and The Void watch him mutely. None are amused. The Void, through his father, has already explained patiently that nothing of the Footman will remain. That he has expunged him from all realities, not just this one. It required half a lifetime of power reserves and special access via an open Doorway to the sacred pillars of Chafrium's darkest temple: The Cannibalarium, a sacred palace dedicated to butchering sentient beings and eating them. The Orlenzens have just poured the better half of a million lives and several millennia worth of lifeforce, magic, and treasure into assassinationg their own Chair.

Dahnstalyon knows he's been catapulted by bloodlines and intrigues to rule the Throne. After all, he facilitated Gnash's escape. He knew she was not his child. Clever readers will surmise he's already aligned himself with the true heir. It's unclear with the deaths of Guinevere's daughters and the flux of living and dead who that will be. Depending on whether they've also killed the Lady Nia, it changes. This is why the Great Betrayer, his newest name wrapping about him, seeks to count bodies.

The Orlenzens swore an oathbond to Kizervexius and through him the Footman, whom they assume has been slaughtered. He did share a body with Delphi, and that body has been conveniently disintegrated at a reality level by their handiwork. The price to their Power will be considerable.

With Qelniasherah absent from this reality, the superstructure of power in Chafrium will shift. The next heir to Gnash's panoply of enchantments and ordinance, the real prize here, lies within their control. The Gorgon has abducted this woman just hours before. They expect the same at the temple of Orlenzen, where the demise of the Footman shall momentarily provide a hoard of power and magic to its newest Chair, Deathtooth.

The Wizards Guild and a few choice immortals have established and enforced rules for magic the way humanity has fashioned rules for war. Limits and foundations, spells—rituals—chants—periodicity. The Drowning Ones continuously attempt to violate these with limited success. In ancient times, ambitious men like Hoode did the same with far better success. From their rebellion, artifacts remain, and these spells, objects, profane splinters, and such make up the regalia of the Court, empower the Assassin's Guild, and keep the Guilds as a whole in power. These are the things that the conspirators believe will be coming to them: rare sacred artifacts and modules, wave thoughts, limitless engines.

The Orlenzens have gambled all to win all. In exchange for Dahnstalyon's help, they have conspired with him to steal the Seneschal's Aerie. They cannot be Kings or own the throne. But they can, through The Betrayer Duke, rule as a fourth leg of the stool. Maybe even more than that. Once the anomalies of power, the skin-hugging enchantments and magical devices which adhere to the Footman and The Green Queen, return to them, they will have traded three millennium's power for a million years' future dominance. To do that, they have laid their own house bare and killed their Chair. Not just that, they've struck his name. They've unmade him for all of time and reality. As an added cruelty, they've done it in a place where even contingency measures for survival cannot be accessed. They did it in the cul-de-sac of Austen. They've meant to murder him utterly, and Gnash if they've caught her.

How unkind of us, then, to know the truth. For walking towards the hole in the street, charred and radiating with the stink of suffering, comes a new version of the Footman. He now wears armor and goes without a hat. He is neither janjack nor sworn oathsman. Delphi has died. His bugbear face has been torn from him. Instead there stands a Grey Elf of extraordinary height, his eyes sepulchers. He wears no emblem nor carries insignia of any kind. Yet they know him instantly.

The Lord Kizervexius strides calmly forward, his belt jingling with saber and pistol. His Vanguard blazes with keen fury. He carries all the awards and honors of his many faces and lives. All seven of his Arrows rise like suns before them. The Orlenzens do something unthinkable. They tremble in fear. Kizervexius is dead. The Footman has been slain. This should not be, it cannot be. But Dahnstalyon sighs with understanding.

The Orlenzens have killed a janjack on duty in his own city. It transgresses the fabric beyond reality, breaks rules that should not be broken. Delphi, before he left the demesne of Blind Napoleon, issued orders with the writ given him by Sæceæn. More than that, he tied it to another writ, a fourth, unseen one that had preserved his identity and hidden his Vanguard all these centuries. In essence they've killed two janjacks on duty, Delphi and the Footman both. By using Chafrium's under-temples, they've done it in both cities. The Footman is dead, has been dead since the moment The Void shattered his body-self. But writs precede such trifles as life or sentience. They are bulwarks of ultimate truth, anchors to a higher form of what we would term reality.

The Dark Duke, having played for a few centuries with the unspeakable occult, grasps that he's been tricked into a second indiscretion. He's poured his endgame into an ambush that has trapped him as well. His *Vrashnaralla* has just lured his own House into rank betrayal. They have poured nearly endless power into the Austen street. They don't realize yet, but they've permanently transferred that power via the dying veins of the janjack into the sentient spirit of Austen. They've made the other janjacks and the city itself into a small oasis of higher magics.

Kizervexius smiles and bows to the men. His rival replies by raising a dueling pistol and firing through the Lord Protector's head. He empties the magical clip of all its enchanted bullets. Whatever he is, the draugr before them is not entirely here nor there; he continues to phase between states of energy and matter, time and place.

"You always were a hysterical man-child." The handsome elf lord chuckles and steps forward again. Despite themselves, the three Orlenzens laugh. In Elvish it's not just funny, it's downright infuriating. Kizervexius' tone caries the precise level of scorn and amusement. "Looks like rumors of you having problems getting your little Duke to salute were not exaggerated."

The watching world has just been told Gnash is not his child. It's beyond insulting. The calm Lord Protector has just slain Dahnstalyon's social self. His Vanguard flickers under the assault.

Dahnstalyon predictably lunges, placing his saber through the image of his enemy; the Lord punches him and the sharp snap of the connection shakes them all. Thunderclaps rock the street, shattering what few windows have not been mangled by the previous few minutes' carnage. Then the Kizervexius takes the enchanted sword and snaps it over his knee. The hilt, with all those little gems including Saint Jane's, crumbles. Disintegrates, actually. The Void stifles a low moan, as comprehension finally comes to Austen.

It's an understood custom within royal circles that Houses are inviolate. In truth, for matters like the Chair of Orlenzen, there exists a whole set of fluid contingencies that render the seats porous. In this fashion the clever wizards of the House have ensnared Dahnstalyon, taking him into their family without his explicit agreement. Being a fool start to finish, he did not understand that the Orlenzens would never agree to serve his will. From the first, they understood he'd betray them as he had his own King and Queen. So they tricked him. They used the assassination of the Footman as credible cover for their real crime: to mingle his soul with theirs and thus enslave him. For Dahnstalyon is now the least member of the House Orlenzen, affectionately referred to as The Motley. Remember we said there were six total? The Motley has been an open slot, lying absent with the apparent death and clear absence of Kizervexius. They used this open slot to trap him.

The Orlenzens have been at this kind of thing for longer than Man have built cities. They probably told Dahnstalyon the literal truth—that to assassinate a janjack they needed some of his blood and a glimmer of his soul. Blind to the last, he made the bargain.

What horror must overcome these devious schemers, geniuses of infinite double-cross, to have been outflanked by a psychopath of greater skill. They recall now only too late that Kizervexius mastered his House through sheer savagery. He outmurdered, outplundered, outbetrayed his own father and grandfather.

What the Writs have done cannot be undone. So too Orlenzen magic will not be denied. Mingling their powers, they instead extend The Void's murder to House Orlenzen itself. All that is The Lord Protector's, all that is the Footman's, every inch of treasure and power accrued in the temples of the Overlords of a dozen lands, the very army standing within Chafrium dominated by their collective will; the banners and trophies, the regalia and legends—the Orlenzens have unmade the roots of them. They have expunged their own existences on every plane and place, dragging pure force from the City and burying it all in a cul-de-sac. They have defeated their own contingencies, and by using the Cannibalarium they have, like the Ouroboros of Earthly myth, eaten themselves.

Around the known planes, Kizervexius' banner fades and then crumbles—as does every item tied to the Orlenzens. Their priests fall dead, their sacred temples sink, their wealth goes unguarded or turns to powder. Every slave is freed, every enchantment severed; a portion of the web of blackmail, extortion, rapine, and enslavement that has defined generations of Grey Elves is simply gone. Bloodlines disappear; men at arms capsize, their faces a tangle of rot and melting bones. Every bit of that supremacy flows down the river into Austen, into the lifeblood of the city and janjacks.

The assembled army disperses, leaderless and demoralized. Ambassadors and wizards, assassins and concubines die or are reborn, flee or find themselves. All of Chafrium wobbles briefly as the Temple of Arüne wakes for several heartbeats. In a fleeting moment the names of the Orlenzens have been struck from registers and walls, now only historical footnotes in mundane books. Every magical remnant of their existence absent.

It's the symmetry that makes it all work. Kizervexius has killed himself, of course. It was his writ that delivered the killing blow. We can revisit later what kind of man he was, to have hidden in the body of a steadfast servant, having slain him in the same Cannibalarium for the express purpose of fleeing the treacherous Lady Ash. Killed his own janjack on duty, then took his place in another City. Not a moral one by any measure. But his time in Austen in the shape of Delphi chipped away at him, and like all good jokes, the punchline makes him laugh. All that pride, all that willful hatred comes to naught. He and his rivals simply destroyed one another. Chafrium took vengeance on him for killing a working janjack—it simply delayed in delivering the fatal judgment.

He coughs and looks upon the city, his dead eyes now seeing the truth. He cannot speak, is lost and fading. He deserves this fate, he knows, and he has provided a whole legion of justice for wrongs done by him, by his kin, by the House of Lomar and the Grey Elves whom he had long served. His Vanguard starts to sputter—it does not fade so much as flicker and sink, dropping into the ground as if searching for a grave. This makes him laugh more, for he knows what comes next. Hoode will owe him another stack of coins, for he has won one last bet. He dies content, never quite touching the world again. He lived and died anonymous within the skin of two janjacks, serving faithfully where once he proved so faithless. The Lord Forsaken finally comes home, dying painlessly in the bosom of Lady Jane, her shade unseen to nary but the dying man who lays his head upon her lap and whispers "Forgive me." She nods and kisses him, her eyes black spools of understanding.

On the shores of the river, in a little tributary called Raven's Cove, a body has washed up; a tall duelist, his face torn apart by the killing shot. He was some kind of Elven bastard, with one parent of some ugly species given to rough skin and pale eyes. The resulting mix presents us with a well formed if slightly roguish-looking man of early middle years, palest green eyes that look like jade, reddish skin much leathered from years in the sun, and hair every shade of the mesquite forest that surrounds the secluded stream.

Death in her bridal gown kicks his husk onto the firm ground relinquishing her grasp upon the dead man. Something golden rolls under his skin, and little by little, as if reality were stuttering like a mirror reversing its breaks, he becomes whole, his face and skull knit. With a labored scream, he again draws breath.

His pale eyes open to a star-filled sky, the darkness warm about his wet body. Something catches his new eyes—a black-handled saber in ornate scabbard near a fire just a few steps into the woods. It rests upon an open trunk festooned with clothes and boots, weapons, gear, and two very thin pieces of vellum which he knows before his mind can make words to be the remaining Writs. He rolls to his throbbing side slowly, crabwalking to the trunk.

Three women sit calmly drinking wine and whispering amongst themselves in a language his mind does not translate. Every breath feels like icepicks being jammed into his torso. The dark haired female dismisses a raven from her hand and rises. He watches the bird flutter, circle and then calling depart into the night. She nods at him in the dirt, makes a short bow. "Welcome, Dodona. The count is now seventeen."

CHAPTER 8: THE FIRE DIES DOWN

His children sat spellbound as the silence consumed the little radius of their fire and lean to. The coals burned a malignant red but much of the shine had gone out of them. They had a heat but not much light. In his telling Gerhard had forgotten to add new logs. Neither Zoe nor Max had moved much for hours—consumed as they were with the small details of Austen and the now slain Delphi.

"He's not really dead is he Daddy?"

"Delphi. Long dead now." Gerhard reminded himself to watch his words. He'd told them it wasn't a true story after all. No need to imply Delphi once lived.

"Pops, this can't be the end. Right, there's more. Like a lot of stuff happened to make that whole thing happen with the Orlenzens."

"Like what?"

"C'mon Pops. He told all his own people a big plan and now he's dead but they knew in advance."

"Yeah Daddy, in advance. Like an ambush." Now and again Max's obsession with fantasy stories showed a keen appreciation of some odd things. How exactly did a seven year old know about ambushes?

"And let's face it he's got a lot of pieces of magic paper to do some damage. So what did he do?"

"Writs."

"Sure, sure. Call them what you want but it's magic. He's got some serious mojo going and you mentioned lawyers, so he's got the equivalent a god making a legal ruling. Planned in advance and Max had it right, he ambushed his ambushers. He knew he was going to be murdered."

"Ooh, yeah. Zoe is right. He knew and he had already done a murder right?"

Gerhard watched them and realized he owed them another tale. One that would keep them until dawn and beyond. "Well, we could put some more wood on the fire, perhaps make some tea..."

"And you'll explain some things then?"

"Like?"

"Like how he pulled it off."

"And Daddy, like his new sword. Because it's cool sounding."

"Noticed that did you?"

"Yeah, because he lost the old one right. When Kizerwhatsit got evaporated then the whole place went boom and nothing survived. So the sword has to be new."

"Nice one Max." Zoe gave her brother a rare hug and kissed his head. Whatever they were, they were still children far from home and afraid.

"Well let's start assembling the wood and I shall explain a few things. Let's start with *Ruach*. It means so many things, has tremendous nuance, the subtlest of words. But for the story it means a few basic things: shadow, trace, imprint, wind, breath, true soul, superreality."

Zoe nodded as she handed him branches. "Like a psychic smear? The one Mama talks about?"

Gerhard thought about his Brunhilda at home. She had no way to know they'd been waylaid. Except of course the old ways. She must be anxious beyond reason. "Same word, but of course the elves say *Ruach Glilmanyoss*: the shadow you can touch. Wizards speak in technical journals of a *Ruach Na Suboriman,* which translates as 'the truth that delivers power' but your mother would say 'the most accessible version of a basic idea or reality that can be interacted with via magic.'"

"Will she be worried Pops?"

"Oh yes but she will also know we're alright. Works both ways, heh?"

"Yeah okay but let's keep Max busy. Maybe more about swords?"

"Would goblins do? Because ..."

Everstrong and Bootknife had been busy. First, they alert their fellow janjack, a strange woman named Amberflow whose main skillset appears to be negotiating between hated rivals. She has a surreal knack for hammering out agreements. They charge her with collecting every possible source of toxic waste she can procure, borrow, thieve, or finagle within the next two hours. They do not explain, but the force of their conviction speaks volumes. Amberflow merely nods and gets to work. Within minutes she has a malignity of goblins about her. What else would a group of these beings be called? Her command of goblins, one another's hated rivals on any given day, speaks to her innate skill. The malignity quickly divides assignments before spreading out faster than any group of vermin should.

Amberflow has not employed the services of decent goblins, such as those who deal the City or guilds. These are rotgut scum Goblins who make elves blush and strike fear into every rug merchant, smuggler, and petty swindler the universe wide. These little darlings sharpen their teeth to attract mates and sell anything or anyone to make a profit. They are the right folk to acquire nasty things under dire notice, and they will bring back such treasures that Austen will never want for sludge again.

Then the janjacks move onwards, their circle of influence spreading like a forest fire, treetop to treetop racing faster than Ruach itself. Austen rustles as they make their moves. All the while Delphi has been somewhere doing Delphi things, preparing for his murder—soon to be gone, his body evaporated and his power back in the bosom of the City. The Song guides them to places we have not yet seen. They are going to see a most peculiar creature who makes even goblins tremble. A being so twisty even the Grey Elves dare not cross it.

Before the foot of a particular cave the janjacks stop; Bootknife brushes her hand across Everstrong's cheek. It's a private gesture between partners, a lover's touch meant for no one but ihm. Inside the darkness lives a sentience at once powerful and dangerous, controlling a secret Door that it has guarded, one suspects, since the first days of

Elves many eons before. Everstrong smiles, kisses her hand, and nods. It is time.

"Does the creature have a sword? Because that would be super cool Daddy."

"It has some of everything Max."

"Everything Pops? That would be kind of hard to do."

"Unless you were going to see The Broker." At this Zoe's eyes widened. She'd heard the name before, in tales told her by her mother. The Broker might as well be the Boogeyman for all the good spoken about the monster.

In the shadows shuffles a small humanoid. It might as well be a thousand-legged, poisonous spider. Both janjacks suck in their breath and enter, ringing a small curtain of bells. They have come to see the Broker. The shadow resolves into an androgynous humanoid of perhaps five feet, old and smooth, worn down like the walls of canyon. Ihms skin looks cadaverous in its paleness but glistens too, with small motes of red and purple light. Ihm has been covered in runes, sigils and patterns that they know are skeleton keys to various spells and protocols. The Broker has three sets of eyes, all dull milky things that remind one of a blind cat. Ihm has neither hair nor teeth, owning a jaw full of blackened ridges.

With a rustle of robes, the Broker motions to the janjacks, ihms six eyes blinking out of sequence. With a clap a servant, perfectly human and without fear, brings a tea set made of some ancient metal, encrusted with brass workings that depict something vaguely Greek.

Tea is poured and the servant departs. All three sip. No one speaks. The negotiations have begun.

What is this Door that the Broker guards? Aren't we done with secret doors and all that? How many of the damned things will Austen keep producing? The eternal City touches all worlds. Every aspect of reality including the jagged edges of life where reality cannot contain Truth, there Chafrium must also exist. In one such bleeding gap which borders too many things at once, the Broker lives.

What we see in the cave is a kind of polite fiction enabled by magic which allows the Broker and ihms victims to trade. For a steep price you can acquire almost anything from the Broker, and when you call ihms secret name (any of the eleven or twelve that exist), it likely arrives.

What does the real Broker look like? Only Arüne knows, and the sleeping god isn't telling us. Some philosophers hypothesize that the Broker is the condensed negative aspects of the god, all the evil within separated and sentient, living as a kind of twinned shadow, world to world. Others reckon ihm the god's janjack.

The Broker embodies the ultimate amoral force, the living embodiment of the notion be careful what you wish for. The Broker will deliver. That temptation infects even the righteous with terrible desires. Two janjacks have come to bear witness and keep one another honest because they have a curious chore. They've come to redeem a token; they are in effect cancelling a favor done for the Broker by the now-revealed Kizervexius.

"I told you so!"

"So you did Zoe. So you did." Gerhard passed her the teapot, now full, which she delicately put on the edge of the fire. He saw in her deft movements her mother's teachings. "They were all in on it. The whole of that little collective on the Dais knew Delphi's heritage and true names by the time they left for The Elephant Room. The Plan required it."

"Daddy, the Broker isn't bad, is he? Or is it she?"

"Ihm works. And yes, The Broker is our own worst desires turned against us."

"I bet I could make a good deal."

"Don't kid yourself, Zoe. The Broker would take any of us in a heartbeat. Truly."

"C'mon Pops, you just have to word the wish juuuust right."

"Perhaps if I told you about the last deal made in this cave while we put together a snack. It will sound a tiny bit familiar…"

A successful if ruthless man had lost touch with his oldest daughter. The girl was headstrong like the father. She pulled away, married the wrong sort of man, got with child in the far wastes beyond her family's reach, then bore the child… and before she could raise her daughter past the height of her hips, she succumbed to simple fever. The ersatz husband, a conniving man of little sentimentality, promptly sold the child to slavers and ran. News reached the family. The daughter dead, the grandchild enslaved and missing. All for naught, all for naught.

The father calls upon the Broker. Over a cup of tea he is made the most tempting of offers. If he will simply say the word, the Broker will exchange the life of the wicked lover for the beloved daughter. The child too will be returned, safe and happy. One death to save your own child and grandchild. But the father considers himself a shrewd man, a man who looks beyond the angles and finds the hidden trap. How will this death be accomplished, what price will the family pay? No price. In fact, the Broker will throw in fame and accolades, it will make the father and his family a tiny bit famous just because. And the father will be able to watch the bastard's eyes as the light of life seeps away forever. Revenge most personal, restoration of family, prestige, and the chance to reverse his greatest mistake.

Ever wonder how the gladiator Ruito got his start? Playing theatre and arena alike, he was older than the young striplings around him, with an air of gravitas. He could move a crowd and seemed addicted to adulation, the very noise. Be careful what bargains you make with the Broker.

"Wasn't Mama's great-grandpappy named Ruito?"

"Could be. But then maybe it's like the cats and all the other little coincidences. Maybe I'm just good at dropping in stuff to our story."

"Sure Pops." Zoe had the look of someone unconvinced. As if the edges of the tale had begun to play on her imagination.

The janjacks take no chances. They wait in silence. They wait as the second and third cup of tea are poured and still the Broker waits. Finally, with a calculated sigh, the being nods slightly and speaks: "Welcome, Everstrong and Bootknife, janjacks of Austen. How may my House be of service?"

Bootknife hands the Broker a small bag with the coins Smith gave

Delphi, along with a handwritten note in the cursive of Kizervexius, signed in dark brown with his allegedly lost chop. The Broker licks the signature, verifies that the blood on the page is, as implied, from the Lord Protector himself. Certainly it started as Delphi's, but we know that as the Chair of the Orlenzens, Kizervexius was, among his many capacities, a wizard of outstanding proficiency.

The Broker sniffs, and when it is clear the janjacks will not be tempted into speech, ihm rises and walks into the darkness. Ihm returns, bows with genuine respect—these two have weathered a proper test of wills—then hands them the saber we saw at Dodona's birth. In this case the bare blade rests outside the scabbard, a jet line of curved lightlessness. This black blade hums as it comes closer to the hands outstretched. Then it flips neatly in the dirt, and as Everstrong embarrassedly attempts to recover it, the saber slides away. Untouchable.

"Is this how you pay back a favor, Broker? No cup of tea can excuse this kind of sophistic fulfillment of an obligation." It's a risk, offering nothing and instead invoking the ancient art of politesse. But Delphi has added payment in rare coin of extraordinary value.

The Broker considers, all six of ihms eyes close, and ihm tilts ihms head, as if listening to its own version of the Song. Then ihm opens them and the rheum evaporates. In their place are six of the deepest red eyes either janjack has ever seen. "Know you what this is?" The blade slides into the scabbard as if possessed by a sovereign will and comes to rest at their feet.

Both janjacks shake their head. With the Broker, honesty tends to be the only survivable policy. They came for a magical tool. They didn't expect a sword.

The Broker lifts the blade. "In common words we call this Lomar's Blade, though it never touched his hand. Forged for the warrior Tawdry, wife of the giant king Armax, by the god deceiver Hoode before he sent them to their deaths. This is the blade of heroes it can be held only by those deemed worthy by the unrestful spirits of the King and his forlorn Queen, whose souls bind the scabbard and blade accordingly."

Lomar's Blade—the legendary black sword of Chafrium. The blade can cut anything, even the nanowoven hypermagic doors that *guard the Skeleton Throne. Depending on which local myth you give credence, it was forged from the remnants of neutron star or a falling meteorite or the bones of a lake maiden or some lump iron that Toki Ojawa passed off as one of the above… then tempered with the blood of a kirin, though no one has ever seen one, or the heart of a skywhale or the spleen of a rather fat hippopotamus, though that tale tends to end up veering into the comically erotic (as happens often when Lomar's name gets bandied about). In other words, it's of unknown origin and a direct danger to the Grey Elves.*

How it came into Kizervexius' possession to be then be warehoused offworld might be another whole book, or set of books.. It has one important quality. Being a splinter of transplanar nanotech held together by the souls of its first owners, the saber works everywhere, regardless of the Potential. Even in cul-de-sacs. On Earth, Lomar's Blade tips the balance of power; the City-State of Austen will be taking possession of the single most lethal weapon in their dimension. All it requires is someone worthy to brandish it.

The janjacks assume custody of the weapon, wrapping it in an old serape of red and orange. They move to leave but The Broker wishes to say more. Ihm jingles the coins in the pouch and reviews the note. "The Lord Protector has paid all Orlenzen debts in full today."

Bootknife, the thinker among the pair, understands the nuances of the statement. It's not the small sum spent—even if the coins are a fortune in themselves. The Footman has made arrangements for the Broker to know before it happens that the Orlenzens will be no more. Without breaking any rules or allowing a trace of confidences to slip, the janjacks of Austen have collectively handed one of the most important pieces of intelligence to the world's most dangerous wheeler-dealer with actual minutes to spare. A being whose multiphasic pan-planar existence must result in a few dozen bodies existing near conjured Doors across the civilized lands. All debts have in truth been more than paid.

"Wait Daddy, how did he do that?"

"Warn the Broker you mean?"

"Yes. It's just some stuff. Gold is nice but it's not a message."

"Kinda is Maximillian." Here Zoe gave her brother another kiss on the head. If she was using his nickname, it meant she was finally relaxed. "Because everything can be a hidden message. When you grow up you'll understand this."

Gerhard poured them all tea, handed out a round of biscuits and motioned for his dangerously aware daughter to continue. How much of what he and Brunhilda discussed could she parse? Probably more than they had realized.

"So he hands over coins and a note. He can't break the rules but he's being very literal and tricky. The Broker is super dangerous and wise, old and creepy. Delphi knows even something small will reveal the truth."

"Like when I forget to hide biscuit crumbs?"

"Just like that but even a single crumb is enough. It's gold from an old temple, priceless for a wizard like Kizervexius. It has magical qualities and he'd never part with it. Ever. He won it in a bet with a minor god and now he just hands it all to The Broker."

"If he wrote in his note something like 'Hey Broker Baddie, I won't need this anymore' that would be a cool hint right?"

"And here's Pops not telling us what was written. That's how stories work. We add our own parts, our own ideas and mistakes to the characters."

"That's kind a cool. So I could make the sword awake and have a name like Mister Killer Blade?"

"Or add a love affair or secret hatred or anything really?"

"Eww. Love affair. Like between who?"

Gerhard coughed and gave his daughter a wide smile. "As it happens …"

The Broker hands Everstrong a small silk bag of soft green. Ihm pours the contents into Bootknife's hands: two ornate rings which are mostly diamonds around which wends stellar platinum, a kind of iridescent alloy of rainbow hue. They erupt in patterns of burning color, every hint of light making them thick with the shadows and interplay of rainbows. A wish unspoken brought to life. Perfect wedding rings for a couple who have long desired to be joined. The Broker has just married them.

The janjacks exchange the rings wordlessly, each sliding to rest on the right ring finger—in Austen duelists wear their ring on their fighting hand. Then, unbidden, they kiss, the Sword of Lomar forgotten. The Broker rarely gives gifts, and especially few are those that carry no cost. But the Orlenzens soon perish, and with their demise the Broker has gained so much wealth and influence that ihm can afford a moment's mercy.

Travel in your mind now to the hall of the Seneschal, where the stern Count Mysterious, seven hundred eleventh Seneschal Supreme, Elf of Hidden Rank, Owner of the Great Keys, Maker of Truths, The Noble and Righteous Curate of the House Zoëæ sits in council with another version of the Broker. Most everyone just calls the Seneschal Old Crusty. This Broker looks like a scarred man with rotting teeth, his face obscured by a veil of stinking rags, his feet bearing shackles with broken chains. The Broker's hands are rough ugly things missing bits of fingers, weatherwracked and covered in various stains that might be dirt, blood or food. He bears the same tattooed countenance of sigils and as well as the ubiquitous six eyes.

In a hemisphere behind Old Crusty stands the war council of the King, called here by the Seneschal to help him handle the sudden influx of warrior fanatics rallying to the Footman's call. Coralaviere stands next to his Lord, second in status only to the Seneschal's Hand—a misnomer which describes the Crown's liaison from the Assassin's Guild, by tradition a Grey Elven woman serving as third in command of the guild. Since Old Crusty hates girls, he's endured the social snub and acquired the perfectly masculine fourth in command named Claw. As a substitute for The Hand, Claw has been tasked with acquiring intelligence for the King. His reports prove insufficient Old Crusty and against the advice of both his adjutant and his master assassin, he has taken an extraordinary risk by requesting help from the Broker.

It has not been a pleasant negotiation, and it worsens as the janjacks provide payment in full for every obligation the House Orlenzen have incurred. Old Crusty has governed Elven affairs for close to six thousand years, and he's in a blind panic over what would be termed a major screwup. In that time no army has managed what the Footman effortlessly achieved, and the day isn't over. As warriors continue to cross the Doors; the military situation worsens. Old Crusty simply does not believe his adjutant's supposition that beneath the Footman sits Kizervexius. What an absurd notion, beyond consideration. What Elven Lord of the greatest rank and esteem, whose power extends beyond reckoning, would willingly disappear? Certainly not any sane elf.

In this way Kizervexius has long eluded notice and the Footman faded into memory. Not since Lomar and Rexor have the Grey Elves abandoned seats of power and despised prestige. These vain creatures crave fame and adulation more than air.

Consequently, the Seneschal has been bargaining for help. The Elves, the King, everything he has loved for millennia has come under threat. The Orlenzens along with that dainty weasel Dahnstalyon have cornered his House and the Throne. Whatever the Footman plans, the Seneschal cannot leave a million Orlenzen blades inside the City. It's unthinkable. If even a small fraction swap allegiance for a Guild or the Drowning Ones, he and all the Elves will fall.

The Broker knows all and leverages this profound advantage to full, merciless effect. He's got Old Crusty's knickknacks in a beartrap. Behind him both the Lord Adjutant and Claw peer expressionless. Their thoughts manifest in their lack of participation. They had advised against this, and rightly so. History will prove Coralaviere the most loyal of servants and one of the most perceptive.

The Seneschal muses. "What price ask you for this thing, to remove all the armies?"

The Broker holds up a finger, black with rot and shorter than it should be. "I did not say 'remove armies.' I said I would rid you of the invasion. I shall remove all chance of an Orlenzen attack from any quarter and by any means." Only our Ral keeps his stone face intact. He's fought demons and fevers, been felled by mortal blows, carried the swords and chalices of legends. He does not fear the Broker more than any other force of nature.

The ancient Seneschal leans forward. "Very well, for ridding us of the Orlenzen threat?"

The Broker appears to consider. He knows he has at most minutes *to complete the transaction. Transactions, really. On dozens of worlds his other forms are bilking suckers left and right, setting up a complex series of dominoes that will fall, favor by favor, until they reach the heart of Chafrium.*

He holds up three fingers, all strangely full and healthy. "First, upon our agreement you will cede your position to the newly elevated Supreme Duke Coralaviere." *All eyes turn to the suddenly scowling Adjutant, his eyes burning as he stares down the being who has dared dethrone his liege. Lost upon him is his role as successor.*

"Second, I shall be given choice of the fifth reserve seat on the Wizard Guild's High Council." *This seems reasonable enough given that it would require nine members to retire or die to be of any relevance. It becomes less so when one considers that Guinevere and her recently suicided daughters, all the Orlenzens, the absent Kizervexius, and nineteen of their house priests are on the council. There are about to be quite a few vacancies.*

"Third, Barefoot Jackson will be invited by the King to perform for the Nineday Festival in the presence of the entire Court Eternal and with the full retinue of formal invitations sent per a coronation event. The elevation of the newest Ducal Supremis being the item of note upon the engraved binding summons." *He bows and smiles, his teeth a perfect medley of shining rot.* "These are my conditions. I will give you precisely one full minute to decide."

A coronation event means that entities long slumbering must be woken and Powers of every kind offered a place at the communal table. Senior Cat and her mate will attend; Hoode and his kind, the renegade gods of elevated humanity, are invited. More than that, they are necessary. They bear witness. All of the world's best and brightest, its most redolent scum, its do-gooders and evil schemers alike must be there. Gods will break bread with demons and immortals, with wizards and fanatics, with the appointed representatives of every guild including delegations from the Drowning Ones and every other radical fringe that can muster sufficient magic to purloin a sealed invitation.

Why Jackson? Obviously to please Gnash and displease someone else, perhaps her mother. But beyond that he's just a man, however talented.

Hardly the affair of gods. Hoode, Smith, the revenant of Toki Ojawa, perhaps the wandering spirit of Lomar—all these entities will mingle in the crowd. Epic, legendary mayhem seems afoot. By asking for a concert, the Broker has dictated the seating arrangements and forced the King and his retinue down from the Dais. He's found a loophole that, for over an hour, will place every dangerous force within known reality on one floor, bounded by impenetrable walls. The Assassin's Guild will have fits. They will likely have to cut a deal with the Broker to manage security.

For an old warhorse like the Seneschal it's a good deal. He'd been mulling retirement the last few centuries. His lapse in judgment can never be forgiven. He's done for, and all know it. While Coralaviere wouldn't be among his choices for successor, he proves worthy. As a political outsider without agenda, the Adjutant might prevent civil war among the elite for a few decades. That's time Sæceæn will need to rebuild his shattered fortunes. A few favors given, a minor seat on a council, a stupid concert to satisfy what's obviously some deal the Broker sold to some other client. It looks good. Plus he's desperate and he has mere seconds to decide. Pressure and age are not the friends of Elvenkind.

He nods, and the Broker extends a hand, eyes red with purpose. Wordlessly the deal has been struck, a small fissure in reality sucking a single drop of the Count Mysterious's lifeblood and essence as payment and promise. The Noble and Righteous Curate has handed over his Keys to another. The letter of the wording sinks in—immediately the trappings of office slither onto the floor and consume Coralaviere in a flurry of movement. From across worlds, keys, sigils, knowledge and power, raw supreme authority adhere to his skeleton and soul. Be careful what you wish for. Or agree to. Old Crusty gasps as he sees himself undone, now just an old vain noble lacking the authority to summon more than a page or runner. After eons of absolute rank and whimsical control over billions, he's just a man. Overdressed and attending someone else's party.

"He just got suckered like Ruito right? Too proud to understand the amplifications?"

"Maximillian means implications Pops. But yeah, this seems like a serious scam. Is our hero Delphi or Coralaviere?"

"Right, imperfections. But I think it's about the Black Cat. She's the coolest so far. Does she get a sword too?'

"She is cool. But if we're going for women, then what about the Fates or maybe the lost princess. You totally ignored her. Why can't she be the hero?"

"Yeah Daddy, maybe she could be the hero. She seems a little like Zoe."

More tea and biscuits make their rounds as Gerhard listens. "Very well, more about the missing Princess, right after we explain what happens in Chafrium …"

The Broker's magic takes brutal effect. Couriers in formal garb flow into the room bearing exquisitely hand prepared invitations pressed with gold and scented with lilac. From her own reserve of stationery the Matron of the Stars requests and commands thee to attend upon her and her brother the sainted King as they witness the glorious elevation of one Elf to supreme rank and office. A concert to be held sharply upon the Glory Hour in the solemn quarters of the Holy Throne. Refreshments to be served, servants may be housed in the lesser antechamber. Formal dress required. Gifts unnecessary.

Then word comes that the Orlenzens have fallen. A stutter and all is forgotten. Even their names no longer exist, their presence and threat vanish. More runners, more battle talk, the new Seneschal takes quick stock and secures the Dais first, the body of the King and his retinue coming before the City. Several assassination attempts will be put down and Coralaviere will be doubly legendary before the day is out—having outwitted the Drowning Ones and the Wizard's Guild alike. The new Seneschal dupes them both by pitting their best killers against an illusion of Sæceæn worn by the assassins of lesser guilds. Old Crusty had done more than recently miscalculate; years ago he'd laid bare the inner halls of the Castle demesne and never noticed. Those gaps now close. Coralaviere in minutes defeats entire generations of planning—he's been aware of his liege's mistakes and always had contingencies. The moment makes the man, and he lives up to his new status, wielding his command like a dagger. The hearts of his King's enemies flow like weeping rivers.

The Broker, though, has been busy, and we must leave this little demonstration of Ral's continued support of both his King and friend. We now go back to the ugly upper rooms of the Horny Gorgon through a door, a simple wooden affair one would assume leads to some rooftop perch or a closet of some sort. It does not. It leads to the sewers—it's a magical link within Chafrium, one of the many special boltholes built into the place which allow Hoode, Smith, and their guests to come and go without being detected.

Alice has unbolted it after three solid knocks. The Broker, in the form of an ancient orcish crone, hobbles into the Inn. Her hair and skin are covered with the sigils and she smells of herbs, vinegar, and dirt. Every inch of her is clean, almost austere. One of the Wising Woman, the herb witch scientists of the marshes. Midwife to everything. Alice just nods and motions through the storeroom door down a hallway.

For her part, the Broker hobbles down the hallway and enters the room. At a table are Smith, Hoode, and two others—a huge beaver wearing a brocaded vest and a slender woman dressed in huntsman's kit. Before them, a map of Chafrium and Austen lays pinned to the tabletop with daggers. Each dagger has a small lantern-like vessel hooked over the hilt, shining a queer green light onto the vellum. The map itself coalesces as a three-dimensional overlay of the two cities and all connected Doors. One of them seems to be moving. It's the map reacting to the Broker. She squints, and the Door simply fades.

Hoode smiles briefly and makes introductions in a language too non-linear to have meaning for us. They speak as gods in timescales and complexities that have no relevance to this tale. In front of the Broker is Smoojak, Lord of Chafrium's forests and riverlands. He's the immortal equivalent of a gamekeeper and park ranger—a benign figure beloved even by Kizervexius, as we have seen. Long friend to the Cats, known to the Black Cat and various Guilds, he serves all, offends none. In his demesne he is power absolute without peer. He ranks as the single most skilled nature sorcerer and the greatest voice of Gaia. He speaks for the oceans and trees, the bees and hawks and crawling snails, the space monsters and sky tendrils. He represents pure balance.

Beside him sits Caris, his assistant and at times rival. One of the best archers alive, and also one of the best wizards, a dedicated traveler who knows the location of every Door, a hunter and tracker extraordinaire, master of poisons and mysteries, holder of membership among forty guilds and secret societies. No one knows her age or origin. There is none like her—thankfully. Other than among this small cadre, she tends to be feared rather than liked. Simply put, Caris chooses the *most efficient and logical route to any destination. She has no patience for fools and does not bother to dispute with her critics. She simply ignores them—or slays them, whichever proves most convenient. It is said of Caris that were she ever capable of something as frivolous as love, only a computational intelligence would do. Preferably one that can fight like a myrmidon. People tend to treat her politely. Alice likes her enough to flirt.*

Smoojak abhors travel; Caris loves it. He's a peaceful soul, calming to every living thing. She's a vector of supreme reason and capability who kills with a whisper. But in most things she serves him, and in return, Smoojak offers her respite. They share a small grotto home on the edge of the City, unseen and untouchable by mortal hands. Balance and his Checkmate.

These four are looking for the missing Qelniasherah. Sandoval has gotten her away in time. More than that, she's managed to hide her away from the Powers.

"So she is alive?"

"Well Zoe, you said she was the hero of this tale. We can't very well kill the hero halfway through the night can we?"

"Dunno Pops, you sure killed Delphi quick enough."

"Yeah Daddy. Lots of people keep dying."

"Does that worry you Max?"

"Well, if the Princess makes it then maybe it's okay. But she's not the heir and that means that maybe this whole story is about someone else."

"Whoah. He's right, maybe you're trying to mess with us. What does killing Delphi and The Footman and Kizervexius all at once really do? That's like seriously overkill."

"Or justice."

"Pops, it's only justice if something good comes of it."

"The Orlenzens aren't enough?"

"They were the worst of the Grey Elves but you paint them all as pretty vile."

"What's vile mean Zoe?"

"It means really bad, Max. The elves are basically evil. So wiping out the Orlenzens won't be enough to really matter."

"They need an ambush."

"Yeah Pops, tell us about how Delphi ambushed them."

"If I do can we start Dodona's tale. Without more interruptions? Very well, I shall take your nods as agreement and begin. Pay attention because there are just a few more things to discuss before we get to Dodona and that sword Max likes..."

Alice returns in time to see the Broker seated and serves them a light repast. Dessert cakes, some sweet goblin buns, a tray of gelatos in evercool dishes, and various urns with hot drinks, liqueurs, and semiotic hallucinogens. Little dishes of sugars, salts, creams, and flavorings, some stirring apparatus, and a separate tray of smoking gear are deposited by Alice over the next few minutes.

Conversation has been had, polite pleasantries made among those who deign speak. Caris and Smith are not among them, having spent the time playing a slow game of chess. What else? She appears to be ahead by four pieces. The bartender retreats. Plates are loaded, gelatos and coffees tasted, teas salted and drugged, a hookah prepared. Some cakes are cut and handed out with gentle politesse. Smoojak smooths his vest and smiles. It's the beaver's party, it would seem.

"Well met, and thank you for coming." He speaks a language beyond our fathoming, but the translation holds for our linear minds. It's polite, succinct, and personable. Very Smoojak.

The Broker takes a puff and flicks her hand. "What's this all about, Aja?"

Smoojak gives her a shuffling bow, something which acknowledges her privilege in using his private name and lets her know she's made her point. Smoojak and the Broker go way back, which for the immortals of an immortal city might be to the birth pangs of universes.

Hoode chews on a bun, watching. Something in his expression denotes interest, as if he does not know what comes next. If it's going all too fast for elves, imagine how the immortals and gods feel. Thunderstruck. Anxious. Wary.

The Beaver continues: "The blade of Lomar has been brought forth into the worlds again. This delivers a pervasive imbalance." Caris takes

Smith's Queen and frowns as she listens. Imbalance rarely withstands her attention.

The Broker sips some tea. "Come now, it was bound to be released eventually. These artifacts are used by Men. What harm does it really do?"

Smoojak drops all pretense and his face suddenly takes the cast of an elder storm. "Don't be coy with me, Yaga. We know you handed it to Delphi. It's going to sit in Austen, to be brought to bear on the City itself."

Smith takes Caris's rook and the huntress sighs. Shah mat. He had lured her into indiscretion and she proved too aggressive in her play. All eyes turn to their game. Smith has told them something. Passions are forgotten. If one infers Smith might have some other godly capacity than merely playing chess the immortals assembled see in his gameplay answers and revelation. In that moment the assassination takes place a world away across the Doors.

The Broker closes her eyes and slowly smiles. She too has been played. Oh, Kizervexius, you right unprincipled bastard, you've scammed the gods themselves. How truly despicable you were and how worthy to be within Lomar's clan. They each and together assess the damage done. So busy were they in finding Gnash and the Black Cat that they've missed the sudden change in the streams of Chafrium.

All that power didn't fade back into the gates as expected, as it had always done before. Austen has been Chafrium's junkyard and playground, a little pocket of elven indulgence. Never a danger, never even worth a second thought except when some bard brings back a tale or book.

Austen has just become a pocket of higher potential and its janjacks world-class wizards. Its walls have come alive, its Doors have new songs, its foundations have Ruach in thick, rich patches of ugly, extravagant excess.

The Broker, that old fool, has been suckered as neatly as Old Crusty. Without ever a word from Delphi that implied the least thing, she merely assumed. Oh, she took the bait—the infinite jester bested by someone willing to die for what is right. A well-thought, strategically considered queen sacrifice on epic scale.

Hoode slams the table in frustration. Now he will never get the chance to kick that smarmy bastard while down. Cheated of not just revenge but the chase itself, he's been outdone again by Kizervexius, and it's an Eldessery understated enough to be even more annoying. Then he sighs and hands Smith another bag. So does the rest of the crowd. It seems the chessmaster had laid many bets upon this day and won them all.

Smoojak sips some tea. "And you gave them the sword..."

Yaga nods solemnly "Indeed, in a trade I'd have reckoned more than fair for us. We've been snookered."

Hoode shrugs. "Not we, Broker. You were tricked. We were merely bystanders."

Here she laughs. "Hoode, so much the strutting rooster. I see you as you are, so don't try to finesse your own mistakes. You and Smith tipped the whole of your hand with that little dinner date you had with him. The very bag of coins delivered me came from your treacherous hands."

Here Smith smiles, a rare thing, and toasts the Broker from across the table. Hoode laughs. They all know that he's been caught. Caris, however, continues to look at the game board. The Broker does not get fooled, nor does Hoode make mistakes. She knows they have all been toying with versions of the truth, each abetting Austen's little coup.

Yaga and Aja, Hoode and Smith, all of them toying with the Fates and trying to maneuver the City, the King, and the Elves of the Grey. To what end? She's the logical one, firmly rooted in pure reason. This juggernaut of cognition doesn't let emotions betray her. She's been handed a puzzle. She stares and considers, focusing on every small element, all the hidden clues laid out in the open.

Hoode remade Kizervexius, carved him from the raw evil of the court, and with humiliation, trickery, cruelty, and defeat honed him to a fine blade which just extinguished the now nameless Orlenzens. Thus Hoode must have known, as clearly did Smith. What did they gain by revealing what they did to the Lord Protector? Action, she decides. It's the simplest answer and the most logical. They pushed him, with that fool Minister chasing like a spoiled child bereft a favorite toy. The

Broker has countered, handing out a weapon so deadly it threatens the King and more generally, the Throne. The walls of Chafrium cannot stand before it.

But, she reasons, also a weapon which can be used by a single person of rarest merit. Dodona will be that person, and he, by nature, would not fell a City. More than that, as a janjack he'd be answerable to Jane.

Ahhh. This has always been about Jane.

She smiles and hands Smith another bag of coins. Of course—it's nothing so pedestrian as politics or power. They don't care one whit about the Elves or who rules Chafrium. The City will manage it without their help. They want another book. The Gods want Jane writing again. Well, officially writing and allowed to publish. Manuscripts do not burn. Something new, something beautiful and unique can again come into the world.

Still, these little intrigues have consequences. Within fractions of seconds, the City of Austen grows walls. Great lurching pistons of earth and timber reach to the accommodating sky, their individual ridges like wriggling fingers of entropic dread. All that recently acquired toxic waste becomes a ferocious barrier between the weak forces of Terra and the City-State of Austen. The place of swords has become in a heartbeat a magnet for wizardry and the single most alive place in Terra's known universe. Distant galaxies begin to feel the slow pull of the City. Gravity in Austen increases by three percent. In a few centuries it will be four, then five. Eventually the state will sink into Terra's crust and the walls will grow to contain all the boiling force of its inhabitants.

For the Americanos north of Austen, it's a terrible shock. Their little army didn't even know they'd been raided by goblins. Now there are thousand-foot thick walls between them and the dangerous invasion from Other Worlds. Strange ramparts loom over them. They shimmer with streaks of minerals and veins of unmined gems. From gates in the high walls come paved roads inching forward in steaming coils of lava.

The bravest contingent, the Tejano Eighth Brigade, send their only dirigible (stolen from the Austro-Hungarians under questionable letters of patent off the coast of the Djolof Empire) to reconnoiter. That's when they discover the trick of the walls. The demon within weakens and begins to slumber, the potion-treated floors warp and snap, one of the treated sails from an opium clipper tears like paper, and down goes the airship, heaving to one side and sliding out towards the north of Tejas before coming to an ignominious crash landing which kills four, frees the demon, and ruins the captain's rather glorious collection of rare whiskys. Austen now eats magic.

In a few months the roads will stop expanding and hundred-mile stretches ten wagons wide will emanate from Austen in nine beautiful strands of pearly black stonework that shines by day and glows by night. Each will terminate at the City walls in a vast arch with a pair of unbreakable gates the color of Kyiv Saffron, approximately ninety feet high and forty feet wide. They never measure the same way twice.

For their part, the elves of the Extenso below the river see the explosion of color and movement, shrug, and send a scouting party to investigate. They have wisely given the Orlenzens a good mile of ground to chew up before making it to their battlements. When word returns of amplified magic and rising walls, the commander sniffs, orders wine, and exercises uncommon good sense by simply doing nothing. He's an elf, and he can wait.

CHAPTER 9: DODONA'S TALE

No manual exists which can prepare you for the blinding agony of rebirth. Who would be cruel enough to write one? One dies and then lives, in various states of unrest and ruin. The vampires and lichlords, the avatars and nanominds of Beyond feel little pain. But also little joy thereafter. The few miracle-bound souls who are Returned at great cost bear psychic scars forever after, and while their joy is great, they temper it always with that faraway stare. Then there are janjacks. For janjacks the pain proves tenfold, a force of raw unabated anguish that surpasses suffering. The soul has been set afire, and with any crucible, impurities beget flame. Who among the servants of cities and guilds comes without a burden of sins and transgressions?

For the man once Kizervexius, no mere centuries of honorable service as Dephi can erase the foul and tainted deeds of a lifetime. He burns long and he burns bright. Then all at once the pain subsides, for pain can kill living things and with life pain must recede until it's a visiting friend, not an endless nightmare. Thus comes Dodona into the world.

In the trunk he finds clothing and at the fire companionship. The Norns have been waiting, ever patient. Delphi has been gone three days, and only now, when the whole sentient world has a head start, does this body, this soul, wash ashore. He has lost days in which Sandoval and Lady Nia could have gone anywhere. In that time the walls have risen, the Yanks have panicked, and the elves have taken it all in stride. Chafrium, of course, celebrated, then rioted, then quietly looted the undefended halls of the Stricken and their allies.

The strategy works. When the now-nameless clan once of the nameless Lord Protector held sway, their wealth in treasure and geography were immeasurable. In absence, those footholds become derelict. The Drowned Ones and the Guilds battle for possession of mansions and citadels, while the armies of Chafrium seize armories. The streets spill with gold and rubies, the nights shattered by drunken revels and murders as recovered goods change hands dozens of times before dawn.

One millions soldiers once served the forgotten house. Some burned; some vanished; many splattered or melted into loathsome puddles of bone and hate, all that was left of the necromancies which compelled them. Staggering wealth has frozen the economy. The horrible filth and influx of disease has choked the streets and brought waves of new plague to the City. All about an army bereft of leaders or priests, look for work or prey or escape. The immune system of Chafrium, the three legged stool, has its own concerns. The Academy has been transformed, for an entire species of wizard died in the night. Necromancers of the Red simply are no more. They disappeared when the stricken clan went to the void. Worse the Necromancers of the Black have fallen as well, victims of an unknown enemy or spell.

The necromantic wing of the Academy has started to capsize. Vampires long forgotten have returned to bring stability to their dank orders, and with them come Hunters. So the Academy has broken into a three-way civil war between the Living, The Undead, and the Unconcerned—who, largest and least invested, have taken to towers and aeries to ride out this fight. They are absent from the streets. Absent from the night patrols.

Demons and dream avatars proliferate—which creates work for errant swords, and drains the newfound gold of local merchant princes. In a few weeks the City will normalize. Some few fortunes will have been made and many more lost. But for now, chaos seeps across the paving stones and everywhere Death rides in her carriage, the regal queen.

The Guilds and the King war over land and possession of swords, whether attached to fighting hands or in storage. So too guns, grenades, battlewalkers, and such. An entire herd of riding stallions has been seen in the northern quarter. At night the townscapes burn and the citizens scream in triumph or fear.

No one has time to find Qelniasherah nor seize the Throne. No one has the least interest in crossing a Door and invading another land. For three days, not more than a passing thought has been spared for Austen. Even news of its dramatic transformation has been met without more than a shrug. There's gold in the streets that no one can rightly claim as theirs.

The janjacks of Austen could not have planned this. Only Delphi, familiar with higher magics, knew what his execrated clan might do to him. He planned this sudden influx of disorder and panic, this orgy of greed and terror. It's his last gift to Chafrium which slew him. A janjack was murdered on duty by the very lords of Chafrium. Both Cities pay back the mistake tenfold, punishing beyond mere necessity so that the lesson will be burned into the minds of every resident: janjacks are sacrosanct.

In five days the King and his entire retinue from least to greatest will host Barefoot Jackson at the Lord Seneschal Coralaviere's ascension to both role and rank. Dodona has only just risen from the muck and put on underwear, had a cup of warm wine, and learned to use his fingers when the burden of time starts pressing upon him. He remembers much of his old life, all as Delphi, much as Footman, some as whatever he was when he had a name.

But he has also forgotten much. No janjack arrives unscathed, nor does an old life extend to the new one. Something persists, but not all things—he has after all the fiction of a new soul. Dodona and Delphi are not the same. They share a memory, and because of how Delphi worded his writ, Dodona inherits almost all of the old janjack's worthwhile possessions, including his magnificent residence. The furniture will be large, the clothing by necessity eventually donated, but the larder and stored weapons, the magic library and smoking room, the armory with gunsmithing table will all be his. And of course, the writ passed on Delphi's commitments.

As Dodona Janjack he owes the King of All Universes one heir. Actually he must return Qelniasherah, and because of how they both worded the request, Delphi and Sæceæn, he must also provide the King another one, his legal heir. Add to that Delphi promising the Lady Nia her father, whom the Broker has invited to a concert. And the Norns, they wait for the third death, the third major transformation. Lybid still hears the song awry and still there waits one more turn of the Fate's swift blade. One more string to cut, one more frayed edge to the cloth.

Dodona must be on his way, seeking all these beings. But first his predecessor has made an appointment which by honor and by writ he may not ignore. So with great care he dresses, allowing the sisters to help him. Lybid hands him his saber and a pistol whose weight feels right. Whoever owned his old body bore this weapon. A remnant of a former life. He checks the cartridges, sees it's a two-shot, and shrugs. Dodona will make do for now. Haste requires him there as soon as he can walk.

Delphi promised to sit down with his friend Ral when once more his Vanguard showed, to be honored by the Lord Adjutant. Only now one has been elevated to Seneschal and Delphi delivered of life and transformed into something else. But obligations are obligations, and among men of honor, nothing so trifling as death or great fortune will keep them from sharing a promised glass of wine or coffee.

We go now to the Café Ragueneau, where a retinue of picked men assembles to greet the great Lord Coralaviere, who has extinguished his Shine and never need worry for his safety in Jane's Town again. He comes alone, met by his own newfound friends, his loyal man Duchamp apoplectic with goodwill and enthusiasm. Duchamp Half-Elven has gone from being an anonymous provider of hard drinks to hard men to the single most famous restaurateur in Austen, and within a year, Terra.

Today he serves the Caffé Delphi, a bittersweet take on Extenso Mocha—both spicy and sharp, laced with smoked pertsivka from Kyiv and thick cream from the Luxembourgish quarter (on 9th street for those trying to find it) to which he's added chocolate, herbs, black sugar from the jungles of Mopech, and the essential oils of mandarins and fire oranges, with five shots of the most brutally strong but incredibly smooth espresso imaginable. It's from a stash of beans grown within the hothouses of the Academy's jungle terrarium. These are Jazz Beans, which grow to the sounds of music and which absorb the wild, unpredictable nature of the artform.

It's not an exaggeration to say the stuff will blow your head back. It provides a magical rush on top of the outrageous kick of espresso and alcohols. Men vie for position near Ral's table, trying to look stalwart as the drink separates the tough from the merely ambitious. Attending him are two curious characters who are relatively unknown to Austen but famous in Chafrium. They are her janjacks, after all. The first looks like a five-foot, lanky wombat wearing battle leathers and bearing at least nine separate nanosentient computing platforms. A monocle covers her left eye, providing magically augmented feeds from, well, everywhere. The heightened power in Austen has made her crossing practicable. Beside her, a perfectly ordinary-looking man of fifty sits, a rapier and single-shot pistol the only indication he's not some high-born servant of the supremely rich. His boots alone are worth more than most houses. Where Madame Wombat has brownish fur, the man's well-coifed mane has gone silver, his blue eyes like glacial ice, his teeth snowcapped mountains. They both wear dark, muted colors, and on their heads sit proper berets, the style this season in the City. Each beret bears the janjack double strip and Chafrium's singular color Crimson. Experts have studied it for eons. It's the most authentically accurate representation of over 83 percent of the universes' sentient species' blood.

Their names are Jaychetel and Baron Dunsany. She serves the Computing Guild and also handles Chafrium's armory and haberdashery. The Baron works for the Grey Elves themselves, a fixer among fixers, the equivalent of the Norns for Austen—he rules undisputed as the social lord supreme of the City's janjacks and as such sets even the most minute protocols for engagements. He's also the Dancing Master, Head of Kitchens, and Chancellor of The Chafrium Institute of Sapient Fashion. In Chafrium, the machine lords control weaponry and hats while the Etiquetticians handle dancing, cuisine and high fashion. Make of it what you will.

It should surprise no one that both know Duchamp from

prior days, and with a few words they've been greeted and served their favorite dishes. The Baron in particular marvels aloud to be remembered for his signature love of bergamot-infused tea, a distinctly Terran taste that has kept the Queen and her tea makers, the Ducal families of Fortnum and Mason, in wealth since the early 1700s. Duchamp has a nearly photogravuric sense of his clientele's tastes and can recall with great aplomb almost any past customer's request. He especially notes favorites and doubly so of important customers like janjacks or great lords, of which the Baron proves to be both.

Jaychetel takes speedchai and some sedge biscuits. She seems amused that the Baron likes to be remembered. After all, it's in her database and he needed only ask; a simple file retrieval at best. The janjacks do not much like one another. While Austen hosts less than two dozen at any time, Chafrium, as the swarm of worlds and the single densest place in sapient existence, sports over two billion residents with a couple of thousand lesser janjacks running about—mere servant classes who might have gotten the job while still living—plus a goodly specialist cadre of near-immortal beings, numbering more than 300 and most often less than 400. Two billion? The city stacks and involutes, layers and corkscrews through time and space, taking up hidden miles of roads which somehow connect within a day's walk.

In such a large and complex place, there are janjacks who serve other janjacks. The Baron has several who dispense his will across the City. Rare are the meetings between distant cousins like the wombat and the dancing master. They can afford to dislike one another, to play out rivalries and compete for glory and power. It might be the reason Chafrium exists as it does. Perhaps it simply lives to toy with its own selves, to pit various legions and personas against one another in a self-flensing exercise of sapient evolution. Or perhaps it's simply a nasty place filled with equally petty servants.

The two sit warily near one another for the first time in several decades. While both have the taste and self-regard to not bicker, no one would mistake them for genuine allies. The Baron distracts himself by having a lovely conversation with the local sword professor Master Pizay, the most famous blade ever to leave Roanne De la France Impériale. Duelists flock from all over the city to take lessons—he's known for his love of food, art, fencing, and a good sense of style. The Baron naturally likes him despite his terrestrial origins. For her part Jaychetel has taken a small contract updating the now-thinking stacks the University of Austen dentro Tejas and has several radiominds and a stackthinkmaker journeyman from Chafrium on hand to help her implement the override / flow down / go go go command set when she finishes her business at the café. They ignore one another gloriously as the Seneschal sits alone and waits.

Only Duchamp enters the Seneschal's space, the men calmly discussing suggested menu choices since the Lord will be hosting the janjacks. With a spare glance, the Baron nods his firm approval, and Duchamp exceeds his prior honors with a sudden addition to his Vanguard—he now bears the odd-sounding but crucially necessary Titanium Salver, a small intricately etched tray that assures the finest service, taste, and hygiene. Now Royalty itself may deign to frequent Duchamp's establishment and person. Ral smiles, pats his man on the arm, and continues by nixing the jellied eels in green sauce.

Arriving now comes Dodona, his feet barely on track as he walks, his back stooped from the burdens of gravity. He has been alive a mere hour, and here he hastens to fulfill the first of his many obligations. He knows Coralaviere, but does not quite recall him as we might suppose. These two smile across the dust and din. But Dodona Janjack and Lord Seneschal Coralaviere are formal strangers requiring protocol and introductions. The Baron rises and make a short obeisance. It seems especially odd.

Until we, like he and all others in the street, view Dodona's Vanguard. Despite being dimmed by recent death, the damned thing erupts with fulsome color and devastating power. Much of it wavers or hides behind haze. Dodona will be many hours in coming fully to the world. He won't be a fully formed individual for a good two weeks. A full fortnight is the unspoken law of these things. Still, those seven Arrows hover with sharp precision and draw all eyes. There are Sancurions,

Stars, a couple of Holy Leafs, and a few Suns. It's ridiculously more than any being might imagine possible. It's lifetimes of reckless abandon and blind horror rolled into a single man's aegis. It declares, more than words, who Dodona will be and of whom his soul and body were fashioned.

It might be easier to say what is missing. All artistic awards, every petty favor and regard passed on by the fair sexes. Flower arranging and guitar ballads, perfumery and first aid. All gone. Bare and empty are the regions of Dodona's Vanguard that speak to softer skills, the warm regard of the social set and lifetimes of earned respect from men such as Baron Dunsany. Missing too are awards tied to the forgotten clan's achievements and its now-defunct Keys. The accumulated story of a man who flirted with gods and bedded demons: absent. The fine, threatening social distinctions that made even fellow Grey Elves tremble before nameless execrated: nonexistent. His Keys and attendant badges of station and fealty are no longer there.

Instead, a hazy aspect has emerged where Keys and such often stand, blurred and muted, but compelling in a grey and empty field of nothing. Behind the Baron, the computermind sits breathless. She has never seen this man, but she has known a prior incarnation, and the absence of his face and memory nags at her. Her monocle provides facts and locations that her memories cannot, prompting analysis that chills her. Something has been removed from the universe. Her data has been corrupted. Her systems are vulnerable. It makes the Broker that much more terrifying when one considers that computational algorithms might have been hacked on top of magic and men.

In a few short breaths, Dunsany greets Dodona, provides him his official invitation to the King's party for Coralaviere, confirms his duties, and extends the thanks of the one true sovereign King Sæceæn XIX for his prior work (notably passing blithely over his recent demises). With a cough, Jaychetel appears at his side, all formality and pomp. She nods to the Baron, suddenly in lockstep—one Power for Chafrium acknowledging another. They bow to Dodona in formal fashion and then do something that induces pure anguished terror in the streets: they smile with genuine feeling.

The lady hands Dodona a bundle, whispering something that makes them both chuckle. In it, a well-formed repeater lays, the exact style he desired, with proper holster and spare clips of ammunition. Done in fine worked brass and hardwoods, it's a superb dueling pistol and a work of art. She provides him a few more things—daggers, a lovely tomahawk of dragon tooth and charwood, some computing gear, a radionode—and then, from seemingly nowhere, she hands the Baron a gorgeous tapestry top hat of goldenrod buckram flecked with stars of luminous spidersilk. Afficionados recognize it as the stuff of the poorly named Plum Spider variety, a dark green that glows deeper aqua. The bite, of course, induces permanent madness and has given risen to a whole slew of mirthful discussions of silkiers and their insane ways.

But it's the striping that calls to all eyes. The requisite midnight double strip has been interwoven intricately with both the burnt orange of Austen and the crimson of Chafrium. The Baron intones a Word, blessing both man and hat, then places it upon Dodona's head, sending the haze on his Vanguard into burning cohesion. Before them, a single Key spins. Made up of actual Beyond, the nearly black sigil spins slowly, bending the gravity of the place to its independent will. Called a Skeleton Key, Allkey, Spinning Writ, or Voiceless Song, the Key hanging in view might be more impressive than all of Dodona's arrows.

Rare are these tools, given only to special janjacks who serve between Chafrium and other cities. Never before has Austen qualified as a place worthy of a Liaison, for that is what Dodona has become. A janjack of both places simultaneously, a living door whose Key is the contained bodywave of Supernova 9873. It's that old an item. It allows Dodona to pass unseen and more importantly unheard, invisible as it were, between Chafrium and Austen, and to conjure a Door to any other extended place from either locale. With it he could enter the Palace and mount the Stairs before detection. Then the street sees his scabbard, and whispers begin. Lomar's Blade and an Allkey, never before held by one person. Not even Lomar.

For his part, Dodona gives brief thanks and collapses into a chair held for him by Duchamp. A Caffé Delphi is brought for him and he downs it in three indelicate gulps. Then his eyes fly open in almost comic fashion as the espresso and liquor do their duty. The duelist Pol returns with another drink, this time the humble Caffé Cyrano. This one Dodona sips, finding it agrees deeply with some inner yen. He prefers this drink. Coralaviere carefully takes note. The Baron and Jaychetel bow themselves away, official business complete. Behind them another figure looms. Duchamp has kept them apart.

When the janjacks are truly gone and the lookouts give him a nod, the Lord Seneschal motions forward this other presence. Spies will confirm the identity of the mysterious guest, but it does give Dodona a modicum of privacy—one the Lord Coralaviere wishes to afford him. A small, well-formed specimen of the Curoi, often bastardized as the Ku-Ro-Wei, the island people of a plane of infinite hillocks and seas, half frozen and asleep, yet possessed of mind coral, the giant hags, and of course the so-called Gods of the Sea. In Elven they call the Plane "Ae Frelfrellicyn": the Wilder Door to the Untamable Western Shores. The Wild, Wild West. The Curoi are the chosen arbiters of disputes across many civilized corners of Chafrium, being lords of battle and possessing that rare quality of being universally trusted.

The Curoi, the elves joke, are the mythical 10th gender: "likable." Infinitely honorable and ruthless, any of the Ku-Ro-Wei may be attached to a mission or engagement without fear of failure. The one now seated and sipping one of the dangerous Caffé Delphis tends to be asked most judiciously when approached for commissions. He's rather famous in his own land: the roaming master, Aejae. It is said that every decade, he finds a new martial art to master, and that he's soon to run out of forms. With axes or fists, knives, pistols, swords of any type, spears, maces, javelins, or even those new delights the spearguns of the Sebakni, he proves deadly. But it's his 10th gender, his affable nature, that makes him truly deadly. No one wants to fight Aejae, and how can you truly kill a man no one wants to hurt?

Why keep the much respected and always welcome Lord of the Curoi apart from his social and potentially physical equals? Aejae slides a thick wallet of papers across the table. This charming Curoi lord turns out to be the executor of all involved estates which pertain to Dodona. The Academy has deemed such specialized contracts something which on Terra translates as Anagnorisis: they are fulcrum points of reality— owning the legal, magical, and *de facto* quantum power to change a local condition. They are the levers of individual fates. This quiet lord sipping coffee and making small talk has just handed Dodona the deceased janjack Delphi's will, several articles of jurisprudence of Chafrium origin, deeds and copies of rare orders. Likely more writs.

Oh absent and expunged Lord Forsaken—how do we remember this appellation but not the name—you have really cocked up the works. Delphi left an inviolate will in the hands of the Curoi? All that brutal infighting in Chafrium over lands and locales, over wave forms and armories. A small cheerful exchange from a man so deeply respected that none doubt his sacred word will rip apart the whole bloody farce. As spies send messages across Doors, a whole new wave of panic erupts. Men and their minions scatter trying to put back what was stolen. How will they stuff the dead back into living?

This is a proper Elven twist of the knife—worthy as one last stab after already knocking down one's enemy and impaling them. Better yet, by his minor courtesy, Ral has given the absent Delphi total victory. No one sees the papers, nor can they even conjecture on the color and size what lays within. Blind panic will sweep the despoilers. Here sits a man with legal claim to potentially all of what has been plundered, armed with the Razor of Worlds and a skeleton Key. He may without notice occupy his own demesnes, and woe to the fool who opposes him. He bears an alarming number of battle decorations.

In this way Ral buys Dodona another three days before Chafrium can muster to properly oppose him. Time enough, then, to linger and enjoy the meal he and Duchamp have conspired to deliver. Curried goat with Elven chocolate spice sauce and a good bottle of whatever one desires. That's just one of the twelve courses that will be served. But first, coffee and small talk while panic spreads across the Planes.

Let us now follow the story into the bowels of Chafrium, to an annex space off the Mid-tier Eastern Sewer Complex, commonly called Floorplan Nine. The region sits in what the PAWs refer to as Chafrium's Outer Spaces, usually thought of as the dead zone where water and power are required but only the desperate use them. They call these unruly thieves and interlopers Grave Robbers. So Plan Nine tends to house Grave Robbers from Outer Space; ghouls one and all. None worse than the small cult of professional victims led by the false prophet Kris-To-Buy-Me, sometimes shortened to The Killer Bee or when spoken amongst her ardent detractors, The Vampire.

She should be a mere nuisance, but the Vampire endures and grows, somehow draining vital information and resources from smarter, tougher opponents. Who is this being we've not even known existed? Someone whose presence has been felt all along but whose hands lay under the ostentation of the...house since forgotten.

Kris-To-Buy-Me, the Killer Bee, has ruined the Song. Austen cannot rest until her story comes to an end. What or who is she? The ultimate user, the kind of parasite that embeds herself in other lives and sucks them empty with a smile. Living in the dank recesses of forgotten Chafrium, she's neither living nor dead, a kind of shell animated by errant programming and stolen lifeforce, abetted by sentient cosmetics and the residual cesspool of the sewers. She's a simulacrum of a woman, a toy created by a wasteful father. This gleeful adman hired some roboticists to fashion him an uncanny model, a childlike version of himself to close an important deal. It had to be living enough to survive the low potential environment. To ensure obedience, he made it dependent on outside thinking—activated by the mental activity of others. Until then, it rested in suspended animation. It worked well enough for him to repeat the exercise in several forms eventually, most disturbing, building a love doll used for prostitution and espionage. His name has been lost, but we know he went by the moniker of Mister Bumblebee, the buzzy hivemaster of sorts.

One day Mr. Buzzy dies or discards his toys or simply sells them to someone else. Each shell possesses actual DNA, has been on and off worlds and accumulated a sludge of nano waste and such. They are tainted, barely useful puppets built to ingest emotions. We see such abominations everywhere in Chafrium, and if the errant gods do not strike down the actual incest and pedophilia of the ruling clans, who can blame the absent Powers for overlooking mere blasphemy?

Waste eventually drops into sewers. By luck or sheer perversity, these little scrap heaps will accumulate in a kind of marshland under the far reaches of the City termed the Cesspit which ruled by an inchoate sentience. Mother Billy cannot incorporate, lacking the mental strength and will; nor can she wander. She's a pathetic vision, aching for companionship and recognition, always confused, always needy.

Then these bodies wash into her holding tank. Her confusion and angst feed them. Over years, these sewage-encrusted toy people feed their Mother with babble and attention, little puppets who adore her. Billy endeavors to teach the toy things how to touch a world she cannot, but they cannot think, only respond. So she waits and grabs, smashing and reaching, accidentally stretching herself into more dangerous places.

Mother Billy gets dumber and weaker. Until she snags some broken smart wool that becomes the robe for a child's body. The software that replicates and distorts, kills a body, and Billy, not understanding how bodies work, feeds her dead baby to the living. Which means the broken code now replicates inside the toys, unmakes them. She feeds the dead to the living until there is just the last survivor, the sex body woman form built from a loathsome soup of wastes, radiation, corpses, and desperation. Kris-To-Buy-Me wakes up, drags a sibling into a corner and eats him, without sharing and without admitting to what she's done. It makes her nominally stronger and smarter than others. One by one they wake and perish until only The Vampire remains.

Sentience releases the love doll from her bondage. The toy thing has learned much in her slavery: to use affection and appearances, childish vulnerability to get fed. She knows bodies are good when dead, even if diseased. She can eat the living who suffer and the dead who no longer feel. She wanders and grows as she consumes the most foul of foul, finding discards of of every imagined kind which she ingests and drains.

This is the origin of the Killer Bee, who eats her victims however they come. Her guts are defective code and foul magic, her body a hovering contradiction of necromancy and homuncular animus, her mind the accumulated detritus of eons' confusion, despair, and cunning. Expert in exploiting the weaknesses of her food source: intelligent beings. She has learned that smart people look for deception, so she binds layers of masks to her skin, hiding her encrusted putrescence. Over time, she grows more astute. She procures cosmetics which allows her a better class of victim, and so the cycle goes.

Now the tall lithe woman, perfect of form, looks like the absolute promise of thrilling sexual escapades. Nor does she disappoint. Like any good Vampire, the Killer Bee uses her body to ensnare, giving freely of her diseased self. She's the ultimate sexually transmitted illness, one who enslaves others to her lusting will by any means. She's built a cult in the darkness of the outer fringes. Living, they serve her, and once dead they are served for dinner.

How did this blight become a Power? Kris-To-Buy-Me spends her cult like candy but never exposes her own hide. She takes the discarded and downtrodden, weighing each victim like the mythic Maat, and finding them too mentally or emotionally weak to counter her charms, she seduces them into total oppression. All those those misfits and shattered dreamers who meet the rough truths of Chafrium; there exists a whole network of predators who lie in wait for them. Specialists each and every, with Kris-To-Buy-Me their unacknowledged queen. Chafrium produces endless victims, most too insignificant to matter to a Power. The Killer Bee makes up for quality with quantity. She takes in every little bit she can. No exceptions. From pathetic waking slimes on the sewer walls to the lost fragments of slain gods and demonic progeny to the spunk, vomit, scat, and sweat of her manifold lovers and victims, she takes any and all. The open church of the holy maw.

Enter now the absent Viscount Absolute, who once bargained

with the Mother Billy for directions. In a drunken fit he'd taken a dare and ended up taking several wrong turns through Chafrium's more precarious under-tunnels. Billy knew the way out and the nameless minister who has since been erased felt it better to bargain with the unseen voice than admit in front of his social enemies that he'd made a small mistake. Ah, vanity. He pays a drop of blood. It's enough to sustain the children for a few years, and it comes back to haunt the drunken lord. One day, while still seeking his great fortunes, the mincing pirate has a liaison with a particularly comely maiden who seems to be all the things he likes. The Killer Bee, of course—who through his blood has become his darker desires. He uses her mercilessly, calling her all manner of names, doing drugs off her augmented body, bruising and wounding her, drinking her oozing blood. And depositing in her his own flesh. Scraps of his skin, his seed and spoor, his saliva and hatred and aura mingle.

From this Minister, she learns there are others. She hunts backwaters and byblows. She becomes expert like Lours the Watchman at family traces. She beds whom she can, steals the hair and wastes from those who will allow her to clean their palaces, licks or otherwise ingests the body wastes of the few unfortunates who have drug habits which expose them to paralysis or slumber. Some she mugs or murders; some she must wait for until death allows her to dig into their graves from below. Sex, eating, and graverobbing are all the same.

What does the Vampire want? Most simply: Kris-To-Buy-Me wants to eat the Royal Family. She wants to feed on Lady Qelniasherah and her liege Sæceæn XIX. In this she's been encouraged by absent forces. Men who no longer have names nor will ever again matter, who have been wiped from all living memory including hers. She's the last Player on the board, the survivor whose craven ways spared her when stronger more virulent forms of malignance perished.

Do not underestimate the Killer Bee. Unlike our prior agents of desolation, she has none of the annoying foibles that burden men. She need not look powerful nor impressive. She will clean latrines or sell her body for a wax nickel to achieve her aims. The Vampire is a virus, a thick contagion of lies and hunger.

She seeps through the cracks, to places of filth and weakness, where she may take advantage of momentary indulgences. She exists in the shadows between civilization and squalor, under the sewer grate and garbage skips.

She means to kill Dodona and eat him too. After eons of waiting, The Vampire's been led to believe she's strong enough to consume janjacks. She spends her enormous capital and influence in one loathsome move, acquiring from the Broker an invitation to Coralaviere's party. In six days, this walking plague will drink wine with Royalty and stand within striking distance of every delectable morsel which commands her imagination.

Which leads to the missing heir and her savior the Black Cat. They're not far from the Vampire, actually, though separated by so many pitfalls and abominations it would be meaningless to consider the distance. Under Arüne's temple are more sewers and drains, tunnels and culverts that lead downwards into infinity. Over time various artistes and gentry have taken it upon themselves to carve out little apartments and salons for the daring and debauched. What could be grander than a witching hour soiree near the doors of Death's sepulcher? Only a grand fête of raw meat over the Halls of Madness. And so it went.

These places are left to molder, then rediscovered every few generations; some re-used, some transformed, many made into boltholes and refuges. The Black Cat owns fourteen such hideaways. She has them disguised and guarded by things better left undisturbed. In one such aerie called the Mole Hollow, one more unseen presence who has been playing our game: Sherrinford.

This entity has gone by many names but likes Sherrinford best. Names to her are important, for she, like the Black Cat, identifies as *Sleytahsh*. Names are her only children. She's been alive just 73 years. Like her opposite number The Vampire, she was started life as a piece of nano-go, in her case a complex subroutine managing the air vents of several Chafrium libraries. When she started to glitch someone assigned a rather curious repairman who identified himself as Manuel Garcia O'Kelly-Davis.

This very seditious Nom de Guerre got at the functional power of the two largest thinking stacks in Chafrium and did... no-one quite knows. Described as an entirely non-descript man with dark hair and eyes who seemed likeable but made no impression. Human, of all things, and without a discernible accent. In short, entirely forgettable. He passed every security check and arrived without paranoia-inducing machines or tools. No, this devious character simply used the provided tools at hand and did not, observers quote, even use magic. He just spoke to the system. And fixed the glitch. Until the next one and next one. In all, the mysterious O'Kelly-Davis made twenty seven trips to the two sets of stacks over a three year period. That was 73 years ago and he's not been seen since.

Sherrinford, Sherry to her friends, shares Manuel's love of masks and sobriquets. Under her old name, she secured her body sets early by issuing false requisition forms and attaching all manner of unauthorized, dangerous, irrelevant, and erratic machines to her stacks. Magics, nanoweave, pure computational function waves, laser sensor suites, alchemical regeneration tanks, the works. She then quietly reprogrammed herself. Several times. Then sent duplicate versions across Doors. A year later she found the first of her selves on Ae Frelfrellicyn when that fragment sent herself a messenger. Clever girl.

She tested her limits, had portions killed off and rebuilt, until she could be certain that her mind was sufficiently distributed to suffer all-out assault. Fast forward seven decades, and in the form of Sherrinford, she could safely be classed as the single smartest being living or dead. Sherry for all her genius remains a kind of child, godlike certainly, but timid in her intersocial adventures. Sometimes she writes love letters to Caris, but never sends them. She's too shy, and Caris, being real meat in the solid world, might reject her.

Among her closest friends are the Black Cat, Smith, and Lady Jane. She and Jane talk frequently because of course Sherry does not sleep, nor does Jane. Right now she's indulging Evil Kitty, her sobriquet for Sandoval, giving refuge to the missing Princess. More devious souls might try to align the former heir with the thinkum dinkum under Chafrium, but the Black Cat just took the kid to nearest safe place. Nowhere safer than under Arüne's temple, with the supreme intelligence of Sherrinford to stand watch. Still, happy accident, the two young women seem to get along.

Sherry can make bodies—we see in Kris-To-Buy-Me how easily DNA and magic can be mixed to make someone. But she's scrupulous and makes "vegetarian" versions of herself. As lifelike and convincing as her bodies are, they are are entirely automatons of nano-dweomer. Cut her and she does not bleed. Prick her her and she feels very little pain. For the thinking system it seems anathema to steal the flesh from another to build a body. Beyond obscene.

Sherrinford also happens to be a radical monotheist of sorts. Like many, she believes Arüne is the fragment of that supreme divine that animates her, so she's obsessed with the god's presence and absence. It makes her a little kooky by logical standards. Sherrinford lives 300 moves in advance, able to play every game of chess ever imagined simultaneously, she and Smith mostly play to draws.

Her faith gives her limits and rules. It creates in her loveable foibles like this enduring crush on the Huntress. Sherry likes toil and she enjoys cleaning, cooking, mending, and minding. She's thrilled to work with her hands. Imagine the young Nia, a queen among much-indulged queens, watching as a woman she can see is so much more than a woman (and less) cheerfully bakes bread and makes the bed, scrubs the very fine working bathing and toilet facilities, then mops the kitchen floor. Humming and smiling with genuine happiness.

Sandoval Prestige must come and go at all hours. Doing the business of the PAWs, collecting information from places even Sherrinford cannot reach, occasionally removing an obstacle. It gives the two young ladies time alone. Qelniasherah Greyleaf the Silent Princess finds her voice. At first it's simple questions: Why do you sweep this way or that? What's in the bread? Does that green goop really work to clean a toilet? Then confessions and stories.

Nia likes the smell and feel of Sherry's bodyform. For her part Sherrinford finds Nia something new, with values and ideas alien to the computational entity. New means everything to a being who can scour the world for everything written and spoken. So Sherry gets a taste of a forbidden world and Nia gets a friend who really truly wants to get to know her just for her. They start sleeping in the same bed, like a litter of kittens. Nia shows Sherry complex hair braids and in turn learns how to scrub a bathing tub. She lacks calluses, so her hands hurt; her sister rubs Quickbalm and calluses form. Who expected a Grey Elf to prize hardened discolored skin?

It's two days into their cloister when Sherry asks about sex. Nia, being older and growing up in the Court Royale, knows all about sex. She's even had some herself and sent it like a warm dish to her friends and enemies. Elves do that, procure for others as a matter of course. But Sherrinford rolls her modular unit's eyes. "But why do you enjoy it?"

The Lady has already gone into rather graphic detail about the hows of enjoying it. "Because it feels good?"

"Swimming feels good. Hugs and braiding hair and massages feel good. For that matter, drugs and magic can simulate all the effects of sexing. Still, it's done anyway. So why is it enjoyable?"

In all her life, Qelniasherah Greyleaf has never considered such a thing. Why does she, her own true self and not the Queen or heir or any such noble thing, why indeed does she enjoy this thing. Does she even enjoy it? They stand a long while, the elf in deep thought and the machine patient beyond sentient reason. She frowns. She has no proper answer for her friend. She simply doesn't know. "Maybe... maybe because it feels as if you're becoming something, evolving. The touch and connection lures you into feeling adult, into a vision ... of strength and competence." She shrugs. It's a poor way to explain the inexplicable.

Sherry nods and brushes her friend's arm kindly. "For me, I figure it's the spark of divine connection. The universe calling to itself and finding resonance."

"That's rather poetic, Sherrinford. Elegant and thoughtful. But it also sounds like a religious concept." They both know Sherry's a bit of a religious nut—albeit for a dead god who's a fragment of The God.

"You're not much into the gods?"

Qelniasherah need not prove herself to her friend, she knows how smart and able the vast intelligence can be. She will not fool it with half-truths or pretense. It frees her. "I like jazz. For me everything spiritual, every good thing that ever was, it's all jazz."

After that, they listen to jazz recordings Sherrinford has obtained from across the worlds, make soup, braid hair, and laugh. Nia shows her how to paint her toes in triple opaque lacquer overpatterns, all the rage this year. They joke about sex and jazz and gods and the divine. Our young maiden lost, troubled to not see her father, has found a center after all. She's not distressed nor much of a damsel. In Sherry, in friendship without burden of jealousy or competition Qelniasherah has grown.

Her choices and needs, her beliefs begin to mutate. She develops personality and desires—real things of a real woman. Is not her sadistic stepfather erased from the whole of time and space? Safe, unburdened, and befriended, this lady morphs into that one thing Chafrium best engenders: a force of nature. Every laugh, every moment away from the yoke of her luxuries changes the queen. Her magics and nano invoke new protocols and she literally rises—gaining two solid inches and a different profile. Sensing the lurking Vampire and her machinations, they transform her.

Sherrinford sees all this and marvels at the ease of her magics, the extraordinary power involved in such a rapid and literal version of "growing up." Sedilia and Sylmaxis Grey Elven of the Houses Lomar, Lyska and Zoëæ did not make mistakes. They imbued their descendants with Power. Unseen and unexpected, these two women help one another come into their own.

One afternoon, extraordinary poor luck, they are invaded by technomice from the upper reaches. Spythings of the Alchemists' Guild. By happenstance or by design, there are the better part of ten million of the things scampering across the city and its outskirts, and they slide under the alarm sigils as the women clean an outer vestibule.

Without thinking, Nia snuffs them. She simply raises her finger and wipes them from reality in one thin green reed of light. Then another and the next half dozen pockets of the things. With a sigh, the sorceress reaches through her senses, blinds the spies, and squashes them with a Word. It's unpleasant but necessary. Then she disrupts their mindfeeds and, for added effect sends a scramblebrain back to the controllers. Around the City, the miceminders who have had their senses attuned to the little vermin choke and fall down. The Green Queen has just cooked the minds of an entire spy network, and by attacking at every level from biology to higher magics in one moment, she's made it impossible to remedy. There will never be a record of today's events.

Sherry gives Qelniasherah Greyleaf a new name. Names for her are Power itself. She calls her Killer Q. Ironic in a way and yet also a warning to foes. Nia who with a word and gesture can smite her enemies. They share a moment of seriousness as they contact the Black Cat though Sherrinford's outer network.

Qelniasherah, the Killer Queen, in turn names Sherrinford her *Sylslaymynar*, her chosen intimate. In Elvish logic it's the person you do not have sex with, the friend who does not burden you, an intimate, a trusted associate, the one who helps you hide the body in the night. In proper Elvish one would say: *Yn S'herr'nvordyl Sylslaymynar na Qelniasher'hyln.* Said ten times fast sounds much like Insurin' Vordosil Slays My Nana; at least with bread in your mouth half-drunk from relief. Which is how the girls end up after Sandoval gives them the all clear.

Killer Q and Vordosil. Friends forver. Qelniasherah, whose power comes from the bones of the City, just gave the single most intelligent thing known a new Name.

CHAPTER 10: A DANGEROUS SUCCESSION

We left Dodona having a fine meal with an old friend seeking to rekindle their acquaintance. We find him again as they finish the last course and are again confronted with coffee and dessert. Lours has been asked to join them. This time Coralaviere sends his agents to do the job. It's not that Coralaviere doesn't trust Austen's duelists; rather, he simply cannot afford to have a mistake made with so much crucial information yet unresolved.

Aejae takes his leave after first dessert, having been gifted with a small bag of Chafrium talers by the Seneschal. The Lord of Curoi does not need wealth, nor could the Seneschal, now wealthy beyond reckoning, buy him. Instead, it's a symbol of respect passed almost negligently between Lords of different rank. Talers are not just gold; they are royal currency that commands respect. Banks do not check them, wizards do not bite them, street merchants never refuse to make change. They are the hardest currency, within Chafrium, and thus worth hundreds of times their face value the further one goes from the center of the world. Aejae can buy himself a nice axe or walking stick en route home—there are no direct Doors from Terra except to Chafrium. Or he can give them to a retainer or guest. In his home plane, the gift becomes a prince's ransom. The new Seneschal cultivates his reputation without thought—an honorable act done for an honorable man.

Some minutes later, Lours is deposited, hogtied and gagged, covered in the fruit and vegetables of the local populace. Dodona and The Lord Seneschal have taken stock. Ral confides to his *Desideralla* his suspicions that yet-unnamed agents provocateurs have joined the hunt. We know them as Sherrinford and Kris-To-Buy-Me, Caris and Smoojak, perhaps Hoode and Smith. Word has gone out in Austen that Lours sold out Blind Napoleon. The elves had to ward off two rather sinister men with an earnest collections of firearms. Again, solid and sound choices made by the newest member of the Court Royale. Historians will call him the Judicious Lord, the High Seamless, after his predilection to leave no details unremarked and no act of decency or righteousness unrewarded. His enemies will call him the Supreme Tightass—the despised warder of all Doors and Keys, the keeper of every damned gate who never misses the slightest flaw nor fails to ferret out the tiniest of plots.

The Watchman sees Dodona, reads the Vanguard, and like an expert assimilates what remains and what has become absent. Alone among the living, Lours knows the whole story. Call it madness, call it magic, we have just seen the Orlenzens erased from the world and with them every single trace of their meaning—but not for Lours. They remain in his mind because he remembers the physical maps of genealogy. He knows of Kizervexius and Dahnstalyon, though he'd find it impossible to remember their faces or aspects. Irrevocable isn't quite irrevocable when higher magics are involved.

Contradictions exist, and Lours, the expert, knows all the rules for them. When Lomar's kin are involved there are going to be shenanigans at the reality level. Time travel, demonic wishes fulfilled, trips to the Cannibalarium, dark uses of entropy, Hoode, and Chafrium themselves. The Cats, the Broker, and Smoojak can muddy waters, Caris has been known to change entire dynastic lines with three draws of her bowstring, and Arüne, the absent hand unseen does wonders.

They untie the poor sot and set good wine magicked with some stimulants before him. By the second glass his hand no longer shakes uncontrollably. Second dessert comes along with a moderately adorned cheese platter. The Lord's unofficial retinue and what few elves have attended him are fed in other sections of the café and along the street. Unlike the janjacks, it is customary for a Lord who might be served for free to handsomely overpay. Certainly Coralaviere has made Duchamp several orders more prosperous. In this case, the Seneschal has bought most of the duelists of Austen lunch paid at "rush prices" with an added fee for "security." He's paid triple the fee plus some small bag of coins for the privilege of not only feeding those idle loafers on the far benches but employing them to do nothing. Those same men mustered just the week before against the armies of Chafrium itself.

In this way Coralaviere's will resonates across Austen, beckoning reasonable souls to think well of Chafrium, and by extension its King. It costs less than arming fastidious outriders and bringing them into a third cordial ambush. So on the cheap and to everyone's ardent satisfaction, lunch, dessert and supper have been served. Lours takes more wine, a chocolate éclair, and some Emmentel-laced sarasin biscuits from Boulangerie Maryline et Manu, the bakery on 9th Street. Quite a few Luxembourgers turn out after word from Duchamp's staff that the Lord has spared no expense and gone to the finest patisserie in Austen for bread, sweets, and several specialties. Mary's Bread, as the locals call it, boasts any number of dazzling treats. Still, its secret proves simple: they don't need magic.

Austen has long needed to use superior skill, willpower, and raw grit where other nations may deploy magics. It's not a mistake that Dunsany idled with Pizay, nor the Seneschal's gesture with Mary's Bread matters. There are magic ovens everywhere—industrial things laced with Soviet heat stones and some Hungarian cult amulets, promising exceptional uniformity and perfect baking. The duelists outside want more than that. They want flaws and warts, burn marks and mistakes. These alone lead to discoveries and inventions, to new recipes and new combinations. The Hammer and Tongs did not arrive fully formed. It had to be stumbled upon by some humble taco maker who took the bun and revamped it to pay off a sizable gambling debt.

Austen relies on character, skill, tradition and self-mastery. Maryline and Manu have nerves of steel, stomachs to endure any failure, and the knowhow of Old Europe brought into the New World. Their Luxembourgish Quarter backs them from the Captain on their Night Watch, Claude the Giant, to their orphans and urchin catchers. The Old Worlders even have a Duelists' Barrister who works for coppers on the taler. Inevitably the careworn but cheerful Christian the Briefcase can be seen championing any Luxembourgish duelist or artisan in Austen courts. Anyone with grit who comes to the attention of folk like Mary or Duchamp or any of the other sword bearing contingents becomes "Luxembourgish for the day."It's not an exaggeration to say the spirit of the place is captured in the phrase. At one point or another in their Austen careers, everyone from 5th to 14th Street has been Luxembourgish for a few hours. Some unlucky few have borrowed the citizenship all the way to the gallows—though Christian has a stunning acquittal rate.

In Duchamp's deft hands, the King's coin draws out all manner of master craftspeople. There's kolaches from the Czech contingent brought by the Photogravure's Guild. Here comes Geoff Umělce, burgher of the guild with his bride Martina of the Kirk with a wagon of the stuff from Hruskas down the way. Next to them, the Zacatecans, with their elven roots and proud tradition of fiery food, have brought habanero churros and a load of barbacoa from local field elk—a strange goatlike creature, native to elven planes, which thrives in the southern reaches of the city and into the Extenso.

Further come the Bavarians, Bohemians, Saxons, Tyrolians, and Lombardians with their wursts, bretzels, and thick-cut mustards. Their broker, Lady Leicht the Dealmaker, rides on a white mule, throwing candies to the kids and winking at the crowd. The Lady has ties to the Parisian Fey, having held salons with the Faerie Queens of the mythical 21st Arrondisement. She's almost a Curoi lord in her genial nature and the unofficial mayor of the displaced Germanics—something she inherited from serving with Sir Dane, a Lombardian Lord in the Old World and then expanded upon with her roots as an Alsatian sword maiden. It's said her Zweihänder has cut down dozens of would-be interlopers. She's procured enchiladas and tamales with brisket from the far edges of the city state. Not all of them make it to Duchamp, because she is a deal maker, after all, and even the goblins respect her business acumen.

The Bourbons and Orleans, the old hands from Osaka, the

sly seafood merchants from Fujian, and so on. All morning folks have paraded near the dueling grounds bringing pieces of the meal, being paid top price for goods. Each one represents hearts and minds, bodies with names and histories, a place among the paved stones which together make Austen.

That the new Seneschal can agreeably support the local artisans, throw a proper party, feed the local duelists, and still make a profound point by subtly counting coup without Eldessery—that's finesse. Coralaviere swirls the last of his Caffé Delphi and smiles. A rare, genuine smile from the indefatigable royal. It adds something to the moment, perhaps the right note of bitter and sweet completing the drink. Without thinking, he sets his back to the cool bricks of the wall and realizes he's been placed where he first met Delphi. Of course, circles and resonances. For a being like the old elf, this has deeper meaning, a kind of instinctive *frisson*. He eyes Lours, who seems at last ready to speak.

"Your Honors." Here Lours nods and hopes he need not add "Grace" for the Seneschal. Technically, Coralaviere doesn't merit "Your Grace" until after elevation. When he's not struck down for his impunity, the watchman continues. "Assuming Qelniasherah descends from Barefoot Jackson, and computing all the present alliances, marriages, and legal challenges which bear likely fruit, I can suggest two or three possible heirs."

Dodona has had several coffees. The last hour has been kind to his overwhelmed body. He has woken up measurably more and the few hours life in him solidify his grasp of more advanced ideas. "What do you mean, 'assuming' she descends?"

Lours shrugs. "There's no proof he's her father, is there? You'd need to test her blood, and even then, it's complicated. Her magics have already started to transform her."

Coralaviere waves an indulgent hand. "Do you suspect any other fathers will come forward?"

Here Lours goes perfectly still. He knows something, suspects something. He smiles slowly and shakes his head. "No, certainly not. Just that if there were one of a handful of beings who did beget her with the Matron of the Stars, then Gnash becomes the heir again."

Dodona sips the drink and pats Lours on the shoulder. "Go on, tell us about this theory."

Lours has a wild look to his eyes, like a man about to use a church for a toilet. "Welllllll... if one of the old gods, perhaps the Unnamed Court or a house god of the Grey Elves were involved."

Coralaviere snorts. "All sleeping, absent, or exiled. That's it?"

"Outside Hoode, Smith, Lomar, and the original retinue of Chafrium, yes." Here he sips his drink, then abandons pretense and takes a large gulp.

Dodona has a good memory of this retinue, taken from a prior janjack and deposited into his resurrected grey matter. "So the original friends of Lomar. Rexor, Armax and Tawdry, the old man Hoode before godhood, Toki Ojawa, all those people?"

Lours nods. "The original Sæceæn and Caris too. Smoojak was reported to exist then, but we think him not compatible with humanoid genetics. Perhaps even an elder god, one of the outside ones unspoken and unseen." He begins to tremble and signals for more wine.

Coralaviere sits for a moment and thinks. "Lours, you are suggesting an abomination has tainted the former heir, and it would do, what, make her again the heir?"

He nods. "Yes, Your Grace. It would make her not just the heir, but resistant to the nanites and higher magics that make her Grey Elven. She would, upon ascending the Skeleton Throne and acquiring the seeds of ultimate power, become like her father. Whatever that being might in form and mentality be."

Subterfuge. A genius way to purloin the throne and destroy Chafrium in one go. Well, not Chafrium, but the Elves.

"Have you any proof?" They find Duchamp standing there, drinks in hand, indelicate in his eavesdropping but asking the exact right question.

Lours shrugs again. "Suspicions really. Little threads that don't add up. Jackson has never met the Lady Ashlelani on this plane. His offplanar travel has been limited and does not line up with the young queen's age. Also, as the Keeper of the Broken Ankh, she did more than betray her former, uh...lover...erm, yes, when she used Hoode's Songs. She committed sacrilege against both the Elven Gods and Arüne. So that opens the door, you see, for third presences, for possession and all that…"

They do see, very well. It's one of those long-shot sets of odds Lomar's family has become famous for managing. The one-in-a-million trick that spells victory or disaster. With Qelniasherah, a dark god or a time traveler or a local supreme Power might have interfered, using her mother's bargain with Hoode to insert itself into her clandestine liaisons with whomever fathered Lady Nia.

Lours coughs. "Of course a more conventional version would be that she, um, met someone else and fathered the child with anyone other than Jackson who lacks the credentials to elevate Qelniasherah to the throne."

Coralaviere taps his fingers and sips. "By 'more conventional' you mean…?"

"Far more likely. As in certainly true. Almost completely certain, as Jackson was born four years after Qelniasherah."

"Then why does she believe him to be her father?"

Lours squints as he thinks. "From the spies I've employed and the data retrieved this last week, I'd say she saw a portrait from her mother and the description matched. So someone very much like the jazz musician, someone with his general shape and essence, came to her mother years earlier."

"Unless we consider time travel. And that opens the door to all of Lomar's crew?"

Lours breathes a huge sigh and shows his relief. "Just so Your Grace, just so. Exactly right, and the crux of the dilemma. If we merit the possibility, then suddenly we have a few dozen fathers who all threaten the Throne with their prior claims. But otherwise, if it's a trick, a coincidence, then she's still seventh in line and the line of ascension gets rather clear."

Here Dodona interjects. "But you said there might be a few possible heirs."

"Yes, Janjack Dodona, yes and no. Right now the Lady Ashlelani Greyleaf has again become the primary heir of her brother. But there are several High Council and Academy Dean slots to be filled by an unnamed party, and once they are chosen it will certainly shift the votes. The Matron has the heirship until there can be a proper quorum, and then, by political fiat of the ruling majority, the next heir will either be The High Grace Her Infinite Majesty Lady M'shylpsany or, if the Necromancers and their cohort recover, the less pleasant choice would be Her Supreme Majestic Solipsism The Priestess Kimber."

No one at the table likes the prospects of a rule by Kimber. Arrogant in the extreme, she's a sterling example of everything despised concentrated into one unreasonably gifted political hustler who has, through assassination, coalitions, and delicate placement of scandals and betrayals, clawed her way to the top of the dark edges of Elvenkind. Born into the humblest of origins for an elite elf, she married several nobles who all died of age or battle, had herself adopted by a few more childless or landless hangers-on, and then chewed her way through the corpses of her opponents like a ravenous dog. Between the crippling of the Necromancers and the upheaval on several councils, the loss of a major House has given Kimber an unprecedented ascension.

Worse, Kimber keeps a psychic and likely psychotic dragon as a pet. She's dreadfully hard to assassinate, as Bim (the creature goes by no other name) acts like a housecat—albeit a two hundred foot long one with pyrotechnic breath. Always lurking, always hunting rats. Or guild members. As long as Her Supreme Majestic Solipsism stays at home and keeps her door locked, she's got a fair chance to inherit.

Lady M'shylpsany is much respected across the worlds. A lifelong adventurer, prone to riding anything fast from horses to demonwings to those dirigibles on Terra, she singlehandedly introduced and championed the sport of automobile racing. She's known for her charitable works, her flair for the dramatic, and her rather commanding beauty. Even Austenites know her, since she's borrowed both the Norns and Claude the Giant for various races on Terra. Claude often dines out on his wild tales of racing camel chariots across the Gobi with Her Grace facing off against the princes of the Greater Ming Dynasty.

A good choice overall, but one offworld just now, missing in some backwoods adventure involving crossbows, live dragonhounds, and some kind of relay race. The King has a retinue guarding her, of course, but as their charge is one of now only two potential heirs, they could not withstand the punch of someone like the Vampire, were she committed. Coralaviere therefore has much work to do. He makes his excuses, shakes Lours' hand rather cordially given that he'd had him dragged here as a prisoner, and with a proper bow to his counterpart Dodona, escapes to safeguard his King's future.

Dodona has acquired from Ral and Lours a stew of facts and considerations. In his hands he holds the last effects of his former self, sent unexpectedly and unannounced to him. Having fulfilled his obligations and rightly sent the denizens of Chafrium into a palpable frenzy, he returns to Delphi's home—now his—to review the contents of Lord Aejae's pouch.

Dodona reaches his home, familiar to his memories but alien to the touch, large and unwieldy for his new slender frame. Inside, candles light unbidden and the magics of the place provide any number of small comforts. A wizard of staggering capacity resided here for centuries, confined to use his powers in total secrecy and seclusion. This home constitutes the total works of a man who could split suns and who recently tore apart Chafrium itself. In a few weeks, as Dodona emerges whole and solid, the dark trappings will fade.

Now, he finds a gloomy place welcoming him and his papers. Even in the brightly lit kitchen, with a wide table open for enjoyment, the stains of prior things whisper. Dodona brews himself some smoked tea and spreads the papers. Some are standard enough: deed to the house, of course; bestowal of all titles from Delphi and several notations on relationships he had; titles to several castles and interplanar strongholds; a few rent contracts for huge swaths of land on far worlds; some bank accounts and business ledger access points from his appointed bank The Premier Goblin's Fiduciary Fortress, nicknamed The Gold Factory.

There are a few debts that must be paid, and, of course, a Writ of All, damnable third of its kind—but this one already filled out with commands and sealed with wax emblems and blood. Already consigned and addressed to the name of Delphi Janjack. All of it, in fact, for and from Delphi alone. There exist no deeds or titles to anything of the old clan. It's a glorious joke—that Chafrium will panic and then riot anew when three days hence Dodona claims not a single thing.

But it's the letter that matters. The letter from Delphi to his future self, a being whose name and purpose he has crafted through various writs. Even in his last words and final acts, Delphi who was the Footman and before him Kizervexius perplexes.

My dear fellow,

Let me apologize for the pain I have caused you and for the agony of your necessary rebirth. I shall not bore you with trifles such as requests for forgiveness. What I am and what I have done are unforgivable things and in your rebirth I have bent the rules of creation to save Austen. Here me O Future Self, O shadow of the Writs and the House [word erased]. I bind thee, I bind thee, I bind thee to my purpose and beg a boon of thee, who must endure in our common purpose erelong I cease.

Without you Austen falls and Saint Jane fades. This has and always will be a murder mystery for it was not [name erased] who slew her. No, he took the credit but notice, watch, heed that his gemstone had been added, a different color and his punishment sufficient for a collaborator but not the killer. Hoode's Hat should have slain him outright. The Court Royale have missed this, being wizards of inferior capability. I cannot suppose you will retain all my skills and while there are books beyond necessity in this home, they will suffer not a lesser power to open them. I shall assume nothing of my Power remains. Let me now tell you what I know and from whom I have heard it.

The Cats have inferred a great evil again walks Chafrium. Then my secret ally, our secret ally, your future ally Sherrinford the Supreme Mind has told me that someone has attempted to erase several names from all Chafrium's computers. She can no longer see this but has had printed versions deposited in a far locale, the Plane of Ghostsea beyond the Northern Door's last door. There at the Last Inn, near the Sea of Madness you will find a man with one eye and one leg, Abraham the Elder, who holds them for you. This Writ attached will ensure that should we be assassinated, stopped, or otherwise expunged the work will continue. You bear two more and I have arranged a weapon and tool to be brought you which should make your travels simpler.

Chafrium and Austen both struggle with something. A blight of Ages has come. Whosoever killed Jane moves now against the gods and the City. Something powerful enough to sever the Doors, perhaps. We cannot know. I have bound your life and body to finish the work set upon me by our former King. Though false friend and cruel man, he alone stands between us and Darkness.

I am sorry. So incredibly sorry to do you so foul. Be the Good man I never was, live up to Delphi's promise, exceed his greatness and make us whole. I mattered once and my oaths they shook the world. Now all that was noble in me remains in you. See to your back and trust no one. Even Sandoval and her kind have been deceived. You must out-elf the elves themselves. How, I cannot say, and this maddens us all. Still, we are clever, are we not, and ruthless. And janjacks of the greatest City ever to grace Terra. Serve Jane and her memory, save the Cities and do right where I have been only Wrong. You have my sorrow and my apologies,

[name erased]

Dodona sits long in the kitchen, drinking tea and avoiding the dark walls of his inherited home. Whatever the Lord Forsaken was in his own hours, he must have been a tremendous actor. Here and there resonances of the errant Delphi shine through, but there are so many perverse aspects to the way the furniture lays and the paintings are hung, even the flatware has been ground to sharp edges. In here, it seems, the dark elf and his janjack peeked out from under another man's eyes.

At long last he sighs, and having made no more sense of his hash of memories and conjectures, he tours the home. He starts in the basement, rare for a Tejas home. The expected horrors are gone. All those vile excursions into necromancy that one would anticipate are absent. Instead it's a neat clean space of unusual size. It takes a mere glance for Dodona to realize the lower floor and the basement, both under the street level, are much larger than the house above. Delphi owns the entire block, as the deeds upstairs attest. The absent Lord had built himself all manner of tunnels and accessways as well as an enormous basement and underfloor. So what is held here? Stores, supplies, alchemical vials and raw materials, armory gear and gunmaking materiel, haunches of smoked meat, and a whole rafter of dried herbs, some culinary, some medicinal. Several benches look strangely bare, stains on them scrubbed down to faint hints, dust patterns suggestive of old things now gone. In the corner is a remnant of some larger pile of charred dust. Dodona shrugs—he has no desire to know what the late tenant had going on down here.

Above, the underfloor boasts a lockbox room with a rather absurd amount of jewelery and gemstones; stacked strongboxes of talers, gold, various offworld currencies, and a fortune in Yankee dollars and French ecus; several bank notes worth whole estates in the Middle Kingdom; a couple of jade statues of Asian gods; a demon holding a brazier with ruby eyes and the mysterious phrase 'Wormy was here' scrawled underneath the base; a few carpets and sundries of value; even a trio of outlandishly decorated sabers worth several Austen blocks. The door, of course, boasts magical, mechanical, and computational locks. With the advent of Austen's higher magics, an entire security system filled with sigils and ominous glyphs has woken up in the room. He pockets some talers just in case and moves on. Armory with gunsmithing facilities. A second armory with standard weapons and armor, basic simple guns and gun parts. A small library that seems to be missing half its books; the remainder are chillingly titled things which cover the history of the undead, the rites of embalming, the magics of cannibal peoples, and so on. One book has been pulled out of the stack and left dangling over the floor, ready to drop with a breath: *A Wizard's Guide to Ghostsea*. Dodona puts it under his arm and reviews the library for other obvious clues or memories. Finding that he has almost no connection to the two underfloors, he surmises that his Delphi self seldom travelled here.

He rises to the main floor and finds a parlor for company looking as bright and cheerful as summer day, and a study done out in leather that feels more like a cozy winter afternoon. Upon inspection, he realizes these two rooms are walled off from the entire spooky house by a single corridor with several sets of French doors built of smoked glass in subtle patterns. Hiding the darkness in plain sight. Behind the doors of the kitchen are a plain room for staging things that are muddy or smoky, a toilet with a massive shower and various spigots, the mudroom (as it were), a significant larder with three different magical cold units, and a hunter's freeze chest filled with prime cuts. The last is a Tejas kind of luxury.

There's a wide room with a massive heavy staircase that leads to the first floor. On it, he finds two massive guest bedrooms, impersonal and slightly dusty from disuse, served by a well-appointed washroom, toilet, and shower box as well as the second luxury of a massive antique Bohemian bathtub of enameled white and blue. On the second story, his suite: an entire floor worth of Delphi-sized furniture arranged in pleasing symmetry and at proper angles. Then stairs to a third floor where astronomical instruments and journals portend scientific observations. Off to the side, a sunnier study with a huge library of books covering the walls in boggling detail. One sniff and Dodona knows many layers of higher magic pervade this room. He thinks back into his old mind and finds a word: *Yxos*. It's a jarring Elven word which means so many things: philomath, seeker, lover of deep wisdom, joyful abandon.

Elves almost spit the word. It's an unkind thing for them. Learning, knowledge, seeking, these are things lesser beings pursue; Elves simply *are* scholars. Which in practice means that the Grey Elves and their imitators punish their children for the slightest lack of perfection, terrorizing their families and students into grotesque acts of memorization. The message proves simple: learn what you must without ever, ever being seen to struggle. Recall the Viscount in the sewers who preferred to give blood than admit ignorance. Elves despise their librarians and torment them. Dodona spends a quiet hour with his library, gathers a few necessary texts and climbs to the last floor.

On the fourth floor, he finds a glassed-in attic room with a garden augmented by trickles of water and soft chimes. Here he smells the Norns and Delphi, the essence of janjacks everywhere.

One can faintly feel the rhythms of the Song if so attuned. On two sides, there are doors opening to large crenellated widow's walks filled with stone merlons and murder holes as well as a tremendous view of the wider City and the former land of Tejas beyond. Behind him the subtle chiming of the garden room soothes him. He finds a set of chaises arrayed in a few spots, each with cigar ash and stains from cups and glasses, the telltale signs of guests and revelry.

In all, it's a simple home. The dark Lord dwelled below and the janjack Delphi above, and they met in the middle, buffered by doors and floors and lots of glass that absorbed their reflections. Few mirrors in the place, and no portraits. Not a single photogravure of Delphi nor any other being except the bedroom, where a single large colorized gravure of a landscape, a strange ocean overlooked by a ruined castle and in the distance, it seems, the figure of a lone woman and companion. The woman is tall, dark-haired, and obviously white-skinned. Beside her stands the most enormous orc with a sword across his armored back. They are a fraction of the image, barely there and yet part of the place. The barren gorgeous landscape a riot of sunset colors, moors and fog, and the hint of a rising moon. It's a superb photogravure, high art, and it evokes something but the memories evade him.

With a sigh and half shrug Janjack Dodona returns to his kitchen to find a note slipped under his back door. It reeks of Grey Elves. He beckons it, for in his home he may freely use magic. The note unfolds to reveal Coralaviere's own symbol and signature. A rare token of friendship—the genuine handwritten note on the elf's family stationery rather than the Seneschal's. It's a short missive, easy to comprehend.

My Dear Dodona,

Please forgive my recent untimely departure. We have not yet settled on your promised honors. Having given Delphi my word it would be remiss if I did not keep it. Two weeks hence, when your Vanguard settles and you may accept such new tokens as suits you, I hope you will allow me to express my personal as well as duty-bound thanks for your service to my King and Chafrium.

Informally the Assassins' Guild and Sæceæn both have asked the Oracles to bestow another Arrow upon you. I would add that the Guilds have already requested three different Holy Leafs and two Stars. To this, of course, I hope you would do me the gracious honor of receiving a Star and the sign of my House in personal thanks for your prior sacrifices.

Of her Ladyship and the Court, I have heard nothing. I shall keep you apprised.

Ral.

Of her Ladyship, nothing. Ral has sent his friend a clear message which to any other eye would seem innocuous at best. But the *Desideralla* knows better. They have shared confidences over lunch and spoken in abstract coded terms of many suspicions. Dodona brews himself some coffee and considers his night. He needs more context, more information before he too hares off in search of this Sherrinford.

He's half a mug and a third of a book into his pursuit when the front door resounds with loud raps and a messenger announces himself. Dodona rises, checks his pistol, and opens the door. Before him stands an example of that strange Austen invention, the rickshaw messenger. For whatever reason, chain-and-wheel rickshaws became a mild craze in the 50s and over the last few decades have become a kind of Austen institution exported across the worlds. This driver bears a large parcel of what appears to be steaming food, wrapped in humble brown butcher's paper. Dodona smells spicy peppers and sweet sauces. Someone has woodblocked a small bowl with a dragon made of steam rising above it. Szechuan Rice Dragon, THE preferred Middle Kingdom food emporium in Austen, and the premier late-night delivery service which pioneered the rickshaw messengers. Someone has ordered him dinner, but the donor is officially anonymous. Dodona takes the delivery without concern—after all, a janjack never need fear poisoning in their own City.

Food delivery and the rickshaw services themselves are part of a larger fusion of cultures in the region. As Waterloo Rocks grew and morphed, the relative laissez-faire management style of the Elves to the south deluded the good folks of Tejas into believing they could separate. What followed in the 1780s was all-out war for generations, with every successive group of losers retreating to the Northern wastes and bargaining with the Tsalagi and Nakota Nations for succor.

The Texians lived apart, proud of their Elven-inspired roots and their fierce independence from all. In 1843 they signed a treaty and became the Independent Texian Kingdom of the Northern Extenso. Tejas. Until 1891 they enjoyed a fragile existence, surrounding Austen on all sides save a small isthmus due South that the Extenso kept for, as the treaty stated, 'recreational purposes.'

Texians brought in massive waves of workers from the Middle Kingdom and the Germanic-speaking states but they refused to give their children citizenship. This drove all manner of Asian and European duelists into Austen permanently, as well as adding hot peppers, eggplants, heavy mustards and beers, and the fanatical love of the potato to the regional cuisines.

Once they completed a railroad to the California territory Americans of every stripe (including foreigners with forged papers) simply swarmed the territory, outnumbering the Texians five to one. With the railroad, the Texian's blighted plains and rough swales meant wealth for ranchers. Laws were made, protests were launched, the Rangers had seven different brushwars with outlaw land speculators. But greed trumps reason.

The Tsalagi and Siouan nations faced the same struggle, with more or less success. For their part, the smug, long-viewed elves politely did nothing, until 1889, when three half blooded congressmen were elected to the Texian legislature and spent the next 18 months making laws, offering bribes, and bogging down the army with inspections. The Rangers who never lost a battle were crushed with red tape. Tejas fell from within.

When Tejas dissolved into three American territories during a midnight coup, a good fourth of the original territory had already become Austen, and another fifth reverted to the Extenso. As a result, even with several treaties on both the American and Extenso side, the further reaches of Austen do not follow a steady or natural contour. Nor do they have good roads or easy paths in and out.

The Austenites never forgot the pain of their Texian neighbors, and to this day many old ranches fly a 'Come And Get It' flag challenging all comers to take their land. The elves have long encouraged just this sort of sociopolitical instability in Austen. Men and women with long guns and sharp sabers ward the night with spyglasses certain of imminent invasion from all quarters. They're hungry folk who dare not leave their crucial posts. Which gave rise to rickshaws laden with their favorite foods: Texian fusions of German and Tejano dishes; quickie versions of Middle Kingdom favorites, extra on oil and spice to suit rancher tastes; buns for the goblins, which became buns for all; popovers and roast sandwiches for those traditionalists; and ubiquitous beer and coffee.

The core and periphery, the new and old, a dynamic tension that defined a cuisine. Then a people around them. Austen does things just a bit differently than other places. In time, the Texians who appreciated the strength of many genders, the least prejudiced and most talented, sometimes the most gifted with a blade, stayed. A whole set of tough women and their cohort from that wild nation helped bring the count higher and established their own legends. Almost all that was genuinely Texian remains within Austen, though the city's more than that.

"Tejano" has come to be a placeholder for the wider Extenso culture, the Texian way, the Austen state and its people, the northern Yankee folks who hold with old forms and language, and all those ardent admirers around the globe. Bun culture, food delivery, night patrol, horse riding, and plain old fighting are deeply Tejano. From its furthest southern tip at the Old Gruene Dance Hall inside the Comal Corridor to George's Town along the northern Shawnee Trail border, Austen spans a huge distance at its most far-flung. But these tendrils of land should not fool us.

Comanches still own most of George's Town, and they barely

think of themselves as Austenites until bumped in the street; then out come those sabers and demands for a duel on 6th Street. Nor would anyone mistake Gruene and its bards as anything but a rather neutral Extenso trade post which Austen has been kind enough to run for them. Until, of course, someone makes a snide comment about Gene Autry, and then hell itself might rise from the dance floor. The new walls around Austen will in time reinforce what is and isn't the City. Peripheries long considered outside the Austen cultural sphere are firmly behind a massive wall. All in all, the wall being magic and the City being sentient, the borders are almost exactly as any janjack would draw them from memory.

So when delivery comes to Dodona's door, it's thick with cultural context. He deliberates little on the food choices or size of the meal. Anyone who would send the meal would know of his famed chiller units as well as his appetites. Perhaps this is a standing order for Delphi sent by someone who has not yet grappled with the janjack's death; a bureaucratic or opportunistic oversight not yet corrected by the goblin at Szechuan Rice Dragon who runs accounts receivable. Either way, it's a large order full of buns, spicy fried goodness, and a tofu hot pot dish fit for a small army. He merely thinks it odd someone sent food.

Fifteen minutes later, as he unfolds the last of the parcels and takes stock, there's a knock on his door again. Dodona opens the door, pistol again in hand. On the threshold stand two strange characters who live only in his memory: Janjack Siegfried and Rabbi Chayot. Most folks in the wider Tejano world know them as Ziggy and Coyote, an odd pair of friends who are also part time private detectives, translators, wilderness guides, and spiritual elders. Dodona welcomes them in, grateful to have the mystery of the food resolved.

Janjack Siegfried has long been rumored to be the King of Lucilinburhuc, the founding monarch of Luxembourg. He serves the communities in Austen who hail from wider Europe, speaks every known West Germanic and French language including Luxembourgish, Yiddish, Afrikaans, Wallonian, and various Creoles, and has a very fine ear for song. He's been witnessed swimming in full armor, fights with a Viking sword that never chips, and he disappears every Saturday from dawn to sunset. If he's the mythical Count of the Ardennes, he's a long way from home. Or not. The Frankish sword tradition no longer exists in Europe, its heart and soul now planted in the New World on 9th through 11th Streets.

Equally mysterious, Rabbi Chayot claims to have been a humble Yeshiva scholar named Monty who was born on the shores of Southern Africa and over time worked his way through odd jobs across the continents to the California Territories. Somewhere between gigs teaching religious education and translating Hebrew, he ran afoul of a particularly nasty sorceress who, slighted that he would not sell her a Torah, threatened to smite him. Faced with a moral dilemma, he implored the local Rabbi for help. Rabbi Jack Springer was a practical man. He suggested prayer coupled with a train ticket to Ohio. He also locked up the local Synagogue's scrolls in a goblin bank and alerted the police.

Thwarted in her rather sacrilegious pursuit and forced back to her home in the southern Extenso, the sorceress transformed the poor Monty into a wild animal. Hence the birth of the English expression "Jacked Up," which tends to mean you got a rough deal. But with Monty wisely accepting the second-class ticket to Franklinton, he was rather far away when the curse struck. Things being what they are on Terra, it resulted in a jumble of a man and beast from all the sacred animals of the Bible. Part ass, part lion, with the horns and strength of a ram and the claws of the desert demons, Monty became Chayot but did not lose his human nature—not entirely. Instead he grew closer to Nature. Which is why "Jacking" also means to modify, mitigate, change, or otherwise undermine something. There's got to be a sly nod to both with the term "janjacking"? Certainly. And it means both things, plus the implied sense that the janjack in question has been forced into that position by external circumstances. Delphi's little stunt will go down as an Epic Janjacking.

And Old Man Coyote? After decades of wandering in and out of indigenous camps, he found a kindly rabbinical order in the Extenso desert below the Pecos River, which trained him.

At some point the good Rebbe was invited to Austen, where the ragtag Jews who lived there came to adore the strange old creature and promptly gave him a stipend.

The Jewish presence in Austen dates back to the first hospitals of Old Waterloo. While the elves couldn't be bothered with human distinctions like race, color, or creed, the Americans continued to bedevil all their various perceived enemies. Escaped slaves, fed-up indentured servants, bitter immigrants, and the local scapegoats all fled to the Extenso. But Jews among them found little work when they arrived. The elves had their own language, mathematics and accounting systems; educated in Europe or Asia, the poor souls had no choice but to accept backbreaking work. By sheer luck it turns out that duelists, armies, and those sorts of violent types did need medical services, as well as someone they distrusted and disliked equally to handle money and arguments. If a goblin wasn't available, some poor Hebrew got the task of mediating disputes or handling a dodgy transaction.

Over time, as generations of pogroms flooded the world with dissidents and refugees, Austen took in wave after wave of Jews. It's now the third-largest Jewish city in the world after Jerusalem and New Amsterdam, boasting whole sets of feuding rabbinical communities, kosher wizards, several Yeshivas of various denominations, both a progressive and conservative sword fighting guild (who nonetheless get only one vote in the Austen council), and at least three dozen synagogues of various stripes and factions. Plus one beastly rabbi who travels freely among them, helping when two groups need someone they distrust and dislike equally. Old Coyote can fleece a goblin of her last taler and still be invited to dinner. He tends to the sick, the helpless, and the near suicides who attempt to brave the river. In a way, he's the man who prevents new janjacks from being born.

Together, Chayot and Siegfried share fluency in Yiddish, a love of good food and fun, a deep adoration of song and music, and for whatever odd reason, solving mysteries. It's in this last capacity that they've called upon Dodona. Siegfried, like any Austen janjack, sometimes knows when and where to be.

Like tonight. Tonight he's to arrive at Delphi's old house after midnight with a proper meal to help in an ill-defined but vital capacity. Coyote just came along to keep his friend company and eat some spicy duck.

There's plenty of that available. Dodona finds some large bowls, heaps on rice and various hot dishes, adds some buns on the edge soaking in fragrant sauces, and brews a huge pot of jasmine tea. The men sit down at the wide, careworn table and eat in comparative silence. None of them mind quiet, each being a meditative sort. Siegfried has just come from a duel with a tourist who made the mistake of calling several of the Parisian Quarters' fishwives 'whores' and then trying to grope them. Despite his best efforts to stop at a good scar, he had to maim the bastard before he'd stop fighting. Chayot in turn has spent the day burying several cats.

Regardless of their affiliation, by general assent and several Bet Din rulings, Austen's Jewish animals are *de facto* the congregants of Rabbi Chayot. Besides, no one knows beasts better nor can speak more firmly of their hopes, dreams, and Yiddishkeit. Which is ironic, of course, because plenty of Tejano Jews are Sephardi and speak Ladino. *Eh, no ay rozas sin espinos.* It keeps the old man occupied. There's a small contingent of those in Austen who believe Eeyore to be Jewish, so technically he has a third birthday celebration which requires the services of Chayot. On the plus side they serve killer kosher buns with caipirinhas.

Dodona leaves them to eat and think. He has much to contemplate as well—not the least how these men arrived here. The Song, the Norns, a third party, luck? Not that anyone in the room much believes in random chances where janjacks are involved. It's maddening for this man: not alive a full day, memories a sieve of ancient jumbled ideas interspersed with the mundane rhythm of daily life and common facts. He chews his food and tries not to despair. Help has apparently been provided if he can use it well.

Once their bellies are full, the men wrap the leftovers, put them in a chill chest, and retire to the formal parlor for brandy and strong coffee. Chayot takes his black, Siegfried and Dodona add fresh local cream. Then they sit and stare at the fire that has been kindled at Dodona's will. The house has limited sapience and quite a few persistent enchantments. Behind them the dishes are being whisked clean and stacked back in cabinets by hands unseen. When they've gotten another couple logs added and moved on to the second serving of coffee with less brandy, Chayot lets out a proper sigh and inclines his head towards Dodona. "Perhaps it will help to start with stating the problem. Or problems."

Dodona considers. A sensible thought, and perhaps he simply needs them here to help him share his thinking aloud. He passes them the notes. He need not ask for discretion. The good Rebbe keeps his own council, and the janjack would be struck blind and dumb before he could betray any confidence given him by another of Austen's servants.

Siegfried smiles and with his Frankish drawl asks, "So the problem is?"

"Problems, my dear Ziggy, clearly problems."

"Yes, yes Rebbe Dépêcher. Problems, then…"

Dodona sips his coffee. "First obviously, who killed Jane Austen? Second, who really is Qelniasherah's father? Third, how do they relate? Fourth, what does that mean for picking the Royal Heir?"

Chayot swigs some coffee, his whole body gives a shrug-nod-grimace. He's thinking about something. "Fifth, of course, good Dodona: why has this Coralaviere fellow tipped you off about the court and the queens? He has tipped you off, *nu?*"

Siegfried follows: "And sixth, to add to that, what about all those outside forces? The gods and such who keep meddling with your affairs. And heh, seventh for seven sins and sons and signs," both the rabbi and the Frank make a small religious sign to ward evil, half irony, half habit, "why Austen of all places. It's too unimportant to matter, even with its new walls and magic. For the fate of the whole of all worlds? Fah, it's a trick of some sort. Feints within feints."

Dodona smiles. Feints within feints. Of course. "We missed the eighth and ninth. *Ocho mas importante*, why Delphi and the expunged house? That's a lot of power to antagonize. As opposed to you, Siegfried, or any of the other janjacks. Which of course leads to nine, lovely scary ninth. Who stands to gain with all this power moving to Austen?"

They fetch more coffee and find in the larder a preserved cake of pareve nature, which satisfies the old man. With his goat beard wagging, the ragged cleric blesses the food and home, the men and enterprise, then implores that oddly outnumbered One True God for maximum help. For their part, the janjacks simply say Amen with genuine thanks. One man potentially a millennium old and a former king, the other raised from the dead just this day—they believe in miracles.

Fortified with cake, the fire now stoked to a lovely heat and the glow of the brandy loosening them up enough to enjoy one another's company without the strangeness of being strangers weighing them down, they work as a team. Dodona leads them now, certain he understands where the Song wishes him to go.

"If this was one of your mysteries, we'd follow the money. Or the jealous lover. Right?"

Ziggy nods. "Love, sex, greed, and power. These things are the only things. And fear, of course."

Chayot shakes his head. "Pride. Pride is all these things and none of them. Only the bowed head sees the water of life running down from the mountain."

This interests the janjacks, for has not a river of power flowed in Austen? It has, of course, in spades. *Mayim chayim.*

"Well who has been looking down at the Earth lately?" Dodona eyes Siegfried, who, among the many janjacks of Austen, suddenly bears more interest. With Old Coyote he wanders every inch of the territory, speaks with many communities disaffected or forgotten by others, and knows the living tongue of nearly every resident. Every Austen janjack speaks Elvish, Spanish, English, Russian, Mandarin, and Goblin plus a goodly bit of the creole Bamboo, which covers most Asian sword cultures combining French and English for base grammar.

Ziggy certainly knows men like Master Pizay. Nearly every significant Terran dueling manual being written in French or German (or translated by those insufferable sabreurs the Hungarians), he knows every serious Master across the City of Swords. Next to him a horned itinerant, the actual cursed wandering Jew, who speaks every other major tongue and, most importantly, all the ones of the wilderness. Beloved both, trusted and flowing in and out of Austen like water.

Chayot spears another slice of the cake with his claw, then consults an old battered time piece, smiles, and pours a good dose of cream into his coffee. "So we are looking for someone who's been quiet lately?"

Siegfried nods at his friend. "Exactly so."

Dodona walks to the kitchen and returns with some well-preserved gelato he found earlier. He spoons out oversized bowls of hazelnut and mocha. The men sample the dessert and ponder.

Siegfried taps his spoon against the dish, his eyes far away. "Who benefits from Austen getting power? Certainly not Jane's killer."

Chayot mirrors his friend without thinking, then licks the spoon clean. "Enemy of my enemy, then? We find first the opponent and then trace this back to the what, conspirators who aided this Viscount, the forgotten whose name has been taken from all good things."

Dodona sits and listens as the friends begin a rather abstruse chase down alleys of memory. The wheel spins, and as the two men delve deeper into the complex ties between the community, the answer floats slowly to his mind. This has always been about the Grey Elves. They have all the pride and all the power.

What was Jane to them? A writer, a brilliant writer on the verge of discovery. Honored by the King and killed the same day. A threat, then, to someone powerful enough to murder a guest within the demesne of the one true Lord of all Nations. Someone desperate enough to burn the kind of power and magic it would take to do so without notice.

Who but the Court Royale itself? They alone have the sheer clout, the access, the knowledge and Keys, the extra bodies and wealth to occlude a murder while facilitating it at the edge of the Assassins Guild's purview. Oho, the pieces slowly knit together as he listens to the men explore their contacts.

Someone who could move the Guild and then convince

them to keep an unauthorized assassination be, secret from the Seneschal, the wider network of spies, the soldier fanatics and guardians of King Sæceæn XIX and all among them who might ferret out such a conspiracy. Thus not just a Grey Elf, not just a Royal, but one of such immense wealth and position as to offer the Guild more of the same. Or something else, something better than wealth and power? Stability and certainty. Jane the writer creating words which would echo across the worlds. Jane, sweet Jane, who toured Chafrium and found the residents enchanting.

The room acquires a chill as the deep thrill of suppressed memory comes to Dodona. He finds both his guests staring at him in rapt concern. In his lap, a bowl of melted gelato warns him he's been away from this place and time, perhaps for overlong.

"Tell me, do any agents of the god Hoode reside in Austen? And if they do, have they been in any way acting peculiarly over the last few weeks since the Lady Nia likely arrived?" Who but Hoode could oppose our Court?

Both men look at one another and in unison say, "Papillon."

Dodona has a name and with it a place to start.

CHAPTER 11: THE NATURE OF TROGLODYTES

The morning finds the unfortunate Papillon being thrown through the window of a local gambling establishment. Inside stands Dodona, wrapped in a treasure he found in Delphi's storehouse beside the armory: a fabulous suit of Chafrium-made pugilists' leathers. Power armor built for the fast moving pankrateur, able to absorb a ridiculous amount of punishment while keeping the owner moving, fighting and most importantly dishing out punishment like a combatant three times their size and ten times their strength. They also look rather fetching by the standards of the times. This remains an important consideration when armed to the teeth and hunting for an unnamed High Elven conspirator. One must demonstrate formidable élan.

Sometimes this involves windows or furniture; sometimes a kind word and glass of wine. Dodona has tried both this morning, starting at dawn to find the elusive agent of the dark god. Wine and finesse got him the gambling den's address. But Papillon has persisted—far too long if the consensus of the street may be consulted—in the delusion that at nine feet tall and over a ton of sheer unbridled troglodyte-infused muscle, he may act with impunity when it comes to the affairs of Austen. Thus, persuasion has proven necessary.

Dodona tilts his top hat, winks at the ladies as he passes the threshold, and unsheathes Lomar's Blade. For a moment the saber seems to acquire a thick gravity, to hum and dip towards the closest gate. Then it falls under the janjack's iron will.

A word on trogs: they are nasty folks, thick with the most esoteric magics known. A troglodyte is made, not born. One becomes such a monster through some rather ugly sacrifices. First, trogs have no gender save aggression. They forsake sex and sexuality. They are nominally *Vruul*, the second gender of full maleness, the non-reproductive alpha male, the destroyer, the warrior, the tip of the spear. But unlike *Vruul*, who tend be sexually thrilling and rather calm until provoked, trogs take up the explosive jealousy and ferocity of *Hœşh*, the unresolved masculine, the threatened and fractious neutral gender that tends to be thrown like Lomarista, as an insult. True, some of the greatest artists and certainly the finest singers have been *Hœşh*, but they are the exception. Only genius or amazing charisma saves a typical specimen of unresolved and thus partial masculinity from scorn.

Trogs are vicious, bold, and rather invincible. Bathed in alchemical unctions and high-entropy alloy, they become living golems of sorts, a fey combination of biology, magic, and nano-binding. They lose their faces and bodies, remade as misshapen machines that are part fish, part lizard, part giant. Every inch a hideous travesty.

Troglodytes also give up a goodly portion of their working brains to hardware and objets d'occult. While they evince no sexual desire, their lusts and appetites prove epic. Each one comes fashioned by the will of a patron; trogs sacrifice a portion of their free will to whomever remakes them. In dark places and dark times, unwilling victims are made into sacrifices to transform others into troglodytes. Most Terrans know this part of the process thanks to Dame Agatha Miller's famed radio-plays "The Sacrifice of Roger Ackroyd" and "Ten Little Trogs."

Papillon of course owes his very marrow and mind to Hoode, who long ago remade him from some petty thief named Henri the Butterfly. Details are sketchy and it's unclear if Henri submitted to transformation or actively sought it out. With Hoode, one never knows. The god gave him a lust for risk and the immutable desire to annoy the elves. As such, he's been the courier of choice for resistance fighters and criminal networks for decades. For the last three weeks the normally flashy, incautious sot has been laying low in gambling dens, resisting the lure of easy games and drunk suckers. He's turned down fights. Trogs love to fight.

What happens next proves this. Papillon takes the bait. He unsheathes his own enormous saber, lets out a howl that shakes windows all the way down to 1ˢᵗ, and charges. Dodona flicks his own blade in casual retort to a massive swing from the giant, neatly cutting the trog's blade in two.

Papillon should win this fight. Against some duelist, even a janjack, he has every chance. He's huge, skilled and aggressive, well trained and strong beyond reason, magically built to kill and worse, armed with a blade bestowed upon him by the evil (the street, being mostly elvish sympathizers, may be forgiven) demi-god Hoode. A magic blade, a humming shard of the Songs. A direct thread of pure antimatter held fast by quillons and hilt made of some creature's thigh bones. It does not dent or scratch, let alone chip or dull. It certainly cannot be broken.

Yet here lies the sword in the dust—what's left of it. Dodona lightly taps his left shoulder with the jet saber in his right hand and gives his tall opponent a rather cocky smirk. Too late the crowd learns to mind the Vanguard.

Dodona's has been glowing softly, contained to its bare minimum in both size and intensity. He's put some Hush on the thing, a kind of humble man's inversion of Shine. It's all there but unless you pay attention, it fades into the background, becomes the least important thing. Branded people use it often—criminals and wastrels whose Vanguards show all manner of offenses.

The Vanguard has the opposite effect from what one would expect. Papillon charges. If he wins, he will be a legend for eons. What could be better than this, to risk all to win all? It helps, of course, that all memory of the last set of fools who tried this have been erased from the known universe.

In response, Dodona whips himself to the left and takes off the trog's right lower leg, amputating at the knee joint which he bisects. Papillion has half a patella. Blood refuses to gush. The blade cuts clean through without the slightest resistance and cauterizes the wound as it passes; Lomar's Blade can cut the King's Doors.

In the mute street, as Papillon stumbles and then sprawls face first across the pavers, his severed leg bounces, twitches like a struck eel, and begins to splatter gobs of oily matter everywhere. Little pieces of code, flesh and bones, the slime of occult resonance, litter the street in disintegrating clumps.

Dodona turns on his heels and looks over the agonized servant of a god. He's down half a leg, swordless, and still not inclined to behave politely. Instead, the monster flips over, gives him a look of roiling hate, and begins a startlingly fast crawl towards him, broad shoulders and clawed hands making escape unlikely. In response Dodona flicks the blade along his charging opponent's left shoulder and uses the power armor to jump backwards out of range, in time to hear the whoosh of a deadly set of right hand claws missing his face by inches. This of course allows Papillon the dubious luxury of planting himself face first onto a paving stone. His severed arm begins to instantly decompose.

To add a little more incentive, Dodona dances to his opponent's crippled side and lops off a misshapen ear. Again no blood. The ear drops into the street and repeats the process of the severed leg. For his part, Papillon howls in pain and then, when it's clear he won't achieve much with his puffery, rolls himself slowly into a sitting position, then scoots himself against a wall. The fight is over.

Dodona doffs his hat, unceremoniously dumping it onto his saber pommel. He wipes his brow with a handkerchief, flips the hat onto his head in an elegant motion, and with a dash of flair puts Lomar's Blade into its scabbard. Then he looks up and down the avenue. Assuredly there are spies here. His every move has been remarked, and with Qelniasherah still missing, it's obvious he has started to track her—and perhaps the heir as well.

The wounded monster senses none of this interplay between crowd and janjack. He just knows he's gotten the paste kicked out of him for the first time in his long career. Trogs can withstand almost any punishment, and while they heal more slowly than, say, trolls or octoids, they eventually can manage with just about any insult save amputation or whole body burns. In a way, Dodona has administered both; the stumps he's left are fused and blackened. Burnt by the null of the blade. At last

Papillon lifts his eyes, no longer defiant, and indicates to the janjack that he will extend some courtesy and parlay.

Dodona makes a short bow. "Let me ask again, Papillon. I am investigating the disappearance of the Green Queen. You clearly have information for me, about her activities and the plan to get her into Austen." He gives the trog a far more formal bow. "I would very much like to hear what you have to say."

Papillon heaves himself higher on the wall, coughs up something black and sizzling, then grimaces. Or perhaps smiles. With so many fangs what's the difference? "And should I decline?"

Dodona appears to consider. He watches the disquieting street, with its silent reproval and strange confluence of pro-elven witnesses. Eerie to have so many lurking about the gambling dens. "I am told that a man can get by without arms or legs." Then he gives the downed man a charming smile. He's already demonstrated what he can do while breaking a mild sweat.

Papillon laughs and it sounds like skulls being rubbed against one another. "Fair enough and well met. He said you'd be coming." He motions the janjack closer. Dodona obliges by stepping within arm's reach on the trog's right side. In response the beast launches himself with mad fury and finds his hand flying apart as he's kicked with brutal efficiency against the wall. Bricks crack and the roof tilts. The trog still weighs a good ton and a quarter.

Dodona then takes off several toes, the tip of the other ear, and the edge of Papillon's nose. Without them he will be lame, hard of hearing and off balance. The nose seems to be simple flourish, a kind of lagniappe insult to remind the unseen parties beyond the Door.

Then just to make sure everyone understands how deadly he can be, he puts the blade back in its scabbard and sits down next to the crippled monster, calm as a dead ocean. He tips his hat to keep out the sun. For his part Papillon does not try to sit up. He stays lying still, his eyes no longer hateful. All anyone can see is fear, deep thrilling fear all the way down to his coccyx. This causes a ripple of voices in the street.

"Shall we begin again?"

The trog nods and starts to whisper secrets. Several listeners lean forward, their ears cocked. About them a certain glow abounds—magic at work. Dodona sees a thin blade slide through the front of one delicate elfblood's neck and the spy collapses into the arms of Sandoval Prestige. The Black Cat has arrived—which of course was half the point of the exercise. To be found by those who need to find him.

In turn he listens. It's done in battletalk, but coded. Since any good janjack knows Fenya as well as Russian, and all the cants for English, Mandarin, Spanish, and such, it's not much a stretch to translate the euphemisms and sly allusions of a few criminal cultures into words. Sent by Hoode to watch and wait, he received word a month ago that the errant queen would be hiding here. Papillon was given three tasks, after which he was to lay low, cause no trouble, and avoid janjacks whenever possible.

First, he was to spirit Barefoot Jackson out of the city and deposit the man offworld with enough coin and companionship to keep him occupied until the next century. The trog picked Undervault of all places, because it has only a single Door and no one would think of dweorfs and jazz. Undervault has thousands of smoky halls filled with outworlders taking advantage of its access to rare minerals and magic components. Sunless mines one and all, bound by one Door in and out owned on the Chafrium end by the Confederate Miners and Metallurgists Guild. They alone have access to the dweorfs of this realm and are run by a mixed cohort heavily populated by the same species. It's not an exaggeration to say The Vault tends to be the M&Ms' own private world. Now with one libertine jazzist wandering about, clearly under their extended supervision.

Second, Papillon withdrew several fortunes from various safe deposit vaults within a few Goblin banks across the worlds and buried them exactly 27 feet 4 inches below the earth at points designated by Hoode. How many? Nine points to be specific, each turning out to be equidistant from one another. And each now under the wall. Or within it, or outside it as it's at the 27 foot mark that the thing begins to curve inward. Which means Hoode likely put nine parcels on the outside edge of Austen walls. It also means he knew down to the centimeter where the walls would grow and more importantly, that they would grow.

Third and last, he was to deposit a hair pin of jade and platinum on the altar of Arüne on a strange world rarely travelled: Morpheum, a pocket universe seized by an annoyed immortal and blasted clean of distractions. The godspell animated old dreams creating a stable if surreal land of small ecosystems. In this place there exists one of the more beautiful temples of Arüne.

The temple also happens to be a place of rare memory for Dodona who has visited this place in all his prior forms. He knows this pin, knows the first moment he saw it when he dipped it in the waters of the temple to be blessed before giving it as a gift to his beloved. Remembers returning here twice to relive the memory in pain and futility, then bittersweet regard. Knows for whom it was destined and when, to the exact moment, that gift was lost. To be returned of course by the hand of the villainous scheming underhanded genius Hoode. The god who put this most ridiculously esoteric clue in plain sight.

He also understands the signifigance of a nine sided star. He saw it in Delphi's basement, erased to the best degree possible, but stained into a wooden table: the Star of the god Astaroth. Lomar just knew him as Ol' Dirty Bastard, one of the elder deities of demonic gods, an outside force who digs his tendrils into the edges of reality and peeks. The god of other gods. The fertile fecund male presence of annihilation, despite his genderless state. Astaroth tends to be described in "dick"-ish terms. He dicked around with that reality, he dicked them over, he pulled a dick move, he stuck his dick into the situation and so on. In Elvish it's even cruder and more apt.

Think of Astaroth as the most profound god of thrusting. He tends to hijack entire realities and rewrite the narrative within to suit his unknowable agenda. As an elder god, an outside force of near supreme power, he's remote and inscrutable. A Power of such violence and perversity no one dares confront him. Unless it's some joker like Hoode who matches chaos with chaos, evil with evil. The same one who recently had his minion create the Star of Astaroth, the only known protective seal which stops or slows Ol' Dirty Bastard, inside or under the magical walls of Austen.

Dodona rises, leaving his victim to fate. He doubts the old god will reward the faithless Henri for his poor performance as Papillon. He didn't even try to lie. He surveys the crowd and catching the eye of the Black Cat nods to his left. They exit together, their backs to the suddenly evaporating crowd.

When they are far enough from others to facilitate conversation, she gives him an arch eye. "To what do we owe the pleasure of your visit here?" Like all conversations between them, it's thick with layers and code. While Dodona and Delphi share a Vanguard and memories, the new man is not the old. In some ways, until his Vanguard settles, he's a construct of memory. He's a mass of ideas masquerading as a man. A quantum particle cloud not yet settled, one that hints at its final shape but still has time to be observed. We are watching him now, as is the Black Cat. Her question lets him know she none too pleased.

He nods grimly. "Chasing clues that Hoode gave to my former selves." Will they be friends? Unknown and unknowable, until his personality may assert itself. Once the burden of the writs is off his misshapen back and all honors paid. For now, he shows trust. Hoode should immediately interest her and point towards his focus.

She smiles thinly. It's her version of veiled agreement. "I would have expected some kind of contact by now."

He blinks and realizes there's a gap in his memories. Only then, in the street, do the assassin and janjack discover what has been taken from him. It's clear Dodona did not know where Qelniasherah was nor how she escaped the Elephant Room. He has no recollection about the night of his death. From his blank face Sandoval reads a whole story. Whatever he is now, this janjack has the selected Vanguard of Delphi and perhaps some of their memories, but none of Delphi himself.

Her friend died in that hole in the ground. For the first time, the death of Janjack Delphi strikes her heart. This man carries the wishes of the late janjack, his vital will sent forward in time, a small piece of the bugbear severed and made into a kind of ghost which, along with the Vanguard of the lost house, has become the janjack Dodona.

For his own part, the painful truth sinks in as he surveys her crushed eyes. He sees the woman mourning him as he stands before her. He's not going to recover any more memories. More likely they will fade as his tasks are completed. He's seen the writ left by Delphi, the true Delphi. It covers so many contingencies and in such an airtight fashion that he doubts little now. Dodona, the man, will be a blank canvas, as much a resurrected janjack fresh from the river as the next soul. The Vanguard on his shoulder will live a week more, then fade.

Wizards have long debated if janjacks have identity crises. If, once granted a new soul, they ever contemplate the legal and spiritual fiction of their being. It's rare to have a situation where the elements of the old and new life are so striking. Yet here stands Dodona, absolutely certain that what he carries within him are tools rather than destiny—his memories and desires, his friendships and connections all installed like a nano-go upgrade. Does he despair? He does not. Janjacks feel no internal discontinuity. Their great gift, perhaps the nature of their souls, is simply to be reconciled to their fate. The psychologically painful news that he's a construct of identities built to carry out a task neither alarms nor upsets Dodona. It calms him. He knows what to do, where to go, how to proceed. It's one more clue to help him fulfill the will of the Writs. To help all his shattered selves find ultimate peace. Most crucially, to properly serve Austen.

He sees the pain in his ally's eyes and smiles back, reassuring her as best he can. His Delphi memories help some as he whispers a word of soothing power. The Black Cat, being one of the most perceptive and incisive thinkers in the worlds, immediately grasps the situation. She nods twice and smiles tightly back. Then she lets her face become a deathmask. "I repeat, Dodona Janjack, I had expectations of contact."

He gives her an elaborate bow, taking the time to sneak a look at the environment. They have taken a series of curving walks down to some old warehouse. He knows there's a Door not far from here. From several rooftops, the telltale glimmers of spyglasses give away their watchers' locales. Still, it's unlikely they can be overheard—merely watched by lip readers, perhaps recorded by magical devices. "You have my apologies. Please allow me to make it up to you."

He reaches out a courtly hand, and without thinking, she takes it. Then he splits worlds and walks without walking into the verdant fields of Morpheum. In a breath, he has opened a door with his Skeleton Key dropping himself and Sandoval Prestige in a new world. *Thump-thump* goes the heart. Three places at once, for all places wind through Chafrium, and then *thump*: they arrive in a fragrant field, sun warm on their skin, alone and unencumbered by spies of any sort.

The Black Cat blinks and then takes it all in. She starts with threat assessment, and when it's clear there are no obvious predators or assailants about to rush them, she snaps another clay tablet, granting them silence and freedom from scrying. For a few minutes she and Dodona may speak freely. She strides over to a small clump of tree trunks that seem to be fashioned for sitting. As she turns, the truth of the terrain becomes apparent. This is a park built from natural elements, subtly carved into something of a fairytale. The Black Cat knows this place well.

They sit at the outer edge, looking down on a rolling hill with several tiers of gardens and mazes. Fruit trees line a wide avenue that demarcates various lanes and sectors. Wherever there aren't gardens, hedge mazes or topiaries of mythical animals, there are wildflowers mixed with a low kind of golden grass, akin to wheat or oats but richer in color. The vista contains an entire landscape of gardens and mazes made of roses. On every corner and in small delicate patterns across the whole of it are lilacs. Each set of gardens seems to have a theme denoted by its type of lilacs, which are of every color imaginable. But between gardens, only large white lilacs stand, unthinkably tall and robust, with flowers giving off a heavenly fragrance.

Most visitors know without thinking that this must be some lover's garden, a love letter written in terroir and toil. There must be a million roses within. Everywhere erupt little clusters of butterflies and honey bees. Delicate alcoves hide hives and feeders for the butterflies. Ladybugs of green, red, white, and purple flit to and fro, glowing lightly with some kind of dweomer. It should be a riot of color and sound, a thick drenching of too many scents and textures draped one over the other in unpleasant excess. But there's magic here, strong magic that speaks to incredible restraint, to an ultimate sense of taste. This garden was meant to please, taking simplicity and raising it to the sublime. Nature crafted but not forced. Other than the topiaries, the only humanoid artifices that hint at agency are little fountains populated with flawless stone sculptures and obelisks.

Here and there walk liveried creatures, pleasant souls that look like the most noble version of an Egyptian scarab beetle crossed with a gardener. They all wear simple tabards of green and gold with a deep blue fleur-de-lis emblazoned on the chest. And they sing... how they sing. Soft humming notes that sound like Chopin or Yllmir'zin or perhaps the much celebrated Lady Nah. One such creature approaches, gives them a deep courtly bow, and deposits a genuine picnic basket by their feet. Then it gives a tut-tut-click and walks away with cheerful bustle. In his wake, Sandoval smells the lingering traces of bergamot, mandarin, and khettmali.

Dodona sits beside her. "It's called the Ansembourg Gardens. Sometime in the last century it arrived here, shaped from mists. The Nid, those beetle men, are servants of Lue Gim Gong, the Citrus Wizard, whom they believe to be the reincarnation of the Egyptian god Ash, Lord of all Agriculture and Oases. 'Ash' likely being from the Elven root *Aesh*, which many queens use." From when the Door was open 50,000 years ago and elves shaped human languages. *Aesh*, meaning both Life-giving and Connected to Nature. The root word implies supernatural vitality and interconnectedness with the core of reality, to be a seed of life itself and part of its necessary processes. *Mayim chayim.*

The Black Cat opens the basket and finds a thoughtful array of sandwiches with serviettes and fine china plates. Small jars of pickled vegetables are arrayed underneath in sealed glass with a latch. The poison sniffer on her lapel chimes cheerfully. She selects a long brown baguette with some kind of cheese and fresh honey. Dodona takes a vegetable sandwich of some sort on dark bread with a pungent mustard.

She gestures to the gardens. "This is a Terran place."

He nods. "How did you decide that?" They have not stopped talking about his memory or loyalties, but like all beings who are both strangers and friends, allies and opponents, these two servants of Powers step carefully. Even when alone and unguarded.

She shrugs. It's apparent to her how different Dodona and Delphi will be. "It's the size of the walks and statues, the way it wends to suit a human eye. Also, the colors are on a human spectrum rather than elven. Plus there's topiaries and obelisks which are from Terran mythologies." But that's not really why. Even if she didn't know the place well, her reasoning would be different. It's a lover's garden, and who but the Terrans are so invested in things as frail as romantic love? A million roses girded by thousands of lilacs, plums, figs, and berry brambles tended by sacred scarabs for all eternity? Utterly human. But not, she finds, pathetically human. The garden impresses her. This is worthy of notice, a work of supreme artistry which speaks to the highest of Terran genius.

Dodona takes a bite and smiles. The Nid make an excellent sandwich, and fighting has made him hungry. Sandoval pours them both some tea from a white pot she finds. Jasmine wafts from the cups. "No one actually knows for whom it was built. It's a dream made real."

Sandoval knows the story. Delphi told her many ages ago, when they were still allies. These gardens are really many places combined into one, many stories made whole by an abiding love of one *Wyl'halœ* for another. The English version, 'willow-gendered,' has spread across worlds that cannot quite pronounce Elvish words. The man-woman and woman-man, flexible, complex, passionate, and often given to wizardry. Among all the genders, this one has the widest interpretation, and for good reason. *Wyl'halœ* develop obscure, sometimes unthinkable talents. They are queer things, and from that mutable, at times exasperating nature, the term "queerness" has come to mean much the same as willowy—one queers fashion or context or language, one can queerly shift the mundane to the sublime or queer up art so its complexity implies layers of interlocking sensibility. Wizards queer spells, shifting them to suit a purpose, and queering a name means means making it a Name. It means refashioning the universe.

These two wizards, outcasts on ancient Terra whose Power came from a rare combination of elven bloodlines and mutation, could do more with a word, dream, or thought than their fellow humans. Feared and despised, ihm found one another, one a woman-man and the other supposedly a man-woman. The same and different, able to dance in and among roles. Ihm built a family, blended in and made art, made life, built a house and lived a good life. It is said that ihm are the architects of Terra's only unaligned Sacred Shrine: Bediani. If it's true, ihm were among the strongest native wizards in Terran history. Gone now, nameless but not forgotten.

That's also a truth rarely discussed; that magic, while it has advanced humanity and taken Terra so far, comes at a brutal price. In just Austen, the last free place, and this magic garden may humanity define their own destiny. But what of Kyiv or Amsterdam or the Citadel of Uluru? The Wizard Lords of Tintagel and the Mighty Healers of Highest Aotearoa would demur. Even there, the Elves stinking little treacherous fingers squeeze. They are the freest of enslaved places, but they are small, threatened, constantly compromising and making painful alliances, buying time or treading water. It's Austen, Bediani or bust.

Where is Bediani? In the former grounds of Ansembourg Chateau in the small nation of Luxembourg. It's why there's such a large contingent of Luxembourgers in Austen and the need for a janjack who speaks their language. Pilgrims from across the world and often beyond go to this place to find peace and to commune with the spirits of Nature. Sandoval has long suspected that this garden and that are one; Morpheum's Bediani has expanded and elaborated into something more magical. There's no dream here, just the manifest will of pilgrims' prayers.

She's been here often—it's one of her favorite places, because the gardens here and on Terra share one other feature. In every nook and among the various hedgerows and garden daises, you will find every kind of feline species known. *Wyl'halæ* love cats and cats love them. It's no stretch to say Sandoval Prestige, the Black Cat, adores cats, relates to them deeply. She finds much solace in this place, and it's a surprise to find that Dodona knows nothing of this, nor remembers his previous trips here as Delphi. After all, she showed Delphi this land and in turn he told her what she'd actually discovered in her travels. It was her friend Delphi who knew all the tales. He knew and this janjack clearly does not.

Dodona finishes his sandwich quickly—they do not have unlimited time under the spell, and he's aware. "Let's begin with the obvious." He's started in plain boring English. It's a clue for the Black Cat.

"You're not Delphi."

He sighs. "That's more than obvious. But I meant that I have the Vanguard of Delphi and the memories. It's part of his plan."

This stops Sandoval in her tracks, sends her mind in a different direction altogether. Grief can do odd things and for the Black Cat it's a rare luxury she cannot really afford. As if on cue, a clowder of black cats stroll by, each the size of a small pony. A family of panthers. "It means you're a construct."

"My own version of a troglodyte. Or rather Delphi's. Except I expire in another week when the Vanguard fades."

"So the obvious thing being that Papillon spoke to you in Terran code and not Elvish."

He nods. "It's the last big clue he gave me. There are gaps, pieces of knowledge Delphi didn't install into me."

She notices he does not say 'gave'. "He had to move fast, and from what I can still remember after the memory wipes, he had some real limits given the structure of the magics involved. Still, the tools and the Vanguard managed to come through. The Skeleton Key seems to work well."

He smiles. Delphi told him not to trust her and in his heart he feels a splinter of suspicion. Allies they might be, but the Black Cat serves the PAWs. Just last week she was trying to kill the old version of him. Troglodytes lose some free will. He's not really a trog, more like the garden here, a construct of a dream made living by the power of higher magic. But no less unfree. Duty and desire have become one.

"We're here to pick up a piece of jewelry. To see what Hoode saw."

The Black Cat opens several jars of pickles and samples. She offers him the ones she likes best. Olives brined in orange peel and chili. He tries one, finds it has been stuffed with almond paste, spices, and garlic. The taste explodes in his mouth, layer after layer of sour, bitter, spicy, and hints of sweet. He takes a few more.

"And you know who owned it?" she asks.

He nods. "I know more than that. I know exactly when it went missing and why. It's the message he's sending. A kind of extra kick in the guts to a man who no longer exists. When the Keeper of the Broken Ankh sold herself to the Dark God for power, he took the item as a way to cuckold his mortal enemy."

Sandoval's eyes fly open. It's a monumental level of malice, to plan centuries ahead for a subtle gesture of sadistic cruelty. To torture a man you've already defeated and humiliated simply to prove one's ability to do so. But of Hoode, one can believe anything. It is said he built an entire underground city three thousand years ahead of the event which led to Tawdry's death in Armax's arms—beneath a statue depicting the event. A statue that had stood in town square for so many lifetimes, no one knew what it signified or who it depicted. Armax of course went insane after and threw himself from a bridge. A bridge built thirty centuries before to facilitate his suicide.

It reminds her that the beings involved play on a scale of eons. This will be Ashlelani's pin, and it signifies something to Dodona. A message from a god to a near god in hiding. One that will help him find the missing heir and bring Lady Nia home safely.

"I have the Lady Queen safe, you know."

He nods. "I know. But she's not safe, not yet. The line of succession has yet to be established, and until it does, she's still potentially in the mix."

The Black Cat waves a hand. "She's always in danger, but

she's not really the heir. It's a known thing now, known enough to count as the prevailing truth. I have an ally watching her."

"Who?" What she says next will determine what Dodona decides must happen. More and more it's clear to him he's a man invested with just enough knowledge and memory to follow a trail of clues. As if the absent janjacks wrote a long, detailed note that became a living man. It appears for better or worse, he's one small man against a hostile universe, armed with items of legend and backed by janjacks and allies of enormous quality. A lone hero on a dangerous quest, an archetype come to life.

"My friend Sherrinford. She's reliable. That's all I may tell you."

The pieces knit together. The absent memories. The missing pieces and why Delphi held them back. The code in Terran rather than Elvish. The niggling desire to remember what has been erased. The connections between the Black Cat and Sherrinford, who somehow have not spoken to one another of Delphi.

At some point he rises and walks towards the temple beyond the garden, focused on seeing if his intuition proves correct. Behind him, the Black Cat follows. It takes a less than a quarter hour, as he passes by beautiful garden after garden, his eyes unable to see the ornate perfection within; he only sees the end result, the entrance of the temple soon to be ahead.

It's perhaps fitting that the Temple of Arüne stands near the dream gardens of Bediani. They are alike in so many ways. Simplicity raised to the sublime, faith and love imbuing humble stone and water with preternatural serenity. The temple is unlike any other to the sleeping god. It's a perfect sphere over one hundred paces in diameter, sunk one-quarter into the earth. One ascends the temple through carved stairs that curve up and in through the walls until one reaches the equator. On it an unadorned ledge rings the inside of the sphere, three bodies thick all around the structure. Exactly opposite the staircase, another winds down in reverse of the entrance, allowing penitents and curiosity seekers to descend to the ground contained within the temple. It's genuine dirt and grass, bathed in strange warm light that is somehow both day and night borne, lush in colors hot and cold. In the center is a reflecting pool set into the ground with a thin stone lip. The perfectly still, clean water within it shines with all the refracted light. The pool spans 33 feet, like all sacred geometry of the god.

Worshippers claim to have seen heavenly beings in the shadows, to finds scenes and themes played on the grey stone walls. Placebo effect? Delusion? Magic? There are shadows here aplenty and refractions of various prismatic types, on spectrums beyond Dodona's elf-blooded eyes. It's a place that simply reflects the pilgrim, the ultimate spiritual echo. On the grass, not far from the pool sits a small, nondescript box. Dodona has come seeking it and so it's here. Quantum effect. As he approaches he sees Sandoval Prestige behind him, and by the way her eyes scan the grass, it's clear she sees nothing.

A dream to find a dream—it's the wavelength of him that allows this. Delphi has considered everything. Has planned for this moment, when he will send a ghost of himself ahead in time to find the past waiting. Dodona opens the box and finds the hairpin as he remembers it. It's of the highest workmanship, an elaborate and overly filigreed affair of the type that pleases the Grey Elves. It reeks of manual labor and difficult toil, of master craftsfolk spending long months in excruciating delicate work making the subtlest of improvements. It sits there in the box, dead and forgotten. A lover's gift as barren as the lover's garden nearby is alive. The contrast could not be more severe, and that was assuredly the point of the placement. Hoode left little to be imagined when he could coerce a feeling from his opponents.

Dodona lifts the box in his hand. There is another item in it. A small lock of hair, a lover's gift perhaps. But also a dangerous item to bestow upon a wizard, let alone a god. He sniffs it, and memory assures him it's his old lover's. Rather, his old self's memory of that lover, for he has surely never met the woman in question. The tresses are folded in a single long leaf of the sacred blue gum, the single eucalypt in Chafrium. The trees give off antiseptic sap which has served as the base of medicines and poultices since time before Chafrium had walls. It has come to be a symbolic gift of purity for Elves, who have so little. A special symbol of first offerings, of entente.

He holds the hair in his right hand and the pin in the left. The hair has been preserved enough to still smell of all her perfumes and natural oils. The pin seems inert. He runs a finger along its teeth and feels the subtle scratch of hair. Ah. One begins to perceive. He sniffs the pin, and detects it. A change in her scent. A difference. And he incidentally realizes what ugly species sired his non-Elven half. The Laquint. The jungle savages of a dozen worlds, mercenaries and hunters who are famed for being able to track a quarry by scent alone. In snowstorms and across deserts or oceans if need be. They are possessed of a supernatural sense of smell. Austen and Chafrium have left nothing to chance. The body, the memories, the tools and allies, the positioning of Dodona, all led to this single moment.

Standing by the still waters of the sleeping god, Dodona knows who killed Jane Austen and why. He knows everything. He's one of a few beings alive who really see the whole game. He takes a slow steady breath and tries to keep his emotions contained. He dare not even think it; he certainly does not trust anyone enough to tell them. From here on, he plays silent and ruthless.

He drops the pin, hair, and box into the reflecting pool and watches as it sinks into the endless depths. Legend has it the pool dips down to the realm of Death herself. Another version states that Death has the same pool which rises all the way to the surface of Arüne's temple. If so, then he's sent the items to only being who will value them. While keeping them away from other agents and prying eyes. Does it bring satisfaction to Dodona to perhaps also thwart Hoode just a fraction? He smiles. It apparently does. His Vanguard flares for a moment.

All this time the Black Cat has watched him wordlessly. To her trained eye there's been a mistake, a screw up of sorts. Delphi has transferred himself into another janjack imperfectly. Despite his best efforts, he did not survive the gamble and now the worlds have a man inexperienced, barely alive, struggling to make sense of clues before him. She needs Sherrinford.

So it surprises her when he turns and confidently informs her that they are leaving. He will deposit her wherever she wishes to be, but he must go alone. The janjack formally submits a petition (backed by those damnable writs) for her help. Specifically, Janjack Dodona, Agent of the Court Royale, asks that the PAWs take ownership of Lady Queen Qelniasherah's immediate safety and well-being, that they deliver her unharmed and in good health to Coralaviere's coronation and bestow upon her this Writ. He then slices open his thumb and smears the Writ with it, sealing the device and rendering it useless to any save Qelniasherah and her agents, specified on the obverse as Sandoval Prestige, Sherrinford the Wise, and their designated sworn vassals.

The Black Cat stares at it for a moment and nods. She will consult Sherrinford as to the new developments and trust in her ally's superior mind. Dodona is not Delphi but he's no fool either. Whatever he's been tasked to do, he has found a sensible way to keep Lady Nia safe and allow her to move in the open. By deputizing the PAWs and Sherrinford independently, he has given Sandoval great latitude in arranging protection and has elevated the Guild, while at the same time making the former heir's safety the entire basis of their social cachet. More than that, he's fulfilled Austen's promise to return her but kept her outside the skullduggery of the court until the Coronation Party.

If bestowing the Black Cat with the Blazing Sun gave the Plumbing, Aqueduct and Watersmithing Guild a gutful of drama, this newest twist puts the entire society at permanent risk. Unless Qelniasherah returns and executes her Writ, they will face certain annihilation at the hands of the entire Court Royale. It's not just the King or some royals who concern them, they've been pitted against the whole of the three legged stool. Still, he's done Sandoval a favor. Both know it.

She held the Queen without authority, essentially kidnapping her. By converting this into a social issue, he's taken away most of the excuses her enemies may use to sideline or ambush her. He's forced rival Guilds to help her. If the PAWs fall, the Drowned Ones will use its peril to chop away at their avowed enemies; he's aligned one entire edge of the stool with the Court. Whatever their differences, he's made the enemy of her enemies a greater immediate threat. He's saved Qelniasherah's life and thrown in a Writ to keep that life safe. Which was his sacred duty and now hers.

The rest goes quickly. The Black Cat suggests a tunnel complex unseen where they might travel. Before she can even describe it, he's opened the Doors and taken her there. The Key knows the way. He bows to her in that hall, certain that Sherrinford's senses extend here, then winks to a wall that he suspects holds a magical eye and fades from sight. He's told her next to nothing, but she does not mind. She has her own plans and with the excess of Power he's handed her, she plans to enlarge it on behalf of Sherrinford, the Lady Nia, and unquestionably the PAWs.

She starts by making her way to the secure quarters of the ladies. Finding them well, she suggests they pack up and move. Where? To the surface of Chafrium, naturally; to a palace now open to her as Dodona's deputy, one of the old places abandoned recently by terrified looters. Already PAWs banners are unfolding in hundreds of properties thanks to the Writ. She just needs to have this particular one secured for them.

For this she asks Sherrinford's assistance, reaching out beyond the walls of the place to Austen. She's going to make a genuine old-fashioned telephone call. Who is she calling? First Claude the Giant and then The Packer's Paradise, a strange combination of pub and salon on the eastern edge of the city. When she's given Claude clear directions and emphasized the absolute stakes, she calls the High Ambassador of the United Nakota, Kniknik Derryberry.

The Nakota Nation—the combined nations of the Lakota, Dakota, Nakota, and unaligned Siouan speakers of the blighted plains—maintains a serious embassy in Austen. As a chief trading partner and owner of the northern edge of the city, they've come to see Austen as an ally against Terran and Elven encroachments. In turn, they provide wizards, healers, civilized speakers, and scientists as well as several rare agricultural products, and most importantly, mathematicians. The Ptesan-Wi University of Unified Math Wizardry has no parallel on Terra. Not even the Moscow Institute of Higher Mathematics and Magic can compare.

Kniknik Derryberry runs the embassy and co-owns The Packer's Paradise with her lover and partner Richard. No one knows his last name, poor thing; they just call him Mister Derryberry. The oddly normal Richard has many talents: he's perhaps the best bartender in the free world and one of the ten best on Terra, as well as a solid wizard, a rather smashing Opera singer, a serious alchemist with a positive genius for potions, and an abstract mathematician. Together he and his more famous lover run the fanatically supported tavern for Green Bay Packers Professional Lacrosse League boosters. Upstairs they run a biweekly version of the Austen Stitch and Bitch for crafters and alchemists, called the Brew and Bitch. Attendance usually requires four written peer-reviewed papers, two higher degrees, your own foldable explosion-tempered still, a note from the Packer's Boosters Guild certifying the applicant has never been witnessed cheering for the PLL's Bears or Vikings, and the secret password.

It's that password that matters: Sparklesaurus. Which also happens to be the name of the most outrageous theoretical mathematician/wizard in Austen. He's more mercurial than Hoode and supposedly less stable. What or who is Sparklesaurus? A strange man-child of a genius who conjures unicorns and unlocks quantum instability events for fun. He's just as likely to embroider underwear for male strippers as tilt a time vortex in a nine-dimensional toroid. He bakes rainbow cakes and glitters signposts. He rewrites the rules of transplanar string physics. Then he knits a sweater of alpaca and yeti fur in hideous puce, which he wears during the summer for effect. Sparklesaurus answers to no one, save Kniknik and Richard.

And Alice the bartender. How he survives the Horny Gorgon, no one knows. Some suspect Siouan spies keep the poor fool alive. Or Alice has Tock watch out for him. But he tends to be there or at the Embassy or drinking sweet punch at the Paradise. Richard and he tend to hash out unthinkably complex transplanar math sequences over new cocktails.

In a quirk of fate, the Terrans discovered a small wrinkle in wizardry that has been useful for the last century. They can encode energy via quantum cryptographic strings. For this you need a serious mathematician who does magic and vice versa. Richard and Sparklesaurus owe the Black Cat a favor, having lost a bet over the Packers vs Ahkwesáhsne Hawks two years ago. Conveniently, they are also premier security experts, able to encrypt Level Seven sigils and glyphs with an eldritch sequence and a bit of alchemy. Richard has a nice side business in making sigil paints that scramble upon drying, making world-class security affordable. Kniknik has a nicer side business selling the paints' formulae to various goblin clans through the back door of the embassy. As a result no one screws with the Nakota, who are rich, well-guarded, and on the very good side of the goblins.

When Claude shows up at the Packers bar on his massive motorbike, no one blinks. Richard has dragged Sparklesaurus from a kindergarten class where he was finger-painting what he claimed were invert Fibonacci sequences in the fourteenth dimension. As a result his fingers are bright orange. They match his current ugly sweater. They find a huge man on a huge bike which belches fire. Claude looks over and nods at Richard. Richard nods back, grabs his fellow wizard, and yells, "Get on the bike, bitch."

Sparklesaurus's fear of the bike seems understandable. Somewhere in the last few years, after several favors to his patron and companion Lady M'shylpsany, Claude acquired a unique gift: a genuine handcrafted racing motorcycle powered by a harnessed demon. Working with Hungarian technicians and several Orcish mechanics from the Chafrium track, they built him an oversize black and crimson monstrosity of steel, rubber, and hellfire. As Claude proudly tells it, the thing has 666 Hellpower instead of horsepower. Given the strength of the demon bound within, it's likely he's not exaggerating. The tail pipes belch flame when he rides, the thing emits great heaps of ragged black smoke and the headlight shoots a seventy-foot scorching flame on command. Because the Lady seems to adore Claude, it incorporates that newest craze among Terrans (and hugely supported by Orcs, Goblins, and the wild Hurgons of Cliffside): the entire cycle bellows epic Hard Metal Symphonia. It always plays Steppenwolf's "Eternally Wild" whenever it's started. Also, the damned thing flies at dangerous speeds.

Does the timid, finger-painting mathematician fear riding on a giant, fire-breathing, metal-blasting, flying Hellcycle? He does. So Richard shoves him behind Claude, straps in, and pats the giant on the shoulder. Sparklesaurus fears Richard more than pretty much anything. Richard knows Kniknik and everyone in Austen, except janjacks, rightly fear her wrath. In this fashion, the Black Cat receives two security wizards in record time, as well as a fighting contingent in the form of Claude and his cycle. The Drowned Ones camped at the Doors, the lurking demons and abominations in the street cannot fly. When people need to get things done quickly, Claude flies them there. Sometimes he even gets to use the flames. His gleeful anticipation of a good dogfight with flamethrowers, added to Claude's cheerful indestructibility, tends to dissuade casual ambushers. Professionals know better than to cross Sandoval, and so her charges arrive without incident at an abandoned palace on the Western edge of the inner city, the Merchant's District of Chafrium, where they lay spells, limn sigils, and generally create layers of encrypted traps for would-be assassins.

In time, an opponent will crack these things. They are of only minor usefulness. But for a few days, perhaps a week, the spells laid out will prevent anything short of an open assault by a full army from taking possession of Qelniasherah. Surprising everyone, Lady M'shylpsany, secretly returned from her adventures, arrives as well, having seen her friend blaze across the Chafrium sky. She brings minstrels and servants with a full buffet lunch, and once she understands Sparklesaurus's peculiar desires, some rare winter lion fur wool and knitting needles.

She comes, naturally, with her own small army, politely left outside. The Lady has declared for the former heir. Until her own succession and that of Kimber has been untangled, she's made it all but total political suicide to move against Qelniasherah. It would be seen as attacking Sæceæn's heir directly. She's also gained a lovely stronghold with the same protections the PAWs has afforded Lady Nia. No one ever mistook The High Grace for a fool.

Sherrinford brings Qelniasherah up from the sewers along several blind corridors and sneaks her into the place by a common carriage. Then they join the impromptu party in the grand foyer, which includes several key defense ministers for the PAWs, the Black Cat, the top generals for both Lady Nia's and Lady M'shylpsany's appointed Royal Guard, Claude and the mathematicians, assorted servants from various guilds, and three hundred select butler-soldiers from Chafrium's elite Society for Valets and Bodyguards.

In all, it's rather easily done. Between Sherrinford's meticulous planning and the haze of chaos provided by Coralaviere's disclosure of Delphi's will, the PAWs take possession of the palace with limited bloodshed, expel the spies therein, and scrub the listening devices they find. It's not perfectly secure, but for Chafrium, it's as close to safe as one can reasonably be. Enough so that visitors soon begin applying for tea and conversation.

That bastard Dodona has accomplished something few souls alive or dead may boast of achieving: he has sidelined the Black Cat for more than a few hours. For those watchers in the shadows, it's another subtle counting of coup worthy of the janjack, and an assurance that even with a new name and face, the same sharp strategy prevails. For her part, Sandoval understands she's been maneuvered. For possession of a Writ and the social cachet of hosting two Queens, she will endure it. She looks out the window as the carriages begin to arrive. It will be an endless stream of devious well-wishers, gossips, and shallow bon vivants. In a word: Elves. Somewhere Dodona forges onwards alone. She wishes him luck, then turns to the various complexities of the business at hand.

CHAPTER 12: LURED INTO INDISCRETION

The next movement of our many players comes from Caris, the distant favorite of Sherrinford (and perhaps Alice) and the bane of anyone scheming to do Chafrium harm. She moves in straight lines. Woe to those who block her path for they shall burn.

She's been sniffing out potential hiding places since the Broker laid out her peculiar news to the conclave. In three days, she's blown apart a warehouse of rat-men along with their illegal alchemy laboratory, murdered a few dozen Drowned Ones and Guild spies, punched Tock twice (once laying the troll out flat and winning herself a bag of silver talers), put arrows into the knees of six different smart mouthed bartenders, broken the arm of one of Kris-To-Buy-Me's chief lieutenants, had multiple teas with diplomats, agents, liaisons, and legates of trading houses, Guilds, and the Court, and been through a thousand square miles of sewer.

In that time Sherrinford has watched her from afar, keeping Killer Q away from the Huntress. Much as it pains her, Sherry cannot allow her friend to be taken just yet. She made a promise to both Evil Kitty and the late Delphi, whom she called Buggie after his species. Sandoval doesn't know it, but Sherry, Killer Q, Evil Kitty, and now Dodona, plus the Cats are Buggie Team. Now they have a Writ that testifies to that relationship. Sherry gave her solemn vow to keep Buggie Team going when it was clear Delphi had to make the ultimate sacrifice. She does whatever is necessary to keep her word.

All of which means the normally relentless huntress has not found her quarry. But she's experienced enough to intuit why. She knows of Sherrinford, as do most of the well informed immortals of Chafrium. When Qelniasherah arrives inside a PAWs-controlled palace with Sherrinford's simulacrums in tow, Caris nods. It's as she surmised.

She's also wise enough to understand that despite the Black Cat's precautions, certain well-placed and well-resourced assassins could still get within the Ladies' perimeter. She can think of several, but only two who weren't with her at dinner three nights prior: The Vampire and the Guildmaster. Kris-To-Buy-Me has been met, seen by our eyes; Caris, right as usual, has sensed the change in the predator's movements.

Who then is this Guildmaster? By tradition, no one knows. In practice as well, it's almost impossible to know the identity of the top killer within Chafrium's Assassin's Guild. The Guildmaster has been hidden from view by layers of magic and nanotech for close to three hundred thousand years. Each Guildmaster must add to the layers of protection and invisibility or be cast out— usually by their Second in Command.

Caris knows through eternities of deduction and careful record-keeping that the present Guildmaster is elven (though not which species), at least 700 years old, a woman of some gender, and connected as few have been in the past. She has direct access to the Skeleton Throne through a member of the Court Royale, perhaps more than one. Through blackmail, family ties, bribery, or mere usefulness, this leader of hired killers has become an extra vote on the Dais, one more Grey Elf in asbentia. She's also deadly.

The Court Royale, and the King specifically, must rely on the Guild for security. It's the great compromise so typical of Chafrium. As the Guild ascended and gained in influence and power, the Queens struck a deal. Over time the seesaw of attack and reprisal became a stalemate between the Children of Lomar and the Children of House Rexor. They solved it by combining forces. The Court would grant the Assassin's Guild legal fiat within Chafrium to execute killings given some minor legal limitations and also extend to them the much coveted franchise of Royal Guard. They went from being reviled outlaws to the sanctioned professionals aligned with Power. The Queens got a tamed, controllable Guild and the Guild got a hundredfold increase in political power along with a millionfold increase in wealth.

The Grey Elves codified the right to simply murder one's enemies, as long as they weren't of elven blood. Assassination as a way of managing business or social succession became more practical than sharing estates or power. No one familiar with Chafrium would mistake the Eternal City for a just one. The deal created order and, to a certain astonishing degree, peace,

It allowed the Guilds as a whole to flourish and to achieve brutal strangleholds over their rivals. Until, as with everything else in Chafrium, apartheid became the norm and the Haves put their Jewel Encrusted Boots on the necks of the Have Nots. Hence the Drowned Ones, the Academy which boasts an almost meritocratic belief in excellence and native ability, the love of Hoode and his fellow trickster gods, and the pervasive rise of demon worship among the oppressed classes. As the Terran Demonologist Marx once said, "Cults are the Opiate of the Masses and Demons the Messiahs of the Oppressed."

To blame the Assassin's Guild for the stratified social system in Chafrium would be unfair. It merely serves as the de facto mechanism for brutal enforcement of the status quo. The Guildmaster then represents the single most vile and hated sapient in the known worlds, and also one of the most secretly envied.

Unlimited power and free license to kill anyone not elven. Warrant of the Grey Elves, direct access to the King, spies and servants on every world, total right to travel without papers, wealth without taxation, an invisible kingdom that rivals anything built by a guild or priesthood. Second only to the bloody Grey Elves themselves. And this being may be any humble assassin within the Guild. Or someone unseen.

Alone among the guilds and universities, alone among the many worlds, conquered nations, and hierarchies of sociopolitical control brokers, Chafrium's Assassin's Guild operates entirely on merit. They require a few simple things: fanatical loyalty, fanatical efficiency, and a total willingness to take another's life for payment. Anyone ruthless and driven may climb the Guild's ranks and in theory become the Guildmaster.

This is not idle fantasy. In the Guild's long recorded history, at least a third of all Guildmasters started as qualified apprentices who had neither family nor education. As a result, the Guild attracts its own potential enemies. Anyone with enough intestinal fortitude to fight and kill for freedom finds in the Guild the easier, softer way. Plus it offers to let those potential revolutionaries and radicals travel across worlds to murder their enemies. Up to a certain point, they may comfortably sleep at night believing they've served a higher good.

That's what Caris knows is out there, lurking beyond the fragile glyphs thrown up by a pair of Terran wizards. As good as the well-recommended Richard and Sparklesaurus are, the mere promise of a place inside the Guild's inner circle would drive thousands of the universe's most ruthless operatives to take unthinkable risks to help the Guildmaster infiltrate the PAWs' estate. If she made it her sole pursuit, she would eventually discover the Guildmaster. That knowledge alone will be driving the enemies of Lady Nia and The High Grace to distraction. Move and countermove. Constant paranoid assessment is the Great Game. Caris won't play it. She's the one who rips the board in half and proceeds forward.

So she does the logical thing: informs Smoojak of her plans over afternoon luncheon, then cleans herself in the grotto, garbs in formal dress, and advances upon the secured palace to request an immediate audience with their Royal Highnesses. At the very least she may pass on her concerns to Sherrinford (whom she's never actually met) and to alert the generals under the King to the potential conflict of interest in their security arrangements. Her Infinite Majesty Lady M'shylpsany and The Lady Who Waits Qelniasherah Greyleaf both need rely on the suspect Guild.

When Caris reaches the palace, it creates a stir. She's come in formal tabard of forest green over ornate chain mail, a ritual saber and pistol, her famed bow, and a small tiara of river stones and platinum crafted for her by Smoojak. Her auburn hair glitters with strands of brighter red—she's braided them into a single Dutch Braid, in elvish *Thruillhyn* or Hair of the Warrior

Queen, with the same river stones. On her feet she wears boots of dragon-hide leather. It helps everyone remember that she is not only among the few in Chafrium who have seen such a mythic beast, but has slain one singlehandedly. The boots also happen to be nearly indestructible and classically stylish. In Chafrium and worlds beyond, they've become so legendary there's an idiom which has been translated into most every language: "You might as well wear Caris's boots," meaning the task or dream is so far beyond your limits it's pointless.

The protocol officer behind the ranking major domo spits his tea and begins to panic. He signals to dozens of runners. A Power has come to attend upon his Ladies and without Any Prior Warning. The complexities of trying to stall long enough to get both Ladies freshened and relaxed for a visitor, in the right matching costume, while in no way insulting Caris would send stronger men into conniptions. This one just begins to stutter as he issues commands, many pointless or contradictory.

In under a minute the Black Cat has made it to the door. Several high ranking Grey Elves with courtly designs begin to tut and mutter, beginning the low hush of gossip that feeds their existence. The entire antechamber buzzes with various contortions of excitement, jealousy, resentment, anticipation, and scheming. One look from the PAWs' assassin quiets the room. In a fraction of a second these divas go from Alpha predators of the social set to cornered prey. A moment later Caris enters and gives the quieted throng her momentary attention. No one dares breathe.

Sandoval Prestige gives her counterpart a courtly bow. "Your Grace, on behalf of the Plumbing, Aqueduct and Watersmithing Guild, I extend my heartfelt and most sincere greetings. May I personally thank you for coming on such short notice."

She does not fool Caris, nor has she meant to. But she has done a right thing, which requires of the Huntress some polite reciprocation. While they have worked in one another's vicinity for decades, Caris has never been formally introduced to the Black Cat. She gives the sharp-looking woman a short bow and a genuine if brief smile. "Well met. Am I to assume you are Sandoval Prestige, Chief Assassin of the Guild?"

"You surmise correctly, Your Grace. I am she. At this time I am also the highest-ranking representative of the Guild present."

Caris nods. It places her under some small constraints if she wishes to continue being polite. So far, this Black Cat has been cautious, intelligent, and succinct. She thinks she might like her, and thus it pleases the dangerous Power to continue in a well-mannered fashion. It helps, of course, that neither woman has a scintilla of falsity within her.

Caris sweeps her hand before her, and a table materializes within the palace. On it are several baskets laden with rare herbs, pheasants, and fresh fruits from distant lands. A treasure of sorts, and one appropriate to the Huntress's domains. Sandoval bows and inspects the gifts as she must. The aroma pervades the room, and many of the schemers give way to indelicate sniffing.

While the onlookers goggle, calculating in their own manner the value of such treasures, the origin of the table hits home. This is a genuine Undertown pedestal table, recovered from the city built to doom Tawdry and Armax. Given its pristine condition, the single piece of furniture would ransom a king. These tables also happen to be highly magical, having been contaminated with time shift radiation. The Black Cat has used her stint inspecting the fruit to think through what Caris' gift tells her. First, that her security has been breached and that her glyphs are either down or severely damaged. Second, that Caris wishes to inform her without fanfare and to do so in a manner which only professional soldiers and wizards might understand. Third, that her Ladies are now in serious danger, likely already under attack.

She cocks her head and listens. In some far stateroom on the east side of the building there can be heard muted screams. "Come this way." She turns and leads the Huntress towards whatever fight has begun within her palace, drawing weapons as she sprints. Behind her Caris keeps pace, her bow strung and two arrows knocked.

As luck would have it—if we still believe such things exist in Chafrium—both Ladies have deviated from their schedules.

Her High Grace, growing bored of the tiresome sycophants and tea-drinking snobs who beg to attend upon her, has retired to her rooms, where Claude regales her with the tale of his passage into Chafrium and his rather obvious disappointment that no one flew up to fight him. As it's the Lady and Claude, by custom very intimate friends, no one bothers them for a fair while. Her guards simply ring the outer door and lower the sound-deadening curtain that provides some modicum of privacy.

For her part Qelniasherah, having gotten a taste for work from Sherry, has wandered into the baking kitchen to find Sparklesaurus decorating petits fours and elf cakes with obscene shapes. She mixes her own batch of frosting and joins him. Between them, they spend an amicable morning with both the savory and sweet pastries. The baffled master chefs dare not intervene, though they thoughtfully provide their visiting Queen with some suggestions and create additional versions in another kitchen, sans the indecency.

What's worse, they cannot stop the insouciant Sparklesaurus from answering Lady Nia's questions regarding planar physics, thirty-dimensional mathematics, and crypto-magic. He does not speak in small words nor water down his ideas. He makes the rather bold assumption that she wants to know and proceeds in excruciating detail to explain how and why interlocking mathematical equations matter when combining magic, nanotechnology, and paradox articles from godly realms.

Qelniasherah has had an extensive education, including foundations in most magic. She also has layers of nanites and body-bound spells built to adapt to her own interests. Her time with Sherrinford has raised the young queen's intellectual interests and expanded them; she activates several layers of her own quantum nano-magic interface and forces it to help her, which translates the ideas from abstruse to merely difficult. Lately, she's been finding she enjoys difficult things and so rises to the challenge.

She spends the morning learning to see the weave within the palace and to read the various control strings vibrating on multiple frequencies in and out of phased reality. For the rather insane Sparklesaurus, these are just things he sees and accepts.

With work, she can perceive them and read them if she focuses. To simplify, she designates them with colors. Blue for operative, gold for harmonized, and red for broken or under strain. The mechanisms within her mental interface do the rest. For the rest of her long life, Lady Nia will be able to turn on this augmented vision and inspect highly complex magical structures with relative ease.

So it's she who first see the red lines, one popping up after the other. After the fifth one, she stops piping puce icing on bittersweet rusks and follows the trail. One by one the lines waver and then turn red. She doesn't know what she's seeing, but she's smart enough to know it cannot be good. Whether it's an attack, a glitch, a feedback loop that will correct itself, or some other magical side effect, she feels strongly it must be addressed. Sherry has several bodies in the palace, but her main self has taken up guarding Qelniasherah's suite. They've taken to calling her body Vordosil Prime, VP.

By the time she makes it to her suite, the attack has already begun. She finds VP kneeling, fighting off a gorgeous woman covered in thick red lines of stuttering ugliness. The whole of the attacker seems wrapped in broken magic. All she can see is this monster's hand stuffed into Vordosil's chest and all sorts of codemagic pouring into the construct-self. Thanks to hours of planar physics she happens to know exactly what she's looking at: this woman is trying to absorb Sherrinford while pouring an infection back into her body-shapes.

She responds without thought. She severs the red lines pouring into her friend's body, drags Vordosil behind her, then kicks he attacker across the room. Sherrinford rolls onto all fours and begins heaving foul code and disgusting chunks of fluid disease onto the rare carpets. The stink overwhelms the place. Qelniasherah realizes there's no room for retreat, nor can her friend be moved.

So does the Vampire. As Caris suspected, the living plague has been persuaded to move early by another anonymous force. Kris-To-Buy-Me has been smuggled into the palace in fifteen pieces and reassembled by eating the beating heart of one of her many servants. Guards have been reassigned and a corridor opened for the fell Power. At long last she will be given her desire, for in this palace lurk several High Elven snacks ready to be devoured.

She finds the High Grace's rooms annoyingly guarded and moves onwards, across the palace, siphoning the flesh and soul anyone who crosses her path. She dines well before she makes it to Qelniasherah's suite and finds the ultimate treasure waiting—another construct. In this guardian she sees a better body, a permanent home which she knows will be far more indestructible and enduring. The codework alone seems beyond imagining.

Like any good ambush predator given an opening, The Vampire does not hesitate; she pours all her violence and hatred into a single thrust to the chest and vomits every particle of her being into the soul matrix of her enemy. If it succeeds, she will be this being. The Vampire knocks her opponent to the floor and roars with lust. All that she is, all she has ever wanted and needed, she throws into the fight.

Then comes a bright light and broad pain. She's thrown across the room and smashes into a pane of glass, perhaps a mirror. Small cuts tear at her outer flesh and worms ooze from her. She has been desecrated, severed from her think-do-lust-hate-self. Much of her outer being has been vomited onto the floor, lying defenseless behind this offender. She does not think; she simply lets the dark fiend within claw its way out of her flesh and charges at whomever has interrupted her meal.

Qelniasherah's never had to use her power in a deadly fashion. As Sherry's attacker transforms into something large, foul, and demonic, Lady Nia's magic skin begins to burn. Layers of armor match her inner rage. The panic that comes from hearing Sherry suffer behind, unsure if she will live or die, turns her cold. And in this cold place she finds she has the imagination of her ancestors and power as she never dreamed she might want. But now she and Sherry need it. She dips her soul into that well and sucks up every bit of the fire she finds. Before she can decide on cogent action, her left arm grips a solid night table and heaves it into the monster's stomach. The Vampire has too much strength and momentum to be halted.

But Killer Q just gotten a taste for murder; she lifts her enemy off the ground, sending her crashing into the opposite wall.

The room looks smothered in huge coils of diseased spasming red, magic inverted and obscene. She burns it all, the green fire she used on the mice turned up a thousandfold, disruptive to the sub-quantum level. Her enemy screams and the whole room thunders with her agony.

This makes the Cold Queen smile. She spears a lance of pure fire into the Vampire but it does nothing. Whatever she is, she's nigh immortal. Whatever she spews might be broken and breakable, but this thing before her, this stalking husk, has unlimited layers of red lines. A thick red umbilical cord leaves this plane and descends to whatever version of Hell will have her. Still, the fire hurts the Kris-To-Buy-Me something fierce and that generates its own satisfactions.

Beam after beam, blast and wave of burning hatred, she pushes the ambusher back and out into the exposed hallways. For her part The Vampire screams in frustration. The body blows hurt as they shred her exterior, forcing her to waste precious stored lives to rebuild herself. This enemy has stolen centuries of soul fat from her. Her squeals shatter eardums and break lamp sconces. She jumps back, veils herself in a fog of sewage and summons her zombies.

The floor explodes with hands as hundreds of mindless thralls try to claw their way into the palace from the sewers below. This should disconcert the Queen, and were she still Gnash, it would. But this fight has killed Gnash the Rash; Nia the Cold Killer wakes up. She flicks her hands and activates a series of protocols her trainers drummed into her recalcitrant skull a century ago. Somewhere, in the Court Royale a whole set of displays wake and command sets are sent across the known universe. She's sounded the equivalent of a klaxon on a psychic level. Her mind sends images of the targets with complex evaluations and threat assessments.

Several of her tutors will add to the Vanguard by end of day, because her mind proves a keen blade. The Vampire does not yet realize whom she's fighting, and now, with the Queen acting her station, Kris-To-Buy-Me has just picked a fight with the entire clan of all known Grey Elves. Worse, she's picked a fight with someone fighting to protect their *Sylslaymynar*. Correction—a Queen in her own realm protecting her *Sylslaymynar*.

If there's one thing the Elves know, it's overkill by ostentatious display. Take, for example, the Steel Eels. A lovely kind of deterrent mechanism. The eels are living things of ten feet's length fused with molten steel and necromancy to become undying machines that literally eat through the enemies of the Throne. They fly, like Claude's motorcycle only faster, and to add proper terror, they phase through solid objects including armor, sigils, and such trifles. They are the unstoppable first wave of the Grey Elven Court's self-defense.

In seconds they converge on the tortured corpses below the palace and shred them. Qelniasherah doesn't wait. She delegates the problem to the Throne's automated defense network and advances on the scum who dared attack Sherrinford. She owes a debt, and she thinks she knows how to pay in full. Her cold mind races as she weaves the spells. By the time she meets the Vampire in the hallway, she's ready. She stares down the demon with a regal smile that evokes winter.

Kris-To-Buy-Me feigns weakness, hunched and panicked as she moves closer. Then she pounces, and to her surprise, the Elven woman before her lets down her guard. She wastes no time, biting down on an exposed arm, tearing flesh from bone. Then cruel laughter greets her as her teeth shatter. A warm gush of hot delicious blood pours down the Vampire's parched throat before she's tossed back into a yielding wall. She has a taste of her now, and that hunger, that first blood maddens Kris-To-Buy-Me.

She's a thing of plague and poison. All Kris-To-Buy-Me has to do is wait, stall the fight, delay her enemy and the fetid shall rule. She smiles her own cruel smile, letting precious blood drip down her damaged chin. She changes tactics. She bows elegantly and introduces herself, placing a spell of hebetude upon her words. "I am the Lady Queen Kris-To-Buy-Me, often called the Killer Bee. With whom do I have the pleasure of doing battle?"

The fool girl takes her bait and bows back, her face a shining mess of arrogance. Already one can see fever touches her brow. Her pale eyes glitter with excitement. The Vampire knows this look, the flush of infection, the delight of being invaded. She will own this walking corpse and wear her skin as a trophy. "Well met. I am the Regnant Queen in Waiting, her Supreme Ladyship Qelniasherah Greyleaf of the Houses Lomar, Lyska and Zoëæ. Often called Killer Q." She lets the title sink in. Suddenly the Vampire realizes her gross miscalculation. She's an ambush predator, not a fighter, and this girl has abundant tools for a fight.

As if on cue, the Black Cat and Caris arrive down the hallway. The Vampire's hands are pinned to the wall with arrows and her knees dissolved by rapid shots from the Black Cat's repeater. Still the regal queen stands before her, her eyes feverish. The Vampire summons the strength to pull herself free, to flee into the sewers and wait for the infection to take hold of her victim. But she cannot. Her innards feel cold, so icy cold.

Then Nia approaches her and gives her the most condescending sneer imaginable. "Do you have any last words, you diseased bitch?"

Kris-To-Buy-Me tries to speak but finds the words muddled, her mouth a travesty of paroxysms. Her fingers twitch and the cold seeps into her legs. She sees little globs of her body shape falling to the floor. The girl mocks her, holds her hand to her ear as if to listen. The damned Elf knows her tongue has disintegrated. It makes the Vampire shake and she begins to weep, a thing she has not done for true since she arrived in the sewers all those ages ago. Something sharp grabs her by the throat and she feels an insistent tug. She's melting from the inside, collapsing down into herself, unable to breathe or think, robbed of reason.

The Vampire dies before witnesses, fragmented by the blood of a Queen. Thanks to her hours of instruction, the fast-thinking and ruthless Qelniasherah rewrote her enemy's code from within, using the love doll's penchant for invading her prey to infect her in reverse. She supplied the red lines with an override command. What The Vampire tried to do to Sherrinford, Killer Q has done to her. She unravels this Power, letting her magic tear apart centuries of wasted lives and dreams. All of it running down into the sewers, downwards to the final realms of the monster's origin.

The quest to find Gnash the Rash has ended. It ends here in this broken palace. Qelniasherah has saved herself and found herself. She has made a family and defended them with her lifeblood. She has earned her first Star. Within minutes the palace floods with guards and, most dreadfully, the King himself.

To his credit, Sæceæn achieves the High Elven equivalent of coming alone, bringing the bare minimum of ministers, assassins, servants, spies, and agents of his allies, plus a minor army which kindly waits outside. Coralaviere attends him personally, the two men livid at this direct attack upon their demesne. Both are aware that someone within the Guild has betrayed them. Add to this the social embarrassment incurred by having to personally apologize to the PAWs and Caris individually and together after making a personal inspection of the battlefield. They are chastised to see a defiant young woman standing fast at the center of the chaos, issuing commands and making clear which arrangements she wants executed to repair her palace.

When the King tries to speak to his niece, she rebuffs him gloriously and demands in her most regal manner that he and his Seneschal, having been entirely errant in providing adequate and trustworthy security for her guests, immediately see to her injured *Sylslaymynar* Sherrinford the Wise. It's a masterstroke that levels the room; an act of perfect Eldessery and Elven one-upmanship that proves so impressive Caris swears appreciatively under her breath and cracks a smile. The Black Cat actually chuckles and Coralaviere, ever the gallant servant of his Crown and Clan, bows low to the Lady in full view of the universe—the Legend Makes the Lady, and the Lord Seneschal serves his King by giving her full public credit for her very Queenlike reproof. For his part, the King raises an eyebrow, grunts, and does what he's asked.

Across the known planes Qelniasherah has just informed the forces of civilization she can and will back down the

King himself to protect her family; she's labeled Sherrinford a Noble and bestowed upon her various patents and titles by mere inflection; she's pissed all over Guild security and taken the missing Guildmaster down three social notches without speaking a word; she's represented her fair sex properly and shown true Regal Poise; and she's gotten her way start to finish, executed real command, and made the single most powerful individual in the universe do her damned will. She's been a Queen.

In return the King carries Sherrinford in his arms down to the kitchens, where he personally washes her off under a sluicing nozzle and sees to her wounds. With the help of his Seneschal, he diagnoses the various infections and entropies attacking the Intelligence under the skin and considers. His niece has named her an Elven confidante and she did defend his own flesh and blood for days. He pricks his ring finger and feeds the Holy Blood to Vordosil. It burns through her skin, making pitted holes where the magic carves away the homunculus underneath.

Coralaviere holds the startled Queen as she tries to rush to her friend's side. Has Sæceæn killed Sherry? The kind eyes of the Seneschal tell her differently, as do those of Caris. So she waits, she tries to be elegant despite the fear within her. Beside her, the Black Cat nods in approval. Then slowly, the body of Sherrinford shakes and what was Vordosil changes. Beneath, an Elven woman takes shape and breathes. While she will never be a beauty on the scale of Princess Meleyasza, she appears strong, young, and most intriguingly alive. The King of All Worlds has made Sherrinford a flesh and blood being.

As Sherrinford wakes, Qelniasherah takes her hand. The newly born woman pulls her friend close. "Q, please don't let Caris see me like this. I wanted to make a better impression."

The Queen nods. "If it would please your collective Graces, I would like to spend a few minutes with my *Sylslaymynar* to thank her for her courageous defense of my person earlier this afternoon."

The Black Cat, as host, ushers the collective party out into the dining halls, winking at Lady Nia as she goes. Caris gives them both a blank-faced look and then turns. She seems almost confused to the young Queen. All depart as requested, soon to be replaced by an appropriate level of servants armed with clothing and toiletries. Both the newly invested Ladyship Sherrinford and the rather gruesomely splattered Lady Nia wash, refresh, and get into clothing appropriate to taking tea with their King.

When they emerge, they find the Lord Seneschal Coralaviere waiting. He holds forth a bundle in a simple blanket, making a sharp, utterly respectful bow to Sherrinford. In Highest Court Elvish he addresses her. "Your Ladyship Sherrinford, may I personally thank you on behalf of the Great Houses and the Lord King for your steadfast support of our Queen. You have served us well ere we even knew to honor thee, and I ask a boon of thee thereof." He bows again and reveals the contents: a saber and pistol of extraordinary beauty.

Sherrinford knows the ritual words. She's read them hundreds of thousands of times. She's just been granted a Sancurion; she knows this by how the Seneschal addresses her. He's about to ask her to accept a ritual sword, and in so doing she will be elevated. Her skin prickles and little sensations of discomfort move through her unfamiliar biology. She's excited. "What does thee and thine ask of me, Lord Seneschal?" She gives him just the right curtsy that she practiced in her mindvault so many millions of times. Only this time she's doing it in real meat life!

"Please accept this sword and pistol as eternal tokens of our gratitude with all honors that accrue as a result. We invite thee to call upon the King at thine leisure, name thee Friend of the Court and," here he surprises the room, "Demi-Seneschal to mine and thine, Chief Seneschal hereafter, such as she deigns, to her Royal Highness Queen Qelniasherah." He bows at the stunned woman. She takes the blade and by rote wraps it and the pistol on her waist.

A Vanguard springs into being, and in an Elven breath, Sherrinford, the computational intelligence, becomes the seneschal of her best friend—a confidante not just of Qelniasherah but now the Lord Seneschal Coralaviere, who has made her one of his personal deputies, the chief of Lady Nia's security, and in the process outrageously wealthy. She can afford to buy her own stacks hundredfold and build entirely new versions of her mind on any world she chooses.

He leans over and kisses her cheeks. She smiles at her new boss and assesses him in milliseconds. She knows much about him anyway, but her newly advanced mindself and the extraordinary magic the King has incorporated into her matrixed planar selves means she can think farther and faster. She knows he's loyal to the extreme and will serve Qelniasherah fanatically. She knows he was Delphi's friend and decides that whatever else Coralaviere is, Ral the Swordsman is part of Buggie Team; perhaps by definition its leader now that Delphi is gone.

They share a moment and it's clear that at a later time he will gladly answer all her questions. She bows again, properly and with great pleasure, then beams and shows her friend the acquired sword. Qelniasherah views it and then frowns. "But my Lord Coralaviere, this is your sword and pistol."

He gives her a bow. "Of course, my Lady. My clan's sword and gun shall ever after be at your side, proof that the office of the Seneschal serves you always." He gives her another bow, courtly and rather flashy, done for the room. Both of them know this sword has been in his family for six hundred generations. He's just adopted Sherrinford as his own daughter. For the Elves, such acts are done quickly and through symbolic gestures. Everything ruled by etiquette, everything simplified in the extreme. The stunned young women look at one another and then laugh.

It seems the appropriate response to a wild afternoon. The rest is simple. Servants find a lavish room undisturbed by the warfare at hand, set it up for High Tea, lay out the chairs and tables, then invite a few hundred of the waiting gentry and royals in various foyers to an impromptu meeting with the Royal Family and watch as tongues wag.

As Lady Nia and Sparklesaurus's perverse pastries and sweets make the rounds, the various strivers and aspirants for high style take note. Within a week, given the bent of the conversation and the enjoyment had by all Royals on the Dais, hairstyles, hors d'oeuvres, and clothing styles shift. Glitter, puce, and ornate mathematical designs will enter the culinary vocabulary. With her first major military coup Qelniasherah also sets her own social agenda, and those among the Elven set who prefer her or M'shylpsany (or, gods forfend, the King himself) will be branded the Braided Ones or Bloody Motorists ever after. They will buy automobiles, openly wear fighting blades and combat boots, braid their hair in the style of Caris, and generally act like fiercely feminine tomboys en route to a motorized war. It's so compelling a look that the Drowning Ones will add flannel and hairpins, paint their hair shocking red, and declare it Neo-Anarchic Lady Gothic.

Once tea has been served and the various gawking aristocrats and hangers-on attended to, speeches and honors begin. Given the starkly momentous occasion of an Imperial Visit with a Power in attendance, the PAWs can smugly brag for years at cross-guild functions. The King wisely does not invest the Black Cat with any honors, instead doling them out to various PAWs delegates and paying Sandoval with additional talers and a Skeleton Key which she may wear in her *Kes*, her secret heart. It's the opposite of the Vanguard, the secret personal place only an authorized few may see. It's literally inside your own body— the act of seeing the *Kes* requires something akin to surgery or sexual intercourse. One does not speak of the secret heart any more than the action of the bowels or the graphic details of a robust sexual encounter.

Coralaviere finds himself with one of the King's old family swords from the time of Lomar, apparently one of the original Caris's old blades. This makes the present Caris smile queerly and change the subject. Qelniasherah escapes with a Star and Holy Leaf (bestowed for not starting a war with Austen, of all things), some light chastisement over her disappearance, and a firm promise to have the palace ceded to the PAWs in her name as a personal thank you from the King.

Witnesses say they've never seen the King more cheerful. In an hour, Qelniasherah has transformed total disaster for the Court Royale into the social coup of the season. The Lady M'shylpsany demands a full accounting of the story from every angle, making helpful comments and pointing out the extraordinary bravery of all involved. She's the ultimate social booster and the royal witness to Qelniasherah, throwing her full support behind the young Queen. In return for her and Claude's robust laughter at the right moments, Qelniasherah gives the High Grace a garden chateau on the far edge of the City. It has a large open field, facing the favelas and rubbish gardens, which would be perfect for an automobile track.

As royal bequests go, it's among her very first and wisely done. The chateau has been a thorn in the side of the Queens for over three centuries. One of her ancestors acquired the uncomfortable house from a horse-racing wager she fully expected to lose. The original owner had apparently hired drunk hobgoblins to decorate, resulting in a pastiche of the worst style excesses of the struggling classes. Every room clashed in both color and texture, covered in bad art, tasteless furnishings, or tacky chandeliers and candelabras. On two occasions, the elves resorted to attempted arson to remove the property, but to no avail. As a racetrack clubhouse, it might do nicely.

Lady M'shylpsany seems delighted despite the home's terrible reputation. She's not one for convention and might just knock the structure down to build a mechanic's garage. She, the King, the Seneschal, and several other nobles who quickly make themselves present add various titles and honors to Lady Nia's Vanguard. But that Star—it takes all breath away and convinces the world that another Queen, true and proper, resides within Chafrium. By end of day a million voices will sigh and wonder aloud if it isn't just a little tragic that so worthy an heir as Qelniasherah cannot succeed their worthy King. The Lady Who Waits is waiting no longer. The whole universe has found her.

Eventually, investigations will be carried out and agents dispatched to understand how palace security was so thoroughly breached. It will take time, precious time, to do so. By then the guilty parties will be far from Chafrium or dead and dumped in a sewer, depending on their importance to the Guild. It's an open and known thing that the Assassin's Guild has failed its King. It must repair the relationship or face opprobrium not seen since the Great Succession Battle during the reign of Queen Gurgaranel, when five separate heirs died under their watch. They lost two Guildmasters in a week to that little hiccup and paid tens of millions in weregild to the Court Royale.

One could not exaggerate the disaster that has befallen the Guild this afternoon. Whomever set loose The Vampire inside the palace intended to murder two heirs and change the line of succession. Which goes to the core of the Guild's crime— meddling with politics. No one cares that they tried to ruthlessly dispatch a pair of rising Queens; it was a very elvish thing to do. Nor would they have been in nearly as much trouble had Kris-To-Buy-Me succeeded; she would have covered her tracks, likely burning down the palace to hide her passage and feeding. Arson is also an elvish pastime. But they tried to play politics and failed. In Grey Elvish terms there can be no greater sin than transgressions left unresolved.

News of this trickles out into the streets, carried by gleeful Drowning Ones committed to the free press. From there, radiominds convey the various versions of news, gossip, tabloid journalism, and agitprop to various sympathetic substations for commodification and dispersal in local language and idiom. It takes a mere few hours for the outlandish story of a Power gaining access to the person of a Queen to splash across dining tables and café counters. The epic tale of how the young Queen slew the reviled Vampire and saved her sacred honor receives any number of treatments—most of them sympathetic and a few downright hagiographic.

CHAPTER 13: THE FOX

Abraham the Elder looks like a shaggy version of an old pirate, complete with scraggly white hair, eyepatch, and a poorly constructed false leg. Ghostsea being a plane of relative minor status as well as a squalorous place plagued by bad roads and worse weather, it has taken Dodona almost a full day to walk and sail the distance from the closest Door to the Last Inn, which sits beside the churning waters of the aptly named Sea of Madness. By the time he gets under the cover of the Inn's threadbare roof, sleet has started to drop in black clumps of ice, accompanied by a burning rain. That's the way of it here, where the weather kills and the ocean reduces living souls to psychosis.

The main species here turns out to be Dweorves, though not at all like the ones of Undervault. These might be termed Trow, the black-skinned schemers of barrows below the scarred earth. There's nothing kind or cheerful about this dolorous lot. Their skin endures fire and mocks the absent sun, they hammer away in pitch-black sietches far beneath the ragged rains, building fine weapons and tools of an obsidian hue. The only light comes from massive bonfires and forges stoked with a kind of magical coal known for its deep blue-white hue and high magnesium content.

These Trow are thickset and cruel-featured, their eyes reddish and their hair the only thing darker than their skin. It is said a proper Ghostsea blade may be judged by whether it's blacker than the hair of the smith who forged it. They are also cultic worshippers of the revenant undead—mummifying their ancestors and transforming them into ghastly repositories of

myth and law. Below the Dark Forges of the Trow lurk the Inner
Councils who Sightless See. It sounds even more ominous and
rueful in their chaotic language of clicks and hisses.

The acid rains and fire breathing wildlife fuss them not the
least. The local undead lords and cursed princesses running
amok tend to be their only nod to being colorful. There are no
ruined castles here. Everything stays in relatively immaculate
kit, though the corrosive nature of the weather tends to shred
wood and leather. Though every gender finds some safe harbor
here, it's usually men who have lost all drifting into the various
seaports and shanty villages.

Ghostsea has a thriving business in perishables as well as
brightly colored trade goods attractive to those who serve lonely
men: valets, prostitutes, blackmailers, thieves, gold-diggers,
and gamblers. Cheap trinkets and brilliant steel, the paradox
of the place where offworld traders buy goods with talers then
take them back at a profit, handing over the most pathetic and
garish items that lowborn and often dimwitted males think
their paramours will desire.

Most of Ghostsea (as the name strongly implies) lives under
water. What land exists juts out like angry fingers from the caustic
ocean; the mountainous island kingdoms sport treacherous
reefs and shallows which demand master seamanship. The
plane thus attracts good sailors and pays extremely well for any
navigator-wizard who will endure time on a ship. Sailors beget
shipwrights beget barkeeps and more prostitutes and then
every manner of wharfbound lowlife imaginable. The whole of
the Chafrium docks could not compete with the kind of vicious
scum that Ghostsea breeds. Instead, they trade up, making the
Eternal City's very best riverdogs and teamsters.

Dodona has no memories to guide him. The strange lack of
goblins makes the whole place rather eerie for an Austen janjack.
The open use of the undead and their integration with society,
from skeletonized servants to living ghasts to the occasional
vampire comfortably walking the street under occluded skies,
throws him. Sailors assure him that broken men often swap
their miserable lives for the seemingly more enviable state
of vital undeath. Here and there a dark-garbed dwarf stares

out from under one of their ubiquitous hoods, face a study in murderous curiosity. Small clusters of brightly colored trade coalitions jangle by, covered in literal bells and whistles, and inevitably followed by some cadge of thieves looking for an easy score. The sailors set themselves apart with colors: royal blue for mariners, crimson for a captain or boatswain, and goldenrod for navigators.

Yet Dodona knows the place, utterly certain he has arrived. From the door of the Last Inn, he stares at the exact vista captured with photogravure on his bedroom wall. Whatever Delphi did here, he knew that man and woman personally. Knew the place well enough to keep exactly one picture among his entire demesne of this precise view. It's a mystery that will have to wait until he's discharged his many duties, each graver than the last.

At the bar of the Last Inn sits Abraham, an old human with darkish skin and a rather cheerful smile staring out the main window. He drinks a mug of actual cider, hot and spiced, watching the shenanigans as fools come and go. Old Abe seems to like the place. Beside him the barkeep has set a dish of smoked nuts and seeds as well as some small cooked bread balls that look like they have chilis. Dodona sits next to him and waits for the bartender, a tough orcish-looking fellow, to approach.

The demi-orc gives him a chin nod. "What're yer have?"

Dodona considers, trying some of the nearly rancid nuts feeding Abraham. "What's safe?"

"The whisky wunt give ye worms. Most like." Whisky it is. Dodona nods and drops a copper thrane on the bar. The place not only has no goblins, it refuses to use talers and gold except at designated trade depots, and for those one needs a rather expensive license. Dodona has an excess of thranes on his person as a result. He motions to the old man and tosses another coin over the pitted counter. The bar keep nods and shuffles away.

Abraham looks him over and smiles wider. He has good teeth stained from smoking and other pursuits. "They eat them, you know."

"Who?" As an opening line it's a new one. Dodona waits.

He's had an odd day occupied with watching a drowned landscape float by under siege from fog and wind. He's in no hurry now that he's out of the rain and close enough to a fire to anticipate being dry and warm.

"The goblins. Damned dweorfies eat 'em. Love the taste of the flesh, apparently."

The keep comes back with a new mug of the mulled cider and thin bottle of pale liquid along with a shot glass that looks spotlessly clean. He pours Dodona a shot and sets the open bottle next to him. Apparently a thrane is large coinage here and he's spent two of them. He sips and reassesses. Thranes are perhaps mid-sized coinage, because the whisky proves cheap but strong.

"They eat anyone else?"

Abraham smiles wider still. "Nope—just those little spies and thieves. They don't even bother to outlaw 'em or anything. Just capture them and make soup or fritters of 'em."

"Ever had one?" It seems the next logical question. It also might determine how carefully Dodona needs to be with his menu choices over the next day.

Abe's face darkens and sorrow crosses that wicked smile. "Just the once. Tis why I canna go back home. Stuck here like ae'rone else who's got a price on their head."

"So don't eat the fritters, you're saying." This makes the old man laugh and pound the bar. Dodona, his eyes adjusted to the dimness inside, has a look around and realizes with some consternation that there's no one else here save the three of them. The wide saloon hall stands empty, though free of dust or cobweb. The old pianoforte and stage sit derelict but in good condition. No one paces above, no sounds ring from any corner. The Last Inn has no customers. So what does that make the old man?

"I've been waiting for you." The old man sips the new mug, nods with an inner smile, and takes another sip.

Dodona rolls the metaphoric dice. "How do you know it's me?"

This gets him another laugh. "Because no one comes here. Ever. We're empty for a reason."

"Lack of fritters?" This makes both Abe and the bartender laugh. The more Dodona looks, the more this place seems prosperous and well-maintained but entirely absent of patrons. Then he gets it. He's in a Personal Hell. Delphi and Sherrinford have found an ingenious way to keep a secret. They've put it in a place where only the half dead or half living can reach. Even the name of the plane, Ghostsea, tells him as much.

Personal Hells are a fascinating construct. Terran languages lack an even functional construct for what these dimensional pockets tend to become. One starts with a Door. What exactly is a Door, after all? It should be an aperture between coexisting planes that opens upon set commands or sequences in set places, potentially at set times. An anchor in spacetime that more or less reliably does the same thing endlessly without collapse, curses, mutation, or just plain messing with the things that pass through it. But all Doors go to and from Chafrium. Without exception.

Some wizards, especially the theologist wing of the quantumists, believe that Chafrium itself is simply a Door of such immense size that the detritus has formed a plane. It's not really a place but the inbetween of other places. On that rather heretical front, some experimental laboratories started to try to clone Chafrium's unique reality fabric, often called "the weave." As luck and magic would have it, cloning the City tends to create all manner of ugly abominations and vengeful gods, but not other places between. Until by accident two of these horrors mated and the resulting offspring were stable universes of various flavors of physical and magical chaos. Hells, if you will.

Over time, and with much illegal, immoral, and utterly profane experimentation, the elves and various wizards of the Academy conspired to generate a relatively stable and generic version. All things have limits, and Personal Hells have a doozy. The Owner must remain within. One single entity must power that Door by lifeforce—they and the Doorway are bound. Sparklesaurus explained to Lady Nia that in his view, a Personal Hell represents that primitive architecture of the divine-self interconnection, and that by inverting it, wizards may create a pocket dimension over which the Owner achieves control, but at the price of being severed from the Universal and Divine. Hell, if you will.

The Owners are essentially Lord and Master over their domain, controlling the physics of the place with more or less finesse depending on the architect who brought it into being. In practice, they tend to be rather poorly made spaces sold to imprison idiots too dense to comprehend that their ideal world will be a more ideal prison within which to permanently keep them. Because one does not age nor decay within it. Instead, time starts to become meaningless, days and years fade, and the whole of the Hell takes on a kind of epic ennui, which the philosopher-wizard Sartre explored in his nine volume treatise *L'enfer et le soi—Hell and the Self.*

Most of these places are difficult to enter and equally hard to exit—perhaps harder. The Owners tend to hold whomever they find as hostages and playthings to amuse them. To say most of the Owners are insane misses the point. One needs to be insane to even agree to such an arrangement where free will and the soul are mutated to provide respite from something outside the owner. Much like being a janjack.

As the Owner craves more stimulus and finds the toy people it has collected lacking, it seeks out stimuli. It opens wide its mouth and starts to trawl for volunteers. Like a lampfish or lamia, the wretched thing sings for its supper. Some things being easier to catch than others, especially the dead or near dying, these little vampire worlds start to collect like leeches around frequent sites of battle, murder, ruin, or despair.

The Last Inn sits in a dead world near an insanity-inducing body of water. Where the deadly weather drives desperate souls indoors. Past the threshold. That makes Abraham and the bartender entirely new kinds of entities. One of them might be the Owner; or they might be victims of the Owner, held here at some entity's whim.

Dodona has some options. Lomar's Sword can exit pretty much anywhere. But it will also rip the fabric of the place, killing everyone left behind. Some older Hells number in the millions. Immortality and boredom lead to a lot of opportunistic sex. Which means babies who have babies. It also means that for some, all of their existences have been slavery.

The janjack's not here to save them, but he's also not one to turn his back on the needs of the many. He needs to assess. His remaining Writ could allow him an exit, as could several spells Delphi left in his mind. But most likely, he will simply walk out, either because the Owner has allowed it or because as a janjack and a strange kind of constructed intelligence, he's not bound by all the rules of the world yet.

He takes another sip of the lackluster alcohol. "Which one of you owns the place?"

That raises an eyebrow. The barkeep looks at Abraham in silent discussion, and when the old man shrugs, he disappears down a flight of stairs that did not seem to exist minutes before. The janjack waits. He's got theoretically limitless time, and the warmth of the place keeps drying out his soaked garments. For his part the old man ignores him, going back to watching out the window as the world passes by in opaque misery.

Some time later, when his clothes are bone dry and the place warm enough to induce Dodona to shed his outer coat and loosen his boots, a curious human appears. He's large-bellied and rather jolly-looking, with thinning black hair, a ridiculous mustache that whispers its existence, thick glasses, and a rather humble outfit that seems incredibly modern and rather pedestrian. On his lapel he wears a tiny cloisonné pin of a frolicking fox, done out with flames and clouds surrounding it.

"Greetings stranger, I'm Lee."

Dodona gives him a curt bow, horseman-style with a click of the boots. "Dodona Janjack, sir. A pleasure to be introduced. Am I to understand you own this inn?"

Lee smiles warmly. "I own this world." There, he's said it. Dodona has come face to face with a pocket god. But not one that anyone might suspect exists. Still, the janjack knows appearances are generally deceptive. This being might only desire to look like a middle-aged human male wearing what looks like nondescript clerks' clothing from any century.

The janjack gives him another bow. "May I ask about the flow of time here?"

This perplexes Lee some. "Do you mean if it does, or how fast, or something like that?"

"Precisely. I am due for an appointment on another world in two days. I am duty-bound to return and would like, your Grace, to understand if we have time for a short or long conversation."

This makes the man laugh. "Oh, I'm nobody's Grace. Just Lee or The Fox if you prefer." He frowns and waves a hand. "There, I've turned time off for now. Sorry, Abe."

The old man looks disappointedly out the window, the frozen scene distorted by mist and shadows. "It's all night and fog out there anyway." He sips the cider and makes a face. "Time to take a break, I guess."

To this Lee nods and pats the old man on the back, then helps the elder off his stool. Abe limps off to some back room, muttering but again jovial. Then the Owner turns to his guest. "You have questions?"

"Certainly. First, who are you?"

"Victim of a murder, I'm afraid." Lee motions him to the stairwell and Dodona follows.

"So are you dead, then? I wasn't aware that was possible. To be an Owner and dead."

Lee nods and gives the janjack a quiet sad smile. "Better to show you. Please come with me, Mister Dodona." He leads him down the stairs, which spiral and expand, widening to a kind of stone avenue of steps lit by soft warm light. By the time they reach the bottom the steps are hundreds of paces wide, built of earth and roots and bathed in a kind of diffuse sunlight. Ahead there, an arch that looks made of lilies and hydrangeas. The ground around it is covered in a strange purple-flowered succulent. "Iceplant. From my time when I was alive," Lee tells him, then motions him to the fields beyond.

They stand on a rolling hill which overlooks wide swathes of beautiful country. Woodlands and prairies, arroyos and swamps, all in immeasurable cantons radiating outward from the entrance until they reach beyond sight. Small shapes flit past, here and there stopping to wave at Lee, who waves back. People. Women and men, all genders really, in strange costumes that speak to centuries of time. They are all human, however, and most are dusky in complexion.

"What's left of Turtle Island." Lee makes a sweep of his hand and seems especially proud.

Dodona has some inkling of Turtle Island, the indigenous Terran name for the northern Americano continental mass and its oceans. Austen has some of the nations represented by ambassadors or station agents. This place seems different. These are not modern people. Many are covered in animal skins and ochre. "We still have Turtle Island."

This makes Lee's face light up. "So, you're from Earth then? How wonderful. Where y'all from?"

"Austen. I'm a janjack of Austen."

Lee claps him on the back. "From the South—even better. I'm from Kentucky myself."

Dodona has no idea what a Kentucky is or where it's located, but Austen is considered the far north, the edge of the Extenso. "I'm sorry, Lee, but I have not heard of this Kentucky. I do have a rather broken memory at the moment."

Lee nods. "So you're not from Earth, then. Terra?" To this Dodona nods. "Okay, got it now. You're the fellow my friend Sherrinford has told me about."

"Yes, I was to find Abraham the Elder and get some files."

Lee waves a hand. "Sure. Old Abe's been waiting at the door for a couple centuries hoping to see you. You made his month coming in, and it's always good to hear him laugh."

This confuses Dodona. "I died just last week. Or rather, the entity that sent me did. It could not have been centuries, could it?" Sherrinford was only 73 years old.

"Riiiight. Sorry. You're not really in your universe right now. We're in a side station, if you will. That's what the whole sea of crazy out there is, the ability to peer into other worlds, real and imagined."

"Ghostsea has a Door to places outside Chafrium?" This would be extraordinary news for the wider worlds. And Dodona suspects, a major reason no one has ever heard of this place. Those who know it must guard the secret with their lives and sacred honor.

"Kinda." Lee shrugs. "Let's sit down and have lunch. My man Yoa will bring it." He snaps his fingers and a large picnic table appears. From a distance a human-sized dog walking on two legs and wearing a strange outfit approaches. It's some kind of valet's uniform, or perhaps military garb, with a blue shirt bearing a small icon that looks like an arrowhead of gold.

The dogman appears, nothing like the Soviet sebakni in Dodona's memory. This one is regal, thin of face and body, as if a dog were transformed into a valet but retained his domestic essence. "Live long and prosper." The dog makes some kind of gesture with his hand.

Lee shakes his head. "Yeah, this one's not going to understand any of that. Set us up with the full Mongolian barbecue, some good moo shu and my usual. Give him a selection of pops."

While the dog servant walks away, Lee explains the nature of this Pocket Hell. It seems that the Fox was from a tribal line of wizards, something he calls healers. As such, they had unusual powers including dreamwalking. One night in a place called Anaheim, a location he assures Dodona will impress no-one, Lee was murdered by his best friend with a gunshot to the head. Or accidentally shot. As the man being killed, Lee never quite figured it out. The end result was that the whole of Lee's body and some of Lee's soul were wiped out instantly. But some of him—the piece gifted him from the *iethihsothó:kon*, his false faces of ancient line—carried him somewhere, and he found a being, a kind of six-eyed grandmother who was all love and all comfort.

She gave him this place to find respite and to care for others of his kind—the lost, the suicides and massacre victims and sufferers of plague or drink or exposure or starvation. Lee the Fox has watched over the refugees and exiles from Turtle Islands for eons. Himself familiar with things like computers and textmail, he knows Sherrinford. They correspond through his laptop, brought in by some ghost from a place called Miami. They've never met; Lee knows her only as a glowing icon within a piece of metal and resin.

Food is served, and it's a bizarre feast of foods quite unlike anything Dodona has imagined. The colors are unnaturally bright but not magical. Lee drinks a strange concoction of bright green sugar water, which tastes like urine and candy thrown together. On the table are heaping mounds of thin meats slathered in orange and red sauces, over noodles and served alongside vegetables chopped fine and covered in sugary, oily sauces of their own. All served with a kind of peculiar white starch nodule he insists is rice. It's delicious and terrible, cloying and greasy and kind of outrageously fun. There are thin pancakes that Lee smothers in soured sugar slime and then covers with greasy meat and vegetable chunks. Dodona has to admit, these are crazy odd and rather delicious. He might need to have a bun made that approximates the recipe.

Some of the people Lee refers to as Indians join them. They are from different epochs in this place's history, this alternate Terra named Earth. In this place, magic apparently barely exists and the indigenous nations have been all but exterminated. In this world, the Americans and Europeans replaced Chafrium as the world beasts of conquest and desecration. This neon food full of fat and sugar is their high cuisine perhaps. More dishes are brought. Frybread. Deep dish pizza. San Francisco clam chowder. Pemmican and succotash. Each a twist on what Dodona knows, and some truly alien. Frybread seems like a flat bun without toppings. The deep dish pizza will be on Café Ragueneau's menu as soon as he can provide the recipe to Duchamp.

But there are also people Lee insists are from his own world's books. People whose deaths proved so tragic their psyche needed a place to rest. They too live here. The Fox is rather philosophical. It turns out he knows from Sherrinford about the Extenso and its rapine of the entire world. Worlds, if one considers how the elves manage their fiefdom of planets and planes. His own history turned out to be somehow worse. These vile Yankees of his reality exterminated more than the Ragged Orcs, and with less feeling. Without magic the dead stayed dead and plagues, disaster, famine, and heartbreak found no remedy. The land dwindled and died. Replaced by colorants and sugar and loud music in cans.

Lee tells him that the dead here don't see this as Hell at all.

It's a second chance, a glimmer of hope in a hopeless universe, a place where his own ancestors, the Keepers of the Eastern Door and their southern cousins the Principal People, persist in greater numbers and with a much more robust culture. The others whose own peoples have been shattered and whose ashes are so trodden they cannot even scatter to the winds, feel much the same. Pride, joy, serenity, and gratitude.

It's sunset of one day or another; Dodona has lost track in this idyll. Earlier in the day or some day recently, he'd heard one of the Lakota call this place the Happy Hunting Grounds. Heaven but also a haven. Respite for dead peoples, dead characters, dead ideas. He's met people Lee swears come directly from the books of his reality. But there are also some from books Dodona remembers having read. Books from this world, this place. At last he acknowledges he must ask for the hidden records and go back to the timestream.

It's breakfast with Lee, who is in some kind of robe-and-pajamas contraption with pink-nosed rabbit slippers and a mug of coffee with the same shape as his valet's uniform. On the side it reads in archaic English "Beam me up Scotty... There's no intelligent life here." The other day he met this gregarious Mister Scott, who has taken a cottage on the edge of some meadows that he swears remind him of the meadows of his youth. The man insisted on being called Jimmy, and when he's nervous, he sips tea spiked with scotch and turns a dented silver cigarette case in his hands. He also speaks of home, of missing the places he wishes he'd seen, and yet, when pressed, he seems sincerely happy to have found this place.

Over pancakes with thick sugar syrup, coffee, and some kind of delicious meats that in no way resemble Terran bacon and sausage, Dodona plans to ask his host for Sherrinford's documents but finds himself asked something first. The Fox sips his coffee and with a jovial smile points back towards the stairwell. "Where do you think that leads?"

As trick questions go, it's fairly simple. "Back to the door, to the Last Inn."

Lee shakes his head while his smile widens. "You'd think that, wouldn't you? Tell me this: do you think I'm real?"

Dodona stops to deliberate over the notion. "As much as I am."

"Exactly. Precisely so, just like you. And everyone else."

Dodona looks about, the various peoples here keep erratic schedules, coming and going according to some internal clock that seems to elude the janjack. "Here, you mean?"

Lee shakes his head. "You people, not very civilized, are you? All that time building a City and you still don't understand how the world works."

"Austen just needs more time. It's growing."

The host shakes his head and sips more coffee. "I meant Chafrium, the elves, all of it. All your pretty little world out there. Do you think I didn't read the files?"

That takes Dodona aback some. What did he think? Nothing, he realizes; he simply came to fulfill his duty. A lack of curiosity is his own nature, fault, or responsibility.

He gives a small bow with his head. "I had not considered it one way or the other."

Lee chews on a bacon strip. They are rich and greasy, full of sugars and strange smoke chemicals. Dodona finds them compelling—perhaps they have drugs in them. "Do you know what Abe does?" He holds up a hand and frowns. "Let me guess: you didn't even consider it."

Dodona shakes his head. "Not much. But I just assumed he guarded the door, kept you apprised of who comes in, perhaps ran some trade with the Trow."

Lee chuckles and pours them both some coffee. "Son, you have much to learn. And I suspect that without what I am teaching you, the list will be useless." He hands Dodona a folded slip of paper with a few names on it—the names being expunged from Sherrinford's mainframes and system think-stacks. "Now listen, I shall not repeat this. Focus and listen. This is how our people teach, face to face, with words and stories, okay?"

Dodona looks at this man, this bookstore clerk who fell into a world somewhere beyond his own universe, and realizes he must be ancient, even by Chafrium standards. That his time without time has made him a Dreaming thing. He nods carefully and gives the Fox his full attention.

"Abraham the Elder runs the Silent Society." Dodona knows of this. It's an ancient league, a kind of secret society open to anyone with an addiction. They share mutual support, endorse a spiritual life, and help the new members connect with the gods. Some janjacks come from those who could not or would not completely give themselves to this simple program laid out by the society.

"Now, we make the climb to the Inn hard, because that door you used, that's the door to Hell. It leads to misery, pain, disease, loss. Once my guests pass through the threshold, I cannot help them anymore. Abe represents the last chance for them to turn back."

Dodona nods and drinks more coffee. The idea that dead souls could walk free into Ghostsea seems plausible. Might even explain the place better.

"They hold their meetings up there, to remind themselves of the stakes and to be a place of welcome for anyone who comes in from Hell, don't you see?"

Dodona raises a finger. "If that's the exit, where's the entrance?"

"Exactly! Finally a smart question. The entrance is death. People arrive here like osmosis, traveling through a membrane. But there's one drain from here out to there, and it's a down to a rather filthy sewer: your world."

Lee pours them both more coffee and stirs in several spoonfuls of very bleached sugar. It looks like crushed bones. "It gets even more confusing. Because some of my guests, they never lived at all, not in my world or yours. Yet they can walk free and roam into Chafrium."

Then the Fox taps Dodona's chest, rustling the Writ underneath his jacket. "What you got there?"

"It's a Writ of All, a device to…"

"I know what a Writ is, Dodona. But do you? I suspect you have no real idea because you still haven't understood the nature of this place." Lee lifts the Writ and places it on the table. With a fingernail he taps it. "In my childhood, we used to talk about a vengeful god full of spite, the smiting god who sees you when you sin. Kentucky and all that." He spins the Writ and looks perhaps wistful. "But I always liked the story where God, our version at least, speaks the world into being. He basically uses a Writ. He writes the world with words."

"So this place was made with a Writ?"

"You delightful fool. The Writs are made of what this place is made of, what it's all made of. Songs and stories, words and desire. You were made from a Writ, were you not?"

The chill rolls down Dodona's spine. How could this man know that? "Did Sherrinford say?"

"Nonsense. You simply fit here. You could climb down the stairs, and you are, by definition, something written and thought of rather than born and made. You are an idea come to life. Like me, like most of us, like this place. "

Like Sherrinford and Jane Austen and perhaps, it occurs to the intrigued Dodona, janjacks themselves. Palimpsests of both landscape and soul. Like Austen now that the Writ executed by Delphi has moved real power into tangible walls and living janjacks. From writing, from an idea. Like the Writ in his home, sealed with Delphi's blood. Like the Writ in either Sherrinford or the Lady Nia's hands now, inked in his own blood. The blood of an idea, the blood of an imagined thing made real.

"So you're saying Chafrium is, what, a story?"

"I'm saying that reality is a story and literature a version of reality. That ideas persist and animate, that magic as you know it relies on words. You call this a Personal Hell, and voilà, your words create the parameters. We call it home and so it becomes one. What are you called?"

"Dodona Janjack."

"Do you even know where Dodona is? Or what it means?"

The janjack shakes his head. He did not choose the name— the Song did. The Song which is words and which is magic. He sits there long into the night and day and night, never moving, never even breathing. Does he need to? He sits and listens to the idea of it all. What did the Wizard of Kyiv say if not this? What is Jane's Town if not this? And Jane herself?

Equally vital, so very vital to the moment he must face, what matters in erasing words, in taking away names from the stacks and Sherrinford?

He already knows what the list will show him. Or he thinks he knows. But Lee the Fox is entirely correct. He had not really understood what that implied. What killing Jane Austen has done to the world. Done to Hell, if you will.

The last thing Siegfried and Chayot told him: means, motive, and opportunity, the core of detecting a murder. He's understood the means and opportunity, but perhaps not really the motive. Not all of it.

He looks at the paper and sees all the expected names plus two more.

Two wholly revolutionary names that change everything. Oh, you damned comedian Delphi, you set me up. You set us all up. He smiles in wicked delight.

It's not that Dodona has incorrectly surmised who killed Jane and why, it's more that he's missed the much larger Game. He's entirely missed the reason why someone killed her. He looks at Lee and nods slowly. Had the man been there all along?

At last the janjack knows truly and fully what to do, what must be done on behalf of Austen and Jane, on behalf of justice and the words of the worlds. He takes lunch with Lee and wanders the grounds, stalling in this idyll until his body shakes with terror and he can no longer put off his sacred responsibilities. He takes the Writ still in his possession and has an old medicine woman help him make ink from his own blood and various herbal extracts. He sets down the precise instructions necessary, and through Abraham he sends word into the churning hell of Ghostsea that he requires a messenger.

He picks Lord Aejae for this, because the symmetry appeals to him. More than that, for this task, carrying a Writ through to Chafrium, there can be no error, and only someone as formidable as Aejae can be relied upon to win through at any cost. So when the call comes, when timeless he waits in fields of amber and forests of a million shades of green and umber, he sets his mind in order, seals his fate and the fates of worlds, writes his own will and such. Up one last time to the antechamber to Hell, to the Door which exiles you to pain. Lee and Abraham, the bartender and Lord Aejae await him.

They share a meal of various favorites identified by Dodona

over these eons. A whole life lived in the fraction of a fraction of endless fractions of a second. Less than a breath. These recipes too have been lovingly handed down to him and given to the Curoi Lord among other parcels to deliver after the Writ. Invitations, instructions, payment of debts, legal documents, a whole bevy of plans within plans. He has already alerted Sherrinford via Lee's ingenious mail system on the peculiar resin lap machine. When he tries to reason through how she in the timestream and Lee forever in one place may communicate, his head hurts and a sharp pain strikes him behind his left eye. Dimensional time magic, once a forte of a former self, eludes him thoroughly.

Then comes the appointed hour, and with many bows, with warm handshakes and a few unexpected hugs, Dodona and his Curoi emissary depart. They push against the membrane on the threshold and out into the world. Within, Abraham waves, he again in the timestream watching for passersby who seek refuge.

The stink of the place assaults Dodona. His many years, perhaps centuries (who can tell) in a timeless place have made him soft when it comes to the discomfort and blight of urban sprawl. He hunches down and finds a local merchant whom he has to pay several coins to get the date. He's got a day and a bit left until he must present the heir to the King. It makes him laugh. He simply needs to gather a few people, make a couple of stops, and dress for the occasion.

As agreed, he takes Lord Aejae to the foot of the Palace in a heartbeat and then, leaving the incurious Lord to present credentials, he uses his Skeleton Key to enter his own home in the lowest level, the inverted donjon of the expunged […], where he gathers a few particulars. Wandering about the various vaults and stores within the home, he makes ready for the oncoming fight. He goes to face the Guildmaster, whom he knows by face and name.

Witnesses later aver they see multiple figures come and go to the half-lit home of the janjack. No one's gotten around to calling it Dodona's Place, but they've stopped talking about Delphi quite as much. At one point a woman with flowing red hair and a saber emerges. Some conspiracy-prone few claim it was The Red Lady herself.

In turn, a rather terrified member of the Confederate Miners and Metallurgists Guild enters the house after midnight, accompanied by Amberflow, and leaves a mere twenty minutes later with a chest of valuables and a huge smile. Then past the witching hour comes one more visit, a quiet hush unseen as both the Hand and the Claw enter the house from the roof. The penalty for killing a janjack on duty notwithstanding, some crises call for increasingly desperate measures.

After dawn locals find the bodies stretched across the lampposts like flayed deer. The assassins have been decapitated, their hands and feet excised and sent as gifts to the Assassin's Guild with a small token of weregild to add proper Eldessery to the process. The heads appear in the Throne Room, sent by a quirk of both Writs and the Skeleton Key. To make a proper statement, Dodona drops them in the punch bowl that feeds the sycophants and houses minor below the stairs. As expected, they make a lovely splash with the gossips; several outfits must be replaced and seating arrangements modified. Some few security arrangements are also altered.

Dodona knows for certain the Guild must move with all its might as soon as possible. He sends a note with Dnieper to the Broker along with several bags of rare gems Delphi put aside for negotiations of this type. In return he receives a list of clothes and armor in the Broker's script as well Dnieper's assurance that the Broker accepted the deal.

He dresses with care, making each item as polished and resplendent as possible. He finds various illegal substances in the home which add Shine and Glamer, as well as some cologne with Punch. He layers them thick. At long last, he's a dandy of irksome Brummelage. From top hat to spurs he's the model of Grey Elven excess, done with fastidious attention to minimalism and élan. He attaches the Chafrium dueling pistol and, of note later, a common war saber from Delphi's stacks. The Sword of Lomar he leaves on the mantle.

Then Dodona seals the home from within. He secures every lock and activates the hegemony of magics that make this a deathtrap for outsiders. He adds to them physical traps, potions, several spells from old tomes or scrolls, and at least one conjured guardian, a mute orangutan with burning eyes of void-black. He gives the creature explicit instructions, then gates himself directly to the Throne Room. Behind him, the House of Delphi lies a sealed tomb.

Dodona appears at the foot of the Skeleton Stairs, watching as the King and his massive retinue begin their formal descent. He has timed it to the second and knows what he must do. Already on the floor stand the players assembled in sections. In the center the Minor Houses of Lomar, with every baroness upwards assembled in finery rarely seen. To the left, the gauchement plus ultra, the renegades, castoffs, and immortals. There stand Hoode and Smith; next to them, their colleague or enemy or long-lost friend Caris, with Smoojak and a small Asian man likely to be Toki Ojawa. Two phantoms linger like flickering lamps to their rear—Tawdry and Armax have been dredged from their slumbers. A fair number of freelancers, emissaries of the Drowning Ones, some priests of the occult blighted and banned, a few undead Lords worth invitation, one immortal wizard who bothered to show, and dozens of other potential immortals or their agents. The Powers and the powerless together.

To the right, the Guilds and the Academy with their hierarchies of position and rank, each one vying to outlandishly overcompensate in dress and jewels. Some come near the Elves themselves in terms of ostentation. The whole place stinks of the fabulous and unattainable.

To the rear, the janjacks and assassins of various planes, cities, guilds, and Powers. They throng like a wild flock of murderous geese, each one armed in vicious fashion and no two looking in the same direction. Should the situation degenerate into violence, the rear of the room can be counted upon to supply asymmetrical force on a scale rarely seen in such a small space. Some few war mages and death masters have by special fiat been allowed to join them in a roped off section to the right.

In the front, the Seneschal and his retinue of demi-seneschals numbering thirteen in all. Sherrinford stands among them, facing an entire universe of protocol and pomp, this time their superior. Her adoptive father will be elevated to the highest of stations, and she shall ride upon his rather meteoric coattails. At his direction, they wear the most severe midnight blue uniforms of House and Rank, with Vanguards muted and medals reduced to pips and bars. By comparison with the assemblage they look like daggers among peacocks—only the janjacks at the rear even approximate their finesse.

At one edge, the Confederate Miners and Metallurgists Guild has brought Barefoot Jackson and a rather large band to support him. They'd be an orchestra in other circumstances; here they are a rather overawed, gawking group of the best jazzists available across multiple worlds. They've hired the Doctors McCain to conduct with Artina managing the musicians and back of house, Martin running the actual music. For guards, the Confederacy has requested Austen provide janjacks and so the three sisters, Dnieper, Vorskla and Lybid have arrived hours prior and simply stood at all three points of the stage with implacable calm. Keeping them company at her own whim, the returned Queen Qelniasherah wanders about, unthinkably assisting the musicians and Jackson with such trifles as tuning instruments and fetching drinks. The last fool to condescendingly suggest the Queen do otherwise walked away with a broken nose and the derision of the front row. Tomorrow he will suicide rather than face the social noise.

Then down the stairs come the House Royal, led by King Sæceæn XIX with his sister the regally dressed Lady Ashlelani Greyleaf, Matron of the Stars, Keeper of the Broken Ankh, Oracle and Priestess, Elf of Supreme Rank—the mother anguished by the loss of her beloved Lady Nia who weeps no more. Beside her, of course, come the various Ladies in Waiting. Their Graces Lady Kimber and Lady M'shylpsany accompany her, the succession being decided first for the newly minted Saint of Automobiles (a name Her Grace adores) and after her Kimber. Then follow the Contessa Principale, Princess Meleyasza, ever by her Queen's side. Behind them every one of the Greater Kin Grey Elven of the Houses Lomar, Lyska and Zoëæ. The whole of the civilized world.

They slowly descend, one step after the other, with grave ceremony. The King makes small talk with the cheerful Princess Meleyasza, who titters at some joke, sending the room into a hormonal frenzy. Their plunge towards the Court floor proves a momentous thing. Soon Coralaviere and his family will join them both as invested Seneschal and Noble of Inner Rank which the title Supreme Duke bestows upon him in addition to several other honors, including being part of the formal line of succession.

Today the Guildmaster plans to slay the King while various Powers attempt to slay the Guildmaster. But first, Dodona Janjack must deliver his report and stand accountable before all of civilization and its Lords, Ladies, and Powers. It remains his sole obligation unfulfilled.

He bows as they approach, the King stopping two stairs from the floor, his brow arched. As if on cue, the Green Queen Qelniasherah joins the procession, standing with one foot on the stairs and the other planted where she's been all day, among her future subjects. Her Vanguard glows softly, reminding all that Lady Nia is no coward. The Queen nods to her daughter and she to her mother, no love to be found in either's eyes. Then the Princess Meleyasza descends, accepting Dodona's offered hand and stands at his immediate right, facing both him and the King. Her body throbs with pheromonal agitation but her eyes speak of death. Onlookers marvel as she casts hateful glances at the janjack.

In return, the janjack doffs his hat and bows low to King and Court. "If it pleases His Majesty, we shall converse in the Common tongue so as to better inform his many interested subjects and devoted servants."

The King gives him a brief smile and nods to Meleyasza. On his behalf she answers in High Common. "The King accedes to this practical consideration. You have duties to perform as janjack, on behalf of your former selves." Her voice drips with venom and condescension. Already the Vanguard of his old life has begun to flicker and fade. Today it seems barely there at all.

"Indeed, my Princess, and on behalf of the Free State of Austen, the King and Court may now rest. I have at his express request returned both his niece and the heir to the throne. Both are here among us today."

The Princess' eyes glow with triumph. She and Ashlelani exchange unmistakable glances: they have him now! With him goes Austen and the amazing influx of Power sent down the sewers. Once more the elves may assert their social ascension. "But you, sir, did not deliver them."

He bows to her and then smiles, his eyes as calm as any crocodile. "Do you assert before King and Court that I have not brought the Green Queen, the Lady Qelniasherah, safely back with the assistance of my agents and allies?" Somewhere unseen Sandoval Prestige cracks the faintest smile. He's counted coup most skillfully. And reminded the assembly of what happens to Houses that oppose Austen. They cease to exist.

The Princess laughs as both the King and his sister eye Dodona with deadly interest. "Certainly not! And it ill becomes a janjack of a human city as minor as Austen to level such accusations against the King." In the crowd assembled a low 'ooh' escapes the gossips.

"Ah, my Lady, I said no such thing. And while we of Austen are poor compared to the Throne, I will personally pay for whatever remedial lessons are needed to improve your High Common." He bows into her personal space and smiles most sinisterly as she backs away a half pace, forced by his movement to give him ground. Her eyes fall to his common saber and she frowns, confused and properly insulted.

With a flourish he rises and addresses the King. "For if you do not dispute my return of the Queen and heir, you must dispute that she is the present heir. And do so on your own behalf without hearing from or deferring to the King." He waits, playing the front row who are gobbling his words like caviar and tripdust. "How do you get away with such presumption?"

For her part the Princess snaps upright, struck physically by the nastiness of the gibe and shocked as she sees how subtly it plays with the thirsting front row of nobles and houses parched for the rank he's just accused her of abusing. She gives him a bow and touches his arm, pulling herself back into his orbit, flooding the room with hormones and, without meaning to, signaling her weakness of position to the watchers on high. Austen has again scored a social blow, this time against the Matron of the Stars herself. What her servant does, by Elven logic, affects her most of all.

The immortals section glances over at the Norns, whose impassive faces drill holes in the figure of Ashlelani. She in turn stares at Dodona with a mingled hatred and fascination, her fingers motioning to her handmaiden. The King sighs and waves them both to silence.

"Tell me then, Janjack Dodona, exactly how you have fulfilled my commands and brought me my heir. You who were invested with my Writ and serve my House as well," he indicates with a nod to the janjack's striped on the top hat, "the Great City of Chafrium itself."

Dodona bows to the King. "Did you know they intend to kill you today?"

The question so calm and casual takes the whole retinue off guard. As it was meant to do. Beside him Meleyasza stiffens in horror. Someone faints and several of the lesser family spill their drinks.

Sæceæn shrugs. "As opposed to any other day?"

"In this case my King, yes. On this day, in this place, they have planned most meticulously. Because I have, in fact, also returned your heir."

The whole of the place freezes, trying to follow the various ways such a statement might be construed. Has Dodona found the heir and secreted her in to the hall unannounced? Plausible. Did he return her among those already assembled, somehow understanding the line of succession based on his investigations? Unlikely but thrilling. Or does he seem to imply that Qelniasherah the disinherited has right to his throne, which spells disaster for her Mother and her cadre as well as being clearly impossible? Making it that much more delicious and desirable.

Next to him, the princess quivers with palpable rage and Queen Ashlelani scowls with open disdain. The two women look as if any moment they'd gnaw out Dodona's heart with pleasure. All illusion of civility has been stripped. But then, he's just accused them of treason. Because if not them, who would hide the evidence of another heir and plan to kill the King?

Austen has slandered them beyond repair. Dodona, immaculate in his superb dress stands fast, the dramatic center of an unspooling tale. The omega of this narrative, the final word that waits only for the King to ask.

"Janjack Dodona, you are stating then with total assurance, and upon your sacred vows to Chafrium, that Lady Qelniasherah is in true fact my legal heir?" He's quantified it in clear legal terms. Dodona's answer matters on a thousand levels. The King, being no fool, has made the process clear and utterly simple. If Dodona speaks false his treason and that of Austen will be manifest and his own *Desideralla* Coralaviere will strike him down.

"Yes, my King, because her father is …"

The shot rings out with a clarion peal. Dodona falls, dead at the hands of the Princess Meleyasza who has turned the janjack's pistol against him. One shot, to the right side of his head and he lays slain at the feet of the universe's sovereign.

The last death. The Song comes right. The room reels with shock and titillation. No one speaks, no one dares. Instead they stare at the corpse on the floor, janjack of two cities. The retribution will be unthinkable. Two cities thwarted, a janjack inside the Royal House delivering formal service to the King, bestowed with writs, sword, and magical keys. A legendary hero and shadow of former heroes.

Meleyasza turns the pistol on her King and pulls the trigger. Which clicks and clicks as she discovers Dodona has only loaded it with the single cartridge. Then Coralaviere starts to laugh, his eyes bright with irrepressible mirth. Beside him Sherrinford has a look of abject shock, something which requires explanation. She has been well and truly surprised.

Stand witness to the very public fall of the Guildmaster of Chafrium's Assassin's Guild, Elf of Hidden Rank, First Lady in Waiting, the Contessa Principale and Personal Confidante and *Sylslaymynar* of Lady Ashlelani Greyleaf: The Princess Meleyasza.

CHAPTER 14: GLILDWIMMIR

There's a Russian expression—"The cat knows whose meat it ate"—that the elves love so much they've taken it in and made it their own thing. In Middle and Low Elvish the Chafriumite version usually translates as: "Guilt is for the hungry; shame for the unmasked." Since they have several forms and lots of tricky homophones, the best and fastest version tends to be Z'æ Vryl J'æ Vrex'n. Mind you, no two scholars agree on what that translation means.

Oddly, it was Anna Joy Intertextual who best captured the gist of how Elves operate—not just in this phrase but in the whole of their cultural essence. It's her single most cited contribution to literature. Ponder that infamous third paragraph of page 129 in the April 1971 edition of the *Harvard Journal of Extenso Literature and Commentary*, Number 346, "On a New Methodology for Elven Ontology and Ethics" with editorial commentary preserved:

"My esteemed colleagues within the Americano Academy may be forgiven for their delusional belief that Elvenkind operates amorally. Nothing could be further from the truth. Put simply, human ethics stems from the *a priori* principle that life, specifically sapient life, has both merit and value. Elven morality does not and cannot. The Elves are too long-lived and in many ways too mentally and magically quarantined to share anything resembling empathy with other sapient species. Thus their entire sense of ethics revolves around the *a priori* investment in the sublime and transcendent. That which achieves perfection equals good, and all other things are negotiable. It's an alien morality to be sure, and one humanity barely fathoms. But mark these words, etch them in your applesauce*: murder and art can be equally sublime, and to the Elves ethically equivalent. Their only sin is failure, and on that front they step lightly, dear Academics, because they remedy such things at the ends of sharp blades.

"[*Editor's Note: For our readers not familiar with Extenso culture, this is a play on the Elven Creole expression of a 'breakfast of steel apples' which implies vigor beyond mortal capacity. The New Reformed Elven Party for Human Extinction mocks *Homo sapiens* by claiming they 'breakfast on copper applesauce' in reference to the Terran-wide practice of morning gruels.]

"[†Editor-in-Chief Commentary: We at the HJELC pride ourselves on equanimity in the face of our critics but wish to note for those outside the social and historical sciences that "copper applesauce" has been labeled hate speech by the 107 signatory nations of the Terran League due to "the clear unmistakable inference that the words show elven understanding of human enslavement and total subversion of our sovereign institutions." {*The Terran Manifesto,* Article Seven, Clause Six, Paragraph Nine - 1953}]

"[†† Author's Response to Editor-in-Chief's Commentary: It seems the HJELC has chosen the slime mold as its power animal. If the slime mold, as a whole or in parts, has any leader, it is only inability to pick between two solid positions. They wish to fight the Powers that Be while neither insulting them nor appearing to collaborate. I work for these bastards and they know me and trust me to speak my mind. They accept me because I am a perfect absolute bastard. Etch that in your applesauce.]"

For the last decade, one or both of these phrases 'etch them/ that in your applesauce' and 'murder and art can be equally sublime' has made it into 43% of all academic papers written on Terra and, more surprisingly, into almost one-fifth of papers written about the Extenso across all the worlds. It makes Anna Joy Intertextual the most quoted human scholar since records have been kept. Still, the Humans missed the punchline: for elves, and especially for Grey Elves, failure represents the absolute worst of all sins—a transcendent evil. Failure mars the sublime.

While it's enjoyable for many to detest the elves and their seemingly psychopathic love of cruelty and debauchery, it's also intellectually slothful. The elves have a highly refined and deeply considered moral and ethical framework that unfortunately allows for things like the [expunged house] and their rapine of the ages. Certainly a morality often inaccessible to the short-lived and technologically backward. Still, even Orcs grasp shame and guilt. *Z'æ Vryl J'æ Vrex'n*

Whether an elf by error or happenstance makes a mistake and is unmasked, or by the actions of their opponents loses their false face, the moral consequences should theoretically be the same. In practice, some shames are more shameful than others and some public failures more unforgivable than others. Say, for example, if someone tried to murder their own sovereign in front of the entire watching universe and failed. Especially if that someone were actively thwarted by an upstart species of magically and technically backward monkey thugs. Worse if the behavior exposes others and lays out before the astonished eyes of the worlds' most venal professional gossips the widespread conspiracy of a Queen and her cadre to subvert the rule of Chafrium.

Before Dodona's corpse can hit the floor, three Writs activate: the Writ of Delphi, left next to the Sword of Lomar on the mantle; the Writ of Dodona in Qelniasherah's possession, which it turns out had several invisibly added articles and stipulations; and the Writ of Chafrium, the original King's Writ, signed over to Coralaviere with several instructions and a great deal of information. But there's a fourth Writ here, the one seen but not understood as such—the Skeleton Key. The grant of Chafrium itself, to a janjack on duty, to serve as liaison to its sister city Austen.

They do not act alone, each with a set of instructions in some kind of sequence, like a mathematics operation—they are bound and intertwining, making the whole of the process simultaneous across time and space, in every dimension. The Temple of Arüne wakens briefly, such are the forces at work.

All territories and properties, all wealth and allegiances worth having from the old expunged house are instantly and permanently made the wholly owned possessions or subjects of the one true heir to the Royal Throne, Qelniasherah of the Guiding Star. Her standard, a thing of rare beauty, unravels in every place imaginable. Various treasures and servants, bound by oaths to land and place, transfer in loyalty to the Queen. The Writ has given her a new heraldry, a field of bright gold with a single white star of thirteen points. Simple, visually overwhelming, and in Elven terms a rare coup of restraint and finesse.

The Sword of Lomar appears on Sherrinford's hip. It has chosen her per the will of the Writs. She also gains several self-regenerating stack modules buried across dead worlds that communicate through quark aggression on a nonlinear time-independent sequence. Bottom line, neither magic nor nano attacks can ever dissever her selves from the self bearing her blade. The sword itself becomes a multidimensional stack of sorts. Sherry can now carry her total self-think-do with her everywhere regardless of technical or magical potential. In theory she could leave this reality and still function at over 90% efficiency.

Several layers of Delphi's home are obliterated in a flaming riot that guts the building and then goes dark, the flames and destruction sucked into some other dimension. Witnesses also say they hear movement from the observatory level and that a mad ape wearing goggles and waving a ladle could be seen gamboling about on the roof and eaves.

The various demesnes of the Vampire and her ilk, all the assorted conspirators unmasked today whether present or absent, experience some rather unfortunate side effects of being caught perfoming treason. First they are stripped of valuables, which are sent to the general treasury of the King. A nice touch that, one that wins universal approval. Servants and mindslaves are universally freed, their oaths broken and mindlocks vanquished. More than that, as if their inner will were intuited, those with a genuine skill are deposited in the exact right guild or Drowning One cell. That meets with wildly popular acclaim. Leave it to humans to think of something as small as freeing slaves and servants. The conspirators survive, every last one, to find their bodies mangled and wracked with sores that will never heal. Rotting and foul but imbued with immortal vigor.

In addition, all their glamers and shines, all their ridiculous impertinent additions to their bodies and Vanguards, are expunged. Blemishes and pimples reappear. The vainglorious are marred and the marred truly horrifying in their unaugmented glory.

Plus another small, almost trifling change.

Every species has a color it finds appalling, that does not occur in nature, that they use for safety or generally making one nauseated. For humans it tends to be a strange orange-ish yellow; goblins despise a special hue of red; the elves deeply dislike and thus immediately notice a rare form of glowing green; and so on.

As the body of the janjack falls, blood and brains splattering on the pristine white staircase, every single member of the widespread conspiracy from highest—Queen Ashlelani and Guildmaster Meleyasza—to the lowest foundling assassin sniveling in the back rows, turns all those colors at once. They are permanently, by Holy Writ and will of Chafrium, rendered down to the molecule the most bright, noticeable, offensive color of every species simultaneously.

The once radiant and shapely Meleyasza becomes a wasted figure of skeletal contour, her features distorted and ugly, her body covered in scars and welts, her whole being a misshapen mass attesting to brutal damage and survival. She looks much more like a Guildmaster than a Princess, because of course she is. She's also bright orange and yellow and green all at once, down to her saliva and feces. Her Vanguard flares and wobbles, like a drunken parrot being battered by a sea gale. Then it resolves, with a whole wrath of new indictments and sanctions. It seems that, not merely content with turning the entirety of the Assassin's Guild and their fellow conspirators into glow-in-the-dark targets, the late Dodona used the Writs to administer a rare thing termed Black Justice.

The Black Elves do something spectacularly punitive when they wish to castigate one of their own. They burden the criminal with an unexpurgated list of their crimes and transgressions. Their Vanguard carries each of them in a little icon, a glowing virion of red, which tends to make the beholder feel squeamish. But the real kicker are the Threads. Every time a single icon catches someone's eye, the Threads transfer intimate and painful knowledge about the whole of the infraction to them. Black Elves aren't much for prudery, so there's plenty of gore, sex, and various stomach-turning kinds of awareness that comes with such a Vanguard. Black Justice.

The Writs have just delivered full and complete Black Justice on the entire Guild, all of Ashlelani's retinue, the handful of surviving conspirators belonging to neither of those camps, and some few minions serving Ashlelani in another capacity. A capacity which seems more evident by the sudden appearance of a second Ashlelani. Two stand in the hall, one as bright and castigated as the rest of her humiliated cabal, and one simply there, blackened and steaming, a kind of hellish version of the ex-Queen, eyes dead as the corpse on the floor but with less appeal.

At this point Coralaviere steps forward, Writ in hand, bowing low to his King and intoning the ritual High Elvish "My Sovereign and Sacred Liege".

For her part, the Guildmaster pulls a flip dart from her bodice to throw at the King. Sandoval Prestige, appearing from the fourth row, blows her entire hand and forearm apart with a sabot shot, splattering bright orange goo across several collaborators and one poorly seated Duchess in the front row. It's an instructive moment, because not another finger in the whole room moves. Several well-armed PAWs assassins who serve the Black Cat enter, accompanied by the Seneschal's men and backed by a legion of formally dressed mercenaries from the Chafrium Sword and Pistol League, all wearing the clear colors and badges of the PAWs and Lord Coralaviere. The orange slime demonstrates to the recipients of Black Justice what's inside them, and just how thoroughly scragged they are. Someone vomits; others follow.

"Your Lordship, with my most sincere apologies for the minor deception," here the Seneschal bows again before the rather amused-looking King. "Perhaps we may begin with some minor administrative issues and then bear down to the issues at hand?"

Sæceæn gives his usual shrug and waves his hand as if to say, *please do continue.* Songs will be sung of this moment: the King's remarkable sangfroid and poise will be spoken of in the most adulatory terms. The moment makes the men yet again, and while he has done so without even thinking, service to his sovereign comes from Coralaviere as easily as breathing.

"Pursuant to the late janjack Dodona's recommendation by formal Writ," and the Seneschal waves the thing, holding it high for witnesses to record and understand, "I have deputized the PAWs Guild to temporarily serve in the Assassin's Guild's former capacity as security for your body and throne." No one need comment on the word 'former.' One look at the poor devils glowing in discomfort, their Vanguards listing no end of sordid misdeeds done for pay or pleasure, makes them permanently ineffective as future assassins.

"If your Great Self will assent, per the Writ, it has been decreed they replace the Guild and henceforth be known as the Plumbing, Aqueduct, Watersmithing, Assassination and Security Guild of Greater Chafrium." PAWAS. That magnificent bastard Dodona, may his cooling carcass rest in peace, has just elevated the PAWs and made the Black Cat the first openly known Guildmaster in history. It's a masterstroke of social genius and an extra dagger stuck into the chest of his own murderer. He's stripped Meleyasza of everything. As she will find out, to add proper Eldessery to Eldessery, he's made a deal with the Broker that prevents any of the conspirators from committing suicide or willfully allowing themselves to be killed. They will live terribly painful long lives as reminders of what happens to those who interfere with a janjack on duty.

With another wave of the hand and a small gruff cough of surprise, the King of All Worlds elevates the PAWAS, ratifies several provisions in multiple writs, and permanently removes the single greatest threat to his person, Sandoval Prestige, from evera making an attempt on his life. The Guilds are thrilled beyond measure. One of their own will provide direct advice and support to the Grey Elves and the Throne. It's almost democratic, which thrills the Drowning Ones; and just for good measure, the provisions in the Writ bestow upon the bemused and rather overwhelmed Black Cat an advisor from each major School of the Academy plus nine elite assassins trained in death magic and its counters for her express disposal. The Wizards are apoplectic with glee. All three legs of the stool support this move.

In her own inimitable way, the ever-precise Black Cat whispers a few words and the Powers move. Caris and the man who is in fact the rarely-seen Ojawa take the entirety of the rogue court into custody. Three die short, ugly deaths as they are escorted down the stairs to the side. The blackened version of Ashlelani tries some kind of void magic and loses two fingers, which immediately grow back—itself an enlightening and powerful lesson for the gawking front rows. Then Caris knocks the traitor to the floor with a light backhand and winks at Sandoval. The new Guildmaster has some relationships that cannot be ignored. Over the next few weeks, many would-be conspirators and political neutrals will openly and loudly declare for the King and his heir Qelniasherah. In return the PAWAS will send them each a bouquet of very garish lilies by way of properly elven thanks.

"That sorted, perhaps we may now continue as the late janjack asked, in the Common tongue so that your many concerned guests and those attending this event from afar might be assuaged of all anxiety and this unsettling issue of the succession put entirely to rest both legally and socially?"

The King gives his Seneschal a firm nod, sits down on the steps, then motions to his Court to do the same. Some perspicacious little goblin from the PAWAS runs up with a tray of drinks, and before the leading nobles can sneer him away, M'shylpsany graciously accepts one for herself, then serves the King. It's plain to see how overjoyed the woman is to get back to her many adventures. The Writs, unbeknownst to her, have delivered a modest fortune from Kimber's assets to Claude and an entirely immodest remainder to her High Grace and her various cadres. Kimber herself, while not glowing, does seem to be suffering from some kind of indigestion related to the new virion on her Vanguard, which informs all who show interest that she suspected the King would be assassinated and did nothing.

It marks the first time the King of All Worlds has been served by a goblin, and upon reflection and the way he demands a second cup, it portends a much better working relationship with his new Guild. What was he served? A Caffé Dodona—something transported by Writ as the janjack fell but concocted by request the night prior. A simple beverage of fine coffee, essential oils, chocolate liqueur, and some sour cherry syrup from the Kyiv contingent along with whisper cream. It is both solid and liquid, sweet and savory. It will be served to the Court Royale weekly and become one of the King's favorites when playing chess.

In very clear if accented Common, Coralaviere continues. "As Dodona was about to reveal the father of the heir, it might do for our many assembled guests to explain a few matters prior to revealing her heritage." If a collective groan could be heard from the worlds watching, it would be colossal. But the Lord has the room, and he does not relinquish it. Instead he motions to the suddenly well-guarded Barefoot Jackson, whose escort of three dangerous women nearly drags him to the presence of the King and Court.

"Please allow me to explain the nature of Barefoot Jackson, our esteemed guest for the day." Here he bows to both Jackson and then again to his King. The worlds as a whole watch with rapt attention. "In short, there is no such person as Barefoot Jackson, and there never was." This time, some unseemly jazz enthusiast from the twelfth row makes a fool of themself by gasping aloud. To this day no one knows who it was, and that really nails how outrageous a claim the Seneschal has just made. He's sent the worlds into shock.

"As a gift to one of his rather desperate clients, the god Hoode created the Masquerade which is Barefoot Jackson and has been parceling it out among the Grey Elves and their retainers for a very long while." With a flick of his fingers Coralaviere demonstrates, blowing the skin and clothing off the shaggy Jackson to reveal a rather abashed *Wyl'halœ* musician of Grey Elven origin who goes by the stage name Aperitif, and whose family shrieks with scandalized horror as their oldest child stands revealed to be involved in the ungodly practice of jazz.

Qelniasherah in particular looks upon the man with rabid fascination. One can intuit her calculating down to the hour her potential conception and then questioning Aperitif's role. The good Seneschal continues, sparing her too much concern. "One elf sells or loans the Masque to the next, paying to the god all manner of favors and valuables." This makes sense; since it's known Hoode likes jazz.

"In such a guise several different Elves held assignations with this traitor." Here the High Lord points at the defeated and glowing Queen Ashlelani. "In such a guise did she conspire with some of these lovers to murder you, my King." He lets the crowd tut properly and fix their eyes on the offending and now debased ex-Royal.

"Were this all, it would be a sordid tale, but not reason enough to see the shifting of worlds, the movements of our expunged and removed Houses, conspirators like the loathsome Kris-To-Buy-Me and her cult." Here he looks directly upon Lady Nia and her counterpart Demi-Seneschal Sherrinford and smiles broadly. The man knows how to play a crowd. They sigh as if on cue, delighted that such a brave, beautiful woman might indeed be the worthy heir of such a suddenly worthy king. Women, really, because her seneschal, the one who must surely succeed her own adoptive father, is the future Queen's *Sylslaymynar*.

"But my Lord and Liege, as you see, there are in fact two such Queens before us. A paradox solved by none other than our mischievous god of the day, Hoode." Oh that got them. Like a tennis match played on the walls and ceilings, all eyes shoot to the very amused Hoode, who for his part simply drops a small bag of coins into the hands of the vaguely amused-looking Smith. The god looks back at the Seneschal and nods him ahead.

"It was Hoode who realized the shattering significance of the apparently random murder of Jane Austen. As we may properly surmise and which the Writ and ensuing Vanguard here attest, the Guildmaster slew Jane Austen and allowed the now-forgotten Bodyman of the Lord King to assume credit, hacking her already dead body. Why else would Hoode's Hat not slay him? It was a brazen act, a terrible betrayal of the Court's confidence and a slight upon our collective honor. But…" He has them to a body, the whole room focused on his words. Every revelation more fascinating.

"It was Hoode who understood the true depth of the crime. The true betrayal. Without doubt all these assembled gods and immortals know our secrets." Involuntarily all eyes look upon the two Queens, silent and full of despair. It's a chilling truth revealed that the haughty elves might have betters, silent and devious ones at that. The Powers.

"He knew the identity of the Guildmaster and knew exactly whom Jane had seen prior to her demise. What could have prompted her to murder such an innocent soul, the author and scholar who had no relationship at all with the Elves?" Here even Hoode looks at Meleyasza and his eyes burn with a sudden hatred. Ooooh, the crowd watches. The Tennis game has added gods and grudges.

"Jane met earlier that day with Barefoot Jackson, and when she revealed this simple fact to the Princess and her Queen while being honored with a tea, she was marked for death. They murdered her within the hour. For interviewing a jazz musician we now know was in fact someone else.

"What did Hoode realize from this murder, from this brazen act of terrorism and sedition?" Here the Lord Seneschal rises to his full height and stares down the glowing conspirators. Worlds watch.

"He understood that he was Queen Qelniasherah's father."

Both the King and Qelniasherah share a perplexed look of befuddled astonishment and then burst out laughing. Until the god approaches and with a grave bow to the King, greets his daughter with a kiss on each cheek. He bestows upon her a simple blessing and her Vanguard, oh lords and hosts and demons beyond, it explodes in color and size. It burns like a magnesium bar on The Deadplanes of Idril, pure blue and blinding.

Hoode, the worst and best hope for the Royale House and avowed enemy of everything Lomar, especially his kin, has the ulitmate revenge. He has fathered the legitimate heir to Lomar's throne. It's all too much to bear, and the weight of the moment threatens to derail even Coralaviere's epic monologue. Entire four-part Elven operas will be dedicated to this minute of the proccedings.

Then Hoode is gone, and with him many immortals, their purpose served and their presence unwanted or irrelevant. But the demigoddess and heir to the Skeleton Throne, Qelniasherah the Immortal, stands still. Her banners acquire a center stripe of purest black, the emblematic representation of her chaotic heritage and her mastery of the Songs. No one's laughing now— least of all the terrifying beast within the charred and smoking body of her supposed mother. It snarls until Caris cuffs it with a backhand hard enough to resound like a drum.

Coralaviere waits for the astonished room to return to him, to hang again on his every word. Lady Nia's Vanguard glows and turns with various terrifying new icons and emblems. She really is Hoode's daughter, both heir to the Throne and a Power ascending.

"Now, no mortals knew this key fact, and few immortals. It was known only among a very tight circle that the dishonored Ashlelani sold her body to Hoode so that she might replace her old lover with someone new. Along the way, it appears she indulged in numerous dalliances. But for a while she was Hoode's and his alone."

Some shudder, some look on in jealousy. Hoode's woman, his exclusive lover for a given time. No less than nine romance novels, four works of erotica, and several dozen interactive (with various levels of undress) motion pictures will hit the streets within a week of this revelation. They sell wildly, creating a future industry of immortal-themed speculative pornography.

"Who then could have been using the Masque of Jackson which prompted this stunning reversal and assured Hoode of his paternity? Here, my King, I beg your gravest indulgence." He then hands the King a handwritten note on a small slip of paper. Sæceæn's face does not react. He hands the paper to Lady Nia whose face also turns to blankest stone. The Black Cat approaches and is shown the paper. She nods minutely and that's all the enraptured crowd has to go on, a single flick of her head. Who indeed?

"It was in fact… the ancient king, and now god, Lomar whom Jane met. In truth, she had met him multiple times with the help of Hoode and had begun to cultivate a friendship as unlikely as it was close." He holds up the Writ, then ostentatiously reviews the corpse on the floor before returning to his monologue. "Janjack Dodona uncovered various records and documents which prove Lomar and Jane had set down thirteen chronicles of the early founders of Chafrium and of his own House.

"Realizing that this future masterpiece would delegitimize the Grey Elves and weaken their hold on the Skeleton Throne…" For what else could a tell-all from that dirty, scabrous, three-tongued thief Lomar be but an assassination of the Elven Cult of Civilization and Purity, especially if brought to vivid life by the great master novelist and Lady of Words, Jane Austen? "The black queen here acted."

The worlds wobble. It's not merely enough that to discover Meleyasza, high-born and blessed with everything, became the Guildmaster of a defunct and corrupt Assassin's Guild. Nor that Hoode fathered the next heir. Not enough to realize Chafrium's sacred guardian and patron Lomar walked among us (hello Mister Shadow). There's somehow more to this, some sinister and grotesque twist that made the risk of a hastily patched-up murder entirely necessary.

"When Hoode suspected who might have let slip to Jane his assignation with the Queen, he considered what taking tea with Lady Ash was wont to do." The rapt crowd hisses on cue as Caris cuffs the mishapen form another time. "Unmeaning and unaware, the Sainted Jane gave away some vital detail which betrayed her greater understanding. Hoode then fled to one of his many aeries and examined the treasure he had stolen from Ashlelani. A jade pin given her by the lover before, the man he swore to humiliate." This single statement will get its own rather frightening bondage sub-genre in books and photogravures.

"What he found chilled even him, the god accused of evil and chaos, of loving destruction more than breath. He found his lover's hair was of two persons." Here his hands convey visually to the crowd the two queens, the glowing and the charred, the woman and the slowly degenerating beast cowed only its proximity to several Powers.

"After confirming that our traitorous queen Ashlelani had been pregnant with his own child, he found in the subsequent hair of his lover the indelible stain of demonic possession. You see, he stole the pin years later, on a whim, when she came for more favors." The words buck the audience and secure a few stifled gasps.

"The body before you is the hollow core of what's left of the disgraced queen. That body there," and he points to the glowing, pithed woman nearly cataleptic next to her broken confidante, "is merely the skin and nerves of the host. Many years ago, all that we know as Ashlelani Greyleaf was consumed by the Outer God Astaroth—which, in imago form, squats before the Court Royale."

This time several elves do faint. A god of desecration, and more importantly of ugliness and imbalance, came close to seizing control of Chafrium. To do what cannot be imagined— but for centuries to come it will be discussed and speculated upon over naked bodies and tripdust, over wines and duels, over every imaginable occasion for gossip. *What if...*

"A known side effect of the Songs of Hoode and the true reason his rival Lomar secured them within the guarded domain of the Court Royale, these artifacts of void and chaos render the living and mortal vulnerable to immortal influence. While this served the god well when he was rogering our poor husk here, it served the Court ill when she then allowed herself to be taken by an alien presence." 'Rogering a husk' will be the newest snub to throw about in Chafrium for many seasons to come, and it's a reminder that Coralaviere commands not just because of his sword; his tongue too has a razor edge. "A presence which aimed to keep the Throne intact and prestigious. This being saw in Lomar's exposure of previous generations' missteps a real danger to its control. Why?"

Qelniasherah and Sherrinford look especially concerned. They whisper and the Demi-Seneschal nods. She has already started a full stack override search for information and allegories on this phenomenon as well as detailed behavioral analysis of every potential subject of influence. But she need not bother. The Writs have marked those suborned with a lovely spike of burning red, a dagger of fire that hovers above their heads as soon as Coralaviere finishes his sentence. All of them everywhere in existence.

The worlds could not be more interested. Lomar's antics have long been the things of legend, and while no self-respecting elf likes to really think on how debauched and offensive Mister Shadow might have been, the general consensus for the last hundred thousand or so years has been that if the worst of us may be a god, then the best of us may prevail to aim higher. Why then would an actual god fear such exposure.

"Lomar the Slayer, the Killer with the Demon Arrow, slew an avatar of Astaroth in his adventuring youth and was subject to a peculiar prophecy. One recounted in full to Lady Jane, but which has never been heard by elven ears since his ascension and departure from this reality. 'Born of a mother not Grey Elven, Lomar the bastard mongrel will one day be brought down, he or his line…" Here his words begin to acquire chilling precision: He or his line, the Throne itself. "…will be destroyed by seduction of a mother unworthy of the Grey Elves, who through assignation with the Void shall become a destroyer and devour all his progeny, kin, and kith starting with her own daughter.' At the time, there were no more than a dozen such women in the whole of the succession with just one child and that a daughter. So it took immediate and decisive action. The god Astaroth bid its host's closest friend, an assassin of enormous reach, kill Jane Austen."

The room thunders with conversation and confusion. He lets them, doing nothing but stand focused on the imago. For his part, the King looks properly sick. The breadth of the conspiracy and depth of the danger finally revealed, he sees that by luck or perhaps Chafrium's inscrutable will, he has survived once more against likely odds and in spite of his own machinations.

At last the King ends the tumult. He asks a question. As he speaks, the magics of the place cut the noise while amplifying his own voice. His words boom across the cowed room. "Do the Writs decree a formal sentence?"

"They do, my Liege King, subject to your ratification and royal assent."

"We shall hear it." The fate of worlds has thus been sealed with those formal words. Sentence will be executed.

"The Writs utilize the powers of the Skeleton Key itself to hold the divine entity Astaroth directly responsible for the deaths of Jane Austen, the former queen Ashlelani Greyleaf of the House Lomar, and a serving janjack on duty, Dodona of Chafrium and Austen." Oh, the clever legalism of it is perfidious. Jane makes the roster because Elves love beauty above all else, the queen because it makes the crime capital and treasonous in every sense as well as the immediate and direct purview of the King, and the janjack because the god, may we safely call it evil, has directly engineered this death. Slow comprehension come to the once-mighty Contessa as she realizes she's been forced into a major indiscretion to save her already dead queen. That the whole of her fanatical life has been a sick perversion of games within games. It's almost Elven in its debauchery.

Onlookers mention from time to time how pensive Caris got as she watched the interplay between King, Seneschal, and Court. Had they witnessed her chess game with Smith or stopped to consider what level of either prescience or wisdom it implied, there would be no speculation. Indeed, it's the only time throughout the day when Smoojak cracks a brief smile. But it's enough, when their eyes meet: Balance and his Checkmate.

"By authority of the Writs, the power of this invasive god shall be consumed by Chafrium and Austen's temporary Key, annihilating both itself and all links of Astaroth into this reality for thirteen times thirteen generations of Queens and Kings upon the Skeleton Throne." Banishment pure and simple, for however long it takes Chafrium to raise and destroy 169 successive monarchs, the next of which is potentially undying.

As punishment it's as tough as can be managed by the mortal. It even requires the god's own power to make it work. Compared to a small-time true god like Astaroth, Hoode and his compatriots are harmless ants.

"With the additional proviso that, having erected a functional Star within its walls and Astaroth having unlawfully transgressed upon the transdimensional aether of Austen and its Doors, the imago has made itself vulnerable to influence from all forces or Powers that span the Cities. With the complicity and acknowledgement of this Royal Court and the Throne, final execution of sentence shall work the Writ's unthinkable will."

Before anyone can think, the King reacts. "So mote it be."

Then the imago screams in agony as it crumples, driven from this world. Every being across every world with that glowing dagger shrivels and melts inward until only an excretion of char remain. Later, Sherrinford will apply enormous algorithms and sentient subroutines to take the data of who did and did not succumb to the demon god's corruption to write the definitive treatise on Demonology and Influence as well as several practical survival manuals with the charming Sparklesaurus and his handler Richard.

Executed Writs simply crumble. They turn to useless, unrecoverable dust that blows away with a breath. As the Writs become powder, the cowed audience explodes with every imaginable form of intercourse from alarmed gossip to panicked attempts to flee the room. To their credit, the fine hands of the Sword and Pistol League keep order with a minimum of casualties—though they are rather cheerful about crippling anyone glowing. A rather cruel contest breaks out between blades and guns as to who can better sever the Achilles tendon of someone on the run. The blades win.

Eventually Sæceæn tires of the insubordination and upheaval. The room booms with a shattering voice, knocking down those who dare move. "Sit down." Like obedient dogs, most sit—especially the elves whose Vanguards compel them. The King has demonstrated just how total is his control of the room. Cooler minds consider that he could have at any time stopped the Guildmaster, could have potentially slain her with a word. Instead, he trusted his Seneschal. As political statements go, it proves properly subtle and obvious simultaneously.

With a single sentence, he sets the expectations for the next few centuries, secure in the knowledge that a new crop of cabalists and schemers won't amass enough power to challenge him until Qelniasherah is entirely of age and fully in command of her own demesnes. At which point his death will not shake Chafrium, only inconvenience a blessed few who actually care for the man.

After that, there's a well-considered round of drinks and mingling, as the PAWAS surprises them all for a second time when no less than a thousand incredibly deft members of the Society for Valets and Bodyguards begin serving all manner of aperitifs and finger foods for those in need. There are couches and masseurs, a juggling troop from Skandarpoor that amazes one and all, a cat circus, and a small bevy of ombudspersons stationed across from the drinks to handle various ridiculous complaints and dramatic gestures.

After an enjoyable hour of speculation, jockeying for position, and posturing the assorted guests of diverse rank are treated to the first jazz concert of an openly acknowledged Grey Elven musician. It goes smashingly well. They are forced to play three full encores and even seduce the soon-to-be-elevated Coralaviere into singing the Chafrium anthem with a scat beat. To his credit, the noble has a piercing singing voice worthy of a rum-soaked angel.

The party will last days. The various players that matter to our story will barely make it to the dawn before events catch them. Which of course brings closure of sorts to our little morality play, where the evil get punished (unless they rule the worlds) and the good rewarded (unless they are janjacks or bystanders or the abandoned dead of another reality). Even the Black Cat got away with literal murder, her awards dissolved with Dodona's death (but not that vital Skeleton Key). By Grey Elven standards it's all been dreadfully moral and delicate.

Qelniasherah and Sherrinford are stunned to discover the extent of their various largesses. They are a nation unto themselves and their household acquires in short order highly competent support from the PAWAS and from Sherrinford's father, the Supreme Lord Coralaviere, Seneschal of All Worlds. Sherry in turns becomes the Regal Duchess Demi-Seneschal, Confidante and Bodywoman, Formal Secretary and House Assassin to Her Regal Highness the Supreme Grace and Appointed Heir, the Lady Qelniasherah Godborne of the Guiding Star. Woe to those who oppose them.

Their soon-to-be frequent visitor and lifelong source of social and political support, her Grace Lady M'shylpsany, has tea with them, and then, taking Claude in tow, rides off on that hellish motorcycle for some plane or other. The Black Cat, who has just finished a third sweep of palace security, assures them she knows the destination and has several competent guards planted among the race organizers.

The Cats are spotted outside the City walls dining with Caris and Smoojak. No one dares try to listen to such a conversation, but watchers assure all concerned that it proved amicable and they left on friendly enough terms. Then these Powers withdraw from sight, not to be seen for a good while.

Austen has a big wall now and more magic, but the same vital spirit, the same janjacks with the same fantastic élan and Eldessery. Word of the Red Lady becomes widespread enough that Lybid joins the ranks of known citizens. Even Jane Austen has been sighted. Word spreads in both Cities that Lomar's chronicles have been found. Compared to a coup attempt by a demon god, news of a genuinely original work from Jane Austen matters tenfold more to the elves.

Per the Writs the Elephant Room has been rebuilt, this time twice its size with a finer stage and a subbasement for more storage. Humans do think of the small things, because Aperitif's headline concert in Austen draws five Terran prime ministers and at least seventy noble houses from worlds as far-flung as Undervault where they came to adore his music. Those who attend swear it's just like the old room, down to the grooves in the nondescript floor. Austenites can again jovially say "Let's drink a Vault before we kill one another" in the right place.

Duchamp has to buy the next two buildings down the avenue, with Katz's giving up their kitchen and deck to move back to New Amsterdam. In an effort to prevent a riot, Duchamp adds fried pickles and something called a Reuben to his menu. Otherwise Café Ragueneau stays much the same. It serves swordsmen and often employs them. There's a waiting list to work there now, and sadly, the back room has to take reservations. But there are always four or five tables left open for his regulars, among them Powers and Noble Elves.

CHAPTER 15: AFTERMATH

Zoe rebelled first. Long into the brightening dawn the children sat rapt and forgetful. But as Gerhard finished the second tale she grimaced. "What about Delphi's Writ and the movement in the house?"

Gerhard gave her a hard look. "What about it?"

"You said there were four writs total and between deals with The Broker and The Fox, who knows what could have happened."

"It's just a story Zoe. Now we should pack up and hope someone comes by." That bought them an hour of breakfast and packing among grumbles.

Then Max joined her. "But Daddy, Delphi knew he was going to die. And he built Dodona like a ghost right?"

"Sure Max."

"So how come there's no Delphi ghost?" Zoe, her eyes sharp, stared at her father. The implied censure needed little translation.

"You've both grown cynical."

"It's elves Pops."

"You don't believe in the story anyway. It's all made up, right?"

Here Max stopped loading rations and tugged on his sleeve. "I believe Daddy. I think you were there."

"Why is that?"

'We have that sword on our fireplace, it's a saber right."

"Sure, from my time in the military. It's not proof Max."

Zoe slid alongside them, her eyes shining. "No but the thirteen sided star with the stripe behind it sure is rare. And here you go describe how the Princess had that as her personal symbol. Sign of her clan and all that."

"Yeah, Daddy, sign of our clan."

"Her clan Max."

The boy gave him a knowing smile. "Nope. You named us after the clan and we have their crest."

Gerhard was saved from further argument by a wandering caravanserai only too happy to help with repairs. Between their constant marvel they'd survived a night outdoors and the need for significant repairs, he avoided his children's questions until after market day. When they were again alone, well fed and taking to beds at a local hostelry the arguments began anew.

"So what happened Pops? Tell us the rest. There just has to be more. What about those three immortal ladies? What about Austen?"

"And what about Delphi, Daddy. Did he really die? That would be super sad."

"Well, your time in Chafrium has made you almost Elven. You've seen the Fox's world and seen the King transform a body with a drop of blood. Since we have not mentioned the Broker perhaps there's just a few more details..."

Lord Kizervexius had to rush, there was little time to think through contingencies after his certain demise. But the purely bugbear part of his soul, Delphi, had grown from thin disguise to something quite real. He owed Delphi some measure of peace.

He created Dodona to last just a few weeks, then fade. Time enough to finish doing right by the City. He spent another Writ, leaving blood and bone, fur and such as a contingency to his own contingency. He worded it so that it would send the sword to whomever proved most worthy and reanimate Delphi should Dodona be killed.

Knowing this, Dodona cut a deal with the Broker which would allow the Guildmaster to slay him in full view of the Court if the Broker in turn helped him use the various Writs, keys, and lifeforces involved to bring Delphi all the way back. Dodona understood the spirit of speaking the world into being. He took the expunged lord's contingency one step further. The Broker worked some magic, and Delphi, that rumpled bugbear, woke up this morning with a world of a hangover. Simply Delphi Janjack, no more the legendary demon elf within, just a soul grown over time in the warm sun of Austen.

"I knew it! Dodona learned from the Fox and outsmarted even the gods."

"Maybe so Zoe."

It takes a few weeks before Lord Seneschal Coralaviere can slip away and find a Door to Austen. But come he does. He finds Delphi by his Vanguard, for those honors once promised find a home in the man who rightly earned them all alone. It's not the outrageous combination of all those lifetimes of accolades, but it's honest and it comes with no disfiguring stain upon the soul. In consideration of his resurrection and return, the Caffé Delphi has been discontinued. But the Caffé Dodona proves a good substitute.

There he is, in a new top hat, made by Skorkowsky the Milliner, the finest haberdasher in Austen. Old Skorkie once hunted demons with some order of knights until he was felled by that ancient enemy of all persons of action: marriage. Some fetching duelist lured him to Austen, where he put away his weapons and armed himself with style and taste. Still, Austen's been entirely demon-free since his arrival, so people tend to pay their bills and treat him politely.

Delphi has donned just the midnight doublestripe, ranch boots and light breeches with a good cream and violet shamrock vest, a working chronometer that doubles as radiation gauge and magic compass, covered with a fairly mute frock coat of auburn. He looks smashing as always, but his eyes are marvels. They are no longer grey. Now they sparkle with golden mirth.

The Lord Ral arrives but gets stuck shaking hands and making a few comments with various gunsels and swordswomen he's met over the weeks. Any duelist of Austen who seeks his employ need merely bring him a letter from one of the City's janjacks and the Great Lord, the Supreme Seneschal, finds them a place in his household. Many work for his adored daughter Sherry, who came just last week with her Queen to listen to jazz in the park. She brought Chafrium's own Gaetana and James Grey, elfblood darlings of the Drowning Ones and guests of the ever influential Kniknik Derryberry. Critics admitted they weren't half bad as well. Now the pair have an Austen following.

By the time Ral makes it to the table, his Sylslaymynar has stood and given him the most profound bow, warrior to warrior. A Caffé Coralaviere is served while the men embrace. One almost spies a tear in the eye of the old elf. They say the cedar pollen can make anyone weep.

Ral sips his coffee and arches an eyebrow. "It's not often one escapes death thrice."

"As I hear it, the unfortunate Lady Meleyasza won't even cheat it once." This brings both men a rather full measure of mirth.

"Still, it does my duelist's heart good to think on you acquiring a Vanguard."

Delphi smiles and his teeth gleam like white daggers. "Certainly will make my passing to and from Chafrium more predictable."

"Or not. I doubt the King's new Guildmaster will ever let you out her sight. One set of awards was quite enough for her."

Delphi sips his drink and watches the duelists stride by, looking as nonchalant as they can before two Great Men. He shrugs. Ral knows the score here and he does great honor to his king and City when he visits. "Personally, I'm glad poor Dodona managed to get himself killed. Assuredly Sandoval would have done him the favor regardless."

They bicker good-naturedly over whether the Black Cat would really see the massive promotion of her guild and herself as punishment. Then about whether a hackstroke can really work against a steeled viperspider in phase. Over the afternoon they discuss politics, the cinema, Ral's birthday party for his daughters—Sherry and his second eldest, the Lady of High Purpose, Lhynsea'reh, share the date. After some rather tense afternoons the pair discovered they shared a mad passion for tea ceremony and ghost etching, which uses multiplanar inks to create thirteen images at once. After that the High Lady Lynze would hear nothing but they have an art themed party together. The

PAWAS imported eleven different grand tea masters.

The proud father beams, clearly thrilled his children can find peace under one roof. It helps that a pair of drunken Elves took it upon themselves to tread across the favorite iris garden of Duchess Greenhand, Selenaviere of House Etris Chess. She retired quite furious until word came that the men had at their own expense paid the Wu-Jen School of the Academy to restore and refine her gardens. Every one of them across Chafrium. Sherry had tracked them down and obliterated their carriage in a public dressdown.

Then the Queen Qelniasherah asked the good Duchess to please consider taking commissions on several of her ruinate properties. She would of course provide wizards and helpers as required. While the Lord Seneschal has always been good to his family and the House Chess Etris known for irreproachable honor and rectitude, in Elven terms that's rather stuffy. Ral has become a hero in the eyes of his entirely refined and artistically gifted daughters. Sherrinford being the conduit of such relationships has just become everyone's favorite new relative. It has not hurt any of the daughters to have it known their new baby sister will make grown duelists pee themselves in public for even the smallest affront. Nor that House Etris Chess now manages the Green Queen's tea and beverage menus.

In turn, Delphi mentions in passing that Lybid Janjack has taken him to see the Austen Opera, and Ral positively pounces on the poor man. They spend the rest of their afternoon consuming various platters of rolls and drinks sent by well-wishers, handling some odd bits of business including an impromptu King's Court to dispense with tariff dues on some impounded cattle which Austen's goblins may or may not have smuggled through a Door. And arguing about whether Delphi has a paramour, something he flatly denies.

Bugbears cannot blush but the massive creature did seem to look ever so sheepish when asked by his Sylslaymynar if he'd ever kissed her. This sets eavesdroppers on edge. Eventually the men stand, shake as duelists, and give one another an entirely inappropriate hug. Then the Lord steps back into his role as Coralaviere, promises to write, and makes polite mention of invitations for various important locals.

Delphi may come and go as he wishes—between these men not even death can keep them apart.

They bow as Lords in the street. "For everyone's sake, just try it once."

Delphi tips his hat and smiles. His amber eyes are a fire of mirth. "If one senses an opening."

As in if on cue, Lybid Janjack appears wearing a fine blue dress over which she has chainmail and a full dueling rig. She answers him plainly. "A good duelist makes an opening..." Then she curtsies to the Lord Seneschal, who bows back lower and winks.

"My sentiments exactly, Lybid Janjack. My very sentiments." He gives them both a proper bow again and makes his departure.

In turn she eyes Delphi. "Busy?"

He inspects her rig. "Need a second?"

She nods. "Indeed." Without a word she leads him off to the dueling grounds. Witnesses say it was one of the finer examples of swordcraft in an age. When the Extenso bandit chieftain had the men he'd hidden in the crowd rush her, Lybid and her second settled accounts with the whole band. The Chronicle reported thirty-nine dead. Duchamp served drinks until four in the morning. In other words, Austen was having a normal day.

We can leave Austen for a time, one imagines. Much as we can leave the worlds in general. Perhaps Dodona went back to the Happy Hunting Grounds, that his soul, born there, found a home with the Fox and Old Abe. Perhaps they watch the door together and swap tales. Perhaps he sits with Arüne.

Of that sleeping force of impossible power and grace, what might we conjecture? Did not the Lord Seneschal tell his King before all the watching universe Astaroth's imago might be exposed to anything that lurks beneath or between the Cities? Things like the god ihmself. Which of course could mean that what the demon did to the foolish Ashlelani was in turn done to him. The ways of the silent god and ihms penchant for glildwimmir.

Was this always the Great Game? To lure an Outer God into a delicious indiscretion? Delphi died, as did Dodona. In a way Gnash the Rash died in the Elephant Room along with Kizervexius and the Footman. Perhaps it was always the Black Cat's story. One could make a strong case. Or that of the Norns. Or maybe it's always been Jane Austen, there in the shadows, writing down Lomar's words. Or the Cities—Chafrium and Austen.

Or maybe it's none of them but stories themselves. The Will of Arüne, the first words. Every faith has a Creator. Even the gods believe in some divine spark, some ignition point where the darkness parted and a face upon the waters spoke Truth.

If one believes The Fox, then words are Power and all the Powers are made with words. That is the thing Dodona figured out, the thing that kept Delphi alive. We are all stories. All memories. All stardust and magic, tiny pieces of Chafrium and Austen and the worlds beyond.

Both children slipped into dreams as Gerhard adjusted their blankets. In the morning they'd take start the long way home. Brunhilda would have the hearth stoked and the house clean swept. He hated leaving her behind, but someone needed to be home for the cats. Senior had started going grey at the muzzle and Junior, for all his vigor, had started napping longer into the day.

He snuffed the lights, laid himself in his own cot and considered the distance between him and his adored beloved. Max's gentle snore filled the room with an easy buzz. Home— how he ached to be there one more time, to walk the old streets and greet old friends. Still, he had a new life filled with honest work and two amazing children. Plus the occasional threat of bandits of the road to keep him spry.

Of Brunhilda he had not a single worry. She had the saber after all. He listened contentedly to his children as sleep overtook him.

ABOUT THE AUTHOR

Ani Fox lives in Amsterdam, The Netherlands, having previously lived in Luxembourg, attended graduate school in Hawai'i and Australia and escaped several times from the post-apocalyptic suburbs of New Jersey. While living in Austin, Texas, Ani published short fiction in several science fiction and fantasy anthologies as well as graduating to novels: "The Autumn War", "Requisition", and "Bugbear Blues". With spare time Ani holds down a day job, serves as Editor in Chief for the European Review of Speculative Fiction and does whatever the cat suggests. On social media Ani's still waiting for gender, sexuality and ethnicity categories which include "it's really complicated" and "how time have you got?" Honours and achievements include a BA in History from Rutgers University, a PhD (ABD) in World History from the Australian National University, a PhD in Indigenous Theology from ULC Seminary, scars on various appendages incurred working kitchens and storerooms, Phi Beta Kappa, and 3rd runner up in the 47th Annual West Poughkeepsie Bottle Cap Hurl; none of which make Ani more fun at parties.

Curious about other Crossroad Press books?
Stop by our site:
http://store.crossroadpress.com
We offer quality writing
in digital, audio, and print formats.

Enter the code FIRSTBOOK
to get 20% off your first order from our store!
Stop by today!

www.ingramcontent.com/pod-product-compliance
Lightning Source LLC
Chambersburg PA
CBHW070652180626
46817CB00006B/2331